THE CORDWAINER

or An American Fairy Tale

CHRISTOPHER BLANKLEY

The Cordwainer

or An American Fairy Tale

ISBN: 0-9838676-1-5

ISBN-13: 978-0-9838676-1-6

email the author at: chris@blankley.net

FIVE
BOB
BOOK
MOB

For Barb

Chapter One

Googly-Eyed Jesus

Seymour Fonk's seminal paper on greenhouse gases forever changed the academic world in 1921, but it wasn't until the droughts of 1927-28, and the resulting global food shortages, that Dr. Fonk's work garnered more mainstream attention. With the 1929 crash and the subsequent 1932 election, the Roosevelt Administration found itself inheriting a pair of twin horrors: Economic collapse and widespread global hunger.

It was here, in these corridors of power, that Dr. Fonk's work truly came to find a receptive audience – an audience desperate for bold solutions to complex, global problems. Almost from the very beginning, the politics of Roosevelt's New Deal became tightly intertwined with the issue of global overheating. So much so, it is said, that Roosevelt himself came to consider the "New Deal" not simply as a new pact between government and the governed, but also a new contract between mankind and the planet – to find common cause, to live in peace and harmony, to sustain one another and to foster continued mutual growth...

> - excerpt from *A Brief Political History of a Warming Planet*

The affair of *The Cordwainer,* and my subsequent meteoric rise to political fame, began the Saturday I returned to Boot Hill, my Class A work chit literally in my back pocket.

I was standing on the corner of Main and H, waiting on the trolley car, itchy in the new jacket and shirt I had just purchased from the Concession Store behind me. Monday morning was to bring my first day at work, as a Foreman at The Shop, and Foremen were expected to arrive in a jacket and tie. I'd never owned either in all my years growing up, or anytime during my four years away at the Big City University; so my first port of call upon returning to town had been the Men's Department of the Concession Store.

The matronly assistant had absolutely insisted that I wear my purchase home. "To show your mother," she'd said, beaming, in some sort of transitive state of maternal bliss. "She will *absolutely* die!"

I doubted that, my mother already being dead – by then going on ten years – but the old bird had been so *insistent*... I wore the suit out. But ten minutes waiting in the sun, and the whole contraption had begun to feel like an irritating hemp noose around my neck. I was altogether too overdressed to be waiting on a street corner for a trolley car on a Saturday. People were giving me sideways looks. But the store assistant had pressured me to wear it. I'd felt obligated.

I was feeling a little down in the mouth and more than a little bit like a fool as I stood there in line at the trolley stop. But fate had not yet had its fun with me – it had not yet decided that my situation was completely unbearable. As I waited there at the curb that early June day, with the first heat of the summer just starting to set in, I happened to look easterly down Main to check on the progress of the electric trolley, only to see a rusty silver wrecking truck come squealing off J Street and accelerate up Main.

You have to remember how unusual the sight of an automobile was back in 1973. Thirty years before, I understand, you couldn't have crossed a street like Main without looking both ways for traffic. But at the height of carbon rationing, during the summer of '73, such a phenomenon was a peculiar sight.

If that sight alone had not been enough to turn heads, the reckless nature with which the vehicle was being driven would have done it. The waiting crowd on the sidewalk in front of the Concession Store let out a collective gasp.

I, alone, was silent. To me, the sight and smell of that particular vehicle loomed large in my memory. I sunk back, attempting to duck my head behind the crowd. That wrecking truck – and the man I knew would inevitably be driving with such insane abandon – was nothing and nobody I wanted to see right then; not dressed in my new jacket, shirt and tie; not standing out in front of the Concession Store, waiting on the trolley; not after four years and enough time and space for me to just begin to regret my days spent in the passenger seat of that truck. No, not that day of all days, two days shy of the beginning of my professional career.

"Shee-it!" A voice screamed from the open window of the truck as it passed, brakes squealing. I dared not look up, but I knew that I'd been spotted. There'd be no other reason for the yell. The wrecking truck stopped in the center of the street, sputtered and settled into an unhappy idle, as the driver's door creaked open. I considered running, all crouched down, back through the revolving doors of Concession Store. But before I could act, before I could flee, the crowd around me began to part. "Shee-it!" the voice came again. There was no avoiding it now. I pulled myself back up to my full height and feigned surprise to see Fluky stepping down from the truck and walking up onto the sidewalk towards me.

"Shee-it!" he said for a third time, somehow making the four-letter word have two syllables. "Ya ol' son-of-a-bitch!" he rolled around a mouth full of chew. He seemed bigger than I remembered, more than his five feet four inches should have let him. Bigger around the middle, perhaps. But it was the same old Fluky, in his stained blue jeans, ripped flannel and cap; smelling of a combination of motor oil and cannabis. "Beanie? Beanie? It's me, Fluky..." he mocked unfamiliarity, then laughed at his own joke. "Damn! When'd you get back into town?" he drawled. "You can't pick up a phone and call an old buddy?"

Fluky. With his backwoods, Tennessee accent; though he'd been born in California and moved to Boot Hill as a child. Fluky. So intentionally vague about his exact ethnicity – sometimes Chinese, sometimes Japanese. 1973 was the tail end of the repatriations – that interminable policy of actively deporting Japanese refugees back to repopulate their radioactive rock. Fluky had been unquestionably born in the U.S. But it was wise for a guy who looked like Fluky not to let the exact nature of his ethnic makeup be too well known, lest a jumpy government official be accidentally within ear shot and prone to fits of excitement.

"Fluky, I just got into town-"

"Ah, hell!" he interrupted, letting out a belly laugh and slapping my shoulder. He held out a hand and shook mine warmly. "How the heck are ya?" I could sense, to Fluky, the last four years had suddenly never happened.

"Good, good..." I replied, shaking Fluky's hand back. I had to admit, it was good to see him. I let myself smile, just a little.

"Ah, that ain't gonna get it done!" he laughed, breaking away from our handshake and wrapping his arms around me in a big bear hug. For his size he was amazingly strong. He picked me clean up off the pavement, with everyone around watching. "Shee-it! Four years!" he continued when my feet had returned to the ground. "Don't look like no college learnin' done hurt you none..." he looked me up and down, noticing for the first time my new hemp suit. "Hell, what you doin'? Standin' there like a five-buck hooker?" he laughed and spit a wad of brown goo into the gutter.

"Trolley..." I pointed off down Main, where the electric trolley was laboring in the distance.

"Shee-it, girl as pretty as you ain't gotta wait on no trolley!" Fluky laughed. "Come on, get in!" He gestured back at the wrecking truck, idling away in the center of the road, slowly engulfing itself in a cloud of choking black diesel fumes.

"Oh, no..." I answered, raising a hesitant hand. "I can wait..." But Fluky was already walking back to the truck, oblivious to my protests.

Every fiber of my being was screaming, "No." I couldn't get into that truck. I wouldn't get into that truck – *back* into that truck. After all those years that I'd been free of it.

I tried to slip back into the crowd, run away, but my foot landed hard on the toes of some old lady. She yelped and I looked left, I looked right, for some possible means of escape. Fluky was already in the driver's seat, reaching across the cab to pop open the passenger's door.

"Get in," he said with a gesture.

I wasn't going to get into that truck, he couldn't make me get into that truck.

Getting into that truck was absolutely, unequivocally the stupidest thing I could do. I was two days away from the real beginning of my career. All the time and energy I'd invested into school was just about to start paying off. I'd be a Foreman.

The Boss. To be seen in the passenger seat of that truck... there was just absolutely, positively no way I was going to get into that truck with Fluky...

...I remembered thinking as I pulled the passenger's door closed behind me.

I guess you could say I wasted my youth.

Well, Fluky and I did, along with Mitty, in that damn old rusty wrecking truck.

The employment bureau, in its infinite wisdom, our sophomore year, had apprenticed Fluky to Old Man Zimmerman. Why in hell was anyone's guess; it put one of the town's only Oriental kids in the employ of one of the town's most notorious bigots. But whatever the logic, it had put Fluky, myself and Mitty into the enviable position of being among the few automobile-powered teenagers in town. We had a car... well, we had a stinky old truck, but small-town girls couldn't afford to be that picky. I'll skip the sordid details, but sufficient to say, without fear of contradiction, we had ourselves a good ol' time. Maybe too good a time.

My grades began to slip. When you spend your nights out driving the town, drinking McTavish and smoking Jefferson's, it's hard to bring your A-Game to class the next day. That damn truck nearly cost me my college career. Halfway through my senior year, my dad wisely took me aside and tried to talk some sense into me. It wasn't hard. He told me: Next time I was out riding around, look to my left and look to my right; look at the fellas sitting next to me.

That was all it took. I bucked up on the books, dodged the old crowd for my last semester, and managed to sneak by with grades just good enough for the Big University over the mountains. I was gone. Free. I fell in with a whole new crowd in the Big City; made whole new friends. Engineering types. Classmates.

Quickly, the nights I'd spent with Fluky and Mitty in that old truck became nothing more than a fond memory. I had little reason to stay in touch, and four years later, with a degree in Mechanical Engineering to my credit, there was no reason at all for me to expect that I'd fall back into my old ways, not the second I stepped back into town. But there I was, not a day fresh off the train and already I was climbing back into the cab of that stinking, rusty old truck.

"You gotta be stupid," Fluky said, reading my mind as I dropped into the seat next to him, closing the door. I began to answer, but my attention came to rest on the four-inch googly-eyed Jesus that was suction-cupped to the dash right in front of me.

I couldn't remember ever seeing anything quite like it in my life. Simultaneously pious and cartoonish. It was self evidently Jesus, with a beard and long hair and robes, but there was no obvious separation of the body and head. He was egg-shaped, with little carved wooden hands clasped together in prayer; googly-eyes jiggling in their glass orbs, cast pensively – hysterically – heavenward. Fluky leaned over, witnessing my fascination, and gave it a flick with his finger. The googly-eyed Jesus began to bob back and forth on some sort of spring attached to its suction base, sending eyeballs googling in their sockets.

Fluky gave me a dirt-brown grin, obviously amused by his small totem, and he put the wrecking truck into gear.

Boot Hill began to roll by.

"Stupid?" I finally replied, a full two minutes later, after the truck took a wild turn onto G, Fluky working his way through the three on the tree.

"Yeah, stupid," he said with joy, working the word *stupid* around in his mouth with his chew.

"Yeah, maybe..." I had to admit.

"Got to be," Fluky said, now sure of his conclusion. "Can't imagine no other reason why you'd show your ginger ass in this town again. Gotta be 'cause you're *stupid*," he spat out the window, "got to be..."

I dug in my back pocket, pulling out my Class A work chit, and held it up between Fluky and the windscreen. "Start Monday morning at The Shop," I said.

He squinted: "What the hell you study at that University?"

"Mechanical Engineering," I replied, refolding my chit and returning it to my pocket.

"That learn you much about makin' boots?" Fluky snorted, giving me a glance as he made a turn onto Yakima.

"Oh yeah, sure..." I shrugged, prying my eyes away from the Jesus' hypnotic googly-eyes. On the corner of G and Yakima a disheveled Indian stood with an outstretched hand. Suddenly, the feeling that I was really back in Boot Hill hit me. My dad's house, Main Street, the Concession Store, Fluky and his truck, were all some half forgotten memory. But that hard-luck Indian – that reminded me that I was truly back in Boot Hill.

Boot Hill, of course, was not officially called Boot Hill. Find it on a map, and you'd think the place was called *Luma*, after that Indian – well, at least his tribe. The Luma had lived or hunted or fished or some such thing in the area for centuries before the coming of the white man, and the town had been named in their honor.

But no one called the place Luma. Everyone knew the town as Boot Hill; not out of some silly Old West, frontier town sort of association, but because the town made boots. Hundreds, thousands, millions upon millions of them, at the Concession's Central Footwear Manufacturing Facility, known as The Shop, just on the edge of town. If you'd bought a pair of shoes in the continental United States pretty much anytime in the postwar era, chances were they'd been made in Boot Hill.

But officially they had been made in Luma. To honor that Indian and his tribe, who were free to stumble into the town named in their honor, anytime, to panhandle off people. Yeah, Indians and Boot Hill made a connection for me, let me know that I was finally well and truly back home.

"Damn! Them injuns make me thirsty..." Fluky stated, reaching back through the absent rear window of the truck's cab, fishing around by the winch, and coming back with a waxy carton of Frau Brau. "Beer?" he asked, holding the carton out to me.

I took it without thinking. He reached back and came back with a Frau for himself. I folded out the tab and popped the carton open, taking a quick sip.

Yeah, I was back home.

Fluky deftly punctured a hole in his carton with the nail of his thumb and squeezed the container like a lemon. A stream of beer erupted from the tear and splashed down his gullet. Three seconds, and the beer was done. He crushed the last of the wax carton in his fist and tossed it unthinkingly out his window.

"Mother fucker!" he yelled, punched the roof of the cab and let out a rebel yell. "Andrew Rice! Rice and Beans! Red Beans and Rice!" he cycled through. Rice, my last name, inevitably lead to the nickname "Beans"; Red Beans because of my hair. I took a swallow of my beer and tried to smile. "How the fuck are you, Beanie?"

Four years with no one calling me Beanie... That had been nice.

"Good, good..." The wrecking truck bounced across the railroad tracks. Almost immediately, Fluky took a sharp Y where Yakima joined Nez Perce. "Hey, where we going?" I asked, but I had already answered that question in my head.

"Where the hell you think we're goin'?" Fluky answered, reaching back through the rear window to grab another Frau. Crossing the railroad put us literally on the "wrong side of the tracks". We had left the small, neat bungalows of the hardworking, God-fearing neighborhoods of Boot Hill and were driving though the maze of prefabricated concrete shotgun shacks that made up Boot Hill's seedier district. I knew only one person who'd ever lived in this part of town – would only ever know one person from this side of the tracks.

"Mitty," I said over my beer.

"Hell, yeah!" Fluky punctuated. "You think you can just sneak back into town and not have a beer with your old buddies?"

"No, no," I began to correct, then realized he was ribbing me again. "How have you been, Fluky?" I changed the subject.

"How has Fluky been?" Fluky lifted an eyebrow while again performing his well practiced one-handed beer maneuver. "Shit, you know they ain't yet invented the itch that old Fluky can't scratch..." He again finished his beer and sent the container spinning out the window.

"And Mitty?"

"Ah..." he shrugged without committing himself. "You know Mitty..."

Fluky turned the old wrecking truck at a boarded-up old grocery store at the corner of Nez and C. He shifted down to second and gassed the truck up the slight grade that was C

Street. I looked back at the boarded-up storefront, at the political posters from last November's election that still hung, dogeared, from the rain-soaked plywood. They were all for Kennedy. None for the Republican, whose name, frankly, now I can't even remember. Most of the signs touted, in large red lettering, the new slogan from Kennedy's latest campaign: "Four to the Future." ("Four" being a not terribly clever play on words for the number of sequential presidential elections he was hoping to win.) But one carried the older, but still popular, slogan: "Nation of Big Ideas" with the stylized likeness of the President against a sky full of his wartime bombers. It was a slogan and poster the Administration had been using from the very beginning, since the 1960 election, when Joseph Kennedy Jr. had so handily defeated the sitting Vice President.

I lost sight of the posters as the old store vanished behind the smokescreen belching from the rear of the wrecking truck. She was really laboring up the grade now and I turned my attention back to the road, then down to the googly-eyed Jesus dancing in front of me, silently praying, perhaps, for our successful conquest of the grade.

Chapter Two

Re-tartared

Fluky brought the silver truck to a halt in front of the large, derelict Queen Anne home perched at the zenith of the hill. It stood distinct from the concrete shotgun shacks that neighbored it – obviously of an older pedigree. A glance further down C, as the street started again to descend the hill, showed silhouettes of similar-style homes. At the top of the hill, we were on the very border of Boot Hill, with the empty boarded-up remains of Pottersville beyond. Here the scrub was slowly reclaiming what Man had once built, and Mitty's home sat right on the cusp of this reclamation. The garbage of the house and whole sections of its construction seemed to be littered over the lawn. The place looked worse than I remembered. Mitty's mother's house had always been something akin to a junk pile, but four years had done it no favors. The house looked positively squalid.

Fluky pulled on the handbrake and killed the engine. The black cloud of the exhaust enveloped us as I hesitated to open my door. "Mitty still live with his mom?" I asked, incredulously.

"He likes to say she still lives with him," Fluky chuckled, cracking open his door with a rusty squeak.

"It still stink as bad in there?" I asked, stepping out of the truck. "She still got all them cats?" Fluky didn't bother to answer. We both stepped up onto the walk and I started for the front door.

"No, you can't get in that way no more," Fluky instructed as he cut across the brown, sandy front lawn. "'Round back."

I hesitated, contemplating the state of the insides if the front door was impassable. The memory of garbage piled shoulder-high returned to me; tight passages cut through the filth; just enough room to move. Presently, a whistle came from behind the house, and I looked around for Fluky. He'd vanished.

"Come on!" a yell came from the rear and I picked a path through the debris with my toes, kicking aside rusting kitchen equipment and sandblasted children's bassinets. Something scurried suddenly from under a pile of rotting winter coats and I quickly doubled my pace, leaping piles of bric-a-brac in great bounds.

I found Fluky waiting for me at the base of the rear stairs. The back of the house, what had once been a sun porch, was now enclosed with plywood. Fluky skipped up the three steps and rapped heavily on the makeshift door, with a rope loop for a handle, that topped the stairs. A muffled voice from inside attempted some form of reply, but Fluky drowned it out with another staccato series of knocks.

I paused to savor the view that Mitty's back porch had once boasted. Feasting pigsty the house might have then been, but once it had been a home of some luxury – a symbol of wealth for some Victorian merchant or locomotive baron. Its vantage point looked down over the whole of Boot Hill and I could take the town in with one sweeping glance. From Main Street and the large Art Deco box that was the Concession Department Store, across the mega-gauge rails that evenly bisected the town; past the Concession Depot where the black worms of the freight behemoths belched black steam into the sky; and out to the flat, football field-like roofs of The Shop rising like stepped terraces away into the heat haze of the scrub. All of it I could ponder without taking the trouble to turn my head. All of it, I realized standing there, from Concession Store to Concession Shop was the property of that one company. The mega-rails, the plots of land, the houses rented to workers – the hearts and souls of those who depended on the Concession for their livelihood – all the property of the Concession. Seeing it all at once, after being away for four years, my eyes saw it all as if for the first time.

"By Washington's wooden teeth, who's banging on my door?" The plywood sheet that served as a back door flew open and the large melon head of John Mitty came poking through. A Jefferson hung from his mouth in a cigarette holder, and despite the dirty gray dressing gown he was wearing, his hair was neatly combed and a scarf was wrapped meticulously around his neck.

Once, back in high school, some girl or other had casually remarked on the similarity in appearance of Mitty and Errol Flynn. It had been true, too... back then, when he'd been, maybe, a hundred pounds lighter. But ten years had passed since that comparison, and now there was little about Mitty's round, flabby face that still resembled the classic movie star. Mitty, however, still wore the rakish, pencil-thin mustache he had grown in his doppelganger's honor; and it still sat – oh so rakish and pencil thin – above his fat upper lip.

"Look who I found." Fluky cocked a thumb back over his shoulder. Mitty looked up, and at the sight of me, his face exploded into an expression of genuine joy.

"Beanie!" he screamed through the cigarette holder. "Beanie, my old fellow..." He came lumbering down the stairs, his bulk creaking the wood. He grabbed my hand in his large, meat-like paws and shook. "Beanie! How do you do? It is a pleasure, sir, a real pleasure!" He pumped my hand up and down, vigorously shaking it and bringing his face in close to mine. "When did you get back to town? How was school? Did you get my letters? How was the weather?" he fired his questions, then thought better of it all. "No, no, come inside. Fluky! The McTavish, and quick about it!"

Still holding my hand, Mitty led the way back up the stairs and through the makeshift door. The purpose of the plywood, I realized as I stepped inside, was to convert the old sun porch into living space. Again, my mind was at a loss to guess the state of the interior of the house for Mitty to have been forced out to the back porch. But the odor, at least on the porch, seemed manageable. A cot covered in numerous blankets sat in one corner, and an old cupboard sat next to it, seemingly serving as Mitty's dresser.

Most of the porch, however, was taken up by a sizable dining table, an antique oak structure covered in notebooks, maps and a number of small figurines. On the plywood wall behind the table a number of other maps had been pinned. Detailed plans of Patton's Iberian campaign, I instantly recognized. It was Mitty's obsession.

There was something about Mitty you should understand, before I go on, before you judge him too harshly.

Mitty was an idiot.

The way he was, it really wasn't his fault.

And I mean he was an Idiot, not an idiot. Capital *I*. The standardized testing – the tests given to all of us during our sophomore year, that had apprenticed Fluky so wisely to Old Man Zimmerman – determined Mitty to have a deficient IQ. Sixty-five, if I remember correctly, which officially classified him as an Idiot, earned him an automatic Class F work chit and a check every month for the rest of his life for sitting on his ass.

Thing is, Mitty never really seemed to me to be that stupid. Eccentric, sure, and dull as a block of sandblasted oak, but not really *stupid*. In the subjects he was interested in... well, he was practically a savant; like the War or the schedules of the Concession trains. But when you strayed too far outside the scope of his interests, or made him interact too much with the public, he *was* an imbecile. I mean, he could barely write his own name or add two numbers together. What sort of work could you do like that? Seriously. But stupid?

Truth be told, the whole idea of *The Cordwainer* was Mitty's – Mitty's Plan. Okay, he didn't design the engine, or really do anything practical towards the success of the project. That just wasn't Mitty. Given a million years and a million dollars he'd have just sat around and talked about doing something. Talked and talked. But the idea – the overarching, grand vision – that was Mitty. And it was everything and anything at all but stupid.

Looking back, it made me wonder: Did Mitty really try that hard when those standardized tests had been given? Stupid, maybe, but I was the guy looking at thirty years stretching out ahead of me with my nose to the grindstone.

Mitty sat down heavily on a raised stool beside the old dining table as I dropped myself into a threadbare, old armchair next to the cot. Almost as soon as Mitty had lowered himself down, he sprang to his feet again and came lunging towards me. For a second I thought he was about to throttle me, but his hands instead grabbed at the lapels of my new jacket, feeling the material.

"That's a singular coat," he commended, admiring the hemp, exhaling smoke from his Jefferson into my face, making me hack. I brushed his hands away from my person, pushing him back out of my personal space. He didn't seem to take offense and snorted as I fanned smoke away from my nose and mouth.

"Beanie here's a college grad-u-ate," Fluky said, head down, digging something out of the bottom shelf of the china hutch. He came up with an opened carton of McTavish and a few dirty paper cups. "Class A right there in his pocket. He done showed me." Fluky poured a dixie cup of whiskey and handed it to Mitty, doing the same for me. The carton, he kept for himself. I sniffed at the noxious, brown liquid that someone, somewhere had the gall to call Scotch and knocked it back in one belt. Mitty did the same as Fluky gulped from the carton.

"Well, where are my manners?" Mitty said, holding out his cup for a refill. "This calls for a toast. To Beans! Red Beans and Rice! Ph.D.!" And they both drank.

"No, not..." I began to correct, but trailed off. It didn't really matter. Bachelors, Ph.D., they all – in the end – really meant the same thing: Class A work chit. Without a college degree, all you could ever honestly hope for was a Class B. Like Fluky. Tradesman.

"And I take it that it's not presumptuous to assume that you've sought employment at Amalgamated Holdings?" Only Mitty ever called the Concession by its real name.

"Start Monday," I confirmed.

"Bully! Just *bully!*" Mitty took a draw off his cigarette and puffed out a gray cloud. With his round face and the cigarette holder he looked like some fusion of the two Roosevelt presidents.

"Bet your pa is just as happy as a pig in shit." Fluky had pulled up an old dining room chair, and sat at Mitty's strategic gaming table like he was expecting dinner.

"Couldn't be happier," I agreed. And he truly was. First Sophie, now me. Two kids out of college and gainfully employed. Sophie in Accounts Receivable at The Shop, and me following in Dad's own footsteps as a Foreman on the floor. It was everything he'd been working towards, ever since Ma died. Yeah, so he looked like a fool, walking around town with that stupid grin on his face, but he had plenty to be smiling about.

"And your starting salary, as a Junior Foreman?" Mitty asked. It was classic Mitty: Totally without social charm.

"Mitty! Ya tartarhead..." Fluky exclaimed before I could answer. I just let my mouth hang open. "You don't ask shit like that! What you get a month for being a mor-*ron*?" he countered. "Fuck..."

Mitty steamed, glaring at Fluky though lowered eyelids, "Retarded," he corrected. "Retarded is now the preferred idiom for my condition. 'Moron' has fallen out of favor."

"Retarded. Tart-a-head. Re-tartared tartarhead..." Fluky paused to laugh at his own joke, letting a guffaw slowly slip. When he had recomposed himself he took a sip off the McTavish carton. "You still get paid for being a damn fool..."

"I merely inquired after the base pay..." Mitty began, than stopped himself, thoughtfully. I think the social nuances of the situation began to dawn on him.

"How's your mother, Mitty?" I asked, throwing Mitty an easy out.

He rolled his eyes and pointed his Jefferson towards the house. "In there, still at the center of her Cretan maze – the horned beast. I've ceased all contact! I moved out here not two years past, the house having become simply unfit for habitation, man or beast. So, I've relocated my HQ out here." He swirled a finger around him. "Fluky helped with the paneling." Mitty slid his cup across the table for Fluky to refill.

"Freezing cold in the winter, boiling hot in the summer," Fluky added, filling Mitty's cup and taking a belt off the carton. The Fraus and the McTavish were starting to do their work on Fluky and his speech was beginning to slur. "Gotta be re-tartared to live out here..."

"I can't begin to describe the conditions beyond that door," Mitty rolled his eyes again. "Though, I believe the mold under the kitchen sink is sufficient to apply as a carbon offset. I just fret that the EPA will declare the whole place a protected wetland!"

I laughed. I could feel the McTavish beginning to warm my belly. Despite the rancid taste, I was beginning to long for another. I looked across the room at my old friends as they chuckled at their little joke. Fluky, drinking sour Scotch through brown, tobacco-stained teeth. Mitty, replacing the spent Jefferson in his cigarette holder, lighting up a new one and taking a long drag.

It was good to be home, I was thinking, as the fingers of the whiskey started to work their slippery way though my veins. Good to be back with my friends. I had friends away at school, sure, but somehow... the shared history that the three of us had together. I could almost feel myself choking up.

Okay, maybe it was good to be back home – maybe I had to admit it to myself that I'd actually *missed* these guys? No, I just couldn't go that far. To admit that I missed Fluky spewing obscenities and drinking himself stupid? To admit that I missed Mitty's pedantic, tiresome diatribes about Patton's northern campaign? No, it was just too much for me to admit to myself, too great a leap.

Nothing I could admit, at any rate, until I'd had at least a few more drinks.

Chapter Three

The Battle of Izpegi Pass

One more McTavish turned into three, then a couple of Fraus followed that, just to keep the edge. Soon, all three of us were sitting at Mitty's table of war, laughing as Fluky recounted the events that led up to the loss of his virginity in the stockroom of Putter's Café.

Mitty had the Battle of Izpegi Pass spread out on the table before us. A particular favorite of his. The battle, like that at Thermopylae millennia before, appealed to war buffs like Mitty, who saw war mostly as a struggle between good and evil, and the continent-wide duel between Patton and Rommel as a chess game played between two titans.

At Izpegi Pass, nine hundred U.S. Marines, only three weeks shy of the D-day landings on the beaches of Asturias, held a pass against two full SS Panza Divisions attempting a counterattack. They were, to a man, completely annihilated, and Rommel knocked much of the momentum out of Patton's Basque Offensive; but the sheer heroics and personal bravery of the U.S. Marines...

Mitty also had a special interest in the Iberian Campaign, and the Basque Offensive in particular. His father, who'd skipped out on Mitty's mom when Mitty had still been very young, had left little behind other than a framed display of his war medals hung in the entry hall of the house. With no other memory of his father, Mitty had become obsessed with those medals. And the War.

Two of the medals were Purple Hearts, two more were campaign medals from Italy and Spain. The final one, however, Mitty came to learn, was a Bronze Star given to his father during the Basque Campaign. It took Mitty many months and countless letters to the Department of Defense during his teenage years to find out the full provenance of his father's Bronze Star; and in the end it had turned out that Mitty's father had verifiability been quite a hero, saving the lives of many of his comrades in battle.

Of course, even a real-life, genuine hero was never going to be good enough for Mitty's imagination. He had soon concocted for himself an elaborate tale of how his father had really been the only surviving U.S. combatant at the Battle of Izpegi Pass; but through some bureaucratic incompetence and a lack of political connections, his father had been denied his rightful Congressional Medal of Honor and had had to settle for the Bronze Star, in an unrelated battle, in recompense.

Well into high school Mitty had still been telling this story. But slowly, as Mitty aged, his need to repeat this tall tale had diminished. I suspect, as he came to accept his father's absence, his need to manufacture heroics for his father had waned. Mitty's obsession, however, with Patton and the War never did. I can fondly recall many a long hour spent with Mitty poring over maps of the European Theater, expertly tracking the many movements of Patton's Third Army and the counter thrusts of Rommel's Nazi Panzas.

With Fluky's story finished, and the last of the McTavish carton gone, Fluky began to meticulously roll marijuana in white cigarette paper from the supply he always kept in a tobacco pouch in his hip pocket. Mitty and I watched silently as the master worked his magic.

The weed was from Fluky's own private stock, a share of the harvest he brought monthly into town off the Palouse. As one of the few people in town whose profession allotted him a diesel ration, Fluky was well positioned to operate as something of an illicit cargo company, moving products back and forth for people who, for whatever reason, were uncomfortable using the official Concession services.

Of course, this mainly meant drugs. Despite America's almost total shift in the last twenty years over to hemp as a cheap, rugged, hardy textile, its smaller, more intoxicating cousin still remained an illegal substance. Pot was big business, as the farmers growing hemp could easily hide an acre or two of the illicit substance in the vast fields of the hardier hemp grown for market.

Distribution, however – as with everything else – was always a problem.

If Fluky had been the type to hold his supplier's feet to the fire, he could have easily become quite a wealthy man, simply exploiting his possession of a diesel ration card. But for Fluky, the weed had never simply been about the money. To him, pot was sacred – used in some sort of religious rite. Seriously. What religion Fluky was *exactly* was hard to say. He was rather closemouthed about the whole affair, but it was some sort of Shinto, Rastafarian, Santeria, Tent Revival kind of Christianity. All of it very secret and strange and closely linked to the forced repatriations of the Japanese Americans back to Japan.

Get Fluky drunk or high and he'd start in on some apocalyptic-inspired, secret society, cult-like crap about revolution, judgment day, and the government being held accountable for the wartime internment of the Japanese and the subsequent nuclear carpet bombing of his homeland. It was all pretty crazy shit. Hungover the next day, Fluky would always play it off as just some sort of big joke he was playing on the rest of us – seeing how far he could take it. But the crazy talk, every time, varied so little in its content, that it started to become familiar simply through repetition. What Fluky really believed, I couldn't say, and he was disinclined to discuss any of it sober.

With the joint made, we lit it up and passed it around, smoking it down to the end. All three of us were soon well and truly blasted; on three quarters of a bottle of Scotch, some wicked chronic, and a miscellaneous number of beers.

Of course, this meant it was time to load back up in the wrecking truck and share our inebriation with the rest of the town. It was a tradition, just like back in high school, cruising around town, looking for girls and trouble.

We made our way out of Mitty's sun porch, around through the yard of garbage, and back into the cab a Fluky's truck.

With an angry growl, the old diesel coughed to life. Fluky reversed back out onto the road, kicking up dirt and sand, and pointed us down the hill towards Pottersville.

We were all talking at once, laughing and carrying on snippets of various conversations. We were catching up with old friends, reminiscing about past excursions in our current state of mind, discussing politics and the past election. Fluky pulled out, accelerating too hard, and followed a winding path down C Street, swerving from lane to lane.

Perhaps nowadays we'd have thought twice about letting Fluky drive in his condition. But back then, when there were so few other operating vehicles on the road... Pedestrians, perhaps, should have been a concern, but we were heading down the hill towards Pottersville, and no one ever bothered to visit Pottersville anymore. No one lived there – hadn't since the Concession put the mega-gauge rails in, thirty years before, and the whole town had upped and moved to build Boot Hill.

As kids, the three of us had entertained ourselves by taking Fluky's dad's .30-30 down into Pottersville and plinking out the windows of old Victorian mansions that lined the streets of the silent ghost town. But that was back in the day when things like cartridges for hunting rifles hadn't been an obscene luxury. Back when the Concession Department Store still had things on its shelves to sell.

But now everything was scarce; from clothes to hardware to the essentials of everyday life – everything except, paradoxically, McTavish and Frau Brau and other liquor. Somehow, the Concession was always able to keep the shelves stocked with booze. Perhaps, once a month, you might have to eat a meal without salt because the store shelves were bare of it, but never did you have to skimp on that stiff drink before and after. Never.

Of course, the shortages, and Boot Hill's complementary surpluses, were the genesis of the whole idea of *The Cordwainer*. As we drove down C into the town of Pottersville proper, I was explaining to the others how the shortages were being felt back in the Big City.

"...I swear, honest to God, three fucking hours people were standing in line. And you know what? In the end it all turned out to just be a rumor. The Concession Store on Pine hadn't gotten any new shipment that day. Not of boots, not of anything. The Manager had just been too chicken shit to tell anyone. He just let them all stand out there on the sidewalk, lining up. Paper says he feared a riot if people found out the rumor wasn't true... He was concerned for people's safety..."

I laughed, Mitty laughed, and Fluky found my story to be almost irresistibly hysterical. The truck listed suddenly towards the sidewalk as he doubled over in hysterics at the wheel. Without thinking, I reached over and pulled the wheel back towards the center of the road, saving us from disaster but upsetting the Frau I was holding in my other hand, spilling it over the lapel of my new coat.

"That right there! That's some funny shit!" Fluky said, regaining his composure and hold of the truck's steering wheel at the same time. It *was* pretty funny. The idea of people lining up for a pair of boots. In Boot Hill it was the one thing, apart from McTavish, there was always plenty of. Hundreds of thousands of pairs. Freight containers lined the roads out of town towards The Shop just full of boots rotting away in the heat. No one in Boot Hill ever went short of a pair of boots. There was no need to. Yours wear out – yours get a little dirty – just pop open a cargo container and help yourself. Every size, every shape, every style under the sun.

But to the roadside of the highway was as far as most boots in Boot Hill ever made it. In other towns – in the rest of America – a new pair of boots was akin to something like gold. Better than gold, truth be told, since you couldn't put gold on your feet.

I suppose, in those other towns, they were making something else. Brassieres, perhaps, and no one there ever went short for one of those. Shipping container after shipping container filled with brassieres there, stretching off into the horizon. But in Boot Hill, it was boots. And shoes and sneakers and waders and galoshes. And pumps and wingtips and loafers and flip-flops and cowboy boots and moccasins. All waiting on the Concession Behemoths, waiting for space on the next available train.

But the next train never seemed to come – space never seemed to open up. What few boots actually left Boot Hill were little more than a drop in the ocean to the size of the need in the thousands of cities, in the hundreds of regions of America where boots were going scarce. And it was a similar story with everything else: Food, clothes, hardware, household goods. The shortages were nationwide. There were too few trains and too few freight cars to ever seriously put a dent in the demand for everything and anything people were running short on. And the Concession, as owners of America's last operating railroad, was to whom everyone pointed the finger – both depended on and blamed.

"You'd think footwear, of all things, would fall under the aegis of the emergency powers," Mitty remarked, his arms thrust out against the truck's dash, bolt solid, hoping to brace himself against the crash Fluky's driving always guaranteed. "I mean, a good pair of boots is no luxury." Mitty was referring to the emergency executive order that President Kennedy had signed after his re-election last year, authorizing a relaxation of locomotive carbon caps, hoping to combat the chronic shortages.

"Boots are way down on the list," I replied, "when folks are still short on food."

Fluky suddenly made a hard turn to the left as if to avoid something invisible in the road and I came crashing across the cab into Mitty, this time completely losing hold of my beer. The rear wheels broke free and the truck came spinning around. We skidded and twisted and for a second, I thought the truck was going to roll. But we skipped to a halt on the sandy cobblestones of Pottersville's Main Street, pointing back up the road in the direction we had come.

"Here we are!" Fluky announced, pulling hard on the handbrake. He opened his door and promptly collapsed out into a heap on the road. Mitty was more cautious, stepping out of the truck like a sailor truly grateful for his return to terra firma. He stooped over the second he stepped free of the vehicle and I thought he was about to barf. But after a moment of contemplation, he caught his second wind and pulled himself back up to his full six feet. He re-lit the Jefferson that had never left his mouth and took a puff.

"Always an adventure, riding with you, Fluky," Mitty said, fidgeting with his cigarette holder.

"Did I hit somethin'?" Fluky asked, still laying in a lump in the middle of the road.

"No, no," Mitty assured, strolling off down a broken, weed-covered sidewalk. "But there by the grace of God..."

The sun was just beginning to set.

We were a block from the old Union Station that dominated the center of Pottersville and we stumbled our way there from the spot where the wrecking truck had come to rest. The Station's grand, Romanesque arched facade had always been a favorite target of ours, with its intricate patterns of stained glass smashing gratifyingly when winged by a bullet. We were weaponless this trip, however, and had to satisfy ourselves with throwing stones.

"Son-of-a-bitch!" Fluky yelled, throwing a rock that hit nothing but air. Mitty and Fluky were drinking the last two Frau's from the back of the truck, but I'd come up empty-handed. "You ready for work on Monday, Beans?" he asked.

I threw a rock but lost sight of it in the shadows of the setting sun: "Hell, yeah," I answered. "Four years of nothing and finally I get to see a paycheck."

"Certainly!" Mitty punctuated, tossing a rock.

"What'd you say you got a degree in?" Fluky threw another rock; this time it hit something large and fragile. "Hell, yeah! What'd you say you studied? Mechanical Engineerin'?"

"Yeah."

"And you're goin' to work at a boot factory?"

"Yeah."

"Lot of need for Mechanical Engineers makin' boots?"

"I doubt it..." I tossed a rock and heard something break.

"Can't you find a real job?" Fluky was picking up a big rock, one that required both hands, and threw it. It traveled all of two feet. "I mean, usin' your degree?"

I laughed. "Sure, sure..."

"Surely somewhere, someone is designing new locomotives," Mitty chimed in, throwing a rock. "Or automobiles... Still..."

I paused. In the twilight the two of them kept throwing projectiles. I picked up a big rock and really gave it a toss. It hit something, maybe stone, but no breaking glass.

"There were thirteen thousand people in my graduating class," I said with an edge to my voice. "I graduated number four thousand six hundred and twelve." I picked up Fluky's beer from where he'd put it down and drank the rest of it. "Ain't no engineering jobs for number four thousand six hundred and twelve." I squashed the carton and tossed it after our stones. "Numbers one, two, maybe three... But number four thousand? Hell, number ten ain't even got a chance in hell."

"My..." Was all Mitty could say. Fluky said nothing.

Fact is, if Dad hadn't pulled some stings – if he hadn't had the inside track and knew who was retiring and when – the Foreman's job at The Shop wouldn't have been waiting home for me, either. In those days, it wasn't like you could just go and apply for a job. To get work you had to know somebody who knew somebody. That was why I was back in Boot Hill. Even with a degree and all the education in the world, all that mattered was who I knew and what jobs they knew about. A Class A chit was all well and good, but if my dad hadn't been twenty years' Foreman at The Shop, I'd have been worse off than Mitty with his Class F.

"Hey, shithead, that was my beer," Fluky said when he turned around and found his beer gone.

"Is there any more?" I asked. We both looked at Mitty. He was drinking the last of his.

"Empty, I'm afraid," he said, tossing the waxy carton idly back over his shoulder.

"Shit, we're out of beer," Fluky said with a serious tone, as if it was the most intractable problem he'd faced all day.

"Have you sobered up enough to drive us back to town?" I asked.

"Hell, no!" Fluky said with pride. "But when the fuck did that ever stop me?"

I couldn't help but laugh. Fluky turned and started off back towards the truck. Mitty and I fell in step behind him.

But it was already dusk. That meant the Concession Store would be closed. We'd be buying no more alcohol that night – not retail.

In the half light of the setting sun I paused in my step, letting Fluky and Mitty walk on. I took a moment to look around me, at the rough stonework of the Richardsonian-style storefronts that lined Pottersville's old Main Street. They were boarded up now, facades sandblasted by the scrub, but the signs of the various stores were still partially legible. Dry Goods, Hardware, Butchers, Grocers. Auto parts and an appliance dealership. Two appliance dealerships, no less, kitty-corner to each other where Main crossed 13th. The inefficiency of it all tickled me.

In Boot Hill we just had the one Concession Store, with departments for all those goods. When they had anything to sell. What town could stand the wastefulness of *two* places, on the same street, where you could buy a refrigerator?

Still, seven-thirty in the evening, back in the heyday of Pottersville, you could have probably still bought a carton of whiskey. Bottle. Glass bottle; it came in glass bottles back then. And if one store had felt the need to close at dusk, perhaps another store would have stayed open later, just to get the business. Maybe people in Pottersville had liked to buy refrigerators after dark...

Yeah, the inefficiency of it all really tickled me.

Back at the wrecking truck I let Mitty be piggy in the middle for a change and made him straddle the drive shaft with his long, chubby legs. Fluky fired the monster to life and ground through the gears trying to find first.

Eventually, we were on our way, climbing slowly back up the slope of C Street. I leaned out the window of the truck and watched the abandoned Victorian homes roll by, contemplative as the booze and the weed began to wear off.

At the crest of the hill, as we passed Mitty's home, I was granted once again a few seconds of the sweeping view I'd observed earlier. All of Boot Hill was laid out there before me, this time in darkness – twinkling lights stretching out to the horizon. Again, the same revelation dawned on me: One town, one company. Owner of the hearts and minds of everyone who lived in Boot Hill. And Monday morning it'd own me, too.

Man, I needed another drink.

Chapter Four

Soliloquies and Snowmen

Of course, you could always count on old Fluky.

Descending back into Boot Hill down C, he swung us across the tracks to a small, well-kept bungalow in the middle of town. I didn't recognize the place and Fluky instructed both Mitty and me to stay in the truck as he hopped out and walked drunkenly up to the front door. After a quick knock, the door opened, and Fluky vanished inside. He was no more than five minutes; the door reopened and Fluky stepped out, Frau in one hand and the rest of a six pack in the other.

"Who lives here?" I asked as Fluky passed the cartons of beer through the truck window. Mitty and I both grabbed a fresh brew and popped open the corners.

"You'll see..." Fluky replied with a wide grin, leaning up against the door. "They're puttin' on their faces..."

They? My curiosity didn't haunt me for long. Presently, the door opened and the plump pink shapes of the Anders Twins came skipping out of the house. I laughed out loud. The Anders Twins, Lisa and Bettie, still as round and cuddly as I remembered. They trotted up to the window of the truck, squealing and making a horrible noise. I inferred they were happy to see me and I was happy to see them. As Fluky swung open his door they piled in, peppering me with kisses.

Everyone was talking at once. Mitty and Fluky for good measure. Hello, how are you, how have you been? One of the Anders Twins positioned herself on Mitty's lap and the other parked herself right on top of mine. Again, the seating arrangement was tradition. I wrapped an arm around the pink cashmere middle of my passenger – Lisa, I think, but it could have been Bettie – and reveled in the familiar comfort. A thousand times the Anders Twins had ridden with us as we'd cruised around town. They'd always been our most eager and reliable company, back in the day. And four years had dampened none of their excitement. Both of them were fussing on me, saying how grown-up I looked, admiring my new jacket. Fluky finished his beer and tossed away the carton, slipped in behind the wheel and started up the truck.

Bettie – or was it Lisa? – had a fresh carton of McTavish. Suddenly, the funk of a mood that had been gripping me vanished. We laughed and passed the whiskey around and squeezed Anders Twins in various inappropriate places. Fluky brought the truck around a corner and parked in front of the old school. Boot High! We all yelled in unison, our alma mater. We piled out of the truck, and while the girls found a spot to sit, the boys attempted to play a rousing game of Flukyball.

Flukyball, named after its inventor, was a sport that could only seriously be enjoyed when you were stinking drunk. It was played on a basketball court – namely the court behind Boot High – and combined elements of basketball, baseball, and probably some shit that Fluky just made up.

It was played with a baseball bat and a number of tennis balls.

A batter stood at half court, with a pitcher under a basket at each end. The batter fielded pitches from both pitchers alternately, attempting to hit the pitch back and through the basketball hoop. A basket counted as a home run; hitting the rim, a triple; the backboard, a double, and simply clearing the court, a single. Strikes were counted and, at least theoretically, score was kept. Of course, the math of the whole game was quickly lost in the chaos of remembering exactly which way the batter was meant to be facing, and balls being pitched at the back of the batter's head when he guessed wrong.

It was an insanely frustrating game, made no simpler by the required level of intoxication. Matches inevitably had to be settled with a "lightning round", which involved tossing the baseball bat up into the air and trying to thread it back through the basketball hoop without smashing yourself in the head.

I never remember anyone ever actually winning a game of Flukyball, other than Fluky, and he always just changed the rules when he thought he might actually lose.

But much fun was had by all. The girls laughed and yelled encouragement from the sidelines. By the time we were done, and Mitty had an apricot-sized welt on his forehead from the "lightning round", we were all sweaty and beat. We collapsed on the bleachers by the girls and Fluky rolled us all another joint.

Our evenings of marauding customarily, and obtusely, always ended in the walk-in freezer of Putter's Café.

Perhaps, in the age of global overheating, it wasn't so obtuse. It was the only operating sub-zero cooling unit left in town, and in 1967 – the date of Boot Hill's last appreciable snowfall – Fluky, Mitty and I had stowed away the final snowman we were able to construct – perhaps the final snowman built in the continental United States.

Actually, it was a snow *woman*, if you wanted to be technical. Dubbed Mrs. Frostynips by Fluky one drunken evening, she had as many curves as either of the Anders Twins. Back in High School, we made a point of visiting her each and every occasion we could, and the staff of Putter's tolerated our loitering in their freezer, perhaps because there was so little in there besides the snowman. For years, most everything Putter's served was made out of cans or dried goods. The only fresh produce Boot Hill ever saw came seasonally off the Palouse, by horse cart, and was sold illicitly in makeshift farmers' markets for hard cash. The rest of the year, everyone had to make do with whatever packaged meat and vegetables came off the Concession trains. Putter's, however, made an apple pie out of nothing but salted crackers that could fool you every time, if you didn't look too hard.

It was there, in that freezer, that Mitty first outlined his plan: Mitty's Plan. I remember Mitty interrupting the general conversation, declaring:

"It is in times such as these," Mitty said forthrightly, drunkenly, blowing out a lung full of smoke, mixing it with the steam from his breath, "that bold action is required."

It was apropos to nothing. Everyone fell silent, unable to retie the lost threads of their conversations. I was cuddling up next to Lisa – or Bettie – trying to stay warm. Fluky was doing the same with Bettie – or Lisa. The McTavish was half gone and

Fluky's joint had given us a case of the munchies. We had a couple pieces of that mock apple pie, stolen on our way through the kitchen, and I was wishing I'd stolen some coffee, too.

"Agh," Fluky exhaled in disgust, "not this goddamn chestnut." He was obviously familiar with this particular tangent of Mitty's. "Three drinks and he starts thinkin' he's J.D. Rockefeller."

Mitty continued, ignoring Fluky, "We define our times, gentlemen, or our times define us. I say we are on the brink – the very brink – of disaster. Lady Fortune is a strumpet that must be courted; she does not acquiesce. To sit here is to be complicit in our own undoing. We have been led, I assert, down the primrose path, my friends, and now the day has arrived that the primroses shall prove themselves to have thorns!"

Mitty returned his cigarette holder to his mouth and let his words sink in. The walk-in freezer was silent except for the compressor buzzing away.

Fluky turned to the Anders Twin cuddled up in his arm and asked: "What'd he say?"

"Primroses ain't got no thorns..." Lisa/Bettie said with a giggle.

"What *are* you talking about, Mitty?" I asked, swallowing a mouthful of pie.

"Ignore him," Fluky interjected, not giving Mitty the opportunity to elaborate. "He's been pitchin' this same dumb-ass idea for goin' on six months now. Dumb-ass talk from a dummy..."

"Funny, he don't talk like no dummy..." Bettie/Lisa commented.

Mitty fumed, shooting daggers from his eyes. He continued, indignantly, pulling the cigarette holder from his mouth, letting his mustached upper lip quiver. "The Sword of Damocles swings precariously about our heads, my friends. The hour is late, there is but one question now to be asked – one question of paramount importance."

"Yeah," Fluky laughed, "where are we gonna get more beer?"

Mitty bristled: "No, no, no!" He thrust the cigarette holder back into his mouth and almost bit it in two. "Are we mice or are we men? Shall we grasp the future in our hands or fall back into the precipice."

"Preci-what?" Fluky laughed, taking a drink of the McTavish.

"Big hole," Bettie/Lisa cuddled up next to me answered.

"Oh." Fluky cocked an eyebrow. "How about you shuttin' your precipice, Mitty?"

"Ah!" Mitty waved a hand.

"Unless you got some wise-ass idea on how we's gonna rustle up some more beer..."

"You say he makes noises like this often?" I said directly to Fluky. "He ever come to a point?"

"Oh yeah, that's the whole nutso part of the deal. Y'all just wait..."

"Then let him finish," I said. I was at the state where I was neither feeling any pain nor the cold of the walk-in freezer. "I want to hear what he's got to say."

"Thank you," Mitty said gratefully, giving me a slight nod.

"Can I eat the rest of that pie?" Bettie/Lisa asked me. I shushed her, and handed her the plate.

There was silence. Mitty looked confused.

"Precipice," I nudged.

"Ah yes," Mitty recovered, "The Sword of Damocles."

"Just git to the meat of it!" Fluky interrupted. "Shit, I swear, ya like a constipated mule."

"If you'll permit me."

"Sure."

"*The Sword of Damocles...*" Mitty started again, stridently.

"...He wantsta haul a load of fuckin' boots over the mountains and sell 'em in the Big City." Fluky again interrupted, stealing away all of Mitty's thunder.

"Damn your eyes!" Mitty exclaimed as the freezer filled with the sound of laughter.

And that, right there, was Mitty's Grand Plan. Simultaneously the most brilliant and stupidest thing I'd ever heard. It was arguably Mitty's only real contribution to *The Cordwainer* – the Plan – but it was genius. It took an idiot like Mitty to be such a genius. No genius in his right mind would have suggested anything so absurd. It was monumentally ridiculous. He might as well have suggested we go to the moon and eat blue cheese, as realistic as the idea was. The Concession had a government-assured monopoly on freight hauling – that was why it was called the Concession – and by extension, just about everything else in the country.

But Mitty had piqued my curiosity.

"I'm sorry," I asked, choking back the laughter. "How exactly are we supposed to do that?"

"He don't know," Fluky laughed, taking a drink. "Tartarhead."

As we all laughed – Fluky, myself and the Anders Twins – Mitty visibly shrank. To us, it all sounded like a joke, but it was obvious that Mitty had meant his speech all with due gravity. He looked injured.

"Horse and cart? Balloon? Rocket to the moon?" I chuckled.

"The-the mysteries of locomotion..." Mitty stuttered out, a lump in his throat. "...have been solved for over a century..." He suddenly found something about his cigarette and its holder that required his attention. He looked up from it and scanned, beady-eyed, between the faces mocking him.

"Ya ever hear of carbon rationin', dummy?" Fluky said, pulling himself up to his feet. "Come on, I'm gettin' cold."

"No, no!" I waved Fluky back to his perch. I wasn't quite ready to let this go. "Mitty's got a good idea." He did, but I was still making fun of him. "Tell us, Mitty, tell us: How would we get a freight load of boots over the mountains? To sell in the Big City?"

"There are trains..." Mitty puffed at his Jefferson.

"Yeah, Concession trains," I corrected.

"Or perhaps that miraculous invention called the automobile..." Mitty added.

And to that I could only snicker.

"Ah, forget it!" Mitty threw up a dismissive hand. "Forget I uttered a word! To expect any curiosity – any vision – from philistines..." Mitty pulled a spent cigarette from its holder and snubbed it out on a block of ice. He reached into his pocket for a replacement and in attempting to knock a new cigarette from the pack, he upset the whole bundle, sending cigarettes spilling over the floor of the freezer.

It was sad.

Suddenly, I was hit with a pang of remorse. I bolted up and quickly helped Mitty scoop up his errant smokes. We were being cruel – picking on Mitty for being Mitty. Picking on the dummy. What was so stupid about his idea, after all? All he'd suggested was that we take advantage of an obvious market imbalance for our own profit. It was the simplest of simple ideas, the very core of commerce. All right, Mitty hadn't even begun to think the idea through. That wasn't his style. There were mitigating factors – the impending heat death of the whole planet, chief among them – but it was no reason for us to laugh at him. Mitty was just being Mitty.

"It's not a crazy idea," I reassured Mitty, without sarcasm as I handed back a fist full of cigarettes.

"Yeah, it is..." Fluky corrected, still huddled up with his Anders Twin.

"It ain't! Mitty's right: The solution to the shortages is so obvious, it's staring us all in the face. We have boots, the Big City needs them. It's hardly rocket science..."

Okay, perhaps I was overcompensating out of pity, but you couldn't really argue with the facts. Now, the details...

"Uh, yeah..." Fluky scratched the stubble on his chin. "I think ya missed a little somethin' in the middle there..."

"Well, of course. But Mitty's right about that, too. What the hell has any of us ever done about it?"

"Done about it? What the hell you talkin' about?"

"Effort. What has any of us actually *tried*?" Fluky and Mitty looked at me with open mouths. I was surprised by my forthrightness, too. "I mean, apart from sitting around and bitching, and expecting solutions from some abstract, remote bureaucrat we can conveniently blame for all our troubles and never have to accuse face-to-face." Now the weed and the whiskey were talking, but I could feel something moving inside of me. "Why can't we be bothered to get up off our *asses*? Seriously. Mitty's right, the answers to our problems aren't *hard*. Hard to implement, perhaps, but not hard to *understand*. Shit, doesn't Kennedy say this is supposed to be a Nation of Big Ideas? Well, what ideas have any of us had lately? Sitting around and bitching, drinking ourselves stupid, expecting answers..."

My diatribe was met with silent stares. Fluky lifted the McTavish carton and Mitty took a puff off his Jefferson. Nobody spoke... Until the Anders Twin, tucked in nuzzled up to my chest, started to giggle.

"You're funny..." she laughed. Her sister joined in. Soon Fluky and Mitty were chuckling along too. Now everyone was laughing at me.

"Hehe, shee-it. What that school do to you?" Fluky laughed, taking another drink.

"Yes, indeed..." Mitty agreed. He had visibly relaxed, now that he was no longer the target of the social ridicule. "Very queer..."

"Hey!" I playfully acted hurt, scooping up a handful of frost off the stacked boxes of fish sticks I was using as a pillow, and tossing it like a snowball at Mitty. I hit him, accidentally, square in the face, knocking the cigarette from his mouth. He responded with a deep belly laugh and an attempt to throw handfuls of frost back at me, unsuccessfully. We were both soon up on our feet and wrestling like children.

By the time the two of us had collapsed to the icy floor, and Fluky was done cackling like a wild hyena, we were both thoroughly soaked to the skin and my jacket sported a new tear at the right shoulder.

"Shit, you guys are crazy..." Fluky laughed.

I tried to pull myself up off the ground, but Mitty grabbed me and pulled me down, pulling himself up in my place. When he was back on his feet, I swung a foot and kicked him hard in the rump, then quickly scrambled away and back to my seat on the pile of fish sticks.

"The profit margin, however, if the task *could* be done..." Mitty said, suddenly serious again, digging around in the frost and coming back up with his cigarette holder.

"Oh yeah, the money..." I had to agree, looking at the damage to my coat. "Anyone who *could* get a load of boots across those mountains, free and clear of the Concession... Well, one crate alone.... A pair of new boots on the black market in the Big City can go for as much as $100. How many pairs in a crate? Fluky? A thousand?"

"Hell, that's a hundred grand!" Fluky said, after a few seconds of doing the mental math. He had suddenly found a new interest in the whole conversation. "Shit, we should just put wheels on one of them crates and roll it," he laughed.

"Them's some pretty steep mountains," I laughed too.

"And full of Polypigs!" an Anders Twins added. The two of them had escaped from the scuffle to the relative safety of Fluky's arms.

"Yeah, Pillypogs!" the other Anders Twin chimed in. "Melanie, at the Concession Store, a friend of her cousin's, she's living in Shadrach, and she says them Pillypogs have been raiding all the way down – all the way down to Shadrach – out of the mountains. Except the government don't want to let anyone know, 'cause it'll cause a panic and all. But they burned some homesteads to the ground, killing all the folks – women and children too. It's horrible, them Polypigs, that the government can't do nothing about them..."

"They need to send the Army!" her sister agreed. "Remember Willy? Will Palmer from History Class? Eleventh grade? He joined up right out of school. He was back home on leave last month and he says all them army fellas do is just sit around, polish boots and peel potatoes. Well, I can't see why they can't put them soldiers to good use and clean out them Polypigs. Goddamn disgrace, if you ask me."

"Too true," Mitty agreed.

"I don't know..." Fluky drawled, looking between the two Anders Twins sitting beside him, cuddling up to him against the cold. He reached back and put an arm around each one. "Them Mormons might just have the right idea... Two wives? Sounds to me like it might have, you know, some advantages..."

The Twins recoiled in disgust, scooping up freezer frost and shoving it into Fluky's face. There was a playful tussle, then all of them were on their feet, chasing around the freezer, slipping and sliding. Mitty and I joined in.

From the outside, someone opened the door to the freezer, perhaps to complain about the noise, but they were trampled underfoot as our chase spilled into Putter's kitchen. More circles around the kitchen equipment, then we were running through the tables of the restaurant itself. It was late enough that the place was mostly closed, but we charged like bulls in a china shop, upsetting tables and knocking over chairs.

Then we were out the front doors with someone behind us screaming unintelligibly. We piled into Fluky's truck and it fired to life. We were suddenly moving with Mitty still only halfway in through the door. We almost completely lost him as Fluky threw the truck around a curve. Both sisters pulled on his arms and the mass of Mitty landed on top of us all. Fluky accelerated then braked hard, sending us all rolling forward into the dash in a pile, the googly-eyed Jesus bobbling, watching on.

The truck came to a halt. Everyone was talking, laughing, and complaining about their pain. When I finally pulled myself up out of the footwell, I became aware of the flashing of the lights and the roar of the passing train. Fluky had stopped at the mega-rail crossing as a behemoth rumbled itself by, pulling an almost infinite line of rail cars behind it.

The train vanished away left and right to both horizons. The locomotive, belching out its black coal smoke, had already passed and vanished into the night. In the other direction, in the dark, the caboose could have been as much as five miles away – the behemoth trains could be that long – rail car after rail car after rail car.

The train meant that a whole shipment of boots was actually leaving Boot Hill. Acres of them, by the ton. Some town, somewhere, would be getting a delivery of boots in the morning. Maybe a few. Where, I could only guess, but in my mind's eye I could imagine people already beginning to line up.

It made me chuckle to think of all the housewives and old-age pensioners, awoken in the dead of night by some sort of psychic premonition that tomorrow, finally, the stores would have something to sell. They'd dress in the darkness and make their way, zombie-like, to the locked doors of their Concession Stores. There they'd wait, lined up patiently with their other sixth-sensed compatriots. They'd wait silently, hawk-eyed, watching, like predators, for the first stirring of life behind the Concession Stores' doors. They'd have no idea what was for sale, just a feeling, but they could smell the blood in the water. Whatever it was, they would buy it. Whatever the price, they'd pay. Boots today, maybe. Tomorrow, perhaps bacon or children's winter hats. It didn't matter. They were circling – circling, ready to feed.

THE CORDWAINER

The train rattled along as I watched it hypnotically through the cracked windscreen of the truck. Minutes passed as I was lost in my little fantasy. When I returned to reality I looked back and realized that I'd become something of a third wheel: Mitty, to my right, was making out with one Anders twin, and Fluky, to my left, was making out with the other. I felt, suddenly, very alone.

I returned my attention to the passing train. Rail car after rail car flashed by. All those boots...

If there was only some way, any way, to get around the Concession and over those mountains. A man could be rich. Very rich. Arbitrage, I remember it being called in school in economics class; though it was spoken of in the pejorative, equated to profiteering. But with the shortages becoming so dire, as Mitty had said, wasn't it all our responsibilities to help out in any way we could?

I mean, to sell a product to people willing to buy it, for a reasonable price and at reasonable profit? What, by all that was holy, could possibly be wrong with that?

Plenty, I would come to learn, once Fluky, Mitty and I really got serious about implementing Mitty's Plan.

Chapter Five

The Shop

I woke up the next morning on the porch swing of my father's house. Why I hadn't bothered to climb into my own bed, I couldn't remember. What had happened the night before after the twenty minutes we'd spent waiting for the behemoth to clear the road was a blur. I remember more drinks, someone's home. And I remembered Fluky hitting a fire hydrant in the truck as he was driving me home. But the details where hazy. At least I was alive, and I'd slept a few hours. The sun was up as I pulled myself vertical in the porch swing. That was a mistake. Instantly, the contents of my stomach revolted to the sudden movement, and came exploding forth. I managed to throw up over the edge of the porch, into the geranium beds.

The front door swung slowly open.

When I came up for air I saw Dad standing in the doorway, coffee cup in hand. He didn't look mad, he didn't look happy. He looked at me over the rim of his cup and took a sip.

"Late night?" He finally said.

I knew he was disappointed in me. *I* was disappointed in me, now that my brain was starting to function again. He turned on his heels and stepped back, silently into the shadows of the house. I was in trouble. Yelling, shouting, I knew where I stood, but when my dad got silent...

I pulled myself up to standing and my knees almost buckled under me. All I wanted to do was head for my bed, inside the house there, through the living room and right at the hall; but my dad was making his slow way towards the kitchen. I dizzily followed. I'd have to take my lumps, whatever they'd be, before I could collapse into the welcoming embrace of my soft bed. In the kitchen, my dad took a seat at the table. I dropped down into the chair across from him, facing my breakfast bowl, laid out ready for me. A box of Tom Mixx cereal – the one with the cowboy on the box – and a carton of reconstituted milk sat between my father and me. A carton of milk approximately the same size and design as the type McTavish came in. My stomach turned.

"Andy..." my father began with a sigh, then stopped, adjusting his horn-rimmed glasses. I couldn't look up from the box of Tom Mixx; the room was starting to swirl.

We sat there in silence as the seconds ticked difficultly by, my dad slowly shaking his head and looking down into his black coffee.

"Tomorrow morning..." he began again.

"I know," I interrupted.

"Just look at your jacket..."

I looked down at the beer-stained, torn hemp of my previously new coat. "Sorry," was all I could say.

"You'll have to borrow an old one of mine." He sipped at his cup. "You're twenty-two years old, Andrew. Do I have to watch you..."

"No," I returned my gaze to the box of Tom Mixx cereal – the one with the cowboy on the box. My vision was getting blurry. "I'm going to bed now," I announced.

"I just, Andy..." my dad added as I pulled myself up out of my chair. "People are going to look up to you now... At the Shop... You're a Foreman, that commands a certain amount of... respect..."

I didn't answer, I just used the table for support and worked my way across the kitchen and back out into the hall. I found the door to my room, closed it behind me, and fell face first, on top of the covers, onto my bed.

This was how I found myself when I awoke an indeterminate amount of time later that day. The sun hung low in the west over the mountains outside my window. It must have been late, I must have slept the day away. Somewhere in the house the phone was ringing. I pulled myself painfully off my bed, the swirling feeling in my head replaced with a thumping pain. I staggered out into the hall, reaching clumsily for the shrill receiver, answering it only to silence the agonizing ringing in my ears.

"Hello?" I asked.

"So, when do we begin?" the voice on the other end asked with not so much as a greeting or prologue.

"What?" was all I could manage.

"The Plan, Beanie, the *Plan*..." It was Mitty.

"What? What plan?" I rubbed the sleep from my eyes.

"For the boots! Across the mountains, to the Big City. Last night, I thought we were in agreement."

"Agreement? Boots? Plan? What?" It was too early – or too late, or my head thumped far too hard from the inside. I wasn't getting it. What had I agreed to?

"You and me, simpatico, concerning my plan..." Obviously I was meant to understand what Mitty was saying. "I've been trying to call you all day!"

"I've been sleeping it off," I admitted, then added: "Ain't you hungover, Mitty?"

"Of course!" Mitty replied dismissively, "but no simple headache is going to dampen my enthusiasm. We have a rare opportunity here, Beanie, a plan of singular ingenuity..."

"What are we talking about again?" I was remembering some talk about the shortages and people laughing at me.

"The Plan, Beanie, the Plan..."

And then it came back to me like a flood.

I dropped the receiver from some height back onto its cradle, letting it clatter and rock back to rest. The phone again began to ring when I was halfway back to my room. I closed my bedroom door firmly behind me, ignoring it. I returned to bed, this time undressing and climbing under the covers, and let the faint shrill of the phone ring on in the distance.

Two minutes and I was back asleep again, with the phone ringing in my dreams. Mitty had something important to tell me in the dream, but I couldn't understand his muffled voice on the other end of the line. Eventually, I was forced to hang up on Mitty in the dream, only to realize I was standing in the corridor of the High School, naked and late for a test.

Monday morning came far too rapidly, and I was still suffering from the aftereffects of my hangover as I pulled on one of my father's old sport coats and ate a breakfast of Tom Mixx cereal – the one with the cowboy on the box – at the kitchen table with my father. He spared me any new lectures on my behavior and improved social status, and I ate breakfast in silence, as Dad sipped away at his coffee.

Twenty minutes later, we were at the end of our street at the corner of Roosevelt waiting on the trolley. That was when the nerves really began to set in. We had our lunch pails with bologna sandwiches and thermoses of coffee. A dozen or so other Shop workers were also waiting at the corner, similarly equipped.

It was my first day of work. I realized I was schlepping to work like every other Joe. No one at the corner paid me a second glance. I was almost invisible. There were terse "good mornings" to my father, but no one paid me any heed. In the old sport coat and slacks I looked like a younger carbon copy of my dad. All eyes looked up Roosevelt for the trolley, and after a few minutes I found my stare also trained down the street in unconscious sympathy. Presently, the trolley rumbled into view, making stops at each corner down Roosevelt to load up on workers. When our turn came, we shuffled aboard to find the trolley already packed with people. There was standing room only and we hung onto the hemp straps attached to the ceiling as the trolley grumbled back to life.

It was a forty minute ride out to The Shop on the very outskirts of town, where the concrete bungalows of Boot Hill give away to the dusty scrub. The closer to the factory the trolley rolled the more frequent the sight of a lone shipping container off to the side of the road became. At first the crates were hardly noticeable, seemingly abandoned and forgotten in the sand. But by the time we were within a mile of The Shop the containers were neatly stacked shoulder to shoulder and two high like valley walls beside us.

It was an impressive sight to see the productive power of The Shop expressed in such physical terms. I could only guess how many years of back stock the shipping containers represented. But the simple fact that The Shop made a hell of a lot of boots at a hell of a clip couldn't be contradicted. That the system fell down so impressively beyond the factory doors was a tragedy of epic proportions. It was obvious to anyone with a pair of eyes that Boot Hill had no trouble producing enough boots to shod the nation. That people were going barefoot in so many towns... Boot Hill couldn't be faulted.

Of course, determining who was to blame for the crippling shortages that were gripping the nation was a harder game to play. There were plenty of candidates to point the finger at: The Concession, with its mega-gauge monopoly on freight; the government back in Washington with its bureaucratic micromanaging of the people's lives cradle to grave; the vicious black-market goons, stealing everything that wasn't bolted down and selling it back the next day for profit. But in any serious critique of how America's fortunes had swerved so outrageously off the tracks, blame had to eventually fall squarely at the feet of the American people.

Perhaps not, candidly, with current Americans, suffering under the weight of a barely functioning nation; but past generations, who'd raped and ravished the land and the air with little idea of the implications or the longterm damage they were causing. The blame, if truth be told, had to fall on the heads of people long since dead and gone; though those still living had to live with the consequences, pay the price. But as a nation, we were the victims of our own excess, squandered a hundred years before I was even born.

The rapid overheating of the planet because of human production of greenhouse gases was, by far, the worst offender. The old coal-burning factories; the automobiles that millions of Americans used to own and drive; the vast deforestation of the planet for construction materials and home heating had all taken an irreversible toll on the fragile planet. If it hadn't been for the global droughts of '27 and '28, the subsequent market crash, and the birth of the New Deal, who knows what sort of damage the planet would have suffered. But luckily, progressive politics and serious respect for hard science came to power in America with the election of FDR in 1932. He set about reorganizing the nation around a green agenda, focusing on the symbiotic issues of rampant poverty and global overheating. The overheating of the Planet Earth was slowed, but the austerity measures required to achieve it...

And forty years later the effects were still being felt. The Concession, so long hindered by stringent carbon caps on its behemoth locomotives, attempted to supply a nation drowning in demand. But to run a company under such conditions, to even attempt to stay profitable, required extensive subsidies and market protections from the government. The Concession had quickly become the last operating railroad in the continental United States – truly the Government Concession of transportation in America. Despite its best efforts – its truly epic attempts to get a handle on the spiraling U.S. economy – the shortages worsened until the nation had reached the chronic conditions that so epitomized that summer of 1973, when I started on my first day of work at The Shop.

The brakes squealed and the trolley came to a rest before the factory gates. We shuffled off as we shuffled on: orderly and in no particular rush. Other electric trolleys from other corners of town were arriving along their branch lines, disgorging workers appropriate in class to the neighborhood it serviced. Trolleys from the wrong side of the tracks brought Class C workers: assembly line cutters and renders and dyers. From the outer, but more affluent, downtown neighborhoods the trolleys brought Class B workers, mostly women; the stitchers and finishers and the low-level office staff. It was only from the central, mainline trolleys that the Class A workers like myself – foremen, accountants and managers – arrived. Only the Class A workers were wearing shirts and ties, the lower ranks dressed in blue-dyed hemp work clothes that could have passed for denim. Everyone made their way through the factory gates and across the small work yard toward The Shop itself.

I followed my father in a state of shocked amazement. The sheer size of The Shop was intimidating. Numerous buildings of various eras and various sizes clustered around the work yard. I remember my father telling me that The Shop had once been a munitions plant back in the war, after weapons production had been moved across the mountains to escape Japanese bombing. The core of that munitions factory was still there, now many times expanded upon. Annexes and processing wings and, in the late 60s, a whole new assembly line building. The Shop had increased output 150 percent since 1958, my father was proud to tell anyone and everyone who would listen. He felt a personal sense of satisfaction in that fact, felt at least a little personally responsible for the success. My dad made straight across the yard for a small, single-story building off to the right. I tried to keep up, but lagged behind as I absorbed the sheer scale of everything around me.

We stepped through a small door to a round of thunderous applause.

I was taken aback, curious about what I had done to merit such adulation, when I realized that no one was actually applauding me. The small room, which I'd later come to learn was the Foreman break room, was filled to the gills with people. There was a small raised platform at the far end of the room on which two men – one younger, laughing; one older, looking sheepish – were standing.

As the applause died down, the younger one continued: "Now, I know we're all going to miss Barry. I know he's been a Shop favorite, particularly with the girls in the typing pool." Laughter. "But retirement comes to us all, and sooner than many of us expect."

My father was sliding his lunch pail into a small cubbyhole off to the left of the door with "David Rice" written on tape in black pen just above it. He removed his jacket and hung it up in the cubbyhole, all the while giving his full attention to the man talking on stage. He laughed on cue with everyone else and stepped in amongst the crowd when he'd stripped down to his shirt sleeves.

I hesitated on what to do. I looked down the row of cubbies but could find none that was labeled with my name. I held my lunch self-consciously in my hand and realized that I was the only person of at least two hundred who was wearing a coat. The protocol was obviously that you wore a jacket to work but removed it the second you stepped through the door. It was little wonder that there was still so much wear left in my dad's old coat. But there was nowhere to hang my jacket and I felt foolishly out of place. I had to fight back the feeling that I should bolt from the room and run the whole ten miles back to town. I was acting like a kid and for the first time in my life I was in a place exclusively the domain of adults. I had to act my age, I realized, unsure of exactly how to inconspicuously hold my lunch pail.

"Now, fifty might not seem that old to some," the young man was saying.

"Put him out of his misery!" someone yelled from the floor to universal chuckles.

The man continued, "...but twenty-five long years of loyal service here at The Shop is deserving of its reward. And today we're happy to send Barry here off to, hopefully, many happy years of retirement, filled with the satisfaction that he is leaving behind a better, more productive factory from his years of service; and a happier, more productive workforce from his inspiration."

There was applause again. The sheepish man up on the stage looked like he was welling up with tears – happy and sad.

"So we'd like to present you," the younger man continued again, "with this watch, in recognition of your long service." He held up a small box with something gold inside. The room erupted again in applause, this time mixed with whistles and cheers. The sheepish man on the stage took the small box and shook hands with the young man vigorously. Then, as spontaneously as the applause had begun, it ended, and a hundred minor conversations began simultaneously.

The sheepish man up on the platform, Barry, looked sad and alone.

The crowd was already beginning to disperse as Barry stepped down off the platform. The man who had presented the watch had already vanished and no one was paying Barry any attention as he moved through the crowd. He was turning over the small box in his hands as he crossed the break room, fidgeting with the lid.

He came straight across the room and right up to me.

"Andrew Rice?" he said, holding out a hand. I attempted to raise a hand to take his but my lunch pail was still in it. I had to transfer the pail to my left hand before I could shake his.

"Yes, yes," I stammered.

"Congratulations," he said, looking everywhere but at me in the eye. "First day of work, I know it can be intimidating, but you'll get the hang of it soon enough. Here." He pushed by me, lifted a jacket out of a cubbyhole and said, "This will be yours." He reached up and pulled off a length of tape that had "Barry Winters" written on it in pen. He pulled on his coat and shook my hand again. "Good luck, keep your nose clean. Pay attention to your father. He practically runs this place, so if you're anything like him..." He was still shaking my hand. The handshake had been going on uncomfortably long. He pulled his hand away self-consciously and wiped it off on his pants. "Well, anyway. Good luck." He spun on his heel and headed for the door.

Suddenly, somehow, I felt like I'd jumped into somebody's grave.

I put my lunch pail into the cubbyhole and removed my coat. I was hanging it up when I noticed a small black box that Barry had set on the shelf inside the cubby. I opened it up and looked at the small, gold watch. Barry's parting gift, ticking away telling me the time was 9:15.

I contemplated running after Barry, but he was already out of sight. My father's voice came from behind me, telling me it was time to get to work. I closed the lid of the small black box and began to return it to Barry's cubby – my cubby. Then I stopped, reopened the box and slipped the gold watch onto my wrist. It seemed a shame to waste it, even for a day, and I tightened the strap in place and checked the time. My father's voice came again from across the room and I turned, reporting to my father for duty.

Chapter Six

The Four-Boxed Form

What I hadn't understood at the time, what might have made all the difference, was that all two hundred of the people in that room for Barry's going away celebration were Foremen at The Shop. Perhaps if I'd known that, what was to happen next might not have come as such a soul-crushing shock. But as it was, I was blissfully ignorant as I followed my father out of the Foreman's break room, up a flight of stairs and along a gangway towards the Managing Foreman's small, glassed-in office.

The Managing Foreman, Mr. Salmon, was an old war buddy of my father's. They had together, unlike so many others, risen up off the floor of The Shop into managerial positions, back before the Employment Edicts – before the chit system. Mr. Salmon was an old family friend, a guest at our dinner table countless times back when my mother was still alive. His portly frame was an unmistakable sight lumbering around town. To work with Mr. Salmon and my father, to be one of "the guys"... It was hard to keep my perspective.

My father held the door for me as I stepped into Foreman Salmon's ten-foot square office, which was barely more than a desk and a panoramic view of The Shop floor. The mass of Mr. Salmon was discussing some figures written down on a clipboard with three men as I entered. Mr. Salmon was dressed in slacks, pulled up high on his gut, held in place by a brown, faux leather, hemp belt, perfectly circling his equator. The other three men were dressed in ties and short-sleeved, pocketed white shirts – the uniform, I would come to learn, of the accounting department.

Mr. Salmon didn't look up as my father and I entered, but continued mumbling to the accountants in low tones.

My father walked up and started to speak without waiting for any acknowledgement of his presence. "Andrew's starting today," he said, "just back from college."

"All the Rices, then, present and accounted for, huh?" Foreman Salmon said without looking up from the clipboard.

"You bet!" my father said happily. "Any time you're ready, you can pension me off like old Barry."

Mr. Salmon snorted at this, finally looking up from his clipboard. He looked me over in my new tie and crisp, white shirt and seemed to approve of my presence.

"The little Rice boy, huh?" he laughed. My father tittered, and the accountants smirked dutifully. "You've got mighty big shoes to fill, you do son, mighty big." He held out a hand. I reached out and shook it. As we were shaking I noticed the Managing Foreman look down at Barry's gold watch hanging from my wrist. He looked up, for the first time looking me in the eyes, and the expression on his face subtly changed.

The Foreman pulled his hand away and I quickly retracted mine, trying to hide the watch up my shirt sleeve.

"Put him on Number Six, Dave," Mr. Salmon said tersely to my father and returned his attention to the clipboard. Without another word, my father and I receded from the tiny office and back down the stairs.

"I..." I started to say, then stopped. My father was walking a few paces in front of me. He was shuffling papers and a pair of clipboards in his hands, arranging them.

"Line Six is a good place to start. Good for learning the ropes," my father said as he clipped a set of papers to one board. "But things can move quick down there. You've got to pay attention. No lollygagging or daydreaming, you understand?"

"Sure."

My father handed back the clipboard he had loaded with pages as we reached the bottom of the stairs. There he paused, turning to face me, to impart some sage advice, as he always did in his way.

"Now, I know what you're like, son, but you've got to keep your wits about you. No goofing off. The Worker B's will take advantage of a new Foreman and try and goldbrick, so you've got to stay on top of them. They know their jobs, but they're always looking for any sign of weakness."

"Sure, Dad, sure..." I nodded.

"I'm serious, Andrew," he said with a gravity that was uncharacteristic. "This isn't school. This is the real deal. There's no make-up exams, re-tests or summer school here. If you can't make the grade... Well, I don't have to tell you how many other kids you graduated with would like a shot at a job like this."

He didn't have to remind me. The thirteen thousand names read out at graduation were a fair reminder. I looked down at the clipboard in my hands and examined the top sheet, determined not to let my father down. I was a well educated, intelligent man, with the full weight of my duty fully explained to me. I was going to try my hardest – I mean, how hard could it be? I'd gotten a 4.0 in differential equations. How hard could making a pair of boots be?

Not hard at all, I would find out.

The top sheet on the stack of papers clipped to the board was a simple cover page, I thought, of four check-boxes. I hardly glanced at it, flipping over to the next page. I was surprised to find that the second sheet was the same as the first: four check-boxes next to four lines of text. The third, the fourth, the fifth page were identical. The entire stack of papers were just the same four-boxed form. I flicked through them quickly, looking for deviation, and looked back up at my father in incomprehension. The look he gave me I couldn't quite read.

"What's this?" I asked, holding up the clipboard.

"Your *job*," my father said defensively. I'd unexpectedly hit a nerve. I looked down at the stack of papers and back at my father. I knew better than to push it.

He turned and started off across the vastness of The Shop floor, moving expertly through the various conveyors and assembly line stations that crisscrossed and dotted the main production floor. I lowered my clipboard and jogged to keep up with him.

"Now, this week, Number Six is working on loafers," he started. "Loafer quotas have been raised by the back office, and we're under pressure to keep up."

I was listening. Not understanding, but listening.

"So, as I said: No loafing about!" he paused in his step, realizing the unintended pun he'd just made. He shook it off and continued: "Not you, and don't let the Worker B's, either. You're a Class A, they're a Class B. Remember that. Never forget it. There's an order to things here, son, a reason for everything. You might not understand it at first, but... Well, it's like the Army. There's officers and soldiers. People to give orders and people to take them. Remember which one you are, son, and you'll be all right."

"Yes, Dad," I agreed, trotting to keep up with him. Large numbers hung over the various assembly line conveyors, large enough to be read from anywhere across the vast expanse of The Shop floor. We were moving quickly toward the massive Number Six, hanging over an indistinct section of the real estate.

"Now this," my father said, pausing and slapping a palm down onto the clipboard I was carrying, "is your progress sheet. Think of it as your metronome. I know!" He threw up a hand as I started to speak. "It doesn't look like much, but it's critically important. Every crate that rolls off the end of your line, son, has to leave with one of these sheets attached. Correctly filled out, signed and inspected. This is your oath here, son, in black and white. You're certifying each crate of boots that leaves your production line as fit and ready for market. Without this form, my boy, there'd be no quality controls on the product that leaves this factory. You're signing your name and certifying each crate of boots this factory manufactures. There's a trust there. You're taking on quite a responsibility with this job, my boy. Think of it as a bond." My father stopped as we approached the Number Six production line and seemed to grow distant. "An unspoken contract... Between you and the greater world beyond these walls... That we manufacture a pair of boots of a guaranteed quality, sold at a fair price." There was a pride in his voice as the clatter of Production Line Six echoed around him. Then he returned to earth and remembered what he was doing.

He began to explain, in intricate detail, the operation of Line Six and the function of each station along its conveyor. But I wasn't listening. I lifted my clipboard and inspected the four boxes that outlined the circumference of my job:

Box One. These Shoes/Boots were stitched and assembled under my supervision.

Box Two. The Shoes/Boots were paired and checked for matching size under my supervision.

Box Three. The Shoes/Boots have been boxed and correctly labeled as "Made in Luma, Washington".

Box Four. This Crate has been certified to contain exactly three hundred and twenty pairs of ___.

...And there was my single point of creativity: The form contained a space where I was to write in the type or style of the shoes. Below it was a place for my signature.

By the time my father had reached the end of Line Six, and finished explaining in detail its function, my head was swimming. He'd introduced each person, by name, as we walked along the line. There were sixty-three women – the line was entirely staffed with women – working Line Six. My father knew each woman's name at a glance and was able to inquire about spouses or children with most of them. Beyond everything else, that impressed me the most and presented the most formidable aspect of my new job. It was plainly expected for a Foreman to know his workers by their first names. I attempted to repeat back each woman's name as I was introduced to her – an old trick I'd learned in college – but soon the names were all swimming around in the soup of my brain. Halfway through, I thought better of it and started writing down names in the margin of one of my four-boxed forms, along with their station numbers. But when my father saw me attempting this, he advised me against it, noting the serial number embossed in the top right corner of each form. "Accounting likes to keep tabs on these," he said knowingly.

Then, as soon as the chaos had begun, it was over. My father slapped me on the shoulder, shook my hand, and told me he was sure I was ready for the task. Then he walked away, leaving me standing at the termination of Line Six, as the women of the production line worked busily away stitching and assembling boots.

I looked at the top form on my clipboard, with the names scribbled in the column, and back up at the women working. I took out my pen and ticked the first box on the form.

And that's how my first day of work at The Shop began.

That four-boxed form, in its entirety, was my new profession. With the insanity of my first day, I'm not sure I really comprehended that fact at the time. I had ample opportunity to look around at the other production lines. The other Foremen, easily spotted in their shirtsleeves and ties, were as unoccupied as I was. They were watching their production lines, but not overseeing them in any serious way. All that bunk my father had pitched about keeping a firm hand on the reins of the Worker B's seemed to be just that: Bunk. The ladies at their stations were frantically working to keep up with the conveyor. There was no opportunity to even converse, much less loaf about.

All of the workers were particularly adroit at each of their individual tasks. Their hands simply flew around them, tossing and turning the parts of the shoe; stitching, gluing or fitting them together. My engineering side quickly got the better of me and, after twenty minutes of watching the ladies do their jobs, I was able to surmise that there were actually four parallel production lines within Line Number Six instead of just one.

The sixty-three women of Line Number Six were actually four teams of fifteen women, with the three extra workers acting as flow control for all four teams. Essentially, Line Number Six had fifteen unique stations with four women working at each station. Theoretically, I suppose, any of the four women at each station could have taken a partially assembled shoe from any of the four women working at the station before her. But they seemed to have worked out a natural rhythm where one worker at a given station fed her completed step to a particular worker at the next station whose pace of production was similar to hers. You could watch, if you paid attention, a single shoe work its way down the line – from disassembled components, to finished shoe – and then watch the next shoe follow the exact same path through the exact same collection of hands without any change in course.

I had Barry's watch and I could time it. One of the four parallel production lines – I decided to dub it Team A – was finishing a shoe in seven and a half minutes. Another, Team B, was taking eight and three quarters. Teams C and D were lagging well behind the others, both taking over ten minutes to finish their task.

Of course, what was truly amazing was that a pair of finished shoes – two of the same size – made it to the end of this parallel, and disparately timed, process at roughly the same time. They had to, otherwise the whole production line, parallelized or not, would have come to a screeching halt. The last step was boxing – putting the pair of shoes in its box – and then adding the box to the crate that I was to inspect. If the partner to a particular shoe didn't make it to the end of the production line at the same time as its mate, there was the potential that the women working the last station might have been left holding a useless, unboxable single shoe. But this never happened. It was the job of the three extra women, those who worked on no particular team, to keep the shoes moving along the line in essentially the correct order. If a shoe, perhaps on team C or D, was lagging behind, they'd hold up its partner that had been moving through either team A or B, and slip a couple other-sized shoes ahead of it in the queue. This way, the boxers and the stackers at the last station were always kept busy. I marveled at it all as I watched.

Back at school we'd have called the whole thing a natural efficiency. There was no need for management at all. I was able to watch and study it that first day, but not once did anyone ask me for even the simplest form of direction. I was the Foreman of the line, but there was precious little Foremaning that needed to be done.

After half an hour of watching the production line in action, I could instantly see the advantages to separating out the four parallel production lines into discrete teams. What difficulties they had in working together was caused by friction between the four teams working within the limited space. If each team could work on a conveyor of its own... But handed limited resources, the women had worked out a system that allowed them to do their job competently, if not optimally. It was impressive.

So impressive, in fact, that I soon realized my total irrelevancy.

In retrospect, I can't exactly remember what expectations I'd had for my father's life-long profession. If you'd asked me when I was younger what I thought a Foreman did all day, I doubt I'd have been able to tell you anything concrete. I remember my father coming home tired from work and talking to my mother about the events of his day, and that had instilled in me the idea that Foremen actually did *something*. What, perhaps I couldn't say, but *something*.

But as I looked around The Shop floor that first day of my working life, it became obvious to me that there was actually very little work involved in being a shop Foreman. It smelled to me to be a serious case of too few Indians and far too many chiefs.

Each production line had a Foreman, doing as little as I was doing. Some of the bigger lines had two. How two Foremen could possibly be needed to fill out a four-boxed form I couldn't comprehend, but I wasn't really trying. I remembered the going-away party for Barry, and that's when I realized that all two hundred people crowded into that room were all Foremen like me. Now The Shop was a large outfit, but two hundred... More people than could comfortably fit simultaneously into the space that served as their break room...

Suddenly, all those shirtsleeves and ties, and the thirteen thousand names read at my graduation coalesced into a clearer picture. Perhaps it was what some people call an epiphany, I don't know. I looked down at Barry's watch and watched the second hand spin slowly around the dial.

Chapter Seven

Barry's Gold Watch

The guilt of taking Barry's gold watch began to overwhelm me.

I'm sure a good psychiatrist would have told me that there was nothing about the watch that really concerned me. After all, it wasn't like I'd actually stolen it or anything. He'd forgotten it and I'd put it on my wrist. If anything, I was holding onto it for safekeeping. In that little cubby, anyone could have stolen it. With me holding on to it, at least I knew where it was. I had always had every intention of returning it. When the opportunity presented itself.

But as The Shop whistle blew, and after the women of Production Line Number Six finally ceased in their toil, the guilt of taking Barry's watch began to eat away at me.

I returned to the break room to collect my jacket where my father happily slapped me on the back and asked about my day. As we both walked across The Shop yard toward the waiting trolley cars, a dark cloud of remorse grew over me.

I was in a sullen mood as my father jovially ribbed me about the events of the day. He was brimming with pride – his first day of work with his son. But I couldn't summon up the energy to be happy for him. That watch, that damn watch... I could feel the weight of it around my wrist. The band was cutting into my skin. I wanted to rip back my sleeve and tear the damn thing off my arm. But I couldn't risk my father seeing it. The shame of it, as I remembered Mr. Salmon seeing it on my wrist. Perhaps he hadn't made the connection. Perhaps I was just lucky enough to be a young man who owned a gold watch. But that look he'd given me when I was shaking his hand. He'd known. I know he'd known.

I had to return the thing to Barry.

At home, my father poured himself a celebratory McTavish and invited me to join him. Instead, I ran to my room and changed into my civilian clothes.

When I was dressed, I put the watch back into its little black box and went to find my father in the living room.

"Have a drink, Andrew!" my dad said as I stepped into the room. He had a glass in his hand and his cheeks looked flushed. It must not have been his first.

"Not right now," I said. "That guy, Barry, the guy who's job I got..." I started.

"Yeah, Barry..." my father waved his glass nostalgically. "Great guy, you know back in the strike of '62..."

"Do you know where he lives?" I interrupted.

"Barry? Lives? What?" my father said, confused.

"Where's his house? He forgot his watch..." I held up the small black box, comfortable showing it to my father now it was out of sight. "The one he got for his retirement..."

"Oh, God!" my father exclaimed, taking the box from me. He opened it and looked at the watch in disbelief. "Poor Barry! All that fuss, must have put it down..." He closed the box and handed it back to me. "I'll find him in the book," my father said and went to get the phone directory.

Luckily, Barry lived less than three blocks away, just on the other side of Roosevelt. I set out immediately to return Barry's watch, while my father poured himself another drink and saw about making dinner. It was a warm evening, but not yet sweltering, and the fresh air calmed my nerves. The whole day had been a schizophrenic experience, perhaps I was making too much of an issue over Barry's watch. Now, however, I had it in my head to return the watch right then and there.

As I walked up the path leading to Barry Winters' small, neat bungalow, I was preparing in my head the little speech I was going to give as I handed over the watch: "Here, this you left behind at work... I know it must have been a crazy day... It looks like a fine watch... All the best, and I hope you enjoy your retirement..." But I paused at the door and hesitated knocking as I became aware of the sound of loud music playing inside.

It was Sinatra. Some slow, syrupy melody. The six o'clock hour was always swing music, weekdays on the single state-run radio station, and Barry had it blaring away inside. That kind of music was still popular with people of my father's generation: Sinatra, Martin, Arnaz – the "ethnic" crooners. With my generation, it was all roots music. The early sixties had seen the "Appalachian Invasion" with a whole mix of bluegrass and fiddle acts. "Authentic" music. Fluky wasn't the only one affecting a backwoods accent that summer, or a dozen summers before it.

Musical tastes had come to differentiate the two generations – those that remembered the War and those born after. The youngsters got their music, starting at seven o'clock, on the government-programmed station that broadcast to the whole nation, but the rest of the day the radio was dominated by music for the old timers, Sinatra and his ilk.

It wasn't music that you normally played loud. I hesitantly knocked on the white, metal front door.

Somewhere inside, the radio faded to background noise and I could hear feet approaching. The door swung open and Barry stood there before me, with a crooked grin on his face.

"Here, you left this behind-" I began.

"Oh, it's you," Barry interrupted, spinning on his heels. He was self-evidently very drunk as he careened back towards his living room, leaving the front door open behind him. I stepped inside, cautiously, holding out the small, black box. I just wanted him to take the damn thing, I didn't want to have to interact excessively. All the anxiety came washing over me again. Did he know I'd worn the watch all day? Had Mr. Salmon ratted on me? I wanted to turn and flee, but I also wanted the watch safely returned. I'd hate myself until he had his damn watch back. The guilt would eat away at me.

Barry took the corner off the hall into his living room and almost fell over sideways. To call him drunk was an understatement. He was absolutely hammered. He crossed the room and dropped into an arm chair beside the radio that was making all the racket. I stepped into the room still holding out the box. The room was in something of a tousled state. Books and knickknacks had been knocked off perches, something glass had been thrown and smashed against the far wall. Barry reached over and clumsily turned the radio back up, returning Sinatra to his original, earsplitting volume.

"I believe you left this!" I yelled, trying to make myself heard over the radio. Barry looked at me and watched my lips move, not comprehending. I held the black box up to his face and he looked at it strangely. He put his drink down on the arm of the chair, took the box, opened it, closed it, then handed it back to me. He said something, but the words were drowned out by the Chairman of the Board.

I stepped around Barry and turned the radio down.

"Keep it!" Barry yelled again, now far too loud.

"What?" I yelled back. We didn't need to be yelling.

"Keep it!" he yelled again.

"But," I lowered my voice, "this is the watch they gave you today. You must have left it behind in your cubby. I found it this afternoon when I went to get my jacket," I lied.

"You can keep it. Enjoy." He picked up his glass and took a swig.

"I... I don't understand," I flipped open the box and looked at the watch. It was a nice watch. It'd cost fifty dollars if you could find one to buy at all.

"Keep your *fucking* watch..." Barry said with bile. He wasn't looking at me, he wasn't talking to me, I just happened to be there.

I was at a loss. I had walked all the way over to return Barry's watch, but he didn't seem to want it. All the guilt I'd been feeling all day, and now to learn that he didn't want the damn thing...

"Here, just take it," I snapped, shoving it into his lap. He slapped the thing away, sending it skipping across the room. It slammed up against the far wall and lay still. "What the hell?" I yelled, suddenly inappropriately angry.

"Get the hell out!" Barry snapped back.

I marched angrily across the room and picked up the box. I marched back and shoved it aggressively into his free hand. "Take it!" I sneered.

"Keep it!" he pushed the box back at me. "You've got my fucking job, keep the fucking watch!" His eyes were clouding up. I stepped back, suddenly shocked by his emotion, as he began to sob into his empty hand. My anger, my guilt suddenly evaporated, to be replaced by pity. He was sobbing not like a man, but like a child or a drunkard. I quickly squirreled the watch away back into my pocket. How stupid of me to bring the silly thing over in the first place.

"I-I'm sorry..." I tried, but it sounded hollow. I didn't know exactly what I was apologizing for. Returning his watch? Stealing his job?

"Ah!" Barry gave me a dismissive wave and began to get a hold on himself. He wiped his eyes with the sleeve of his dress shirt and took a gulp of his glass. "I'm not blaming you. Do you blame the lion for eating the gazelle? No, it's just the law of the jungle, that's all."

"I-I-I," I stammered. "If I'd known..." But I didn't know how I was going to end that sentence.

"Oh, hell!" Barry said, realizing his glass was empty. He awkwardly began to pull himself up out of his chair. "You need a drink?" he asked.

"Yes," I could only answer with the honest truth.

He refilled his glass from a carton of McTavish and poured a full measure into a second tumbler on a side table. He returned to his chair handing me my glass. "Twenty-five years," he ruminated as he sipped at his drink.

I took a long slow belt of mine, emptying the glass.

The foul-tasting, sour whiskey burned as it went down. I gritted my teeth and swallowed hard as I let the drink settle itself in my belly.

"I really don't understand," I said earnestly, that first drink fortifying me. "I've only done your job for one day, but..." I gulped, looking down into my empty glass, "it hardly seems worth shedding tears over."

Barry was silent, sipping meditatively at his drink. I turned and helped myself to a refill at the side table, pouring a double and talking a long gulp.

"I mean, retirement seems better than being on your feet all day," I said between mouthfuls, my back turned to Barry. "Do you want to keel over and die checking off four stupid boxes on a pile of stupid forms?"

"You don't understand," Barry said, his voice suddenly weary. I turned around to see his head lolling. "Twenty-five years..."

"You should count yourself lucky," I tried.

"Twenty-five years..." he repeated, as the drink got the better of him. The glass slipped slowly from his hand, but I was attentive and ready. I stepped forward and caught it in mid fall, spilling only a little of its contents. I put the glass back on the side table, along with mine, next to the McTavish carton.

From deeper in the house, from some hiding place, a middle-aged woman took this moment to emerge. She obviously knew from long practice exactly the right moment to show herself and when to remain hidden. With Barry quietly snoring, she appeared in the room, turned off the radio and silently began to tend to her husband. She didn't acknowledge my presence, or appear to even see me. She simply wiped a little spittle from the corner of his mouth, removed his glasses, and strained to lift him from his chair. I gave her a hand, pulling Barry up, and we carried him between the two of us out into the hall and down towards the master bedroom.

With Barry disposed of on the bed, she silently and without thanks started to remove his shoes. I took my leave, exiting the bedroom, then the house through the open front door, closing it silently behind me.

Then I remembered the watch in my pocket.

I contemplated stepping back in the house and leaving the black box by the door. Perhaps Barry would reconsider his revulsion to it when he'd had a chance to sober up. It was, after all, a very nice watch. It wasn't like you could just go out and *buy* a watch like it. At the very least he could sell it for quite a handsome sum. He might be repelled by the idea of the watch, but I'd wager he would be less emotionally disgusted by cash of the same value.

But I didn't turned around. I took the watch out of its box, noting that the crystal was now cracked. But it was still ticking and I slipped it onto my wrist. This time I did it without guilt or discomfort. There'd be no more feeling sorry for Barry. It was my watch now, I knew, if Barry didn't want it. Just like the job at The Shop would always be his.

You can't own something you don't value.

As if by magic, Fluky's wrecking truck came rolling to a halt in front of Barry house as I stood there at the curb, looking at the gold watch in the evening light. I looked up from the watch face and saw Fluky smiling at me through the passenger window. He leaned over and unlatched the door.

"Ya pa said you'd be here," He said, straightening himself back up in the driver's seat. I stepped up into the truck and dropped into the passenger seat, closing the door behind me. Fluky fished behind him and came back with a carton of Frau.

I accepted the beer.

Chapter Eight

Horse's Ass

I'd drunk two beers by the time Fluky pulled up in front of Mitty's place. Mitty climbed in beside me through the passenger's door and instantly began talking about "The Plan".

"According to my estimations," Mitty had a small notebook of coarse hemp paper open in his hand. A page was covered with his jittery, illegible, spider-like scrawl. "A crate of boots, as prepared on a production line of The Shop, contains a thousand pairs of boots."

"Eight hundred," I corrected, reaching back behind Fluky to find Mitty a beer. At least that much I had learned that day.

"Ah, that complicates things..." Mitty said, pulling a stub of a pencil out of his shirt pocket. "Oh, thank you," he said distractedly as I handed him a beer.

Fluky put the truck in gear and started us rolling down the hill towards Pottersville. Mitty recalculated his figures, intermittently pausing to take a sip of his beer. The sun was setting breathtakingly over the mountains as we motored down the hill into the old ghost town. We sat in silence as Mitty concentrated.

I looked at Barry's watch. I was already late for dinner with Dad. There'd be hell to pay, but I wasn't worried. I just couldn't face another second of pretending. I didn't want to think about the day I'd had at work. I didn't want to think about anything.

"Correction," Mitty finally spoke. "A crate of boots, as produced at The Shop, contains eight hundred pairs of boots. A standard Concession mega-gauge boxcar is sixty-four feet by thirteen and half feet by ten feet in dimensions. That works out to forty-eight crates per boxcar, or thirty-eight thousand, four hundred pairs of boots per boxcar." Not bad for a dummy. "If, as Beanie reports, a pair of boots is selling, west of the mountains, for as much as one hundred dollars a pair, that's a little under four million dollars for a single boxcar of boots."

"Four fuckin' million?" Fluky exclaimed.

"These are just back-of-the-envelope figures, you understand, but I think my mathematics are correct."

"Shit, them Concession bums are crooks." Fluky spat.

"That's black-market prices," I corrected, "the Concession doesn't sell them for anything like that. Two bucks and change last time I actually saw a pair of boots for sale."

"Yeah, well, still..." Fluky grumbled.

"And you can pick numbers out of the air all you want," I reached over and shut Mitty's notebook for him. "They're just that: numbers. We ain't got a box car and we ain't got a crate of boots and we ain't got a way to get even a single pair of boots across the mountains. So you can dream and talk and drink beer all you want, but we ain't any closer to four million bucks scribbling it down in a notebook than we'd be not scribbling it down."

I finished my beer and crumpled up the carton, throwing it out the rear window.

The cab of Fluky's old wrecking truck fell quiet.

I opened another beer. With two large scotches and three beers in my belly, my head was swimming. Any guilt, any pain I might have been feeling was well and truly lost under all the booze. Acrimony, however, I still had front and foremost. Mitty and his stupid ideas. It annoyed me just to hear him talk. What an idiot! A boxcar full of boots across the mountains... The fool! There was so much wrong with the whole idea there wasn't much left that could be right about it.

"Well, we have this truck," Mitty said softly, reopening his notebook to a clean page. "It has a towing capacity of, what? Four tons?" He was writing with the ridiculously small pencil. "And a pair of boots weighs..."

I grabbed the pencil from his fat hand and unceremoniously tossed it out of the passenger's side window. Mitty turned to me and gave me an expression of shocked horror. I gave him such a murderous glare that he said nothing. He simply closed his notebook and returned it to his shirt pocket.

"There ain't even anything like enough diesel in Boot Hill to haul just us-all across the mountains, to say nothin' of no cargo of boots," Fluky continued, watching the road, having not seen my little exchange with Mitty. "Old Man Zimmerman gets a ration for this here truck, but that just for salvagin'. Cleanin' up the town. All them old cars in old driveways just rustin' up. That ain't good for the environment. Someone's got to haul them off."

"I cannot stomach the sentiment that this enterprise is impossible," Mitty said, emptying his beer. He reached back behind through the rear window and came back with a fresh one. "The Concession rails run directly from here straight into the Big City. It's a three-hour journey."

"Concession rails and Concession trains," I said as the truck was rolling into downtown Pottersville. The sun was below the mountains now, and the eerie silence of the ghost town was intensified by the dark. "Concession cargo and Concession rolling stock. Can you think of anything that ain't owned by the Concession, Mitty?" I asked.

Mitty shrugged.

Fluky brought the truck to a halt in the square in front of the old Union Station. He killed the engine and it coughed unhappily to a drawn-out halt. We disembarked from the truck and stretched our legs, Mitty and Fluky searching around the cobblestones for some good throwing rocks. But I wasn't in the mood for breaking glass. I finished my beer and walked up the front steps of the old station. For the first time in my life, instead of entertaining myself with mindless destruction, I decided to open one of the the massive oak doors that fronted the derelict building, and I stepped inside.

The main concourse of the station, with its grand arched ceiling and sturdy, marble columns, was littered with broken glass, rocks and other debris. Evidence of animal and human habitation was all around. Many of the benches on which passengers had once waited for trains were splintered and smashed. It appeared, long ago, there'd been a large bonfire set in the center of the floor.

I wasn't sure what I was looking for, if I was looking for anything at all. I kicked over a bench and tried to pull a plank free from it, only to be impressed by the solid nature of its construction. I'd need an ax. I gave up on that and went to explore deeper in the station.

"...I mean, with four million dollars on the table," Mitty's voice echoed through the cavernous hall, continuing a conversation, as he and Fluky followed me into the station. "We should at least give the scheme a little effort."

"For four million bucks, we should hijack ourselves one of them Concession trains," Fluky laughed. "For that kinda green, I wouldn't be opposed to a little thievin'."

"What I was suggesting was legitimate commerce," Mitty's voice echoed, "not larceny."

Fluky laughed again. "I was just funnin' you, Mitty."

"Yes, quite," Mitty answered, concern still in his voice.

The two of them were across the concourse, picking their way down the large, marble stairs. I was standing in front of an old ticket counter, looking up at an automated timetable board listing trains and their destinations on routes that had not run for over thirty years.

And that's when the lights switched on.

Not literally – in my head. I suddenly saw the universe in a whole new light.

"Say, where'd they used to run trains from this station to?" I yelled out, my voice bouncing back at me off the marble walls. I was looking up at the timetable at an entry for a 3:15 to Seattle.

"Well, the Northern Pacific Railroad famously ran stock from Saint Paul to Tacoma," Mitty began. He and Fluky turned to see what I was looking at, and the realization of what I was driving at visibly passed over their faces. "Oh," Mitty said, looking up at the table.

"Shee-it," Fluky said and spat on the floor.

Suddenly we were a whole lot closer to that four million dollars.

The three of us stood there looking up at the ancient, dusty old board. We were all mentally processing the full implications of what we were looking at. I felt a little bit not unlike a fool. It had never occurred to me that there might be *another* railroad that crossed the mountains. Perhaps that was the greatest feat ever performed by the Concession: They never had to act to protect their monopoly, everyone simply took them for granted.

Like an immutable law of physics. The Concession owned everything – there was no commerce outside of the authorized and approved business of the Concession. They had us by the hearts and mind and therefore had us all by the balls.

But right up there in front of us was the evidence that the Concession had not always ruled the roost. Long ago, once upon a time, there had been commerce outside of the aegis of the Concession.

"We is gonna get *rich*!" Fluky put into words what we were all thinking.

"Bully!" Mitty agreed.

"It still can't..." I stammered. Answering one question had created a legion of new ones in my mind. Would the track still be usable? Was there track still at all? Did it truly stretch all the way to the Big City? It had, thirty years ago, but thirty years was thirty years. Where precisely did it pass through the mountains? "There's just no way," but I could not peel my eyes away from the dusty old timetable.

Fluky and Mitty had no intentions of simply pondering the questions. Behind me I heard feet scuffling through the detritus across the concourse floor. They were moving, as quickly as was safely possible, towards the platforms. I spun and picked out a path, attempting to follow. If the track was still there – I could hardly dare to wish it – then there was a real chance. By the appearance of everything, Pottersville had simply been abandoned. There was no reason to think that the old Northern Pacific hadn't been similarly forgotten.

Fluky whooped in joy as he sprinted out onto the platform. He leapt down onto the tracks, between the rusty old rails, and rapped on one with his balled fist. It rang solid. He skipped, jumping from tie to tie for a few yards down the track. He whooped again and tossed his cap into the night air.

"Hell! We's going to be *rich*!" he yelled into the darkness.

"Bully!" Mitty repeated next to me, still up on the platform. He puffed on his Jefferson and nodded approvingly. Mitty liked what he saw.

I went back to Fluky's truck, ostensibly to grab a celebratory beer for everyone, but in reality to let my head clear a little. Suddenly the impossible had become disturbingly possible. I half didn't believe what we'd stumbled upon: A realistic and serviceable method to smuggle boots from Boot Hill to the Big City.

Of course, like all great ideas, the first question to pop into your head is why hadn't anyone thought of it before? Perhaps they had, and there was some simple but impassible obstacle that we were not yet seeing. But I was able to answer that question for myself before I'd even fished the case of beer out of the truck: Tracks were one thing – even if they did actually stretch all the way to the Big City – a train was another.

The intractable problem, as with the shortages themselves, was power.

Producing power meant burning carbon. Burning carbon meant contributing to global overheating. The production of power was tightly controlled by the government, to save us all from melting away along with the polar icecaps. We might have found a path by which we could cross the mountains, but we were no closer to possessing the power with which to surmount such an obstacle.

Mitty and Fluky had come to the same conclusion by the time I returned with the beer.

"Perhaps you were correct before," Mitty was saying to Fluky as I handed out the cartons of Frau. They were both sitting on the edge of the platform, their feet dangling down over the tracks. "If we had access to a Concession train..."

"Nope, no good," Fluky replied, opening his beer. "That right there, that's Stephenson gauge," Fluky gestured with his Frau at the tracks below him. "56.5 inches. All that Concession stock, that's mega-gauge: 78.75 inches." Fluky burped. "Not gonna fit."

I was impressed. But mechanical know-how had always been Fluky's specialty. I dropped down on to the edge of the platform next to them and opened my beer.

"What the deuce?" Mitty replied. "That's hardly to be believed."

"Still, there it be..." Fluky said distantly.

"Why 78.75 inches?" I asked. It was a queer figure.

"Two hundred centimeters," Fluky answered. "It's all metric now-a-days. Now 56.5... That there is a tall tale." Fluky snorted.

"What?" I asked over my beer.

"Well, see," Fluky began solemnly. He always loved to tell a tale. "Them tracks right there, they got themselves a *long* pedigree. You see there was this fella, Stephenson, over in England that invented the steam engine – he's the fella the gauge is named for. He invented his engine to pull stock, that before he thought up his engine, was being pulled by horses. And you know the thing about a horse's ass? It's 'bout yay big." he held his hands about two feet apart. "Get yourself a pair of horse's asses and what you got? 'Bout 56.5 inches." He paused to let the gravity of that observation sink in.

"Bullshit," Mitty observed.

"Well, horse shit, yeah," Fluky continued undaunted. "Guess they gone and found ruts in Roman roads back there in England dating back two thousand years where the ruts are exactly 56.5 inches apart. Roman chariots, I deduce, had the same track spacin' as that there Stephenson railway. And you know what else?" Fluky nudged me knowingly.

"No, what?" I said dutifully.

"'Bout the time old Henry Ford gets around to inventin' the automobile, he's got to run them down roads that been carrying horse-drawn wagons for years. You wanta guess how far the wheels turned out to be on the Model T? That's right," Fluky said with self satisfaction. "56.5 inches."

"Oh, I've never heard such garbage," Mitty scolded.

"Swear to God!" Fluky raised a hand in oath.

"Happenstance," Mitty said stoically. "Everything in your vignette can easily be explained by coincidence."

"Coincidence?!" Fluky sounded hurt. "That there's the God's honest truth!"

"Fortuity," Mitty said dismissively.

"Why, you tartar-headed son-of-a-bitch-" Fluky was about to pull himself up to his feet when I interrupted.

"So, you're saying you can drive a car on these tracks?" I asked, pulling Fluky back down to sit on the platform. He was shooting daggers from his eyes at Mitty, but slowly my questions penetrated his brain.

"Hell, yeah!" He said, changing moods. "Well, not all cars and trucks are as thin as the Model T, and road tires ain't gonna do you a damn bit of good; but yeah... Slap on a set of train wheels and you got yourself a four-door locomotive with rack and pinion steerin'."

I was silent. I just looked at Fluky with half a grin. It hadn't clicked for him. He emptied his Frau and reached back to open up another carton. He took a sip of the fresh one and turned back to me. I was still staring at him, my lips ever so slightly curled.

"What?" he asked, looking at me like I was crazy.

"No!" Mitty suddenly exclaimed from behind Fluky. He'd gotten it.

"Oh, hell, no!" It hit Fluky like a wave.

We were all at once up on our feet and running; back out through the concourse to where we'd parked Fluky's truck.

Sure enough, after we'd driven the wrecking truck around the station and spent a few minutes lining it up just so on the tracks, we had Fluky's truck balanced uncomfortably on top of the two Stephenson gauge rails. It wasn't perfect – the old 1952 International Harvester was a lot wider than a Model T – but the tires sat precariously perched on their inner edges, with the width of the tracks well within the wheel wells. It could be done, we realized. With some modifications, a standard-sized truck like Fluky's could be made to ride on the Stephenson gauge rails like a train.

After we were finished with our experiment, we returned to our perch on the train platform, popping the corners on the last three Fraus in the case.

"Forgive me," Mitty began after a long silence. All of us were staring at Fluky's truck sitting on the rails. "What have we learned here? We can drive the wrecker on these Stephenson gauge rails. But how is that getting us any nearer to our goal? Isn't running the wrecker that many miles still prohibitively expensive? If enough diesel could successfully be procured."

Neither Fluky nor I answered. We just sat in silence and stared at the truck.

"I mean, I know I am – officially – not the sharpest knife in the drawer, but if I'm missing something..."

Carbon.

It was all about carbon.

We were one more hurdle along in our steeple chase. Tracks right in front of us, and a train. Even without saying a word I knew what Fluky was thinking. We sat in the darkness of Pottersville drinking our beer and contemplating the last obstacle that needed to be navigated if we were ever going to see our plan become a reality. And this one was a whopper – an obstacle bigger than all those other obstacles combined. But we were so close to it, everyone could almost taste it. That four million dollars in Mitty's notebook was quite an incentive. There just had to be a way, there just had to be.

Carbon.

Mitty was right. Despite his IQ, he could see the massive obstruction that still presented itself. We might have a track, we might have a train, but we still lacked an engine. The Big City and four million dollars were still just as far out of our grasp as they had been at the start of the evening. We'd been clever, very clever, and if only there was an engine that ran on wits. But what we needed was power, and power meant fuel, and fuel meant carbon.

And there all our cleverness could do us no good. There simply wasn't any carbon set aside for the likes of Mitty, Fluky and me.

Not us and a load of old boots.

Chapter Nine

H_2O_2

The horse-drawn milk wagon was lumbering slowly down the street as I made my way home. Fluky had dropped me at the corner on Roosevelt so as not to wake anyone on the street with his engine, and I hoped I could sneak back into the house without disturbing my father.

I was uncomfortably sober and the sun was beginning to rise in the west. Fluky, Mitty and I had spent the rest of the night out in Pottersville, tossing around ideas, trying to get ourselves at least one step closer to a working idea of how we were going to power our locomotive. We'd come up dry. We'd discovered the unused Stephenson gauge tracks; Fluky could construct serviceable rolling stock from the almost infinite supply of rusted and forgotten automobiles salvaged at Zimmerman's yard; acquiring cargo for our trip would be laughably easy; but an engine... There was just no engine that could possibly be constructed that didn't require fuel we didn't have access to.

And then there was the whole moral aspect to it, as well. Fluky had suggested the perfectly workable idea of burning the dry timber that constituted the venerable buildings of old Pottersville until we reached the high timber of the mountains. There we could cut what fuel we needed to power ourselves over and through the pass. It *would* work. I could design and Fluky could construct a simple external combustion engine, but the byproduct: Carbon dioxide.

We were, after all, motivated entirely by greed. We could make noise about duty, and taking it upon ourselves to attempt to alleviate some of the suffering caused by the shortages, but it was all so much steaming horse shit. We wanted to get a cargo of boots across the mountains so we could sell it at a profit. We all wanted to be rich. The idea of four million dollars was quite a carrot hung out in front of our noses. Barry's watch around my wrist and the prospect of another day working on the floor of The Shop was quite a stick whacking me in the ass. It was plain and simple greed – there was no other word for it.

Now, greed in itself was nothing I objected to. Nothing wrong with a little enlightened self interest. But could we, in good conscience, make the rest of the world suffer from our greediness? Some folks would get some boots that they otherwise might not, but the whole planet... How many degrees were we comfortable overheating the planet to line our pockets with gold?

The sun had almost fully risen by the time I opened the front door of my father's house. To have expected that I could just sneak back in, at that hour, was foolish. I walked through the hall and passed the kitchen where my father was sitting with the morning paper, sipping his coffee.

"Andrew," he said, not looking up as I stood in the kitchen doorway.

"Dad," I answered.

"Fifteen minutes or we'll miss the trolley," he said, and left it at that. I went to my room and changed out of my clothes, back into my shirt and tie and old coat. I met my father by the front door, where he stood with our lunch pails prepared. He handed me mine and a mug full of coffee.

Up until that moment, I'd managed to survive all my life without coffee. All my years growing up, all those all-nighters pulled before a big exam in college, I'd managed to get by without ever needing the pick-me-up of a cup of coffee. But I was about to start the second day of my professional career without a dinner the night before, no breakfast, a belly full of whiskey and beer, and not even ten minutes of sleep. I took the cup of coffee and drank it down in a series of thirsty gulps. It tasted vile, but I choked it down. I handed back the mug and my father put it down on a small table beside the front door. He stepped out and I followed, walking back up the street towards Roosevelt.

Later in my life, after I finally gave up the booze, coffee would come to replace it as my overwhelming addiction. I think back to that first cup of coffee and how seriously it gave me the jitters. If I'd only known, I'd have turned the offered cup down. But the caffeine hitting my system had its intended effect. I was awake and alert as I boarded the trolley, wordlessly, with my father. I could feel my father's seething bubbling just below his skin, but I dared not poke at it. Even an apology might have set him off.

My second day of work proceeded to unfold very much the same as my first. I watched the Worker B's beavering away on Line Number Six and ticked off my boxes as the crates at the end of the line filled with boots.

But the effect of the coffee quickly began to wear off and I was soon overcome by the full weariness my night out in Pottersville had earned me. I found a stool and perched myself upon it, fighting desperately the desire to sneak off and lay down for half an hour.

Eventually, I simply had to get up and move. Watching the repetitive motions of the Worker B's building footwear was hypnotizing, I just couldn't watch it. I took the opportunity to explore around the floor of The Shop a little, scouting around. I was acutely aware that my presence was not required at my station for my subordinates to do their jobs. If I wandered off for ten minutes or ten hours, I knew the output of The Shop would not be affected in the slightest.

Pottersville and the Northern Pacific, Stephenson gauge and horse's asses. It was all bounding around in my sleep-deprived brain. I could feel, almost taste, a solution to the power problem just at the periphery of my comprehension. If I could only concentrate, I was thinking, I could put the idea squarely into view. But my mind was too tired to get a handle on anything. The riddle of Mitty's Plan broke down to just another four-boxed form. One, get boots. Check. Two, find tracks. Check. Three, build train. Check. Four... That was the box I just couldn't check: Build an engine. There had to be an engine – some sort of engine – to carry Mitty, Fluky, myself and a cargo of boots across the mountains. If I was only just a little bit smarter, if I could only just get a little sleep.

I walked across the main floor of The Shop and took a large corridor that connected the primary structure with one of its annexes. I was heading nowhere in particular, just following my nose. In this case, "following my nose" turned out to be literal.

As I walked the length of the corridor connecting the two buildings I became aware of a definite odor. I couldn't place it. Something akin to rotting flesh and lye. Thankfully, the odor was hardly noticeable on the main floor, but as I stepped into the annex building, the aroma quickly became overpowering.

There were large vats here, and men in white overalls wearing masks. A catwalk circled the walls and I climbed a nearby ladder to get a look down into the vats. Up there the fumes were even more intense and they began to burn at my nose and throat. But I got a look down into the large swirling vats of... well, I could only guess – some caustic liquid. Large bolts of hemp were being unfurled beside the tanks and submerged in the clear, stinking broth. The men with the overalls and masks were patting down the sheets of hemp and making sure the cloth was well and truly soaked. In one vat near the far wall of the annex, two men were attaching hooks and lifting out a thoroughly soaked sheet of hemp and pulling it into the air to dry on pulleys. The sheet had turned white, from its natural mud brown, with a slight pinkish hue.

I suddenly realized what fluid was below me in the vat.

"Mask!" came a muffled yell from along the catwalk. I looked up and saw a masked man waving at my angrily. "Mask!" he yelled again, and pointed repeatedly at a sign hanging from a support beam. It showed an icon of a man coughing and another of a man breathing comfortably behind a clean gas mask.

I got the hint, as if I needed one, and started to descend the catwalk. My eyes were watering and the burning sensation in my mouth made me want to spit. I couldn't get out of that foul annex fast enough, but I'd seen everything I needed to see.

Back on the main floor I found a seat on an empty crate and paused to catch my breath. I wiped the tears from my eyes with the end of my tie and spat a mouthfull of bile behind the crate as discreetly as I could manage.

Hydrogen peroxide. Strong stuff, I could tell by my level of irritation. Hydrogen peroxide was an excellent bleaching agent. Hemp was naturally an unattractive brown color. With hemp the predominant cash crop in the United States, and the hinterlands surrounding Boot Hill prodigious producers of it, hemp was essentially the only material available to The Shop from which to fabricate its boots. This required hemp to wear many hats, so to speak: cotton, wool, faux-leather. Over the years, The Shop had gotten pretty good at making silk out of the proverbial sow's ear. I had a pair of cowboy boots back home that you couldn't tell apart from real snake skin. But the whole process required many steps of dying, rendering, forming and stretching. Dying the hemp white was an understandable and obligatory first step.

And very well suited to my needs.

I looked down at the clipboard in my hands and examined the four-boxed form as I struggled for my breath. Four boxes and four steps. I had three checked off and only one more to go. Hydrogen peroxide. The words rattled around in the recesses of my memory. What was hydrogen peroxide, other than a bleaching agent?

I flipped over the topmost form and began scribbling frantically on its back with my pencil. Before I was fully aware of what I was doing, the schematics for an engine were already on the paper in front of me. Hydrogen peroxide, H_2O_2, besides being a strong bleaching agent, was also – I could recall from a fourth-year seminar – a powerful rocket fuel. That in itself was of little usage to Mitty's Plan. It wasn't like we were going to ride a rocket over the mountains. But I recalled exactly how hydrogen peroxide worked as a rocket fuel: Exposed to a catalyzing agent, it decomposed, exothermically, into water and oxygen. H_2O and O_2. So exothermically, in fact, that the water was inevitably produced as steam.

And what use was steam? Oh God, all the use in the world! I could hardly contain my excitement. Steam was for running steam engines. Right in the annex – right behind me in massive vats that could drown an elephant – was my fuel. Fuel to make power, power to pull a train over a mountain, over a mountain and to a Big City as ripe and ready to be plucked as any apple ever to grow on any tree!

And not an ounce of carbon in any of it! Hydrogen peroxide in, water and oxygen out. Clean, sweet, wonderful water! Fresh as they day that it fell from the sky. No carbon dioxide, no global overheating, no moral angle to the enterprise at all!

I'd found it! I'd found my engine.

All the rest of the world faded away as I sat there etching out my schematic. My hangover, the lack of sleep, my empty belly didn't bother me. Nothing would stop me until I had finished my task. Twenty minutes passed as I covered the back of the whole sheet with my design.

That's not entirely true: The design wasn't really mine, I didn't invent a four-stroke, tandem compound, dual-stage piston steam engine. They'd been in use for over a century, and it was a design I could re-create from my studies from memory. And I still feel, to this day, that the design was a sound application of hydrogen peroxide as a monopropellant. What happened in Pottersville – what almost derailed Mitty's Plan before it had even really begun – were design errors outside of and additional to the fundamental working of my engine. I had no experience with hydrogen peroxide as a fuel source, I doubt there was anyone alive in 1973 who really did, and the explosion... Well, I'm getting ahead of myself.

When I was through with my schematic, I jumped to my feet and almost cheered in joy. I expected a round of applause from the surrounding factory, so monumental I felt my accomplishment had been. But the work of The Shop went on uninterrupted around me, oblivious to my self-evident genius. Worker B's were working away at boots at their stations; bending, fitting and stitching. A pang of isolation hit me as I looked at the design in my hand. I folded it in half three times and tucked it away in my shirt pocket. I had neglected my station at number six production line long enough.

I passed the rest of my day dutifully completing my work as instructed. Crates came off the end of my production line and I soberly inspected each for compliance with my four-boxed form. Having found the crate complete and correct, my four boxes fearlessly marked, I signed each form and attached it to its crate with a small staple gun. It was then the job of a small army of heavy-shouldered porters to seal each crate and cart it off on a dolly for who-knows-where. Beside the road leading from town to the factory, I guessed, for very few boots made in The Shop ever made it much farther.

When the whistle blew at the end of the day, I could barely keep myself from sprinting for the break room. Jacket and lunch pail in hand, I waited impatiently for my father. He appeared, eventually, walking and talking with a clutch of other Foremen, laughing and making plans. I had to remind him three times that the trolley would not wait for him to finish his conversation. Eventually my father had gathered his coat and lunch pail and we were on the trolley heading back to town.

"You seemed to have held together well," my father said when we'd found a seat and he'd had a chance to look me over. I was tapping my foot irritably, but otherwise awake and alert.

"Second wind," I commented.

"Good," he said with satisfaction. "I don't approve – I've spoken to you before. But after last night, to be able to stand to a full day on the floor... I'm impressed."

I didn't want to get into it with him, to insult his chosen profession, to suggest that I could have slept half the day and still got my job done. It wasn't the time or place – there'd never be a time or place. Now that I could see light at the end of the tunnel, now that I had four boxes on my Mitty's Plan form ticked off, I didn't need to lose any sleep over what a dead-ended life my father had lived. That I didn't have to live it, that it had given me the education and brains to find another way, was all that mattered. I could never attack my father for living his life. He was happy in it.

"I have to go out again, before dinner," was all I said. "To see Fluky."

"No!" my father quickly commanded. "Not two nights in a row!"

"No, no, not like last night. I'll be back for dinner."

"Son-" he began, but stopped himself.

"I swear!" I pleaded. I'm not sure why I thought I needed to ask permission. Old habits die hard.

We rode the rest of the way home in silence.

At home I changed and rang Fluky's parents' home. His mother informed me that he wasn't home, that he hadn't returned yet from work, but that many Tuesdays he played cards in the back room at Putter's and today being Tuesday... Putter's was downtown, on Main, and a good half an hour's walk each way. I'd never be able to make it there and back by dinner. Trolley service was always spotty at this hour, with runs still bringing workers back from The Shop. I'd have to run, I realized, and then there was always the chance that Fluky wouldn't be there. He could have been at any one of a dozen Tuesday night card schools that met in town. But I'd have to chance it.

I'd moved the four-boxed form with my schematic on the back from my work shirt to the pocket of my jeans. I had to show it to Fluky – show him what I had produced. Mitty, I knew, would be unimpressed. Solutions always presented themselves to Mitty; someone else always arrived, at the eleventh hour, to pull his bacon from the fire. If I told him we'd be riding a rocket over the mountains and landing in Pioneer Square, he wouldn't have batted an eye. Trains, engines, facts and figures, they were all someone else's problem.

But Fluky would comprehend the enormity of what I had created. In the world of achievable things, this was where Fluky resided. If I could explain to him my design, if I could show him that conquering the mountains between Boot Hill and the Big City was an achievable goal – with his mechanical expertise and my designs – then we could really do this. We could really get cargo across the mountains and to market on the other side, completely circumventing the Concession and its monopoly. If we could do it once, we'd be wealthy, but if we could make the trip multiple times...

The horsepower of the engine I had down on that sheet of paper was nothing like that of one of the Concession's behemoths. There'd be no five-mile long trains on our railroad. But even just one crate, the product of two hours on my very own production line, would net us... What? Fifty thousand dollars? And my engine could haul fifty crates, at least.

All that money... it was all right there on the back of that four-boxed form. I had to show it to Fluky. I had to make him understand.

Chapter Ten

Pressure Stages

I sprinted all the way over to Putter's in under ten minutes. I arrived at the front door of the café drenched in sweat. It was a balmy evening, as the real heat of the summer was starting to set in. The restaurant portion of the café was almost deserted, but the bar was humming with activity, as Worker B's and Worker C's from The Shop mixed for an after-work drink.

I spotted Fluky at the bar, talking to a young line seamstress dressed in coveralls. He was drinking draft Frau from a glass and evidently being very charming to the girl. I pushed hurriedly through the crowd that choked the floor of Putter's Café bar and came up behind him.

"Fluky," I said, resting a hand on one of his shoulders. With the other I was taking the four-boxed form out of my back pocket.

"...And I says to this guy, I says-"

"Fluky!" I said louder, pulling him around. He came about, shot me a dirty look, then bodily shook me free from his shoulder.

"So I says-"

"Fluky, this is important," I interrupted again. This time the young seamstress shot me the dirty look and Fluky turned fully to face me.

Murder was in his eyes, "Are you deranged?" he asked.

"Look at this," I ignored him, opening up the folded paper. I moved a few glasses on the bar and began to spread out my schematic.

"Later, Beanie," he said, turning back to the girl.

"No, now!" I grabbed the scruff of his oily, plaid shirt. He grabbed my hand and for a second we wrestled. By the time he'd gotten my hand removed from his person, the girl had faded back into the crowd.

"Shee-it!" Fluky spun around to me. In one swift motion he had my arm behind my back and was twisting it painfully. Again, Fluky was remarkably strong for his size. Fast too.

"Ouch! Shit!" I cried as I felt the tendons in my arms ripping.

"I'll snap your arm off, I swear to God," Fluky hissed. But his grip slacked and he eventually released my arm. His point made, he reached to the bar and picked up his beer. The schematic was still spread out on the bar. He paused to look down at it. "What the fuckin' shit is this?" he said, squinting in the poor light of Putter's bar.

"Our engine," I said triumphantly – well, as triumphantly as I could mange rubbing out the soreness in my arm.

"Our what?" was all Fluky could manage.

"Engine."

"Yeah, that's what I thought you said..." he looked again at the diagram, not making head or tails of it. "This is what you had to show me? Right this minute? Are you as re-tartared as Mitty?"

"No, you don't understand-" I began.

"No, I don't," Fluky interrupted, pulling himself up on his toes, looking around for the girl.

"This is the engine that will get us to the Big City," I continued.

"Uh-huh."

"With as many as fifty crates of boots..."

"Yeah," he took a sip from his beer but wasn't listening.

"It's a four-stroke, tandem compound, dual-stage piston steam-"

"Yeah," Fluky interrupted. He'd spotted the girl. "It looks great. Why don't you show it to Mitty?"

"No!" I exclaimed, loud enough to get most of the bar's attention. I grabbed Fluky's shirt again with my sore arm, risking getting it broken off. I pulled his face close to mine and said in a hushed tone: "It's a steam engine, Fluky, but it uses hydrogen peroxide as fuel."

Fluky just looked at me in incomprehension.

"Like they use-" I realized I was still speaking too loudly. Our little wrestling match had stalled conversations all around us. I lowered my voice to almost a whisper, "Like they use at The Shop to bleach hemp. Thousands and thousands of gallons of it. Just sitting there. This engine right here," I said, jabbing a finger down onto the schematic on the bar. "Runs on that. hydrogen peroxide. With no carbon emissions."

Realization dawned on Fluky's face.

"You're shittin' me." He smiled, returning his attention to the piece of paper on the bar.

"No," I said eagerly. Conversations around us were starting up again. I pointed out the pictograph on the schematic that represented the fuel tank, "Hydrogen peroxide. H_2O_2. When introduced to a catalyst," I traced a finger to the first chamber connected to the fuel tank. "Here. It produces water, oxygen and plenty of heat. Enough, in fact, to turn the water into steam." My finger moved over the first of the pair of pistons, "Driving the high pressure stage." Then the second, "And then the low pressure one. Notice they're in opposition. Here's a camshaft, very much like an internal combustion engine, but here there are two power strokes, forward and back, then..."

"Wait a minute," Fluky interrupted, turning away from the bar. "You really think you can build this?"

"No," I answered, "I think you can."

Fluky nodded, took a sip of his beer, and returned his attention to the drawing.

I continued, "Then the down stroke of the high pressure stage is the exhaust stroke for the lower pressure stage, then the values change thusly," I pointed to a few spots on the diagram, "and the final stroke of the low pressure stage is pulling fuel into the catalyzing chamber via the vacuum created. The peroxide reacts with the catalyst, creating pressure, and the whole process begins again."

Fluky was quiet for a long time, studying the drawing. He finished off his beer and, when the barmaid came by, ordered another. I ordered one too.

With his fresh beer, Fluky looked up from the schematic and said to me: "I don't get it."

"It's an engine, Fluky," I said with frustration, starting my monologue all over again.

"No, no, I get that," Fluky conceded. "But this here thing is going to get us over the mountains? Without diesel? Without coal?"

"Yes."

Fluky shook his head – not in disagreement, but it disbelief, "But carbon..."

"It doesn't produce carbon, Fluky. Just water and oxygen. That's the chemical reaction: H_2O_2 to H_2O and O_2. Get it? No carbon. No carbon in, no carbon out."

"Hell..." Fluky scratched his head under his hat.

I was staring at him, staring at him hard. God, Fluky understand what I am saying, I thought. Please understand. If I can't explain it to you, then you can't build it. I just didn't have the mechanical expertise. An engine like I was planning, like the one I had down on paper, would require a first-class welder to construct. And there was only one person in town with the talent or equipment to weld anything, and that was Fluky. Please, Fluky, please understand...

"And you say this hydrogen pryrockside..."

"Peroxide," I corrected.

"Is just goin' spare, up there at The Shop?"

"Thousands of gallons of it," I embellished.

"Then why don't the Concession run their trains off the stuff? If it's so plentiful?"

I laughed, folding my schematic back in halves, "Well, it's basically rocket fuel..."

"It's what?!" Fluky almost screamed, jumping to his feet.

"Rocket fuel. In the concentrations we'd need to us it. During the war, the Nazis used it to fuel their V2 rockets. Ask Mitty."

"You wanta build a rocket-powered train?!" Fluky yelled, overcome with disbelief.

"Not rocket powered, steam powered." I began to unfold the four-boxed form again.

"Ah!" Fluky let out a sigh of disgust. "You had me for a second, you son-of-a-bitch!" He slammed his beer down on the bar, threw up his hands and stormed off across the crowded barroom floor.

"Fluky?" I called after. "Fluky?" I hurriedly took a large gulp of my beer and returned my schematic to my pocket. I pushed through the crowd, trying to keep pace with Fluky. I lost sight of him as he cut across the restaurant and out the front door.

"Fluky!" I yelled as I broke out into the early evening air. Fluky was already beside his truck, the only vehicle in the parking lot, opening the door. "Wait up!" I hollered. "What's wrong?"

"You're just as bad as the tartarhead! You and Mitty, you make a fine pair," He said through gritted teeth, over the driver's door.

"What?" I had legitimately missed the cause of his sudden anger.

"Rocket-powered trains," he said fumbling with his keys and the ignition. "You know, for a minute there, I was thinkin' we might actually be able to get this sucker off the ground. Then you show me that dingus," he pointed dismissively at my pocket, "and I'm right back down on the ground. Lower than the ground." He hit the starter and the truck grumbled to life. He continued, yelling over the idling engine, "You're just as bad as that dummy, with his maps and his battles of Izpegi Passes!" he bellowed. He said something that was drowned out by the revving engine. "Pig in poke!" I understood as he slammed the truck in gear, rooster tailing in the gravel of the old, unused parking lot, accelerating back on to Main Street.

Chapter Eleven

Fluky Signs On

I didn't hear from Fluky again for three days. I didn't attempt to call, thinking it best to let things lie after our exchange outside of Putter's. I also didn't bother to fill Mitty in on the details of my engine design, knowing the whole deal was off if Fluky wasn't on board. It seemed unnecessarily cruel to get Mitty's hopes up, and he'd be of no use in helping to convince Fluky that the engine could actually get built. Potentially exactly the opposite. A sound endorsement from Mitty would be more than enough reason for Fluky to sign off on the idea, permanently.

I busied myself with my job at The Shop, exploring the rest of the complex and determining exactly what resources I had available. I had no more epiphanies, however. There were no more revolutionary means of propulsion lying hidden in the recesses of The Shop. Our train, what would come to be called *The Cordwainer*, would run on hydrogen peroxide or it would run on nothing at all.

It was Saturday evening when I again heard from Fluky. He called late in the evening, as I was listening to the radio with my father, and invited me down to Putter's for a drink. It was Saturday night, after all, and my father was enjoying the *Dean Martin Variety Hour*, so I found my coat and headed out. I don't believe my father noticed me go.

I found Fluky again in the barroom. He was in a booth, all alone, drinking a beer from a glass. I bought a glass for myself and joined him at the table, pulling off my coat.

"So tell me straight out," Fluky began before I could say hello. "No shittin'. You think that rocket-powered train of yours can really work?"

I thought for a second about whether to correct him again, but I decided against it, "Yep," I said.

"Seriously?" he said with gravity, leaning forward over his beer. "You, me, the fathead, and a cargo of boots. All the way over the mountains and into the Big City?"

"I think it can work," I replied honestly. "If you can build my engine, I think we've got a fighting chance."

"At four million bucks?" He said hopefully.

"Well," I hedged. "That was Mitty's figure for a mega-gauge boxcar. We could never haul such a load with the horsepower we're talking here. I was thinking closer to 25 crates..."

"What that work out at?" he asked impatiently.

"Probably a square million."

Fluky let that sink in.

"Are you on board?" I asked eventually, after I'd given him ample time to contemplate.

He looked at me with an expression on his face I couldn't quite gauge. He began, "So Wednesday mornin', after talkin' to you the night before, I goes to work like always. We've been cleaning up this lot of cars on the west side of the tracks. All them little shotgun shacks got something rustin' away 'round back. City is sick to death of it all, says they're all a hazard. We can get a writ from the judge on folks that don't want us towing off their old Studebaker. You know, there's still some folks think that the oil is gonna come back? They're holdin' on to their old car for when the shortages end. Damn fool, tartarhead white trash bastards...

"Anyway, Wednesday morning I'm in the yard cuttin' up with a torch the wrecks I'd hauled in the day before. Had a good day – got six without no complainin'. Nothing special in the lot. Fords, a Chevy and an old Hudson. Choppin' 'em up with a torch, as I said. Not rightly sure why I bother. Supposed to break them down small so the Concession can haul off the steel – make 'em into new stuff – maybe new cars. Ain't no iron mining no more, too dangerous. Too much carbon. Gotta recycle the steel we have. But you know how it is, the Concession ain't hauled off a load of steel for years. No space on the trains, no trucks to get the scrap from the junkyard to the terminal. So here I am burnin' up diesel, riding around town, hauling off old cars that no one can ever drive no more, choppin' them up so I can make a big old pile of junk, that no one's ever gonna make any smaller. That right there, that's what I was doing that Wednesday morning.

"Then that son-of-a-bitch Zimmerman, he comes on out of his hut. Bastard has a little hut that he holes up in all day. Too damn old and too damn ornery to do any work. Sits in there and counts the money that the Concession pays him for makin' that there pile of shit a little bit bigger – nah, forget that, counting the money the Concession pays him for *me* makin' that there pile of shit a little bit bigger. Bastard comes out of his old hut and starts cussing at me. I'm runnin' my torch, watching steel split, so I can't hear the fucker. Anyway, he comes on around and is cussing at me an earful. Ain't exactly sure what he's all bent out of shape 'bout – still don't rightly know. Anyway, he's callin' me a chink bastard and a lazy no good slant-eyed motherfucker. I feel like windin' up and clocking the old coot. But I don't, you know, 'cause by now it's been goin' on six years of this crap. Everyday – everyday that old piece of shit gets a burr in his ass, he comes around cussing at me."

Fluky paused take a sip of his beer. I'd almost completely forgotten about mine.

"You know, he was in the war?" Fluky continued. "In the Pacific. He was at Guadalcanal, the evacuation of Hawaii; got shot in the head on the Baja by some Jap. Got a metal plate up there now. Can't get too close to magnets. Reminds me at least once a week that the happiest day of his life was the day Truman nuked Japan. That son-of-a-bitch knows what I am – says he can smell the difference between a nip and a chink – and to sit around and say that shit... But I got to sit around and take it. You know why? That old bastard's got me by the balls. There ain't no other place for me to go. Not in Boot Hill, not to work with steel. I got a Class B chit, sure, but what the hell am I goin' to do? Sew boots on the floor of The Shop? Hell, I can weld as tight a seam as any motherfucker that ever built a Sherman tank; I've kept that old wrecking truck running for almost ten years without nothing but rusty old spares to pick from; and I got to stand there and take whatever crap that old bastard want to pitch? Yep. If I ever want to work another day with tools, and not just sit around on my ass like that tartarhead Mitty, I gotta just stand there and take it. Fuck.

"But you know what? In the past I always just let that shit roll off me. I could look at the miserly old fuck and think: Yeah, flap your lip, you bastard, when you die I'll get everythin'. Yeah, that's always what I was thinkin', when he'd start in on me: insult my race and my homeland and anythin' else he can fuckin' think of, that old bastard, but someday, he's gonna *die*...

"I know that ain't Christian – both comin' or goin'. Love thy neighbor, the prophets say, and don't sweat the trials and tribulations of this life, for the majesty of the promised land will soon be on us all. But shit..."

Fluky paused again to sip at his beer. The tone and manner of his speech subtlety changed and grown much more inward.

"I know I don't much talk on it. Faith. I know you ain't got none, so I don't whittle you on it. But for me it's a sustainin' thing. I *know* that God has a plan; that he threaded this world through with *kami* out of the grace of his love; that it surrounds us all and protects us and guides us. But hell... That his people have to suffer such burdens... There may be grace in the afterlife for those who love Jesus, but...

"I mean, ain't ol' Kennedy always saying that despite our troubles, we're still a Nation of Big Ideas? Ain't that what America is 'bout? You ever hear an idea in your life bigger than Mitty's? Bigger than this here rocket train of yours? Shit, Jesus may walk this earth in body and spirit and the fruits of the earth may be given, we might fill our stomachs and be happy, but... Ain't Jesus busy takin' care of the old widows and the little babies? Can't we take a little somethin' off his plate? Seems like if we can provide for ourselves, ain't we tasked with the duty of doin' it?"

Fluky leaned forward in the booh, the vigor returning to his voice.

"So, there I am, Wednesday morning, listening to Zimmerman pitch his shit, and something inside me moves. I ain't sayin' it's the hand of God or nothin' – I ain't blaspheming – but somethin' right here," he tapped at his chest, "moved. What am I doin'? Hopin' the death of that old shit-heel for? For what? A measly diesel ration and a pile of steel nobody nor nothin' is ever gonna use? What am I makin' in this life? For the glory of God? Nothin', that's what, nothin'."

"We create our own providence," I said, unsure if I was offending Fluky. I wasn't sure – Fluky was always a mystery – but I think he was slowly screwing up the courage to sign on to Mitty's Plan. But I could have easily been way off base, it was hard to tell with Fluky.

"Hell, I don't know," Fluky continued, "if you can really make a rocket-powered train, I don't know if such a fool thing should ever be attempted, but I *do* know God don't want me pitchin' shit and hatin' on my neighbor. Not like Old Zimmerman.

"Hell, maybe we'll all blow ourselves to hell!" he smirked. "And then I can ask Jesus what he might be wantin'. But, hell, ain't we got to *try*? Ain't we got to do *somethin*? Instead of sittin' around and waitin' on perdition?"

I raised an eyebrow, and looked at him expectantly.

"You know Mitty," he went on, changing gears. "You know what a pulp brain, horse's ass he is. But ain't he tryin'? I mean, really, in his way? You can't fault the fool for that. What you said back there in the freezer," he thrust a thumb back over his shoulder. "You was right. Ain't we supposed to be a Nation of Big Ideas? Well, what idea is bigger than this 'un?"

He trailed off and sipped at his beer, thinking.

"Then you're in?" I asked, getting to the nub of it.

"Yeah," Fluky said with a slight grin. "I'm in."

Chapter Twelve

The Cordwainer

If life was a picture show, all the hard work of a project would be easily abbreviated by a montage. A montage of sweaty, hardworking men laboring away at tools, sizing, cutting and generally looking serious, perhaps occasionally tossing each other an encouraging thumbs up. The montage would encompass and parenthesize all the hard labor, as great works of artisanship and engineering coalesced into something approaching a working device.

If only real life was a simple as a picture show.

In our movie, the one we were living and breathing, we suffered a number of intolerable false starts and dead ends. I can scarcely blame anyone other than myself. Fluky – correctly, as I estimated – was a first-class man with machines and tools. But he was not a "high concept" kind of guy. That role I was required to fill. And it was a role I was only barely able to live up to.

The problem was communication. The schematic I had on the back of my four-boxed form was, being charitable to myself, rough. There was very little there for Fluky to work from. Lame pencil drawing at best. While I considered my design brilliant – still consider it brilliant – actually communicating its brilliance to someone else proved to be a task I neglected to invest time or spare patience for. And without that task done, well, all other tasks were forced to the wayside until everyone understood exactly what it was we were all working on.

Our first prototype turned out to be little more than a hunk of inanimate steel. Fluky had hit on the idea of using a pair of old engine blocks welded together for both expansion chambers and pistons. We would basically double my design. Two pistons in one block and two pistons in another, moving in the cylinders bored for internal combustion, with the cylinder of the opposing engine block directly above containing the catalyst. The high and low pressure pistons were parallel instead of in opposition as intended in my original design, but the whole thing was otherwise compact and quite innovative.

In practice, however, it required doubling of the crank shafts and the cams. This turned out to be a confusing clockwork mess, with chains and jury-rigged gears. After a week's time invested, we could barely turn the whole contraption over by hand without something flying off. It would have never survived the RPMs required for a fully functioning engine.

We wrote that one off as a learning experience.

For our second attempt, we stuck with the notion of using existing engine blocks, but this time we put a single crank shaft between two blocks welded flat to a car chassis. We quadrupled my design for this attempt, with a high pressure then a low pressure piston alternating along each block. We opted for an external expansion chamber, fashioning one out of a used propane canister. Fluky made a clever manifold out of copper piping that would have been trivial to time, but the weakness of our new design instantly manifested the second we pressurized the system. We were only using an air compressor, nothing extravagant, but the copper solders self evidently were not going to stand up to pressure generated by a hydrogen peroxide system.

We scrapped that design, too.

Two weeks were wasted and we had nothing but scrap metal to show for it.

We had to take a step back and attempt to understand what it was were were trying to accomplish. Fluky and I confabbed over beers one evening after work. We sat in the bar at Putter's and were able to agree after much arguing and finger pointing that, perhaps, we were both overthinking the issue. We were trying to be clever – too clever, and clever in multiple directions at the same time. We needed to focus on constructing an engine that was sufficient for our task, but no more than we needed. Clever technical solutions to engineering problems were all well and good, with infinite time and infinite resources, but we had a timetable. Cleverness always required just that little bit more cleverness to reach a practical, functional design; one more innovative solution to a problem that was, if truth be told, only created because of the cleverness in the first place.

We were over-engineering our engine. Being smart for smart's sake. We had to focus on the simplest possible solutions to the simplest possible problem. Break the task down into its individual component tasks and solve each one in turn, as simply and completely as allowed. We were giving ourselves a crash course in practical engineering, Fluky and I, and it was eye-opening to realize how little my education had prepared me for it. So much for all the book learning.

For our third prototype, we stuck with a simple two-piston design, as originally outlined in my schematic. We kept the parallel pistons from our first attempt – that made sense – a single crank had the advantage of simplicity, and the closer we mirrored the function of an internal combustion engine the less we had to re-engineer parts to fit roles they were never intended to fill.

One of the four cylinders in the block we designated the expansion chamber. Here again we opted for simplicity. With a metal slug welded to the base of the cylinder, the thick walls of the block would take whatever pressures were created by the expanding peroxide. And the existing engine head was already pre-drilled in a configuration quite similar to what we required.

The last cylinder we filled with a condensing coil. The low pressure stage would evacuate quicker with the vacuum created by the cooling water. Fluky re-piped the exhaust manifold to channel steam from the expansion chamber to the high pressure piston. Lower pressure piston to condensing coil, and lower pressure piston back to the expansion chamber, we plumbed with heavy, braided hose. The hydrogen peroxide was to be fed to the expansion chamber via a length of plastic tubing, a small supply of which Fluky had miraculously spirited away.

This engine passed our preliminary tests. We hand cranked it, pressurized the whole affair, and tested our custom-lathed cam shaft for timing. After three weeks of laboring away, we had something very close to a prototype.

Of course, even if the engine did work, we needed a train in which to put it.

Here, Fluky went insane, working all sorts of strange, long hours at the junkyard. I had nothing to contribute to this portion of Mitty's Plan and Fluky never asked for my opinion. Early on, we had agreed on rolling stock of three freight cars, an engine and rear caboose. A freight car, I figured, roughly the size of Fluky's wrecking truck, with no engine, cab or winch, could conceivably carry eight crates the likes of which I watched every day rolling off the production line at The Shop. That would be 24 crates, very close to the 25 I was aiming for, and well within the manageable, if plodding, pace of an engine that might, perhaps, produce 80 to 100 horsepower.

How, exactly, we were going to modify rusty, dilapidated old road vehicles to function as rolling stock, I hadn't put much thought into. I wouldn't need to. Fluky took the task on with relish. In the junkyard, Fluky found the chassis for three 1953 Ford pickups. They had already been stripped of their bodies, cabs and engines. Fluky removed the rear axles, cut them down to the required 56.5 inches and welded them back together. Reattached to the chassis, the shorter axles looked peculiar, but the wheels still had plenty of room within the wheel wells to move. He found spare rear axles and welded them in place at the front, replacing the rack and pinion.

Onto these axles, Fluky put regular street tires. This seemed peculiar at first, railroad cars usually rolling on steel, rimmed wheels, but Fluky's solution to that problem was wholly unique, and among the cleverest pieces of jury-rigging I was to ever see.

Tires, of course, were no good for train tracks, the rim of the wheel being the guide that kept the train on the rails, but Fluky didn't want to give up on the traction that road ties provided – even on steel rails. We were looking at a hill climb, after all, of unknown and perhaps steep grades. Fluky wanted poorly inflated rubber ties to give absolutely the best possible grip to the track, wrapping them around in rubber. But what was going to keep the car on the track? A simple guide, just like a train wheel, but not attached to the wheel itself.

Fluky welded a crossbar of steel, parallel with the ground, attached to two tire jacks, adjustable with a third tire jack at its center. This bar could be lowered down below the bottom of the car, between the two rails the tires would be riding on, and adjusted to the point where they where almost touching, but not quite, their tips to the rails. If the car began to slip left or right off the rails, the crossbar was there to keep it on the tracks. It took some calibrating to find the sweet spot where the bar allowed the car to still move freely but didn't allow for too much shimmy, but after a few hours of testing we stumbled on the right setting.

The genius of the design was that the crossbars served multiple purposes. Cranked tight they functioned as brakes. Pulled in and all the way up, the chassis and axles were still road worthy. But the true wizardry of the whole dingus didn't reveal itself until after *The Cordwainer* had started its actual attempt. Out on those rails that hadn't seen use for over thirty years, we derailed our train on at least a dozen occasions. We would have been completely sunk, but we quickly learned that if we cranked out the crossbars totally, then cranked them down, setting them fully on the top of the track, we could lift up a five-ton freight car and drop it back on the rails with little more than a simple block and pulley. It was a life saver – it was more than a life saver – it was an absolutely critical piece of machinery that none of us had had the foresight to actually build. But the crossbars did the trick.

And all of it was created by Fluky, laboring away on his own late into the night.

All this time, I was still working days at The Shop. I'd come home on the trolley, catch a quick bite to eat with my father, then ride a bicycle over to Zimmerman's junkyard where we were working in his largest garage. Mitty, without fail, would join us every evening, though there was little work for him to actually do. But he was a first-class tool hander, and we employed him mainly in that capacity. He would prattle on constantly about the War and Patton and the Iberian Campaign. Fluky had a radio in the garage and we'd sometimes turn it on, hoping that Mitty might get distracted; but unless it was the bluegrass hour, Mitty was always more interested in listening to his own voice than the radio.

He'd occasionally discuss exactly how he was planning on spending his million dollars (I hadn't had the heart to tell him it'd be significantly less), but usually he just kept prattling on about the War. Intermittently, Fluky and I would have to shush him to discuss some technical detail, but by and large we went about our work mutely. There was so much to get finished, and so few hands to do it. By ten o'clock I'd call it a day, and Mitty and I would head on home. But Fluky would stay up for two or three hours more working on the rolling stock or a perpendicularly difficult problem we'd encountered with the engine. Some nights I think he didn't sleep at all.

But the train that would take us up and across the mountains was starting to take shape.

A month after we had begun our labors, in the heat of a bright July day, Fluky towed the first of his completed freight cars over to Pottersville for a road test.

With the crossbars raised, we were able to maneuver the bare chassis onto the tracks just behind the Union Station, where a road crossed over the rails. We lowered the crossbars into place and tightened them up to the rails, moving the chassis slowly forward. With the freight car free of the street crossing, we were able to correctly position the rails. And after a few minutes of tentatively maneuvering, we were soon racing up and down the tracks, the freight car running handsomely on the rails.

Fluky and I were pushing. Mitty rode on the chassis, ostensibly to control the width of the crossbars, but mostly because he was in no shape for running. Back and forth for three hundred yards we pushed the car, trying to pick up as much speed as two people on foot could provide. Mitty sat bolt upright on the car, cackling in joy as the the cravat around his neck snapped behind him like a fighter pilot's.

After three complete trips there and back, Fluky and I were beat. We screwed the crossbars into braking position and collapsed back onto the skeleton of a freight car, popping open a few cartons of Frau.

We were flush with our success, laughing and telling jokes. It was only natural, that presented with so few obvious obstacles to our eventual success, our talk soon turned to how history was going to remember us.

"A train needs a name," Fluky said, "a good one."

"Something fitting for the ages..." Mitty agreed, looking off towards the horizon.

"We can't name her yet," I disagreed. "We haven't even built her." After all, we were just sitting on the chassis of an old '53 Ford pickup with some steel welded on. It was hardly a train.

But everyone sat there for a long moment, thinking. It wasn't hard to guess what everyone was contemplating.

"*The Prometheus*," Mitty said theatrically, breaking the silence.

"Ah, hell..." Fluky didn't approve.

"No, see," Mitty said excitedly. "Prometheus stole fire from the gods and delivered it unto mankind. It's apropos."

I laughed, "Yeah, he also got chained to a rock for his trouble and a bird ate his liver. Sounds like bad luck to me."

"Oh, balderdash!" Mitty dismissed. "No one remembers the fire, everyone remembers the liver..."

"*The Boot Hill Ass-Press*," Fluky volunteered, laughing at his own joke. "Get it? Ass-Press?"

"Oh, God," was all I could say.

"Ass? Press? Get it?"

"Yeah, yeah, got it."

"*The Booty Hill-*" Fluky was riffing.

"Thanks, Fluky," I interrupted.

"Well, then you name the damn train," Fluky said, finishing off his beer.

"How about we build it first and then we can give her a name," I brooded.

But Fluky and Mitty weren't going to let it go.

"*White Lightning!*"

"*The Hermes.*"

"*The Luma Flyer.*"

"*The General Patton.*"

I shook my head to all of these, "If you've got to give it a name, make it appropriate. We're trucking boots over a mountain to sell on the black market..."

"*The Midnight Marauder,*" Fluky said with an air of conspiracy.

"*The Outlaw Cobbler,*" Mitty tried.

"No. For a start, a cobbler *repairs* boots, here in Boot Hill we make them." I was being pedantic. "If anything, the train should be called *The Cordwainer.*"

And there it was. I don't believe we ever actually agreed on the name. But after that day, for the rest of the project, we all simply referred to the train that was slowly taking shape as *The Cordwainer*.

Of course, I think Mitty thought it was some Greek god, and Fluky insisted on calling it *The Cordwiener*, but I didn't care. I had every hope that our adventure would take us across the mountains and back without drawing the slightest bit of attention – from the authorities or history. I was interested in money, not notoriety. Notoriety, I reasoned, would get us all a one-way ticket to a dark jail cell somewhere, though the further along in Mitty's Plan that we got, the more I tried to reason out exactly what law I thought we were breaking. There was no law against building a train from junk, and no law against running one if it didn't produce any carbon. There was also no law against buying boots at cost and selling them at a profit, though this was obviously frowned upon by the powers-that-be.

What was it about Mitty's Plan that I felt was so wrong? I felt a need to be secretive, though no one had made even the slightest suggestion that something like *The Cordwainer* was anything illegal. Still, I was cautious not to mention Mitty's Plan to anyone I didn't have to, and I had advised the others to do the same. Perhaps I was being paranoid, perhaps the people of Boot Hill would have welcomed our efforts as an affirmation of a can-do, American attitude – but somehow I doubted it.

I knew, deep down in my core, than if *The Cordwainer* was ever going to roll on tracks, we would have to play our hand very close to our chest. Maybe I couldn't put my finger on exactly what about Mitty's Plan was illegal, but I knew for sure that I had grown up in a world where such attempts at self aggrandizement where strongly discouraged.

After all, who were we helping except ourselves? How did our actions in any way enrich the community?

Who were we to think we could be rich?

Chapter Thirteen

Form 24-01

While we were making solid progress on Mitty's Plan, my hold on my position as a Foreman at The Shop was slowly starting to slip away from me. I was doubly confused by the whole situation – the job, paradoxically, proved to be both childishly simple in its duties and confusingly complex in its nuances.

Returning to work Monday, flushed from the victory of our successful test of *The Cordwainer's* rolling stock, I took it upon myself to implement a few of the simpler optimizations of Production Line Number Six I had identified watching the line in action.

What could have possibly possessed me, I could only guess. No one had even minutely hinted that such a thing was at all within the portfolio of my position. But I was, at heart, a problem solver – I felt like a problem solver, with so many victories under my belt back in Zimmerman's junkyard. After everything I'd achieved in the last few weeks, the optimization of my production line was small potatoes. The girls would be happier, the output would increase, I'd actually have something to do... everyone would be happy.

How much more foolish could I have been?

My first change was the simplest: Move the girls who organically formed a team closer to each other on the line. The Worker B's initially looked at me like I was insane. Some of the older women had been working at the same station on the same line for upwards of twenty years. They looked at each other in confused silence. Did I have the power to make them move workstations? No one seemed sure. Begrudgingly, they rearranged on the line as I had instructed them, and after twenty minutes or so of working in the new configuration, every girl on the line was looking up at me and shooting me wide grins. A simple optimization of effort had made everyone's lives demonstratively better.

If I'd stopped there, perhaps no one would have ever noticed the change and I could have achieved a substantial good at little to no cost.

Of course, I couldn't just let it go at that.

My second change was where all the trouble began: The three extra Worker B's on the production line, the girls who seemed to belong to no specific organic team, the ones who attempted to pick up whatever slack formed on the line for whatever reason, these girls I instructed to step away from their workstations. I told them to move wherever they felt they could be most useful. They were soon flitting up and down the production line, watching for bottlenecks or lending a helping hand when a Worker B became overwhelmed. They were my flying squad, shoring up the production line wherever it began to give.

And it all showed results. Timed with Barry's golden watch, I was seeing boots coming off the line thirty seconds quicker than before my optimizations. But it was within the comparative times of the four organic teams that things really improved. My worst two performers, Teams C and D, who'd taken more than ten minutes to complete a pair of boots before, had rocked up to eight minutes forty-five and eight twenty respectively. With my "flying squad" able to move up and down the line and pay extra attention to these under-producing teams, I was getting some great results. The girls were joking and laughing more, they had more time to loaf about and chatter than they did before, and they were still making boots faster.

The problem was, the three girls I'd moved off the line, my "flying squad", were suddenly finding their jobs very physical. No one on Production Line Number Six was a young pup, and these ladies were quickly finding themselves winded. They didn't need to be on their feet the whole time, much of their job was simply watching for bottlenecks, so I made the fateful decision to allow them to sit down. I gave up use of my

Foreman's stool for the purpose. If they were able to rest between bouts of activity...

But the sight of Worker B's sitting down on the job drew angry glares from across The Shop floor. No one else was sitting down – only Foremen. That my production line was producing boots at a rate far superior to any of the other production lines, no one could tell. All they could see was that my girls were sitting down on the job.

If I'd only left well enough alone, if I'd only not been such a goddamn smart ass. If I'd only just done my job and drawn down my pay and left well enough alone.

Then no one would have come looking for Form 24-01.

The first suggestion I got of the coming storm came two days after I'd put my optimizations into place. I was home that evening with my father, letting him beat me at chess. We were playing on the World War II Patton chess set I'd earned collecting Tom Mixx boxtops my whole eleventh year. It was the summer after my mother had died and I had developed a disobedient streak to overcompensate for the loss. I'd taken to not eating my breakfast, as my father never bothered. That was until he told me about the Authentic, Collectible World War II Patton/Rommel Chess Set that you could get if you sent in twenty boxtops of Tom Mixx Cereal and $1.99.

Of course, after seeing the set in all its color-printed glory, I started eating my breakfast again. Even augmenting it with a few bowls of cereal when I got home from school. It only took me two months to collect enough boxtops; and I helped my father dutifully put each one in an envelope, with a check for $1.99, and mail it off to Cedar Rapids.

Two weeks later the chess set came. I unboxed it and set it up and spent hours just looking it over. Patton, understandably, was the white king; Rommel, the black; Old Glory the white queen, the swastika the black. A pair of Omar Bradleys were the bishops for the good guys; a Nazi General I could never identify was the bishops for the black. Sherman and Panzer tanks were the knights, P-52 Mustangs and Stukas were the rooks, and a slew of Doughboys and Wehrmacht infantry were the pawns. My father sat me down and proceeded to teach me chess. By the time I was fifteen I was consistently beating him, and by my seventeenth birthday I was charitably letting him win.

But you know what? Looking back, a World War II chess set seems like a mighty strange product tie-in for a cereal with a cowboy on the box... but I ate my breakfast every morning for the rest of my childhood after that, my disobedient streak forgotten. My father had won at least that game.

"Foreman Salmon says you've made some changes to Number Six..." my father began out of the blue, moving a Panzer tank.

"Hmm," I grunted, not looking up from the game.

"Says it's caused some chatter on the floor. Rumblings."

"Hmm." I moved Old Glory.

"Tells me you've got girls sitting down..."

We both looked at the board for a silent minute, both taking sips from our tumblers of McTavish.

"What? Sorry?" I looked up.

"Girls sitting," he repeated. "Down."

"Yes, yes..." At the time I didn't understand the trouble I was in – that my father was trying to break it gently. "My 'flying squad'" I said with pride. "Productivity is up fifteen percent. I had one team make a pair of boots in six minutes today. Can you believe that? Six minutes?"

My glass was empty. I got up and went to the bar for a refill.

"That's-that's... Great," My father stammered. "But son, *sitting*?" My father said the word like it was the most vile sin you could perform against nature.

I turned around from the bar, finally grasping that my father was dressing me down.

I said defensively, "Yes, they're watching for bottlenecks. They're moving all day. They don't have to stand to use their eyes."

My father climbed to his feet and walked over to join me at the bar. He began to refill his glass, but it was only half empty.

"You've got to understand how it looks, Andrew. Worker B's sitting on the job. The girls on the other production lines don't get to sit. If they look over and see a girl on your line resting on her laurels. Well, I mean, next thing you know they'll all want to sit down."

"Perhaps they should!"

"Now, son..." my father condescended, putting a hand on my shoulder.

"Number Six is making boots faster than any other line!" I knocked his hand away.

"Number Six has always been the fastest-" my father began.

I interrupted, "Yes, and now it's faster."

I found my seat again and slumped over the board, pretending to study it, but I couldn't remember whose move it was.

My father sat back down in his chair. "Andrew, remember what I said your first day of work: This is the real world, not school, there's no second chances. Making changes, rocking the boat, you're only causing problems. Maybe production is up on your line, yes, but what about the others? What effect on morale will watching girls sit down on the job have on those other production lines? What will happen to their productivity? We're all in one big boat, Andrew. That your production line produces more than another... well, it's not important if the total production of The Shop goes down, now is it?"

"Just tell me one thing," I thrust an accusing finger across the chessboard. "Have I done one thing out-of-line? Have I done anything that is not within my powers to do as Foreman of Number Six?"

"No, but..."

"Then don't berate me for doing my job!" I jumped to my feet, putting my drink down on the board. My father grimaced and rubbed at the stubble on his chin. "You should be copying what I've done, not pissing on it! You old fools wouldn't know a good idea if it bit you..." But I was already storming off out of the living room, looking for my coat. "Give me a month and I'll shave another ten seconds off a pair of boots. Give me four empty production lines and I could quadruple output with the staff I have!" I was yelling from the hall. I'd found my jacket. I put it on and paused in the doorway to the living room. "How about that? How about I show everyone how lousy you guys have been running things? For years. How would Mr. Salmon like that, huh?"

My father didn't reply. He was looking down at the chessboard.

"Yeah, that's what I thought!" And I stormed off out of the house.

The next morning I was called into Foreman Salmon's small, glassed-in office. His bulk was sitting behind his desk as I entered. He pointed to the ancient aluminum chair that sat across the desk from him and I sat down. He shuffled some papers on his desk and didn't look up at me, making me wait.

Managing Foreman Salmon's office looked out across the full expanse of The Shop. From here, he could see the entire goings-on of the factory. I could just make out Number Six production line working busily away at the far end of the floor. Mr. Salmon coughed and appeared to find the piece of paper he was looking for.

He began, "I'm sure your father stressed to you, during your initiation, the importance of the inspection forms you daily complete." He held up a sample four-boxed form, showing it to me. I had my clipboard across my lap, inch-thick with identical forms.

"Of course," I said, glancing between the sheet of paper and Mr. Salmon's face.

"Did he mention that each is individually numbered?" Mr. Salmon's fat finger indicated the embossed serial number in the top right corner.

I opened my mouth and closed it. I wasn't exactly sure where this conversation was going. Hadn't I been called into the boss's office to discuss my optimization efforts?

"Yes, yes, he did," I blurted out, realizing I was staring at Mr. Salmon like a fool.

"It's very important that we keep track of these forms, you understand. Internal accounting."

"Yes..."

"Good, good, I'm glad we had this talk," Mr. Salmon said, standing up from behind his desk. I rose to my feet, too. Mr. Salmon held out a plump hand and I shook it in confusion.

That's it? Mr. Salmon's body language was telling me the interview was over. I turned and started for the door.

As I was reaching down to turn the handle, Mr. Salmon added, "So, if we can just get 24-01 – for completeness – we'll be right as rain."

I paused, "I'm sorry?" I asked, turning back. "What?"

"Form 24-01."

"Form..."

I looked down at my clipboard, at the barely legible serial number – more indented than embossed. My top form was number 25-73.

"...24-01?" I parroted.

"Yes. That'd be great." Mr. Salmon was sitting again, shuffling papers around his desk.

"24-01..." I said again, like an idiot. "24-01?"

And then, as if my eyes suddenly leapt ten miles out of my body, I had a vision of my engine schematic, pinned to a board in Old Man Zimmerman's workshop. The four-boxed form I'd sketched my engine design on the back of, it must have been-

"Yes, Form 24-01," Mr. Salmon said slowly to me, like speaking to a child. "If you can get that over to accounting, they'll be overjoyed."

I was dumbfounded. None of this had been about my efficiency efforts? Nothing about the girls sitting down? They just needed a crummy form back that I'd misplaced?

"Is there anything else?" Mr. Salmon asked and I realized I was standing, thinking at Mr. Salmon's door.

"No, sorry," I said and turned the handle, slipping quickly out.

Managing Foreman Salmon, like so many Generals, was reticent to attack his enemy in a frontal assault. I had not yet fully comprehended as I walked away from Mr. Salmon's small, glassed-in office that his request for Form 24-01 was only a feint; that his true target, as I had suspected, was my efficiency efforts on Production Line number Six. Why the ruse, I can only surmise. Perhaps he thought I'd have been unable to lay my hands on the errant form, and therefore had cause to officially discipline me. I didn't know.

My father had explained the importance of keeping track of the four-boxed forms, and other than that single exception, I'd kept a good handle on the paperwork entrusted to me. That I was still in possession of the form, but disinclined to part with it, I can guess that Foreman Salmon was unaware.

If I returned that form to accounting with the schematic of my engine on the back... well, at the very least it would create a whole lot of unwelcome questions. I needed to keep hold of that form. I was going to have to find a way to get accounting to let me off the hook for the loss of the form, and lucky I was positioned well to get exactly that done. After all, Sophie, my sister, worked in Accounts Receivable. I had pull. Family connections.

Of course, Mr. Salmon – and my father – weren't going to let the whole sitting-down-on-the-job issue drop without seeing me disciplined. But their first round, I was thinking, might just fall short of the mark.

Score one for productivity.

But now, in hindsight, I realize how foolish I was being. My whole attempt to optimize line Number Six had been a fool's errand from the start. If I had possessed half the brains I credited myself for possessing, I would have seen it. But in my myopic, childish attempt to make my work meaningful. I was butting up against the very fundamental purpose of The Shop:

The Shop didn't make boots, it made jobs.

If I'd bothered to open my eyes, I could have seen it. All those crates of boots boxed by the side of the road leading up to the factory – millions of boots that would never be worn by anyone. The Shop had been overproducing footwear for decades, more than could ever be shipped to market, even without carbon controls. But that wasn't the point. The Shop didn't make boots to sell. It made boots to keep hands busy. To keep people employed. To keep people happy, to keep their minds off the shortages. To keep money in people's pockets so, at least, they felt rich, even if there was little or nothing for them to buy.

The Shop made work, not shoes.

That I didn't see this was unforgivably short-sighted of me. If I'd been able to grasp the full social-political meaning of The Shop, I would have understood why my father and Mr. Salmon reacted so violently to my efficiency efforts. Making boots faster or better was helping no one. I was just sowing dissatisfaction, rocking the boat. The longer it took to make a pair of boots the better. After all, why really make the boots at all if no one was ever going to wear them? The *process*, that was what was important. The labor. That was what was keeping the world turning.

I could blame it on my age, or my inexperience, but I'd be lying to myself if I did. It was, fundamentally, a world I was not cut out to occupy. It takes a certain attitude to make things poorly, to make them slowly, to make them for the sake of wasting the effort.

It was an attitude I didn't possess. I was a man, after all, who still believed he could build a train out of scrap metal, power it with steam, ride it across the mountains to make his fortune in the Big City. No, I didn't have an attitude compatible with Boot Hill or The Shop. And never would.

Chapter Fourteen

Pee Stick

It was with this "ah shucks" naivety that I walked upstairs the next day to the accounting floor of The Shop to see my sister, Sophie, at her desk.

Sophie had always been the true genius of our family. She was two years my elder and had graduated before me from the Big City University, also with a degree in Mechanical Engineering. She'd been my inspiration to follow that path – her ability with machines. When she was ten she had taken the family radio apart. Not a particularly unique feat, but she was actually able to put it back together again. At twelve, she had adapted an old automobile to run strictly on McTavish. She was amazing with anything mechanical.

She had graduated magna cum laude from University, within the top one hundred of her class, and had actually fielded offers for jobs in the engineering profession. But she had gotten married in her senior year, to a guy in her class named Alan, whose job prospects had not been as outstanding as her own. When our father had suggested they both return to Boot Hill, that he could find employment for both Sophie and Alan at The Shop, they'd taken him up on his offer. They'd settled down into the leisurely pace of Boot Hill and a small concrete bungalow not far from my father's.

They had been working together at The Shop the two years I had been away finishing my degree, Alan in transportation, where he'd made himself almost indispensable, and my sister in accounting, handling the books. If she found the work stimulating, I could scarcely imagine, but the pair, at least outwardly, appeared happy. My sister and I had always been close – after our mother had died, she'd stepped into the motherly role as best she could – but since returning to Boot Hill, we had hardly had a chance to see one another. Mitty's Plan had come up and Sophie had her household duties to see to on top of her normal work day.

Perhaps over the years we had drifted apart some. It was only natural. But that morning, when I stopped by her desk to enlist her help with my little Form 24-01 problem, I could have hardly anticipated her reaction:

"You're fucking kidding me?!" Sophie said loud enough that all the short-sleeved, tie-wearing accountants could hear her. She looked up from her balance sheet and gave me a look of disgusted horror.

"Will you keep your voice down?" I said through my teeth.

"I will not keep my fucking voice down!" She said. She wasn't. "Three fucking weeks on the job and already you've fucked it up. I cannot believe you, Andrew. You're like a fucking child! Running to me every time you made a mistake. Well not this time, Andrew. No!" She wheeled her chair away from her desk and pulled open a drawer. She started digging angrily around inside, still cursing. "You're a grown adult with a grown adult job. If you've forgot a fucking form, tough! There's numbers on those damn things for a reason, you pecker-head!"

The third drawer she tried, the one top right, had what she was looking for. A pack of Jefferson's and matches. She grabbed them, slammed the drawer shut and sprang to her feet. Without another word she stormed off across the accounting office, pulling a cigarette out of the pack and putting it in her mouth.

I followed after her, trying to make calming noises, but she strided determinedly ahead. She threw open a glass door and stepped out onto a high balcony looking down over The Shop's main yard. I followed. Blue-shirted workers moved below us.

Sophie lit her cigarette and took a long drag.

"Jesus, Sophie!" I said as the door closed, feeling free to talk in the breeze. "Who stuck a finger up your ass?"

"I'm just sick of it, Andy! Every time you make a mess it's me who has to clean it up!"

"It's just a stupid form..."

"Yes! A stupid fucking form *you* lost. It's your problem. Don't come crying to me."

"Sophie..." I was trying to keep my temper.

"Fuck!" she yelled off the balcony. "It doesn't matter, anyway. There's fuck-all I can do to help you, regardless. I've been given my thirty days."

Thirty days. Termination. The Ax.

"What?" I almost laughed. "They? Firing *you*?"

"No, no, not fired..." she said, suddenly calmer. "Maternity..." She took another drag on her cigarette.

"What?!" My eyes almost popped from their sockets. I was going to be an uncle! "Are you sure?"

"Yeah," Sophie said unhappily, like the news was a death sentence. "I went to see Doctor Reese last week. He had me pee on a stick. I guess they can tell from that – the pee stick..."

"Have you told Dad?"

"No!" she snapped angrily. "And neither will you. I'll tell him when I'm ready."

"But," I began, looking back through the glass at the short-sleeved, tie-wearing accountants. "Thirty days? Doesn't it usually take nine months?"

Sophie had finished her cigarette and she snuffed it out in the sand ashtray beside the railing. "Dead men's boots," she said. "And pregnant? You might as well be dead. You know there's a dozen guys just waiting to step into my job. And the thing about guys, you know? They don't get pregnant. I guess I shouldn't complain. They only gave me this job 'cause of Dad. Easy come... And Alan is still down in transportation. He'll be up for a promotion in a year..."

"But... but," I tried to think of something clever, comforting to say.

"So you get an idea of how much I give a shit about your fucking form!" Sophie found her anger again, swinging back open the door. "We've all got problems, Andrew," she said, stepping through.

I let the door close behind her, loitering on the balcony. I looked down at the yard below, at the people moving about.

I let the news sink in.

I was happy – I was going to an uncle – but my sister... it didn't seem right that she was going to lose her job because she was pregnant. I was a guy, I'd never have that problem, but if you were going to pick an employee to fire, between my sister and myself, you'd be a fool to keep me. Or Alan, for that matter. The tartarhead. Wasn't he sort of pregnant, too? Wasn't he expecting a kid? If they had an ounce of sense they'd fire him and keep Sophie on. But I guess that wasn't the way it worked.

Still, it seemed like a colossal waste. Sophie was a genius. A genuine one, not like me. She was going to make a great mom, but to make a mom all she was going to be...

It didn't really seem fair.

Chapter Fifteen

High Test

The prototype of my engine was ready for its initial test about the time I learned that I was to become an uncle. Fluky called that evening to tell me that the last of the welds looked good. This left me with only two remaining obstacles to hurdle before my engine could run: Acquiring metal for the catalyst and a sufficient quantity of fuel.

The expansion chamber of our hydrogen peroxide driven engine would require a small, but not insignificant, amount of silver. Formed into a mesh, this would catalyze the peroxide, stripping off the extra oxygen, producing water and oxygen along with a whole hell of a lot of heat. Finding a source for silver presented a problem. Luxury items that might have once been manufactured from silver had long ago vanished from the shelves of the Concession Store. They were, after all, unnecessary extravagances for people who were going short on essentials – food, clothing, boots – but they had not totally vanished from the top shelves and the back corners of the closets of America.

It occurred to me that I had access to quite a substantial source of high-grade silver. In the china hutch, in the dining room of my father's home. My mother's silver was still there, untouched for over a decade. The stuff she only ever pulled out for special occasions – Christmas, Easter. My father never used it; he didn't entertain. It was my mother's pride and joy. It had been my mother's mother's. Or my mother's mother's mother's – something like that. It had to be a century old if it was a day, made back when people still ate off china with solid silver flatware. I remember it being quite beautiful, the last time my mother had set the table for guests.

I had a small pang of conscience surreptitiously breaking into the china hutch. My mother had loved that silver so. When things had started to get tough, after the war, it had been her only luxury; a reminder of better times and a world that was now lost to the fog of memory. I wasn't going to need much. A knife and a fork would be plenty. I stole a whole place setting so it wouldn't look so suspicious. There were still seven more, but if my mother had still been alive... well, then I'd never have touched it. But she wasn't, and I did. Perhaps she was looking down from wherever she was and shaking her head in disgust. But then again, perhaps she was smiling.

If we succeeded with Mitty's Plan, if I was able to freight boots across the mountains and came back with enough cash to buy Boot Hill twice over, wouldn't that stand as a better memorial to my mother than an old box of silver hidden away in the back of a china hutch?

I was rationalizing, I know. But still...

The fuel was a slightly trickier problem. Hydrogen peroxide I could find in spades. The Shop was drowning in the stuff. Large, mega-gauge sized tanks sat stored in the freight yard of the factory; vats of the stuff sat stenching up the processing annex. Late one evening, Fluky, Mitty and I drove up to The Shop in the wrecking truck, hopped the fence, and helped ourselves to a number of old, cracked mason jugs full.

But the peroxide used at the factory, I estimated, was only ten to thirty percent in concentration. That would be of no use to us. Hydrogen peroxide as fuel would need to be eighty to ninety percent pure. HTP. High Test Peroxide. That was rocket fuel, the stuff that Nazis had used for their V2 rockets – the rockets the Germans gave to the Japanese, with their foothold on the Baja, to rain down on San Diego and Los Angeles. The act of war that would eventually provoke Truman into the nuclear carpet bombing of the Japanese Islands, effectively wiping them off the map.

It would be simple enough to purify the peroxide through distillation. Water boils at 212 degrees, where hydrogen peroxide boils at 300. It'd be like making moonshine in reverse. But hydrogen peroxide vapor is highly combustible, so Fluky and I set about constructing a vacuum distillation rig. If we could lower the pressure enough, the peroxide would boil without requiring much heat.

Old Man Zimmerman had an electric air compressor in his shop. We salvaged a length of copper piping to use as a condenser and we set one of the old mason jugs on a hot plate to warm slowly. With water pumping through the condenser and the air compressor sucking, we started to get water out of a spigot at one end of our contraption. The process was slow, but we were getting good results. We kept boiling our mason jug slowly, running the compressor and periodically testing the pH of the mixture. When it got really acidic, below a pH of 3, we called it good.

What the actual concentration of our eventual product was, I could only guess: Pushing ninety percent, at least. It sure stank to high heaven. We corked it up and went about melting down the silver knife and fork and pouring them into a crude mold we had fashioned, approximating the size and shape of a grill. It was rough, looking like something that a five-year-old had made in Kindergarten, but that was of no consequence. All it needed to do was react violently with hydrogen peroxide. Looks were the last thing we were concerned with.

As the week-long holiday celebrating the Fourth of July approached, we started making plans for a test run of my high test engine. We had, early on, decided it best to wheel the prototype out of Zimmerman's yard and over to Pottersville for the actual test. We planned to take every safety precaution. Fluky wanted to rig up the prototype to a freight car and test the engine in a practical scenario, but I quickly kiboshed the idea. We just needed to test the engine – test its ability to turn chemical energy into mechanical. Its ability to produce power, we could test later.

Besides, running the engine on a track would have required an operator, to start and stop the engine, and I didn't want anyone within a hundred yards of the prototype when it first ran. HTP was powerful stuff. If man ever went into space, like in the picture shows, he'd do it in rockets powered by HTP. If anything went wrong... We were all going to be a long way away when my engine took its first breath of life.

Our physical remoteness to the actual test presented itself as a whole new, different technical hurdle. If we couldn't start and stop the engine manually, just how were we going to get the thing to run? Fluky, true to form, came up with a simple and elegant solution: We'd test run the engine for thirty seconds, about the length of time it took a bedside alarm clock to wind down its spring. We would simply set the alarm clock to ring at a predetermined time, enough time to allow us to escape to a safe distance and observe. Then when the clock started ringing it'd pull a switch with its hammer, completing a circuit, opening a solenoid fuel valve. As the clock ran, it would wind up a string around its key, shortening it, until the string pulled another switch, breaking the circuit, shutting off the valve.

It was an insane, Rube Goldberg sort of jury rig, but in a dry run using a light bulb instead of a solenoid, it worked perfectly.

We spent the Fourth of July watching the fireworks and getting drunk. The next day we nursed our hangovers. By July 6 we were prepared for our test. We hitched the rolling cart to the back of the wrecking truck onto which Fluky had mounted my engine, and we started the truck up, heading out for Pottersville. We got an early start, before 8:00 according to Barry's watch, and we saw barely a soul as we drove through town. It was a holiday morning and no one but us had a reason to be out of bed so early. The heat of the day was already starting in and it was going to be a warm one, I could already tell.

Luckily, Fluky had saved a case of beer from our Fourth of July celebrations, so we'd be well oiled for a day of toil. Mitty and Fluky had already cracked open a couple of cartons as the old wrecking truck smoked up the hill towards Pottersville. I refrained. My drinking had dropped significantly since we'd begun work on the engine – there just hadn't been enough time. Mitty's Plan had that going for it, if nothing else.

We had chosen the Pottersville Town Park for the site of our experiment. It sat directly in the center of town and was the largest expanse of space available to us without driving out into the scrub. Most of the park had gone to seed and become overwhelmed by brambles and desert grass, but the center still boasted a large flagstone square, dominated by a statue of Mr. Potter, the town's founder – a name otherwise lost to history.

We set my prototype engine there, next to Mr. Potter, wheeling the engine in from the street on its cart, taking the strength of all three of us to move it. We were hot and exhausted by the time we had the contraption in place and paused for a Frau for each of us. When our drinks were done, we set about wiring up our test run.

The HTP we left in the mason jug, raised up above the level of the engine, letting the fuel naturally siphon down into the engine. We attached a large wooden fly wheel to the crankshaft, on which Mitty had painted a bright red circle off center. The logic was that from fifty yards away we'd be better able to estimate the RPMs of our engine watching the big dot spin than simply listening to the engine purr. Fluky busied himself setting up the strings and springs of his Rube Goldberg timer, gesticulating away like some mad puppeteer.

Once Fluky had indicated all was ready, I checked over the engine one last time, wiggling the manifold and tubes to make sure everything felt solid. Satisfied, I told Fluky to set the time. Barry's watch told me it was 8:47 in the a.m. I told Fluky to set the alarm for 8:50 exactly. When he'd done so, all three of us rapidly sprinted tangentially away from the engine like it was a ticking bomb. We only returned momentarily to recover the case of beer.

By 8:48, we were standing by the iron railings of the park, looking back at the silent, still nest of tubes, strings and wires that constituted our engine. Fluky handed out the Fraus and we all popped the corners.

"So, if this sucker works," Fluky began, "what's the next step? Strap it to the rolling stock?"

"Yeah, I guess..." I was watching the engine intensely, not really listening. If I'd been a praying man, I'd have been spending those last moments begging God for a little providence.

"Well, once that dingus is bolted on, I get to drive it, okay?" Fluky said.

I looked at my watch: 8:49. "What?"

"For the first test run, I wanta drive it."

"Drive it?" I didn't understand. "It's a train, Fluky. The tracks drive it."

"I know. Still... handle on the throttle and all. I always wanted to drive a train."

"There's going to be more than enough chances to play engineer, Fluky, when we're making our ascent."

"Still... First time. I think it should be me. Hell, I've earned it."

"Sure, sure, whatever."

"Will there be a whistle?" Mitty asked. He was watching the prototype as intently as I was. "I think there should be a whistle."

We stood there in silence, collectively holding our breaths. Any second now...

"A whistle?" I suddenly realized. "What a damn fool-"

Then the alarm sounded.

The ringing echoed through the empty streets of Pottersville. It was a haunting, eerie sound, bouncing back on itself. For a second I thought Fluky's timer had failed us, for the engine just sat there inertly. Then there was a hiss of steam as some seal pressurized, then that large wooden wheel began to move. It mostly jiggled at first, not really turning, but then the red dot started to move. It began to turn clockwise, slowly building its speed. One revolution, then two. I let out my breath and laughed out loud. Fluky slapped me on the back and Mitty put and arm around my neck.

Two revolutions became three, then four, five and then the wheel was turning too fast to keep track of. Steam was pouring out of the exhaust and the whole contraption was rapidly vanishing in the cloud of white. The spinning wheel was creating a vortex, swirling the steam into a funnel. I glanced down at Barry's watch and saw that we were approaching ten seconds. Fluky and Mitty were jumping up and down next to me whooping in joy, when...

Boom.

The engine exploded. No, I can't say it was an explosion, as there were no flames, but the shock wave of the blast knocked the three of us back up against the iron railings. The prototype – or rather where the prototype had been – was enveloped in a mushroom cloud of steam.

I'm not kidding. As I pulled myself up off the flagstones, the explosion still ringing in my ears, I saw a genuine, authentic mushroom cloud rising up into the sky. Just like in the newsreels about the bombers over Japan.

Fluky and Mitty pulled themselves up to sitting positions next to me, groaning in pain. It looked like everyone was okay. Mr. Potter, however, considering his closer proximity to the explosion, lay on his side, smashed into pieces on the flagstones.

I shook my head and tried to pop my ears. I didn't know if the echo was in the streets or in my head, but I could still hear the explosion.

Shock turned to surprise and then turned to fear in the span of moments. We didn't pause to examine the wreckage of our prototype engine. We leapt to our feet, slipping on the flagstones, and sprinted for the wrecking truck. If the explosion had been as loud as it seemed – as the numbness in our ear attested to – and the mushroom cloud as vivid, then there was no doubt that the entire town of Boot Hill would have woken up to it. I could already feel the eyes peering down from the hillside, searching the ruins of Pottersville for the source of the explosion.

We were in the truck and moving before I'd had time to think. Fluky was heading back up the hill, toward Boot Hill on C Street. That was a bad idea. If anyone was coming from Boot Hill, they'd be coming down C, and we'd run right into them. I instructed Fluky to turn around and take the long way back to town, around the rise that split the two towns. We rumbled off into the scrub to vector into Boot Hill from a different angle.

When I'd had a chance to catch my breath and the ringing in my ears had started to fade, I realized that we'd left a whole lot of evidence behind us.

There was nothing we could do about it.

"What the hell happened?" Fluky finally asked, twenty minutes into our drive, when we were well out into the scrub, pulling back onto the highway.

I had nothing to say.

There were a thousand things that could have gone wrong. The engine had been a prototype, little more than a functioning mock up. A weld could have given, a hose could have broken, I could have been woefully inaccurate in my calculations. But later, I would come to learn that the most likely explanation was a BLEVE.

A Boiling Liquid Expanding Vapor Explosion. Basically, the engine didn't explode, the mason jug full of HTP did. And perhaps not for the reason one might think. In fact, the fragile nature of the mason jug might have been a blessing, allowing the engine to run as long as it did.

But, in all honestly, my design was particularly susceptible to this type of catastrophic failure. I still feel the basic design was sound, but the problem came in that final stroke, when the low pressure stage was used to pull fuel into the catalyzing chamber. This technique created a dangerous under pressure in the fuel tank. I had hoped to suck the fuel into the engine, eliminating the need for a fuel pump, but that low pressure stage instead acted on the fuel tank like our air compressor did in our vacuum distillater – lowering the pressure and the boiling point until the hydrogen peroxide evaporated. This created intense pressure in the fuel tank until the container ruptured and... boom.

If anything, the mason jug's inability to hold a tight seal acted as a release valve on this process. If I'd chosen a more substantial fuel tank – steel, for example – the pressure would have been many times greater at the point of rupture. Even fifty yards' distance between us and the explosion might not have been enough to save us.

We sneaked successfully back into town from almost exactly the opposite direction than Pottersville. Fluky, off on an early morning trip in his truck, was nothing unusual, and little was said about our absence at the time of the explosion.

But a lot of speculation abounded about the source of the bang and the subsequent steam cloud that could be seen from town. Many suspected that there'd been an accident at one of the nuclear reactors over in the tri-towns of Shadrach, Meshach and Abednego, but the cloud was south of the city, not west – in the wrong direction.

By and by, the town Deputy, Aesop, and his ancient white pony were sent over to Pottersville to investigate. He was in no rush to do so, being almost as ancient as his mount, but Aesop constituted the whole extent of the law in Boot Hill (apart from Fluky, there was very little need for any) and the task fell to him.

That evening, just before dark, he rode back into town and stopped in at Putter's. We happened to be at the bar, washing out our wounds with round after round of McTavish. The Deputy reported on the fallen statue, but could not rightly say what had caused the explosion. He found some shrapnel and deduced that it had been an unexploded Japanese bomb.

That was a good enough explanation for most everyone in town, and it gave them all plenty to talk about over the long Fourth of July week. It was a lucky break for us. If there had been anything even faintly recognizable left of our engine, or the town had sent anyone competent over to Pottersville to investigate, there might have been trouble.

But as it was, the testing of *The Cordwainer's* prototype engine, despite being a total and complete failure, drew very little extra attention to exactly what we were attempting to do in Old Man Zimmerman's garage.

We had been knocked down, but we weren't knocked out.

"What the hell we gonna do?" Fluky said, despondently, after we'd listen to Deputy Aesop's report to the whole of Putter's Bar. Everyone was chattering away and we were huddled up in a booth at the back, drinking our whiskey.

"Surely, this is a minor setback," Mitty added cheerily.

"No," I interrupted. "No, the more I think it over. The design... There was something systemic. A fatal flaw." I didn't know about BLEVE at that time, but I suspected. My instincts were good.

"Then we're sunk," Fluky pouted, finishing off his glass.

"No, we..." Mitty tried.

"All that work for nothin'. What a fuckin' waste. You two tartarheads. Getting me excited."

"Yeah, I can't build us an engine," I admitted into my glass.

"But, but-" Mitty stammered. The look on his face was like someone had told him Santa Claus wasn't real.

"And what am I gonna do with them five Stephenson gauge rail cars?" Fluky laughed, though he blatantly didn't think it was funny.

"Oh, we're going to use them," I said.

"Huh?" Mitty perked up.

"What? Push 'em?" Fluky raised an eyebrow.

"I said I can't build us an engine," I smiled. "But I think I know someone who can."

"Who? What?" Fluky looked at Mitty like he might have answers. "Who?"

"Sophie," I replied.

"Li'l Bean?!" Fluky exclaimed, with a look on his face halfway between surprise and lasciviousness. Fluky had always had an inappropriate fascination with my sister, ever since she'd blossomed at twelve and Fluky had developed an unhealthy fascination with girls. I guess she was attractive, in a librarian-takes-off-her-glasses-and-shakes-down-her-hair-and-suddenly-she's-Rita-Hayworth sort of way. But Fluky idolized her. Sophie, for her part, found Fluky a disgusting mess.

"What the deuce? Sophie?" Mitty added.

"Yeah," I nodded, "Sophie. She can build us our engine."

"Seriously?" Fluky raised an eyebrow. "Ain't she got a day job?"

"Not anymore. The Shop laid her off."

"And you think she'll help us?"

"Yes, I think she will..." I replied. I think I knew my sister, knew what motivated her. A challenge like this, it was exactly the kind of thing she loved. Tell her something couldn't be done and she'd go out of her way to show you exactly how to do it. All I had to do was tell her I *couldn't* build an HTP powered engine and she'd be hooked.

Of course, if I'd known it was she who'd ultimately betray us, I never would have suggested getting her involved.

Chapter Sixteen

Li'l Bean

"I knew that was you!" Sophie said across her kitchen table the next evening, as she sipped at a cup of coffee, smoking a cigarette. I'd stopped by to test the waters about bringing Sophie in on Mitty's Plan. I'd left Fluky and Mitty behind – they would have been of little help – and I'd just filled her in on my progress so far. Sophie was smirking. The explosion in Pottersville, my HTP engine, it all amused her. "What were you thinking?"

"You see, Mitty has this plan," I began.

"And Fluky, too?" she interrupted. "Of course. Those two would have to be behind it."

"No, it's not like that." I tried.

"Anytime anything explodes, guaranteed, Fluky is behind it. After High School? After almost costing you college? You're still palling around with those dummies?"

"No, you see-"

"You guys could have killed yourselves," she scolded.

"Yeah, but we didn't!" I raised my voice. Alan was in the living room, listening to the radio. I didn't need his input on this conversation, so I lowered my voice back down to a sensible level. "Look, the HTP engine," I continued. "I think the idea is sound. Now, my implementation was wrong, but I was thinking..."

"What?" Sophie looked at me, suddenly suspicious.

"Well, you were always the engineer in the family. Maybe if you took a look at my design." I produced Form 24-01 from my breast pocket, unfolding it. I handed it to her and she barely glanced at it, dropping it onto the table.

"Well, that won't work," she dismissed.

My heart sank.

"If you'll just look-"

"You created a low pressure catastrophic event in your fuel cell, didn't you?" she said, and I realized she *had* looked at it. I picked up my schematic and looked it over.

"Yes, maybe..." I studied my own design. It was suddenly alien to me.

"But that's secondary," she continued. "Your basic principle is flawed. It's a pedestrian design, attempting to adapt an existing technology to a fundamentally new concept of an engine. No wonder you almost killed yourselves."

"What?" My feelings were hurt. "What's wrong with it?"

Sophie shook her head and stood up from the table. She walked over to the coffee pot and refilled her cup, "Best to forget about it," she said.

"But..." I swallowed hard, collecting myself. I needed to remember the reason I was there. "But you – you could build a working engine?" I asked.

"What *for?*" she said in disbelief, returning to the table.

"Well... To build it..." I tried.

Sophie paused, the coffee cup halfway to her lips. There were very few souls on earth that that sort of logic made sense to. Luckily, Sophie was one of them.

Sophie returned her coffee cup to the table, leaned back in her chair, and reflexively rubbed at her stomach. She was glaring at me, weighing me up, attempting to deduce my motivations.

"And Fluky and Mitty are helping you with this?" she asked.

"Despite what you think, there's no one better in Boot Hill with tools than Fluky. And Mitty is moral support."

"A pervert and an idiot," she said.

"We built one engine," I countered.

"Yeah, I heard the explosion."

I couldn't judge her expression, what was ticking over in her head. I'd intrigued her, at least. There was that.

"24-01," she said, nodding at the sheet of paper on the kitchen table.

"Yeah," I said, refolding it and returning it to my pocket.

I left my sister's house without anything really being decided. She asked a few more questions, mostly about Fluky's rolling stock, and I answered to the best of my knowledge. I didn't go into detail about the ultimate goals of Mitty's Plan. I didn't think it relevant, and knowing my sister and her world view, I didn't think it would help.

But I think I'd managed to touch on something inside her, perhaps that little niece or nephew that my sister was presently incubating. The change to design something revolutionary obviously lit a spark within Sophie. With a long career of motherhood and housewifing stretching out before her, I think the idea of one last... well, *accomplishment* enticed her. At least, I hoped it did.

It was three days later, in Zimmerman's shop, when I got my answer. Sophie appeared with a rolled-up sheet of drafting paper in her hands. Fluky, Mitty and myself were working on the rolling stock. We might have lacked an engine, but there was still plenty of work to be done on the two untested freight cars. My sister walked in unannounced. Fluky was the first to see her, freezing on the spot like he'd just seen a ghost. A silly smile formed on his face and Mitty and I had to turn to see what he was smirking at.

"Sophie?" I asked in disbelief.

She didn't answer. She walked over to the shop's workbench and started clearing a space.

"Li'l Bean..." Fluky said like a shy schoolgirl. I didn't think Sophie heard him.

"Call me that again, and I'm leaving," She said. She'd heard.

The three of us walked over to the workbench where Sophie had unrolled her drafting papers. She weighted them down at the corners with tools and stepped back so we could see them.

It was the most complicated thing I'd ever seen in my life. Meticulously drafted schematics for a... well, I guess it was an engine, but I could hardly make head-nor-tail of the design. It made my schematic, the one drawn on the back of Form 24-01, look like a child's crayon drawing. My jaw fell open.

"Hell, that's pretty..." Fluky was the first to speak.

"What is this?" Mitty said around his cigarette holder, looking up at Sophie. "A spaceship?"

"This is your engine," Sophie said calmly, her arms crossed in front of her.

"That?" Fluky pointed an oily finger at the schematics.

"An engine to take us to the moon?" Mitty looked back at the papers, craning his head.

"You said you wanted a hydrogen peroxide engine," Sophie said defiantly. "That's what I have here."

"But," I finally spoke. Some of the design was starting to come into focus. "This is a turbine. We need an engine to haul freight," I said, flipping a sheet over, looking at another part of the design.

"Yes," was all Sophie had to say to that.

"It would never generate enough torque," I began.

"It doesn't generate torque," she interrupted.

"Then what-"

Sophie brushed my hands away from the schematics and flipped through three sheets. Here was a flywheel and a generator and HT tables going to...

"The HTP is just the primary mover," she began, "it's ill suited to the task you're attempting to use it for: Cargo. It is well suited, however, in a turbine design to power traction motors, as you see here." She pointed to the schematics.

"It's electric?" I asked.

"Electric motors provide the torque."

"Where we gonna get electric motors?" Fluky interjected.

"I have some ideas..." Sophie didn't elaborate.

"What's this?" Something about the schematic caught my eye. A tank, secondary to the peroxide tank, bypassing the catalyzer.

"Diesel," Sophie said without fanfare.

"What? Diesel?" I squinted and stared hard at the drawing.

"For shorts bursts of power. H_2O_2 reacts to create H_2O and O_2. I think you understand. It makes a perfect oxidizer. Diesel may be scarce, but I believe Fluky has a ration. When extra performance is necessary, diesel can be injected into the turbine, tripling output."

"It's diesel powered, too?" Mitty looked confused.

"Yes, in a way."

The three of us looked down at the drawings, attempting to find anything there that we could remotely understand.

"Hell, there ain't no way we can build *this*," Fluky finally said.
I looked up from the drawing, up to my sister, and smiled.
Yes we can, I realized.
"Yes we can," I said.

Chapter Seventeen

Black Cadillacs

I think that moment, gathered around the schematics, marked the high point in Sophie's commitment to Mitty's Plan. We showed her what we'd accomplished with the rolling stock, which disinterested her, and our vacuum distillation rig, which positively terrified her. I think the only fact about the whole project that impressed her was that we'd survived so long considering the ham-fisted way we'd gone about our first attempt.

Sophie put us directly to work, that very day, constructing her engine as she had envisioned. There would be no jury-rigging and adapting automobile parts for this attempt; almost everything would need to be fabricated from scratch.

Luckily for Mitty's Plan, it was Sophie giving the orders, specifically to Fluky. Half of what she wanted, if anyone else had requested it, Fluky would have told them to go fuck themselves. But Fluky followed Sophie around like a sex-starved puppy. Fabricate an expansion chamber from sheet steel with airtight welds? Yes ma'am. Weld the blades onto the turbine cone at twenty degrees, not thirty? Yes ma'am. Somehow find enough copper wire and hand wind a generator core a thousand turns? Yes ma'am. The work she could get out of Fluky was prodigious, without even as much as a please or thank you. The heights of excellence Fluky's hormones could push him to... You just had to marvel.

Much of the construction of Sophie's engine I was absent for, however, as events back at The Shop – after we all returned from our week-long Fourth of July vacation – required my attention. It appeared that some of the Worker B's, over beers and hot dogs and burgers, got to discussing the efficiency optimizations I'd implemented on old Number Six. The boost in productivity, the fact that idle workers were allowed to sit, all went down well with those who did the actual laboring at The Shop. My understanding is that these casual conversations began to turn into a genuine desire to improve working conditions as the week-long break progressed. A small group of the more motivated women met two or three times more before Monday rolled around, in their homes or at Putter's.

Now, since '62, and the general strike that had paralyzed the nation, trade unions in America had been banned. That was the genesis of the chit system – a compromise between labor and the government, effectively abolishing organized labor in exchange for rigid assurances of job security.

What the girls of the production lines were attempting to do smelled suspiciously like unionization. When word got around about what they had been discussing, people began to panic. Many of the upper managers and Foremen – Mr. Salmon and my father included – still held vivid memories of the '62 Strike, and they had little interest in seeing any of its excesses repeated. The violence, the acrimony, the National Guard patrolling the streets...

So, when work began again on Monday morning, tensions were running high. Productivity was way down, on my line especially, as Worker B's darted back and forth between production lines to secretly confer. My attention was all but totally consumed with the details of Mitty's Plan, but even I could see that something was about to happen.

Nothing transpired until halfway through the lunch hour. I was up in Accounting, standing on the smoking balcony with Sophie, discussing the tension on the factory floor and a few details of *The Cordwainer* engine, when I witnessed a most peculiar sight: Through the main gates, into The Shop's yard, pulled two low, black automobiles. Large cars, looking nothing like any sort of automobile I'd even seen before. I have already mentioned that Fluky's truck was one of the few moving vehicles left in Boot Hill, but it was over twenty years old. These cars looked new. Shiny, and chromed like something out of a distant memory.

Parking in the center of the courtyard, the two black cars each disgorged three black-suited men. From the distance of the

Accounting balcony I could barely make them out, but even from that great distance I could tell they looked clean cut and official.

The law had arrived to put an end to the Worker B's small revolution.

It turned out, however, that the black cars didn't contain the law – at least not in any type of government form. Word quickly spread that the six black-suited men were actually agents from the Concession. Some investigative arm that the company ran internally. The black-suits strolled out onto The Shop's floor and were quickly spirited away by a very nervous-looking Foreman Salmon. For the rest of the afternoon, the six men remained in Managing Foreman's office. Half an hour before the end of shift, a young, pimply faced accountant came around the floor, gathering up various and sundry Worker B's, mostly from my line, taking them off, one at a time, to Mr. Salmon's office.

I learned what happened next from Sophie, when she came that evening to warn me that I was next.

"They summarily fired them all," she said, "without warning or severance. 'Conspiracy to Disrupt Production'. I guess there's some law. They could have faced criminal charges, but I think the black suits just threw that out there to scare everyone. Fact remains, however, there are now twenty open positions for seamstresses on the floor of The Shop – and twenty women who've had their Class B's downgraded to Class F's."

"Oh, God..." I reacted in genuine shock. I was sitting on my father's couch in his living room. My palms began to sweat. "It's all my fault," I realized in terror.

"It is," Sophie didn't pull any punches. "And next, those Concession goons will be coming after you." She thrust a manicured finger at me. "Word is Salmon rambled on about your 'efficiency improvements' – how you've been disrupting The Shop. But, since you weren't in on the unionization, they can't pin anything on you. Mark my words, though, the men in the black suits aren't finished until they can nail your ass to the wall."

"But, I increased productivity," I said weakly, rubbing my wet palms on my pants.

"Oh, I'm sure they'll take that into consideration," Sophie said sarcastically. She looked me up and down, grimaced at what she saw, and left the house without saying good-bye.

Tuesday morning came, then Wednesday, then Thursday and Friday, and the ax didn't fall. I went to work each morning, with my father, who was mute on the whole subject of the firings.

We took the trolley in each day, and each day I expected to be called up to Mr. Salmon's office. But nothing happened. I dutifully watched Number Six make boots, ticking off my boxes as the crates came off the end of the line. I was many girls short now, including my two members of the "flying squad", but I made no effort to reorganize or optimize my line. No one working on Number Six asked me to. Everyone kept their noses down and worked doubly hard, simultaneously trying to show their worth and not stand out from the herd.

What was taking them so long? The six black-suited men never again appeared on the floor of The Shop, but their cars were often seen driving around the streets of Boot Hill, apparently patrolling. They stopped, occasionally, at people's homes and asked cryptic questions, not appearing to listen to the answers. They predominantly made their presence known without taking any actions – simply hovering over Boot Hill like a gathering storm.

They had a disruptive effect on everyone, but it was me that everyone genuinely expected them to swoop down on. But they didn't, they just circled. Waiting.

But we didn't let the presence of the Concession goons slow down work on *The Cordwainer*. If anything, the pressure doubled our efforts. For the first time since Mitty had presented his plan in the freezer of Putter's, I understood why we had been operating with such secrecy. If simply the whiff of labor organization could provoke such an aggressive reaction from the Concession, what would the general knowledge of Mitty's Plan elicit? I dared not speculate. Unionization of The Shop might cause the Concession some pain, perhaps, but Mitty's Plan was an assault on its very bottom line.

If we succeeded in our attempt – if we made it to the Big City and sold a cargo of boots – we would be humiliating the entire organization, the very infrastructure of America itself. After all, if a trio of stupid kids could get product to market, people might begin to wonder what was wrong with the Concession? It might force people to ask a lot of uncomfortable questions that the Concession might not like to answer.

The thought of humiliating the Concession pleased me, as its cloud of wrath hung over me – its vultures circling in their black cars. The thought motivated me anew. If I could stick a finger in the eye of the Concession, if I could cause it pain, however small, it might at least be a partial payment for the twenty jobs they had taken.

All of this, as we worked away on our new engine, sat poorly with Sophie.

I had been intentionally vague as to our intentions for building her engine. I knew the greed of Mitty's Plan would rub Sophie the wrong way. A genius she might have been, but above everything else, Sophie was a follower of rules. Not stupid, ignorant, pointless ones, but the big, life-affirming, socially cohesive ones, were important to her. Everyone had to sacrifice for the greater good, she firmly believed. And while it was possible to make the argument that Mitty's Plan was to help a few people, its primary purpose, above all, was to help ourselves.

That didn't sit well with Sophie.

The cat escaped from the bag one long evening while we were attempting to fit the turbine cone into its housing. It was all custom work of Fluky's and he'd assed up the measurements somewhere along the line. We had to cut it down to size. We were swinging the medieval looking contraption that was the turbine back and forth, in and out of its housing, as Fluky marked each poorly sized blade, then sized it down with a grinder.

Sophie was sitting at the workbench, making some minor adjustments to her schematic.

Mitty, as always, had perched himself on a stool and was monologuing about the war, "...if the British had just stuck it out with Churchill, they would have been in such better straights, by and by. But everyone in the government was so damn-blasted ready to make peace with Hitler – after the Irish Campaign, the whole damn-blasted country was – and the special election of '42 just opened the door to Mosley and his BUF chums. Then the bombing of Parliament – which historians have clearly determined to be a false flag operation – and it was child's play for Hitler to justify SS thugs patrolling the streets of London. For the safety of the British People, of course. It was that easy in the end to topple the Great British Empire. Hitler didn't have to fire a single shot. Now Russia, that was a different matter entirely..."

"How about you stop fightin' the war and get me a hacksaw," Fluky said. We had the turbine jammed halfway into its housing again, for the third time that evening.

Mitty rose from his stool with the deep sigh of the hard put upon and crossed the shop floor, over to the workbench. He stole a glance down at what Sophie was working on as he retrieved a hacksaw from its place on the pegboard.

He delivered it to Fluky, leaning in close, "Psst," he hissed. Fluky ignored him. "Psst!" He spit through his teeth, this time right in Fluky's ear, and loud enough for the whole shop to hear.

"What?!" Fluky recoiled, wiggling a finger at his ear. "You big tartarhead..."

"The girl..." Mitty cocked a head towards Sophie.

"What about her?"

"Is she getting a full cut?"

"A what? Cut?" Fluky began to work the hacksaw across the jammed turbine blade. "Cut of what?"

"The *profits*," Mitty was trying to keep his voice low.

"Huh?" Fluky had an eighth of an inch of steel removed now and the turbine came loose, swinging, suspended from its A-frame. "Oh," and Fluky grasped what Mitty was talking about. He looked over the top of the turbine at me. "Beanie?"

"Of course," I said quickly, not looking up from my work.

"A *full* share?" Mitty questioned.

I looked up and met Mitty's inquisitive stare. I glanced between him and Fluky, wondering how large a can of worms I'd just opened. "Yes, a full share," I clarified.

Fluky, without a world, returned to hacksawing away at the turbine.

"Then, I believe, it is befitting that I hand these out now..." Mitty said louder for all to hear, returning to his stool and fetching a roll of crumpled papers out of his inside jacket pocket. He came to each of us in turn and handed us a slip of paper – Fluky, Sophie and myself. I looked at mine in my oily fingers. It seemed to be some sort of hand-written stock certificate with a crudely drawn American eagle in the top left, and a curly border all around scribbled with green crayon.

"The Luma, Seattle and Pacific Railroad?" Fluky read out load. "What's that?"

"What's that?" Mitty replied, feigning offense. "Why that's... that's us."

"We's a railroad now?" Fluky laughed.

"I believe it to be appropriate," Mitty said defensively, "that this whole enterprise be conducted above board. I have taken the liberty of incorporating us, with myself as Chairman and Chief Executive Officer. Beanie, I hope you will accept the position of President. Fluky, Vice President of Operations..." I put my stock certificate down, tuning Mitty out, and returned to the turbine. "I have made the initial private offering of two hundred shares, each with a cash value of ten dollars. Here you have your initial stock option of a single share." Mitty indicated the slips of paper he had handed out.

"What? You want ten bucks for this?" Fluky waved the stock certificate in front of his face, fanning himself.

"The purpose of incorporation is to raise capital. Our railroad is going to need operating funds."

"You know what?" Fluky said, crumpling up his certificate. "You can shove your stock certificate up your ass." He threw his balled up slip of paper at Mitty and it bounced off his chest.

"Fine! Fine!" Mitty bent over and picked up the crumpled-up share, un-crumpled it and returned it to his stack. "But I want no belly aching from you when it comes time to dividing up the profits! You threw away your share! We all saw it. It's my share now!"

Sophie, who until that moment hadn't looked up from her schematics, suddenly perked up and looked over at her stock certificate that Mitty had placed on the workbench. She studied it intently for a second, then spun around on her stool.

"Wait a damn minute," Fluky continued. "You said you drew up two hundred shares? Why the hell I only get one?"

"That's the initial stock option. You may purchase more, based on performance."

"What!?" Fluky stepped away from the turbine to point an accusatory finger at Mitty. "Performance? You see me here buildin' this damn engine? And you wanta give me stock options based on performance?"

"You... obviously have..."

"Hell, what the hell work you done the last couple months, tartarhead? Sit there on ya brains and start up imaginary railroads?"

"Fluky, leave it alone," I interjected.

"Leave it alone? This dummy is sittin' there wantin' me to pay for the privilege of workin' for his damn railroad, while he's flappin' his lip about shit no one gives a damn about, and I'm supposed to leave it alone?"

"Fluky..." I rolled my eyes.

"Hell," Fluky stepped up to Mitty and grabbed at the wad of hand-drawn stock certificates in Mitty's fist. "If there's gonna be two hundred shares of this damn railroad, I want 'em all..." They wrestled over the pieces of paper for a few seconds, then started to shove each other.

"I'm sorry, am I missing something?" Sophie spoke up, causing Fluky and Mitty to pause in their struggle over the stock certificates. "You boys are thinking that you're going to make a *profit?*" Her eyebrows and lips curled in disgust on the last word.

We all looked at each other, gripped by confusion. It was Fluky that finally spoke, "Well, yeah. You ain't thinkin' we're doin' all this outa the goodness of our hearts, are ya?" He let out a single nervous, mirthless cackle.

The look on Sophie's face told us all that, yeah, maybe she did.

She spun back around on her stool, returning her stock certificate to the workbench, and turned her attention back to her schematics. Fluky and Mitty both turned to me and looked at me inquisitively. All I could do was shrug. If Sophie had yelled, if she'd called us fucking idiots, if she'd thrown something across the room, I'd have known how to deal with it. But silence...

I went back to attempting to fit the turbine into its housing.

Chapter Eighteen

Supply and Demand

As the month of July passed quickly by, the reality of the journey we were preparing to take started to set in. Mitty's Plan, which we had undertaken in the beginning, honestly, as something of a lark, was starting to look like something we were actually going to have to try and attempt. The logistics of it all were suddenly quite overwhelming. The engine, the rolling stock, producing fuel – we had made a lot of progress in all of these areas – but the sheer number of other details that we hadn't even begun to address almost prompted us to cancel the whole thing.

Most prominent in all of our minds was actually acquiring the boots we were planning to sell. Laying our hands on them was not a problem – there were freight containers full of boots lining the road out to The Shop, just laying there unguarded – but purchasing a large number of shoes was a different matter.

Exactly who could we go to and place an order for ten thousand pairs of boots and not raise any suspicions? Despite our secrecy and our fear of how the authorities would react if they discovered the details of Mitty's Plan, I honestly think that everyone involved with *The Cordwainer* considered it a legal venture. We weren't thieves. In the end, to get *The Cordwainer* rolling on its tracks, we understood that we might be forced to perform quite a large number of petty thefts, but the boots themselves... well, if we stole those, was there any way to maintain the pretense that we weren't embarking on something that was anything other than a simple criminal enterprise?

But can you steal something with no value? It was an honest question. If, as I had come to surmise, the value of the boots made in Boot Hill was in the labor needed to make them, not in the product itself, could it be said that the boots themselves had any real value? The intrinsic value that footwear has when it's on your feet, sure, but realistically no one was ever going to wear a boot that had been rotting, forgotten in those storage containers beside the road. Not unless *The Cordwainer* took them to a place where people were short on shoes. The Shop made them, not for anyone to ever wear as boots, but as a way to keep a population employed and distracted. Weren't we imparting to the boots their only real value by putting them on *The Cordwainer* and taking them to market? Could you steal something that no one would miss? Yes, perhaps, the Concession would not share my view, but were we really being *thieves*?

Then, we had to consider the hydrogen peroxide we were about to help ourselves to. There was no store where we could go and purchase such a product in the quantities we would need them. The five thousand gallons we eventually stole was a literal drop in the bucket to the amount in the mega-gauge tankers stored behind The Shop.

But more so than the boots we took, the H_2O_2 would have eventually been put to use. I feel safe in the assertion that if the adventures of *The Cordwainer* had managed to remain a secret, no one would have ever noticed any peroxide missing. But it was still theft. Pilfering perhaps would be more accurate, but stealing all the same.

In the years since the affair of *The Cordwainer,* I've been asked by many people if I still feel that the enterprise was justified, considering the scale and scope of the larceny required to accomplish our goal. And while I try not to stand as an example of how stealing can sometimes be right, I cannot think about the thefts without framing them in the larger context of the Concession's stranglehold on towns like Boot Hill.

If anyone had owned anything at all other than the Concession, perhaps stealing would never have been required. We could have built our train and crossed the mountains legally, purchasing everything we needed on an open market. But no such market existed, so we were forced to improvise. Was that wrong? Perhaps. But never in the intervening years have I been able to muster the strength to feel guilty about what we stole. Role models perhaps we are not, but I can hardly call us hardened thieves, either.

What really came to concern us, however, as the departure of *The Cordwainer* neared, was the risk posed by the Polypigs as we crossed the mountains. The Polyamorous, Bigamist, Mormon separatists had been operating all that summer in the mountains outside of Boot Hill. The state newspaper was increasing full of the military's attempts to flush these outlaw gangs out of the hills, as they'd been flushed out of Utah, Nevada, Oregon and Idaho. None of us was sure of the path the old Northern Pacific took through the mountains, but it was a fair guess that our path would take us through the middle of Polypig-infested territory. Fluky and Mitty suggested, and I reluctantly agreed, that we were going to need to arm ourselves, lest we lose everything to bandits before we had even seen the slopes of the western side of the mountains.

Fluky went to his Cannabis chums and came home with three .38 caliber Smith & Wesson revolvers wrapped up in a sack. He showed them to us one evening while we were working on *The Cordwainer's* engine. Unfortunately, he was only able to acquire two rounds of ammunition – bullets in those days being far scarcer than guns – and one of the cartridges looked significantly corroded. It was hardly an arsenal, but it was all he could rustle up. It would have to suffice.

As July was coming to a close and Sophie's engine was beginning to near completion, the need for the traction motors to complete the design became critical. Her engine, essentially, was the first stage of a two-stage design: Hydrogen peroxide reacted with a catalyst, which produced steam, which turned the turbine, which generated electricity. The electricity then needed to run electric motors – Sophie had specified one per car of our rolling stock – which would propel our cargo of boots and ourselves up and over the snowcapped mountains, and down to the Big City.

But as the first days of August arrived, we had begun no work to construct these motors. Sophie, when questioned, dismissed their absence as unimportant. But I pressed the issue, and

Sophie relented, loading us all up into the wrecking truck and taking us to a remote fenced-in lot on the wrong side of the tracks I had been completely unaware of until she drove us there.

Inside the fence we found a cornucopia of old, rusting trolley cars of the same make and model as the one I rode daily to The Shop. There were at least twenty, parked in amongst the brambles. Some seemed very old, some almost new. Sophie instructed us to salvage whatever electric motors we might need from the trolleys there scattered about. She assured us that all the trolleys, if otherwise well used, were still perfectly serviceable.

The Luma Transit Authority, she said, received a new trolley car, annually, every April like clockwork on a flatbed Concession car – a new trolley, ever year, if they needed it or not. This was where the old ones – and sometimes the brand new ones if it was just too much trouble to trade out a trolley – were abandoned.

We had our traction motors, and after a dozen trips to and from the LTA yard, we had them bolted to the chassis of our freight rolling stock, driving both fixed axles by the means of chains. On top of all of this, Fluky constructed the hoppers we would be filling with the boots, out of corrugated sides of old delivery trucks. Some of the old advertising was still visible on the iron. One car sported an advertisement for Jefferson's Safe Cigarettes. Another the logo of a long forgotten haircare product. The last of the three cars had an epic mounted silhouette advertising Tom Mixx Trail Ready Cereal.

This advertisement I had to stare at for awhile. I could barely remember the advertising campaign from when I was a child, back when there was still the need to influence people's purchasing decisions. The cowboy on horseback and his trusty cereal, providing all the energy he needed for a hard day working the trail. It seemed comical now, but it was still the cereal I ate every morning – the only cereal available at the Concession Store. Tom Mixx? Would you have been happy being the last Cowboy Cereal left on the shelf?

With all the pieces of *The Cordwainer* puzzle falling into place, we made the collective decision that the time had come to move our whole operation out of Zimmerman's junkyard and over to the ghost town of Pottersville, in preparation for our departure.

An unannounced visit one Sunday afternoon by Deputy Aesop precipitated the move.

He came riding into the yard around three o'clock on the back of his slow, old white pony, all dressed up for duty, pistol at his side. We only had a moment to rapidly throw a tarp over the partially completed engine before he was close enough to make out what we were up to. We tried to look busy, working at tools as the Deputy dismounted. He made his slow way into the large workshop, looking gingerly around.

"Afternoon, boys," he said as he came in out of the sun. Fluky was sitting up on top of the turbine housing, swinging his feet leisurely over the side.

"Sheriff," Fluky nodded.

The Deputy moved, all hunched over with age, and did a circle around the shop. We all waited quietly while he had a look around. *The Cordwainer* freight cars were plainly visible, but unless you knew what you were looking for, it was almost impossible to tell them apart from the rest of the junk filling Zimmerman's yard.

After almost a minute, the Deputy returned to the front of the shop, apparently unable to find what he'd come to look for.

"Boys," was all he said as he stepped back out into the yard and back up onto his old pony.

What he'd come to the junkyard looking for, I can only guess. It was obvious that something about Mitty's Plan had drawn the attention of someone in Boot Hill, and it was more than enough to put the fear of God into the three of us. That night, we hooked up the rolling stock, one at a time, and towed them under the cover of darkness over to the terminus of the Stephenson gauge tracks in Pottersville. There we mounted them onto the rails, all in line at the platform of Union Station. It cost us all a night's sleep, but when we were done, we had, for the first time, the whole *Cordwainer* fully assembled and pointing in the direction of the Big City.

It was a heartwarming sight, the sort of thing that sets the hairs on your neck on end, seeing the machine set up in its entirety. The cargo hoppers were still empty, true, and we lacked fuel or even a fuel tank to hold it, but the frame of our train was on its tracks, and it required no imagination to see that *The Cordwainer* was a real, solid thing – a train that was going to take us all across the mountains.

Moving the operation to Pottersville had a secondary advantage: peace and quiet for the mass refining of hydrogen peroxide that we still needed to achieve before *The Cordwainer* could depart.

Sophie had put an end to vacuum distillation as a means of purification. She said it was recklessly dangerous and downright stupid. She wanted to refine the industrial strength peroxide we had access to at The Shop into high test via fractional crystallization. Basically freezing it, in a number of steps – I was hazy on the exact details. What I did understand was that the process would require a professional-grade cooling unit, nothing we could jury-rig together ourselves. And there was only one of those in Boot Hill.

"Not Mrs. Frostynips!" Fluky had exclaimed when we broke the news to him that we'd have to steal Putter's freezer coil, if only for a few days, to process the peroxide. "Ain't there another way?" he'd begged.

"We all have to make sacrifices, Fluky," I consoled him. I was thinking of my mother's silverware. I had had to steal two more place settings to fashion a new catalyst for Sophie's engine, our last having been blown to bits along with our first engine and the statue of Mr. Potter.

"But Mrs. Frostynips? She ain't never hurt a soul."

"She's already lived more than her alloted time," Mitty commented, solemnly. "That a woman of ice and snow might live for six years... She will always live on in our hearts..."

"Ain't there no other way?"

It broke my heart to see Fluky so distraught. But we needed that freezer coil, or *The Cordwainer* would never leave the station.

That Saturday, there was a fiddle band playing in the bar at Putter's. The place was packed with young people; the whole town under thirty seemed to have turned out. No one was manning the kitchen. With no demand for food and girls dancing out on the floor, the cooks were loitering in the doorway to the bar, watching the show. Mitty, Fluky and myself easily slipped in through the back door. And while Mitty and I tapped our toes to the banjo player, Fluky quietly unbolted the electric coil from the wall of the walk-in freezer. Twenty minutes, and we had it in the passenger seat of the truck. We let Fluky have a few minutes of peace, alone in the rapidly warming freezer with Mrs. Frostynips. When he emerged, he looked like he'd been crying.

With the band still playing, Mitty and I sent Fluky and the freezer coil off in the truck, opting to walk home instead of clinging to the hitch of the truck for the whole ride home. As the clamor of fiddle and upright bass faded into the distance, Mitty and I turned onto C Street, casually chatting about Mitty's Plan. As we walked and talked, we became aware of the low rumble of an engine behind us. It was too even, too dulcet a noise to be Fluky's truck. We turned to see one of the low, wide, black cars I had first seen in The Shop's yard turning off Main onto C, and falling in behind us. We paused in our step as the car rolled up, the driver's window automatically rolling down.

In the car were three clean-cut, black-suited men. They turned to face Mitty and me as the car slowed to a halt. They were young, probably not much older than Fluky, Mitty or myself, and they gave off the strange vibe that they might be brothers, or triplets, or something. They almost seemed to move in unison – of one mind.

"Evening, gentlemen," the driver said, the car idling.

"Nice car," Mitty commented, looking over the long sleek chrome.

"Out for a stroll?" he asked, ignoring Mitty.

"Taking in the honky tonk," I said, then cocked my head up C. "Heading home."

If the Concession man believed me, or if he suspected we'd been up to something else, he didn't let on. "Andrew Rice, correct?" he said, looking me up and down.

"Yeah," I replied guardedly.

"Yeah, we've heard about you," he said and smiled. The Concession man in the back seat let out a small chuckle.

"Number Six." It was an innocuous thing to say, but somehow he made it sound like a threat.

"Yeah, what of it?" I asked, leaning forward, putting a hand on the door of the low, black car. The driver looked at my hand like it was an offensive invasion, then at Barry's watch around my wrist, and then back up at my face with a smile.

"Be talking to you real soon," he said, and then the window of his door began to raise under my palm. I quickly pulled my hand back, out of the path of the closing glass, and the car pulled away, the engine rumbling.

"Nice car," Mitty said again to the receding taillights.

I slugged him as hard as I could in the shoulder.

Chapter Nineteen

Sophie Opts Out

The theft of the freezer motor from Putter's Café set into motion a chain of events that would ultimately lead to the premature departure of *The Cordwainer*. Fluky, Mitty and myself were to flee Boot Hill, tails between our legs, escaping our imminent arrest.

My first indication of the encroaching danger was at The Shop that first Monday morning in August, directly after the theft of Putter's freezer coil and my encounter with Concession men in their black car. I was called into Foreman Salmon's office and told to take a seat.

We were alone in the office, Mr. Salmon and I, but the presence of the Concession men could keenly be felt.

"Now, you know how important family is to us here at The Shop," Foreman Salmon began. I didn't like the sound of where a sentence like that was headed. The ax was inevitably about to fall – for my optimization efforts on Line Number Six, and the rumbles of unionization that it had caused. It had to be coming. Perhaps, when the theft of the freezer coil was discovered Sunday, the Concession men had put two and two together. I didn't know. I doubted that I ever would really know. "Your father has worked here – worked for me – for almost twenty-five years..." Mr. Salmon continued.

I was barely paying attention. I had form 24-01 in my back pocket. I'd spent an evening with a gum eraser removing as much of my failed schematic as I could. If I'd wanted to, I could have just reached back and handed over the errant form – it might have been seen as some sort a peace offering – but I couldn't bring myself to do it. If they were going to fire me, if that was how they dealt with innovation and progress, I almost welcomed the chop.

After all, before the month was out, *The Cordwainer* would be fully tested and operational. Potentially, in a month, I could have a cool two hundred and fifty grand in my pocket. I wouldn't need Foreman Salmon's lousy job, or any other job for that matter. What could I buy for two hundred and fifty grand? The mind boggles. The whole town of Boot Hill, part and parcel, that was for sure, and still have change left over.

I could have handed over form 24-01, yes, I could have made an effort to save my career, but a large part of me wanted to get fired. The hours at The Shop were starting to interfere with my work on *The Cordwainer*, there was still all that peroxide that needed to be processed.

Fire me, please, I was thinking when I only half heard Mr. Salmon say, "and that is why we believe a week's suspension is appropriate..."

A week?! Suspension? For all the chaos I'd caused? I was almost insulted.

I sat silently, my mouth half open as Foreman Salmon finished his little speech.

I almost laughed. They were so feckless, they couldn't even seriously punish me. One week of suspension? For what I had done? I should be fired. I almost told Mr. Salmon so, but managed to hold my tongue.

When Foreman Salmon finished, I rose from my chair and dropped my clipboard down on the table. Before I did, however, I removed form 24-01 from my back pocket and clipped it to the top of the stack. I don't think Mr. Salmon noticed, and it was not really an act of contriteness. I simply wanted to be rid of it, I realized. It was his form, after all, not mine. With my schematic on the back now erased, I had no more use for it – or for the job that went along with it.

The trolleys wouldn't be running back to Boot Hill until that evening, so I decided to trek my way home on foot instead of waiting, wallowing in my supposed shame. It would take most of the day, and the trolley might still beat me home. The sun was blazing in the sky, but I set off regardless. By lunchtime, I had cleared the forest of freight containers full of boots that surrounded The Shop and was well out in the open of the scrub when I caught sight of Fluky's truck rumbling up the road towards me. He was kicking up a cloud of dust; he must have been moving fast.

He didn't slow down until he'd shot right past me, only realizing it was me waving by the side of the road after he was two hundred yards further on. He skidded to a halt, swung the truck around and came rolling up beside me.

He started yelling before the truck had fully stopped, "Them black-suited fellas!" he yelled across the cab, out the open passenger side window. "They're at Zimmerman's junkyard!"

"What?" I opened the door and pulled myself wearily into the truck, happy to be off my feet.

"Them black Cadillacs!" Fluky continued, putting the truck in gear. "Pulled up 'front of the junkyard, ten this morning. I was out, towin' in a wreck, but I seen them when I pulled on back. Dropped my load and hightailed it out here after you. What the hell you doin'? Walkin' home?"

"I got suspended," I said.

"Suspended? What, like in high school? They can do that?"

"I guess... Is everything out of the workshop at Zimmerman's? Everything having to do with the train?"

"Yeah, yeah, think so." Fluky had the truck up to its full speed, hurtling through the scrub.

"Are you sure?"

"Hell, I don't know. I didn't know there was gonna be an inspection... How you think they found out about us? Huh?"

"We don't know they know anything," I said resolutely.

"But they-"

"Deputy Aesop was sniffing around, too. Just 'cause they're suspicious doesn't mean they know anything."

Fluky fell quiet and drove. I might have reassured him. I wished I'd reassured myself.

Fluky slowed the truck down once we hit Boot Hill proper and when we reached the gates of Zimmerman's junkyard, he rolled the old truck slowly past, giving us a good look. The two black cars were there in the yard, but there was no sign of any Concession men out in the open. Fluky kept the truck rolling, pulling past the gate and around the block. I had him pull up and park, killing the engine, so I could consider our options.

"Ten o'clock, you said?" I asked, craning my neck back, looking at the high fence around the junkyard.

"Yeah, 'bout then."

"Right when I was called in to talk to Salmon..." I said.

"Yeah," Fluky agreed thoughtfully. "So?"

"So, they knew I'd be at The Shop. Where's Mitty?"

"Hell, how the hell should I know? Fighting the war with his tin solders, probably."

"No one's in Pottersville?"

"No... Oh sh-it! The train!" Fluky reached for the ignition. I grabbed his hand to stop him.

"No, no. If they knew about Union Station they wouldn't be here at the yard."

"But it's all just sittin' there out in the open..."

"Yeah, and we'd lead them right to it."

Fluky relaxed. I let go of his hand.

"What we gonna do?" Fluky finally asked, looking back with me at the fence of the junkyard.

"Nothing's changed," I began. "We've all still got work to do." Then a horrible thought hit me. "Fluky, where's the freezer coil? Where?!" I almost screamed.

"At the station!" Fluky said defensively. "All piped up like Li'l Bean instructed."

"Oh, thank God!" I sighed in relief. Thank God we'd had the foresight to move the whole operation to Pottersville – thank God that Deputy Aesop had so ham-handedly come snooping around.

"So, maybe we should lay low, you know? If these black-suits have caught on to our scent..."

"No," I said firmly. "If anything, we need to move up the schedule."

"But everythin' we need now is out at The Shop."

"Yeah," I agreed. "We'll make a run tonight."

Freed from my responsibilities as a Foreman, I was able to focus my full attention on the imminent departure of *The Cordwainer*. With the ever present threat of the Concession goons, we worked almost exclusively at night. We took the precaution of no longer driving Fluky's truck up and over C street into Pottersville for all the town to see. Mitty and I started trekking out into the ghost town on foot after dark, and Fluky got into the habit of only driving the wrecking truck the long way around the hillside, where anyone following him would instantly be obvious.

On our first excursion – nighttime raid – on The Shop, we went in search of fitting containers for the transportation and storage of our HTP. Mason jugs, this time, would be a dangerous eccentricity. We found exactly what we needed in the motor pool of The Shop: A pair of large, thousand-gallon aluminum tanks that had once, perhaps, had some sort of agricultural role. What purpose they served at The Shop was a point of conjecture, but they would serve our needs very well. We made two runs that night, back and forth to Pottersville. We filled both tanks carefully at the spigot of one of the large mega-gauge H_2O_2 tankers, and hauled them back to the station.

It took two more nights and two more trips hauling one of the tanks full of peroxide back and forth between The Shop and the other tank we had mounted to the nose of the engine car of *The Cordwainer.* In between, by the light of the day, I ran our fractional crystallization rig to purify the peroxide from 30 percent to 90 percent. How it worked, I never really understood, but it required a pair of coaxial copper coils and precipitated large quantities of freezing cold water. Sophie had instructed that a small amount of ammonia be added to the purified peroxide to stabilize it before we added it to the tank, and I did this dutifully with each batch.

By Friday evening of that week, *The Cordwainer's* fuel tank was full. I tested its pH and it came out as highly acidic. This I assumed meant we were right in the neighborhood of high test. I planned to wait for Sophie to get her final approval, but altogether I was feeling well prepared.

With our fuel runs complete, our night raids from there on out concentrated on filling our freight cars. We uncoupled each car in turn, hauled it out in its entirety and loaded it up directly from the cargo containers abandoned out in the scrub. The boots were in relatively good condition, even in the containers that looked like they'd been out in the open air for years. On that Saturday night we were able to fill two whole containers, and Sunday we filled up the third.

When Monday rolled around again, we had our cargo of boots fully loaded into *The Cordwainer*, her fuel tank sat filled to the brim. All we had left on our agenda was for Sophie to look over Fluky's handiwork and the initial tests of her turbine engine. Since we had moved the whole operation out to Pottersville, Sophie had been mostly absent from the work site. Fluky felt that he'd followed Sophie's instructions to the letter, and I'd looked over the whole engine myself with a keen eye, but we all felt it fell to Sophie to drop the switch the first time *The Cordwainer's* engine turned over. It was her engine, after all.

That Monday evening I walked back into Boot Hill to pay her a visit. I'd taken to spending my nights in Pottersville. I hadn't wanted to go home and face my father after the suspension. I was mostly working nights, sleeping days, with all our evening burglaries. It was refreshing to return to Boot Hill on a lazy summer evening with no nefarious aims in mind. The front doors of all the small, neat bungalows sat open and people had extended their living rooms out into their front yards. There was a whole street fair feel to summer evenings in Boot Hill, with neighbors casually chatting and children playing in the streets. With all the anxiety of Mitty's Plan, with all the trouble out at The Shop, I'd forgotten about that side of Boot Hill – the Boot Hill I'd grown up in. Poor and hard set upon people might be, but it had always been a great place to live.

I knocked on my sister's kitchen door. She was working at the stove in an apron and turned to look at me through the glass. She let me in with a finger pressed to her lips and moved to close the connecting door between the kitchen and the living room.

"Now's not a good time, Andy," she said, tending to her cooking.

"She's ready," I said, sitting down at the kitchen table.

"What's ready?"

"*The Cordwainer.*"

"The what-" and then she remembered, "Your damn train?"

"It's ready, in Pottersville, at the old Union Station. We're ready to test the engine. We all thought, since it was your design, that you should have the honor."

"You'll need to process some peroxide before we can test it," she said, taking something off the heat.

"All done," I said happily. "I got suspended at work, I've had some time."

"How much have you processed?" she asked.

"A thousand gallons," I said with pride.

"A *thousand?*"

"Enough to get us to Seattle."

"Are you *insane?*" she turned to me, wiping her hands on her apron. "It was a fun project and all, but you can't be *serious?*"

"Serious?" I was confused.

"Playing Rockefeller with your idiot chums is one thing – stock options and profit sharing – but you don't actually think you can get across the mountains in that thing, do you?" She tried to laugh but nothing emerged.

I opened my mouth and closed it again. I was speechless. It was Sophie, my surrogate mother, talking down to me. I felt like a child. "Did you think this was all a game?" I eventually said.

"Build the engine just to build it, you said. I believed that. But to actually risk your life trying to get across the mountains with a load of old, stupid boots. Now, that's just foolish."

"But in the City," I began, "a pair of boots can sell for-"

Sophie snapped at me, suddenly angry, "Money! That's all you ignorant, selfish children care about! To make a buck. The other two, I can forgive it, they know no better, but you, Andrew, I'm ashamed. I thought you were raised better than that!"

"What's wrong with making a buck?" I asked, in all honesty.

"What's wrong?" Sophie almost choked on her indignation. "With all the problems this country is facing, Andrew, and you want to know what's wrong with making a buck? It's crooks like you who got us into this mess. Look at this," she opened the pan she had been cooking with, showing the brown, gelatinous goo she'd prepared. "*That* is supposed to be food! *That* is what I have to feed my husband this evening. People are going hungry, Andrew. Not the poor, not the idle, but hardworking, everyday people are short on food. And you ask what's wrong with making a buck? You selfish little snot!"

"But we made an engine that produces no carbon," I tried to defend. "Don't you see the potential in that, Sophie? If it can carry shoes it could carry food."

"Exactly!" she thrust a finger at me. Her eyes looked insane. "I build you an engine and do you use it for the betterment of anyone? No! You only think of getting rich – just you. You disgust me, Andrew. You and those two dummy friends of yours."

Sophie turned back to the stove. I reached for the door. I had almost reached it when I thought better of it. "Isn't Kennedy always telling us we're supposed to be a Nation of Big Ideas? Well, what idea is bigger than this one?"

"Big ideas to help people, Andy, not line your own pockets!" Sophie said, her back still to me.

"But lining our pockets *is* the idea, Sophie!" I fired, stepping back away from the door. "The train – the engine – that was always the point. The reason to do it. If people thought of this sort of stuff out of the goodness of their hearts, don't you think they would? The idea, Sophie, the motivation is everything."

Sophie turned away from the stove and looked at me, scolding me with her eyes.

"And nothing motivates better than a chance at improving your lot in life. Back a man into a corner and don't give him an out and he's a dangerous thing. But give him some room to move, let him explore and there's no telling what he'll achieve. I'm sorry, but I was never cut out to work at The Shop, Sophie, and you weren't either. That you could design that engine, that we – together – could build it. That's something, Sophie. Don't we deserve to see the fruits of our labor? Reap some reward? If we can build it, if we're smart enough, don't we have some sort of right?"

Sophie was quiet, staring at me, unemotional. As always, when she was quiet it scared me, just like Dad. Yelling, screaming I could handle, but silence...

Then I realized what she had done.

Deputy Aesop, the Concession goons, sniffing around Zimmerman's junkyard. She'd sent them. She'd tipped them off to Mitty's Plan. And here I'd just told her where *The Cordwainer* was, where we had moved it to. She'd ratted us out. Because she disapproved of our motives, she'd sold us out to the authorities. There was no look of shame on her face, no guilt. She looked at me silently, with still, cold eyes.

"No, no you didn't..." I said, the horror rising in me.

"The rules apply to us all equally, Andrew," she said, slowly shaking her head. "None of us are above the law."

"But what are we doing that's *wrong*?" I asked, slowly moving towards the door.

"You need to think of others before yourself, Andrew," she said. "If we all went around just looking out for number one..."

"But, but you're my sister..." I tried, backing up.

"If you haven't been doing anything wrong, Andy, then there's nothing to fear," Sophie said. She was growing visibly smaller in my eyes, receding away from me. I reached back and unlatched the door, swinging in open.

"But you built the engine, Sophie. It's your engine."

"Exactly," she said coldly. "And I will see my engine used as I see fit."

But I had turned on my heels and I was sprinting away; around my sister's small, concrete bungalow and down the street. I sprinted all the way to C Street and along it, up the hill towards Mitty's house.

It felt like my lungs were about to explode by the time I was knocking on the makeshift, plywood back door.

Chapter Twenty

Traffic Jam

"Phone... Call... Fluky..." I managed between gulped breaths. Mitty looked at me through the smoke of his Jefferson. I had barged past him, into the old sun porch.

"The phone is in there," he indicated towards the house itself and the old back door. "I'm reticent to use it, outside of an emergency. What's wrong?"

"Sophie," I panted.

"Your sister? Little Bean? Is she all right?"

"Traitor." My wind was beginning to return. "Sold us out to the Concession, gave up Zimmerman's garage."

"I don't understand."

"Stupidly told her about *The Cordwainer*, in Pottersville. All ready to go. Now it's just a matter of time..."

"Yes, told her *The Cordwainer* was ready for testing – it's her honor after all." Mitty wasn't understanding. "Quite a piece of craftsmanship, if I do say so my-"

"No, no!" I grabbed Mitty by the lapels of his dirty dressing gown. "You don't understand. It was Sophie! Sophie! The Concession goons, in the black car. At Zimmerman's... That night at Putter's... She tipped them off. Now they'll know about Pottersville, they'll be on their way! If they find the train, they'll find everything: The shoes, the tankers, the peroxide. Everything we stole. We're not just going to lose our jobs, Mitty, we're going to go to jail!"

"Sophie? No, she built us an engine..." Mitty couldn't fathom what I was saying. I could hardly blame him, it was ostensibly insane.

"I know, I know!" I raised a hand in surrender. "You've just got to understand that the whole game has been blown. We need to call Fluky, make sure he knows that the black-suits are gunning for him."

Mitty's expression shifted slowly from confusion to terror. He took the cigarette holder from his lips and said gravely, "What are we going to do?"

"We're going to get *The Cordwainer* out of here," I replied.

"To where?"

"To where?" I parroted in disbelief. "To where? The Big City, of course!"

As Mitty vanished into the house proper to make the call, I rummaged around amongst Mitty's possessions looking for anything of use. A bundle of dirty blankets, some canned food, and three quarts of McTavish was all I could muster.

Up until that point, I realized as I attempted to collect anything of Mitty's of value, I had been thinking of Mitty's Plan as an expedition we would undertake over the mountains to the Big City *and back*. The permanent nature of our exodus from Boot Hill however, at that moment, dawned on me. We would never be coming back. There was nothing left in Boot Hill for any of us now except charges in front of a circuit judge on multiple counts of grand larceny. I would never work another day at The Shop; Fluky's days working for Old Man Zimmerman were over. We would either escape that night from Boot Hill aboard *The Cordwainer* or we'd wake up tomorrow in a jail cell.

We weren't ready – we just weren't ready.

The fact that we hadn't tested Sophie's engine was separate and apart. We had prepared no supplies. No food or water or bedding or clothing. The departure of *The Cordwainer* had seemed remote and distant. There had seemed no need to lay on provisions. But now the departure was imminent and we would have to satisfy ourselves with whatever we had at hand.

Mitty returned from the filth and squalor of his mother's house to inform me that Fluky wasn't home. That could only mean that he was in Pottersville, tinkering away at the train. That would mean his truck would be down there, too. We'd have to make the trip on foot. Would there be enough time? If the Concession goons came in their low, black cars, they might beat us to old Union Station. If they set eyes on what we'd accomplished, there'd be no hiding anything. *The Cordwainer* was just sitting ready at the platform at the station, loaded with cargo. Mitty and I would have to beat them down the hill and into the old ghost town. There was no reason to believe that Sophie had placed a call exactly the second I'd run out her back door. Perhaps something I had said might have moved her, given her pause. I couldn't count on that charity, however, and I rushed Mitty to dress and collect up what things he felt he would need for the journey.

"Do you want to say good-bye?" I asked, once we'd collected up what sacks and bags full of provisions we could find. I pointed back towards the house, into Mitty's mother's home.

"No," Mitty said without emotion. "Did you?" he asked.

"No," I had to admit. If there had only been time.

On the large, old dining room table Mitty's figurines were still positioned, ready for battle.

"Don't you want to take those?" I asked.

"No."

"We won't be coming back."

"I know."

And we left by the makeshift, plywood door.

Down the hillside, down C Street, into Pottersville I jogged, with Mitty puffing away behind me. As we neared the Union Station we became aware that the work lights we had rigged up were burning away inside the station. Fluky's truck was parked outside. Mitty and I came storming across the concourse, out onto the platform lit by the bare, yellow incandescent lights Fluky had strung up to a utility pole outside. Fluky had a cowling off something on the engine and was leaning forward, almost completely consumed by the machine. When he heard our approach, he gingerly pulled himself vertical and started to wipe grease off his hands onto this shirt.

"Think I found that there voltage blip in the-" he paused when he saw the load we were carrying. "Plannin' a camp out?" he chuckled.

"The guns, Fluky, where are the guns?" I said ominously.

Fluky stopped laughing. He didn't say another word, understanding the tone and manner of my request. He turned and walked the full length of *The Cordwainer*, to the caboose he had built out of an old woody, 1940 station wagon. He reached through the window and came back up with the sack of guns. He returned and handed it over to me.

I fished around and found the best of the three revolvers. Into this, I loaded the two cartridges – both the healthy and the heavily corroded one. I swung the cylinder closed and held the gun in front of me, feeling the weight.

"Shee-it, you're finally gonna put Mitty outa his misery..." Fluky joked, but he did not laugh. It took someone like Fluky to joke at a moment like that. I tucked the pistol away into the belt of my pants.

"We leave in twenty minutes," I commanded.

Mitty didn't comment, he simply went about picking up our sacks and loading them into the rear of the caboose.

"Wha-what?" Fluky asked, watching Mitty. "You're jokin', right?"

"*The Cordwainer* departs now, or she'll never depart at all," I said.

"But, but, but, we ain't even tested the engine."

"I know."

"Remember what happen' to the first one?"

"Yes, I remember."

"I sure as hell don't wanta be on that thing when this one pops..."

"We don't have a choice, Fluky." I started to move along the train, checking on the freight cars, testing the hoppers for sturdiness.

"What the hell's happened that now you're in such a hellfire rush?"

"The Concession goons – the black-suits – they know about *The Cordwainer.*"

"What? How'd they know that?"

"Sophie told 'em," I said, trying to keep my voice steady.

"Sophie? Li'l Bean? Why'd she tell 'em?" Fluky was following me, trying to understand.

"It's hard to explain," was all I said. "But she told them about Zimmerman's. If she'd known we'd moved the train here, the game would already be up."

"Li'l Bean?"

Fluky paused to let that news sink in.

I was satisfied with what I saw. There was no faulting Fluky's craftsmanship. He'd built a train – an honest to goodness freight hauling machine, out of nothing but scrap car parts and loose steel. I gave the caboose a quick once over. It was quite plush. I hadn't realize what care Fluky had put into its construction. The back seat was pushed back, almost to the rear doors, and the front bench seat was turned around to face backwards. There was a low table of plywood at about window height between them. It had all the feel of a comfortable restaurant booth, like one at Putter's. I'd later come to discover the table latched down, level with the benches, to form a sleeping surface, and the engine compartment – now lacking its engine – contained a small kitchenette setup and supplies. Fluky, it seems, had just about thought of everything. Thank God for all of us he was always so prepared, thinking ahead. If we'd had to make our odyssey across the mountains with just the tinned beans and whiskey I'd been able to scavenge at Mitty's...

"Surely we got a little time, I got the voltage regulator all-"

"No," I said, looking at Barry's watch. "We've got fifteen minutes."

"Shee-it, it'll take me two hours to get this here regulator back together!" Fluky sprinted off towards the engine.

"Well, you got *fifteen minutes*!" I yelled after him.

Of course, I had no idea how much time we actually had. It was a good thing too, because it would take us almost an hour before *The Cordwainer* was even starting to look like it was ready to move. We drained the last of the diesel fuel from Fluky's truck and transferred it to a baby tank that sat next to the mother peroxide tank on the engine car. We passed over the whole length of the train and greased every joint and every axle we could possibly grease. There was no avoiding the cold hard fact that *The Cordwainer* was as ready as she'd ever be to make her journey. And time was running out.

By the end of the hour, we took a moment to familiarize ourselves with her controls. Fluky and I sat in the cockpit of the engine, looking over the panels that Fluky had rigged up. She was going to be an embarrassingly easy machine to operate, despite the technical brilliance required for her construction. There was a twist value, which controlled the flow of peroxide out of the tank and into the expansion chamber. Next to it was a fuel temperature gauge with a strip of red tape stuck to it indicating the temperature it was critical to keep the engine beneath. On another panel was a switch, two ammeters either side of a knob, hooked to a potentiometer that regulated the power output to the traction motors on each car.

On a third panel, set apart from everything else, was a tantalizing red button. I had to restrain myself from automatically pushing it the second I sat down in the cockpit. "What's this?" I interrupted Fluky when he was only halfway through explaining the potentiometer to me.

"The diesel injectors," he replied, trying to draw my attention back to the amperage knob.

"Diesel injectors?"

"Yeah, remember? Li'l Bean's schematic. That shoots the diesel directly into the turbine. Boom! Boost of juice. But you got to keep an eye on the temperature gauge here, and not use too much, or you can scrap the whole engine."

"Why'd you have to make it red?" I asked, fingering the button.

"I don't know, seemed appropriate somehow..."

Mitty came alongside the engine and lifted his bulk up onto the running board, sticking his face into the cockpit. "I've done a thorough inventory of our supplies," he said. "Six cans of beans, ten cans of stew, five gallons of water, two boxes of salted crackers, a box of Tom Mixx, three quarts of McTavish, and a carton of Jefferson's. How long are we expecting this trip to take us?"

Fluky and I looked at each other. The thought had never occurred to me. We hadn't even plotted out a route, we were that unprepared.

"Two, three days..." I wildly guessed.

"Then we'll need more Jefferson's," Mitty said authoritatively, dropping down off the running board.

Eventually the moment came when we could stall no longer and the engine of *The Cordwainer* had to be started. The evening had rolled on into early night, and I was confident that my sister would have by then informed the Concession men – and perhaps even Deputy Aesop – of the location of our unlawful, capitalist enterprise.

The honor of first attempting to start *The Cordwainer* fell to me. After our first attempt to test run a hydrogen peroxide engine had ended in a mushroom cloud, Fluky and Mitty were understandably disinterested at being near our second attempt to do the same. And for this attempt, we had over a thousand gallons of peroxide sitting in a tank not four feet from the expansion chamber, and almost sixty gallons of diesel fuel, too.

Fluky and Mitty found cover in the archway leading to the concourse. I doubted, if the whole affair exploded, that such slim cover would have done them much good. An explosion of that magnitude would easily bring down the whole Union Station and the buildings for a few blocks in all directions.

God, it was times like that I wished I was a praying man.

As my hand reached out for the fuel valve, trembling with anticipation, Fluky's voice came echoing through the station, "Wait!" I almost leapt out of my skin. I frantically looked over the controls, out across the engine, to locate the emergency. Fluky came sprinting up and hopped up onto the running board beside the cockpit. He reached in and slammed something down hard onto the top of the control panel. When his arm pulled away, I could see that it was the googly-eyed Jesus, in all his egg-shaped glory. "For luck," Fluky said and gave the Jesus a flip. It was still bobbling back and forth as I reached for the fuel valve again, turning it slowly on.

Nothing happened.

The large flywheel, which bisected the axis of the turbine/generator combination, didn't budge. I was getting zero readings on both ammeters, north and south of the potentiometer.

The engine didn't work.

"Nothing!" I yelled back along the length of the train. The googly-eyed Jesus was just finishing its oscillations. It stared at me, disapprovingly. Fluky and Mitty emerged from cover, hesitant to approach. My mind was racing with all the potential faults there could be in such a complicated system. Vacuum lock in the fuel line... Perhaps the peroxide was pooling in the expansion chamber, not touching the catalyst. Maybe I'd overdone it with the ammonia – could you make hydrogen peroxide too stable? Perhaps the turbine was jammed – no, that'd just explode...

"Turn the dingus!" Fluky yelled along the full length of the platform.

"Dingus?" I yelled back. Which dingus? The damn train was ten thousand dinguses all bolted together.

"The flywheel!" Fluky specified.

"The what?"

"Flywheel?"

"Why?"

I could hear Fluky's exasperated grunt down the full length of the platform.

He came running up, "You ain't gettin' no fuel into the expansion chamber. The fuel pump, it's just a dealie on the turbine. Got to get the whole thing spinnin' to pump fuel."

"What? The fuel pump's where?" I asked, confused.

"Ah, hell..." Fluky pulled himself up onto the running board of the engine, shimmied along, then climbed up onto the cowling, straddling the turbine. He took the flywheel in both hands and gave it a shove clockwise. It spun for perhaps a quarter turn and came to a halt. "You sure that valve's open?" he yelled back.

"Quarter turn!"

"Open her up full!" he instructed, and I did as I was told. Again, Fluky got a grip on the flywheel and pulled it around with all his might. This time it went a full turn before it began to slow. Then, deep down underneath me, there was a sound not unlike an animal awaking. The whole engine palpably lurched as the flywheel began to pick up speed.

Fluky didn't wait around. With unexpected grace, he leapt free of the engine cowling, landed on the platform, did a half roll, and sprinted away. A soon as the flywheel began to pick up pace, a stream of steam began to shoot out of the long, tall exhaust pipe above the engine.

We had power!

I looked down at the gauges and could see electric potential north of the potentiometer. Three hundred amps and climbing. The temperature in the turbine was climbing too, and I backed off on the fuel valve, turning it down a quarter turn. The amps hovered just below three hundred, and so did the temperature at six hundred degrees.

It was working. The fucking thing worked! I was flabbergasted. I watched the flywheel spin on its axle for a whole minute, waiting for something to go wrong. But there was nothing. I marveled at how remarkably quiet the engine ran. After becoming accustomed to the noise of Fluky's wrecking truck, the comparatively silent grace of Sophie's engine came as a pleasant surprise. Cautiously, I reached down and turned the potentiometer ever so slightly.

The whole train lurched suddenly forward.

I cut out the voltage as suddenly as I started it, and the whole train lurched to a halt. Everything shook – the boots in their hoppers, the links between the cars, the cockpit I was sitting in – I almost fell forward over the controls. She had some pep, I realized, and straightened myself back up in my seat. I attempted to turn the potentiometer again. Again, she started moving forward, but this time I did it with a little finesse. I turned the knob, barely five degrees around its full sweep, and *The Cordwainer* slowly began to roll forward along the tracks.

All aboard, I said to myself in my head, feeling like an old time engineer. The Nine Fifteen, leaving for Seattle, stops in Shadrach, Meshach and Abednego! Then I remembered, standing up and leaning out of the cockpit, not everyone was actually aboard.

"All aboard!" I yelled back down the platform.

Fluky had never made it back to cover – he had paused, halfway down the platform to watch *The Cordwainer* take its first breath. Mitty, however, came sprinting out of the concourse archway. The train wasn't moving much over two miles an hour, but for Mitty that was quite a serious sprint. Both Mitty and Fluky, at the last minute, leapt onto the running board of the station wagon caboose. Mitty almost tumbled, but Fluky caught his arm.

We didn't make it two hundred yards before the engine car derailed.

It was at the crossing, where C Street came across the tracks. I think the front crossbar was mis-configured, running too low, and the front wheels popped clear of the tracks. I flicked the switch next to the potentiometers and the whole train shuddered to a halt. I was down out of the cockpit as Fluky and Mitty came running up the side of the train. We stood in the dark looking at the wheels of the engine car sitting tangential to the tracks.

"Ah, shit..." I said looking down, my heart sinking in my chest. So close, but yet so far from success.

"Don't worry, I gotta plan!" Fluky said confidently, then hopped up onto the engine and began cranking the crossbar up and then extending it out. I was bewildered, I had not yet seen the technical genius of Fluky's crossbar guides in action. As he cranked the front bar down over the tracks again, the front wheel lifted up in the air, weight of the engine and all.

"Get the block and tackle from the caboose," Fluky called to me. "It's in the back."

I sprinted to the back of *The Cordwainer*, opened up the rear doors of the station wagon, and pulled out a heavy duty block and tackle and a length of rope that were stowed under the rear bench. I was carrying it all back to the engine when I saw the first pair of headlights crest the hill at the top of C Street.

I had the perfect vantage point to see all the way up the long, straight road – all the way through old Pottersville and up the hill to where Mitty's house sat at the crest. A pair of headlights lit up the clouds momentarily, then swept down, lighting up the grade down the hill. My stomach almost leapt out my mouth.

What did emerge was, "They're coming!"

Mitty and Fluky popped up like prairie dogs from inside *The Cordwainer's* engine. "What do I do with this?" I asked, holding up the block and tackle.

"Tie it to the sign post," Fluky pointed to the "Railroad Crossing" at the edge of the road on the opposite side of the train than she had derailed on. I tied one end of the tackle to the sign post and hooked the other end to the chassis of the engine. I was straightening out ropes when I risked another glance up the hill.

There were a lot of lights up there now.

I went back to my ropes, thinking little of it, rushing to get the train back on the tracks. But the full implications of what I had just seen began to dawn on me. I paused and looked back up C again. There were far more that two pairs of headlights at the crest of the hill, so many they were starting to blur together.

They were like moving spotlights in the darkness, dancing back and forth up against the abandoned Victorian homes flanking the street.

At the time I didn't understand – had no way to know – but I would later come to learn that the first automobiles that crested the hill between Boot Hill and Pottersville were not the two low black cars of the Concession goons. When Sophie had raised the alarm, after I'd fled from her kitchen, she'd attempted to put in a call to the Concession men about the location of *The Cordwainer* by calling Deputy Aesop, who that evening had been having dinner at Putter's. He'd taken the call calmly, promising her that he'd relay the message, and then he'd sat down again to finish his supper.

Now, Deputy Aesop was never one for keeping a secret, and he'd proceeded to explain to most everyone in the restaurant exactly what Fluky, Mitty and I had been up to over in Pottersville.

Turns out, Mitty's Plan was one of the poorest kept secrets in history.

It's not like it's easy to keep a secret in a town like Boot Hill. Most everyone knows most everyone else's business, like it or not. Apparently, the trials and tribulations of our attempt to construct a train for hauling boots were well known to the community. Word was there was even a pool going on our chances of success.

Mitty had been of no help. After one or two drinks in the bar at Putter's, he'd start telling everyone about how he was going to be rich when he came back from the Big City – what he was going to buy and how he was going to live. One or two drinks more and he'd give up most every detail of everything he was privy to. Which was most everything.

When then Concession men had come to town to break up the unionization, the rumors of the illicit railroad had kept them snooping around. It had been only the natural reticence of the community to cooperate with authority that kept the Concession goons from marching directly into Old Zimmerman's workshop and discovering our train. Most everyone in town was aware, to one extent or another, of what we were up to late at night in the junkyard. And when the news broke that *The Cordwainer* was finally ready to roll, and that the

Concession men were racing to Pottersville to shut the whole operation down. the town of Boot Hill did the most miraculous thing.

They created the first traffic jam Boot Hill had seen in thirty years.

Out of old garages and sheds, a whole fleet of vehicles emerged. Some running off whiffs of gasoline, jealously horded for decades; others converted to run on alcohol, or rigged with electric motors. It turns out that Fluky, Mitty and myself were not the only gearheads in Boot Hill. A dozen, two dozen, two score other projects like ours were all being worked on in parallel to *The Cordwainer.* Not trains, of course, but restorations of classic cars – conversions to alternate power sources.

There were enough cars in Boot Hill to jam C Street all the way up the hill, past Mitty's house and down the other side. When the Concession men got word from Deputy Aesop about our train, they had attempted to make all haste over to Pottersville to shut us down. But they hadn't made it any further than C Street, as cars pulled out into the road in front of them, blocking their path. Horns were honked and responded to with horns that hadn't sounded in twenty years.

The traffic jam would not slow the Concession men down for long, but it bought Fluky, Mitty and myself enough time to man the block and tackle, pull on the ropes and slide *The Cordwainer's* engine back onto its tracks.

If I'd only known at the time what the town of Boot Hill had done for us. But it wouldn't be until many years later that I'd learn the whole story. The fact was the odyssey of *The Cordwainer* would have ended before it had even begun if it had not been for the people of Boot Hill.

Fluky made some minute adjustments, taking some measurements under the chassis, making sure it wouldn't derail again. The lights at the top of the hill started to break up, separate and stream down the hill. I was already in the cockpit when Fluky finally pulled himself up onto the running board.

"My turn," he said, climbing up into the cockpit.

"What?"

"My turn to drive. You've cocked it up once already."

"You're blaming me for that?" I laughed, making room for Fluky, letting him get into the engineer's chair.

"Hell, yeah," he said, tuning the potentiometer to zero, flicking the switch back to on, and slowly dialing up the speed again.

We were rolling again as I climbed out onto the running boards that stretched the full length of the train, along the side of each freight car. Our lights in the Union Station were receding into the darkness behind us as the strobing clutch of headlights came dancing down the hill and intersected with the tracks. I couldn't make out in the distance exactly what transpired when the Concession goons finally reached the Union Station. But by the dancing headlights over the roofs of the building and the occasional horn echoing out through the empty streets of Pottersville, it sounded like an awkward scrummage of cars and people were frustrating the Concession men's attempts to give chase.

I shimmied along until I was at the station wagon caboose, and I swung in through one of the open windows. Mitty was sitting at the table looking at a map with a pen light in one hand. He looked up as I sat down on the bench across from him. I smiled a smile at him I think will still be plastered to my face a year after I'm dead.

"Now," Mitty said, tapping the map with the pen light. "Where does this train take us again?"

Chapter Twenty-One

Shadrach, Meshach and Abednego

Five or six miles away from Pottersville, Fluky brought *The Cordwainer* to a halt. He feared another derailment if we proceeded in the dark and the stretch of track we'd so far navigated was heavily overgrown. The odds of encountering a felled tree or an uprooted section of track seemed pretty high. Fluky thought it best to proceed in the daytime, when at least we would be able to see obstacles approaching, and have more light to work out solutions to overcome them.

The heavy brambles felt like a good spot to lay low. They provided good cover for us to layover and spend the night. It would be a long walk through the thicket in the dark for anyone trying to follow us, and we rightly concluded that we were safe for the evening staying put.

But before any of the crew of *The Cordwainer* could get any sleep, there was the matter of Mitty's map to be attended to. We had left Boot Hill so unprepared, that we had never had the time to fully chart out our course over the mountains. Mitty's map was potentially as old as the tracks we were running on, but it did show the course of the old Northern Pacific Railroad in some detail – from Boot Hill all the way to the Big City – as it ran some thirty years ago.

First along the tracks were the tri-towns of Shadrach, Meshach and Abednego, Boot Hill's nearest neighbors. These towns weren't on the main mega-gauge line, but were serviced by a spur line, because of the twin domes of their two nuclear reactors, Sodom and Gomorrah, which dominated the towns. These two massive structures produced much of the electricity used in the northwestern United States. In the Northern Pacific days, they had been farming communities, but now they mainly housed and supplied the workers at the nuclear facility. The Concession nuclear facility, like everything else – another series of company towns.

How the Stephenson gauge rails navigated the tri-towns, I couldn't fathom from the map.

From there, we'd cross a large section of open territory in the shadows of the reactors that was planted for hemp or corn. There was an old logging village on the map, called Johnson City, as the country began to gain altitude. Here, I assumed we'd start to see the tall pines that sat thick on the ground of both slopes of the mountains we planned to cross. There, high in the hills, was another settlement, an old mining town called Lode.

Next, the tracks crested the mountains through a pass on Mitty's map that was vaguely outlined, on down the west side of the mountains, though countless small farming communities – mostly orchard towns. At the big lake east of the City, we'd turn north into suburbs and push toward the center of town. We'd meet up with mega-gauge rail again here, I knew from experience, and run in tandem the last few miles into the freight yards that dominated the south part of the City.

Where we'd stop, where and how we'd unload our cargo, I hadn't even begun to contemplate. But the Big City still seemed so far off, at the end of such a long journey, that I didn't put the effort into worrying about it. There was a lot of wild country between here and there.

Full of Polypigs.

And I knew, without a doubt, that we hadn't heard the last from those Concession men.

We folded down the table in the caboose and lay out under the pile of Mitty's dirty blankets I had scavenged from the house. I didn't get much sleep, but I rested better knowing I had the .38 Smith & Wesson within reach. Even if I only had two bullets.

When the sun came up I opened my eyes to see Fluky already awake, eating Tom Mixx out of a billy can. He was chewing happily away and I noted that he appeared to be in good spirits. He might have even washed his face and hands – for the first time in a dozen years, I would have had to guess.

"Mornin'," he said through a mouth full of cereal, seeing that I was awake. I looked around at the thick wall of thicket that was surrounding the caboose. I hadn't realized it was so thick, so close in, the night before – not in the dark.

"Get any sleep?"

"Hell, no," Fluky said, dropping his spoon into his can and sliding in behind the seat into the old engine compartment. "Let's get this train movin'." He leapt to his feet, climbed up and out through the sunroof and moved on all fours across the top of *The Cordwainer* toward the cockpit.

We put three more miles between us and Boot Hill before Mitty woke up.

He'd slept like a baby. He pulled himself out from under his blankets, reached around for his cigarette holder and maneuvered, bleary eyed, a cigarette into it. The first drag revived him, and he looked around puffing away as the brambles scraped by against the sides of the train.

"Golly," he said with a smile, climbing to his feet. "I positively forgot where I was..."

Ah, to have the brain of a dummy.

We didn't break clear of the brambles until well after noon, out onto the open plains that surround the tri-towns. The dual domes of the nuclear reactors loomed large in the distance, only slightly dwarfed by the mountains behind them. The smoke from the chimneys of The Shop were barely visible on the horizon behind us. By dark we would be within walking distance of Shadrach, Meshach and Abednego.

The track had been fair to very good so far and we'd had no more derailments. We paused once, before breaking out of the thicket, to move a fallen tree off the tracks. Fluky had been manning the cockpit all morning, and after I'd eaten a little lunch of cold canned beans, I'd climbed up to the front of *The Cordwainer* to relieve him.

"We'll be into the tri-towns before long," he said, as he gave up the engineer's chair to me.

"I think we should hold up outside in the scrub and roll through after dark," I said, looking at the gauges.

"Tricky... If we derail in town..."

"Better than rolling down Main Street on a Tuesday afternoon," I countered.

"Yeah, I guess," Fluky said as he vanished back towards the caboose to get his lunch.

We settled on my plan. As *The Cordwainer* got closer to the tri-towns and the twin domes of the reactors grew to fill the sky, we realized that the old Stephenson gauge rails really did cut right through the center of the most southerly town – Shadrach. I had joked about rolling down Main Street, but from the cover of a group of trees on the end of town it looked like that was exactly what we were going to have to do. The rails joined up with a second set of rails, perhaps for a trolley car, and ran down a wide street east to west through the community. I could make out the bulk of Shadrach's Concession Store facing onto that street.

There was nothing we could do about it. The rails ran where the rails ran, even if that meant right through the center of town. We'd wait for dark. At least we could do that.

We watched trolley cars come and go as the evening approached, returning people from work at the reactors. Shadrach appeared to exist in the same sort of rigid chit social structure as Boot Hill. Some trolleys were obviously bound for wealthier neighborhoods, full of shirt-and-tie-wearing accountants and foremen. Other trolleys rolled by with blue-shirted workers in hardhats, taking a different spur, perhaps to Meshach or Abednego.

As the evening rolled on, a crowd of people began to gather on the streets. The sun set and the crowd didn't seem to disperse. It was hard to tell what was going on from our vantage point more than a mile away, but the street we were preparing to travel down appeared to be a busy one. By seven in the evening there was no sign that the crowd on the street was dispersing. It was mind-boggling. Did no one have work in the morning? Was there nothing on the radio to listen to?

By nine o'clock, Fluky came up to the cockpit and stuck his head in.

"We're just gonna have to roll on down in there," he said.

"It looks mighty busy," I said, squinting. "Maybe in a hour..."

"We can't sit here forever. Eventually, we're bound to be discovered. Best we have a full head of steam when it happens."

I bit my lip.

I waited another fifteen minutes, but the crowd seemed to be thickening. Whatever was happening, people were lining the street now, both sides. It was intolerable. We couldn't go back and we couldn't go forward. We'd lost almost half a day sitting in that grove of trees. Fluky was right, if we got caught sitting still we'd be in trouble. The Concession, undoubtedly, had a map too. They could see as well as we could where the tracks of the old Northern Pacific lay. There was no great secret to be kept now we were underway. If the Concession caught us... well, they would catch us. Whatever was going on in Shadrach it was none of my concern.

Little did we know that what was happening in Shadrach was all about us.

The town was gathering along the length of that street to watch *The Cordwainer* roll through. Word had gone ahead about our departure, and people had started to coalesce, after work, to watch us pass through town.

With no sight that the crowd in Shadrach was going to disperse, I opened the valve to the expansion chamber, got a good head of steam going and turned up the potentiometer, moving the whole rig slowly forward. We rolled boldly into town up the center of the street, at no more than five miles an hour. As we approached, I began to realize how large the crowds on each side were. Hundreds of people, it must have been the whole town. Old men and women, young children, blue-shirted workers still wearing their helmets. They all stood silently as *The Cordwainer* rolled down the center of their street.

It was eerily quiet as we split down the center of the crowd. I sat in the cockpit with my hand on the gun, watching the crowd for any signs of reaction. But there were none. They didn't seem to be there to stop us, they didn't seem to be there to cheer us, they simply watched as we passed with their wide, cold stares. No one made a motion, no one made a sound. There was just the sound of *The Cordwainer's* flywheel spinning.

We rolled to the far end of the street without incident. I looked back to see the faces of the crowd still silently watching us steam off out of town. Fluky and Mitty were sitting on the roof of the caboose, looking back also. I turned up the amperage, and let *The Cordwainer* pick up speed; the silent faces and the lights of Shadrach receding behind us.

I left the cockpit and shimmied back along the running boards.

"Did you see that?" I said to Fluky when I was on the hood of the caboose.

"Pretty freaky, huh?" he agreed.

"...Though I walk through the valley of the shadow of death..." Mitty began to quote.

"Yeah, no shit," Fluky nodded.

"Guess word's gotten out about our little trip."

"Hell, we is celebrities!" Fluky laughed.

"Or outlaws," Mitty corrected.

"Ain't they about the same thing?"

"I..." I began, but stopped. There was a noise. For a second I thought something was wrong with the engine, but then I realized it was off to the side. The train bumped, like it did when it crossed over a road that intersected the track, and just for a second I caught a glimpse of headlights on the perpendicular road. "Shit!" I screamed and tried to climb to my feet, but fell on my ass. Fluky leapt like a small animal from the caboose onto of the rear-most freight car. He vanished into the darkness, heading up toward the cockpit.

I pulled out my gun.

In the darkness behind us, a car swerved madly off the road the tracks had intersected. They pulled out onto the tracks. It was a black car, low and chromed. It tilted, balancing on the two rails for a second, then slid off and straddled them – one wheel inside and one outside tracks. Its engine roared and it began to gain ground of us, headlights illuminating Mitty and me on top of the station wagon caboose. I was about to panic, raise my gun, when Fluky reached the cockpit and punched his fist into the large red button on the panel. *The Cordwainer* lurched forward, suddenly accelerating with a burst of power. I fell forward, flat on my face on the roof of the caboose. I was vaguely aware of Mitty vanishing down through the sun roof. I struggled to regain my feet.

We were moving fast now, the night beside the train rushing by, but the black car behind us was keeping pace. In fact, it was slowly gaining ground as, below me, Mitty began to throw things out of the back of the caboose. He was cursing, I could hear, but I couldn't make out what. An empty can of beans, then a wrench came flying out and bounced off the hood of the black car. It was getting closer, its engine screaming loud.

I pulled myself up to my knees and leveled the revolver. I took aim between the pair of headlights and pulled the trigger. My gun made a small, wheezing noise and then popped. Not a bang, a pop. I looked at it in my hand in disbelief. Just my luck!

I was well lit up by the headlights of the pursuing car. Someone inside leaned out the passenger window and fired off a shot from his own gun before I had a chance to take a second shot. Something stung me bitterly in the right temple. My head snapped back.

My God, I've been shot! But there was no time to think much about it. I was sliding sideways off the roof of the caboose. If I hadn't flailed out with my arms at the very last second, and miraculously caught onto a running board as I fell, I'd have vanished into the darkness.

The engine of the black car behind me roared.

I was hanging by my fingernails from the running board of a speeding train. My head was splitting in pain. I looked back to see that the black car was almost completely on top of *The Cordwainer*. A black-suited man was pulling himself out of the passenger side window with a gun in his hand and up onto the hood. Reflexively, I raised my pistol and again pulled the trigger. I wasn't aiming. This time the gun went bang.

The bullet must have hit dead center in the middle of the black car's chromium grill. The engine began to billow steam. The man hanging on to the hood vanished into the cloud as the engine struggled to keep pace with *The Cordwainer*. It began to lag. As the distance between the train and the car grew, I could hear the engine of the black car beginning to falter. First a hiccup in its earsplitting roar, then a cough. Its headlights began to shrink back into the night as Mitty appeared at the window of the caboose to grab my arm. The engine of the black car gave out a single, painful, mechanical, angry yell, then braked suddenly behind us, throwing the Concession goon riding on the hood head first onto the tracks.

Mitty pulled me up and into the caboose, where I collapsed out over a bench, my head bleeding freely. I hadn't been shot, at least not directly – the Concession goon's bullet had ricocheted. But the throbbing in my head told me I had been.

I passed out there, on the back seat of the caboose with the Smith & Wesson still in my hand, Mitty blowing concerned smoke down into my face.

Chapter Twenty-Two

The Ghost of Tom Mixx

I awoke on the hard ground, the stars twinkling in the sky above me. I sat up suddenly, only to be forced back down flat by the throbbing in my head. I could hear the crackle of a campfire and I rolled onto my left side to look over at the embers. By the fire, the still mounds of Fluky and Mitty were sleeping nearby. I attempted to sit up again, this time cautiously, and I raised a hand to my bandaged forehead.

It was a clear, warm night. Wherever we were, we were still within sight of the massive domes of Sodom and Gomorrah – I could just make them out silhouetted against the night sky off to east. We were camped at the brow of a small, grassy hill, *The Cordwainer* sitting silent, inert, perhaps two hundred yards away.

I let out a soft moan as the pain in my head readjusted itself. I kicked off the dirty Mitty blanket that was covering my legs and attempted to stand. My legs would not cooperate. Instead, I crawled closer to the fire and took a drink of water out of a billy can that sat by the fire. It tasted vaguely of old coffee. I contemplated waking up Fluky or Mitty, asking them how long I'd been out. An hour? A whole day? But they were slumbering peacefully away and I thought better of disturbing them. I was still wearing Barry's watch. I tried to see the tiny date dial on the face, through the cracked crystal, but couldn't make anything out in the darkness. I tilted it towards the fire, but I was no better off. I thought of Mitty's penlight in the caboose of the train and attempted again to climb to my feet. This time I was more successful and I wobbled for a second by the campfire.

Presently, I took a step, then another, and soon found that I could walk under my own power. Dizzily, I made my way down the slope of the low hill towards *The Cordwainer*, holding my head sensitively in my hands. At the caboose, I opened one of the side doors, reached in and pulled the penlight off the table, clicking it on. I shined it on my watch and saw that a whole day had passed since the shots at the railroad crossing. How far had we traveled in the interim? It was hard to gauge with only the domes of the reactors as landmarks.

I flicked off the penlight and was returning it back to the table when I realize that I wasn't alone.

I spun around to see a shadowy mounted figure not twenty yards away from me, the horse standing idle, the face of the rider cloaked in darkness. My mind instantly thought of Deputy Aesop on his ancient white pony – that he'd somehow tracked us and found us – but the mounted figure was too rigid in the saddle, too erect. The Smith & Wesson was sitting on the table by the penlight in the caboose. I leapt for it, grabbing it up and turning to face the silhouette.

I still couldn't make out the face of the rider, but now I could see the gleaming six gun in his hand, leveled at me.

"Howdy," the figure said, the gun not faltering.

"Err... Hi..." I replied. The revolver suddenly felt very heavy in my hand. I let it droop slowly then gave in and dropped it into the grass.

"Nice night," the figure said, his pistol vanishing away into a holster at his side, almost as quickly as it had appeared. He prodded his horse forward and the two slowly resolved into view. The rugged features of a rugged face looked down at me from the back of the bay stallion. The man removed his large Stetson and looked up at the stars, squinting. "Ain't a cloud in the sky," he said, "but still ain't too cold." I attempted to speak, realizing we were talking about the weather, but nothing emerged from my mouth. "That's quite a contraption," he went on, nodding at *The Cordwainer*.

"Yes, yes it is," I said slowly. He held up his horse and dismounted. His spurs jingled as his boots touched the ground and I saw he stood a good few inches taller than six feet. He looked, somehow, familiar...

"You folks on a camp out?" he asked, tending to the horse's bridle.

"What? No, I..." I touched my forehead. The bandage.

"I'd be much obliged if you folks got some coffee..." he said, looking back up the hillside towards the fire. Fluky and Mitty were still snoring away.

"Yes, yes, sure." I reached down automatically and picked up the handgun – not to use it, but like I was cleaning up for a guest. I returned the gun to the caboose's table and trotted back up the hill towards the campsite. The cowboy in his boots followed behind.

At the fire, I tossed some more firewood onto the dying embers and balanced the water can in the center of the fire. I was digging around amongst the supplies as the cowboy sat down beside the fire and removed his gloves, warming his hands.

"You're out late?" I asked, finding the instant coffee, adding it to the water.

"Got a gross a cattle on yonder," he said, pointing north. "Beef on the hoof. Grazing them higher up in summer, when the grass is long. All of this is Concession land," he continued, "but they don't mind none, no one's using it. Says it's contaminated – from the reactors – but it don't seem to hurt the cattle none. Good grazing, and folks tend to avoid it."

"Sounds lonely."

"Yep," he smiled. "I ain't, as they might say, one who craves the company of his fellow man."

I laughed. I found some cold beans and canned meat and offered it to the cowboy. He gratefully accepted.

"Why you folks out here?" he asked after a few mouthfuls of stew. "That there some kind of train?"

"Yes, we built it," I said with pride. The coffee was starting to boil.

"My, ain't that somethin'. And you brought it out here for a camp out? From Shadrach?" he asked.

"No, Boot Hill."

"Well, that there's a long haul."

"But we ain't camping," I corrected. "We've got a load of boots, there in the hoppers. We're heading for the Big City. To sell." It felt good to speak of Mitty's Plan with no thought to secrecy. The cat was out of the bag and I could speak with justifiable pride at what I'd accomplished. The cowboy was suitably impressed.

"Well now, ain't that somethin'... Folks at the Concession ain't gonna look at that too favorably, I hope you know."

"Yes, I know all too well," I said, touching my forehead.

The cowboy munched away at his beans. I found it hard to believe that Fluky and Mitty were still sleeping. The cowboy and I were making no attempt to be quiet, but they just lay there, slumbering, not three feet away.

"Exactly how many boots you got in that there whirligig?" he asked, craning his head around, looking down the hill at *The Cordwainer.*

"Ten thousand pairs."

"Heck, and you're taking them all the way over there?" he pointed up into the darkness, at the mountains looming silently above us.

"Yep."

"In that thing?" he pointed back down again at *The Cordwainer.*

"Yep," I stressed.

He laughed, shook his head in bewilderment, finishing up the food on his plate. "Better you than me," he went on. "Ain't ever been very good with machines."

"I got these two to help," I indicated the sleeping lumps of Mitty and Fluky. The cowboy didn't seem terribly impressed. I poured out two cups of coffee and traded the cowboy his empty plate for a full cup. He took a sip of his, blanched at the heat, and put it down in the grass to cool. "Bet you had to raise holy hell to get that contraption out of Boot Hill, loaded for bear."

"Yes, it was quite an adventure," I said.

"Folks just don't appreciate the entrepreneurial spirit no more," he replied.

I sighed, thinking of Sophie. "Guess they think we're being selfish, trying to make a buck."

The cowboy scoffed, "Good for you, son. Selfishness is something this world needs a little more of..."

I raised an eyebrow, squinting at the cowboy, and took a sip of my coffee. Hot.

"Now greed, I agree," he went on. "Ain't ever done no one no good. But selfishness... A selfish man has to learn to appreciate things, what he's got, what it's worth. Looking out for number one, that makes a man independent. Go expecting things from other people – things you ain't earned – that's greed. But a man who can stand on his own two feet and understand the value of the things he's labored for, that's a man with the right to be selfish. If all they can cuss you out for is bein' selfish, son, then you're doin' all right. Now, if you been greedy..."

"Well, they weren't exactly our boots..." I admitted.

The cowboy laughed, "Well, this ain't exactly my grazin' land, either." He tried his coffee again, found it acceptable, and drank it down in a long gulp. "That don't make it greedy for me to take a mouthful of grass."

"Some folks would call that stealing."

"Yep," the cowboy said with a nod. "And it ain't for me to say it ain't. Fella's got to decide for himself. However, a fella can't just stand on the say of others. You of the mind that you stole them shit kickers?" he asked.

"No," I said with all honesty.

"Then there you go." He wiped his mouth on his sleeve and leaned forward to help himself to another cup of coffee. I finished mine and put the cup down. It tasted vile. "See, the law's got the nerve to be callin' a lot of things stealin' that really ain't."

"Doesn't make it right, though," I countered.

"Don't make it wrong, neither," he fired back. "Ain't nobody can decide right from wrong but ya'self. Lots of folk might *want* to tell ya, but they can't decide it for ya."

We passed into silence as I thought on what he was saying – attempting a response.

"It's different out here," I finally said. "You're free to make up your own rules."

"Yeah, yeah, you can say that." The cowboy rested back on his haunches, sipping at his scalding coffee. "Can also say I got a mess *more* rules out here, than folks got livin' in civilization. Hard livin' out here in the open. Comforts of town, that's a kind of freedom – freedom from want, freedom from need. If ya ain't ever had an empty belly ya don't know what a noose that is around a fella's neck. That a rule, believe you me. Out here, there's a whole mess of rules like that – rules you don't want to be goin' around breakin'. Breakin' them rules will get you in big trouble real quick. Big trouble and dead."

He went on speaking, looking up at the stars, as his coffee made whirls of steam in front of him, "Though, folks are all to quick to be mistakin' freedom for liberty. They ain't the same thin', ya know. Freedom – now, freedom is the lack of chains holdin' a man down. Real-life chains, for sure, but also them chains like the empty belly I was speakin' of. The essentials of life. Man ain't free if he has to grub around for essentials, them can be chains holdin' a man down, just as tight and hard to break as any chains of a jailer or a tyrant. But liberty – liberty is the power to *do* things – things a man wants to do. And here, out here, in that respect, we got the townie well and truly beat. Out here, on the land, we can be free or we can't be. But what we really got – what we got a whole sky full and all a man could drink for a thousand years – is liberty. A man's fate is his own fate out here, nobody else's.

"See, what you got in town is a predisposition to organize things that ain't got no earthly reason to get organized. Hell, I love my momma, yes I do, and I love Jesus. But on a Sunday I don't get all fired up 'bout sittin' around with folk and talkin' on how sweet and nice my mother is. Why do folk have to go and do that for Jesus? Ya think he wants ya to? Hell. Ain't nothin' but an excuse for some fella to get up in front of everyone and tell 'em what to think. Jesus ain't wantin' none of that – that's why he wrote what he got to say down in a book, like a sensible sort. It's all right there, written down, if a fella wants to know what Jesus wants. Ain't got to go and ask no preacher.

"And then there's them City Hall types that's just as bad, with their spittin'-on-the-sidewalk laws. How can folk get a damn thing done with that kind always interferin'? No parkin', no sittin', no cussin', no breathin'. It gets to the point that a fella can do nothin' but keep his hands in his pockets – except some lady folk might take offense at that, too. Now, I'm all in favor of everybody being civil – my momma raised a good boy, who knows his pleases and thank yous – but when you start a-thinkin' it's your business to tell other folk how to behave... Ain't no reason for it.

"It all gets to the point in town when a fella is facing other folks every way he wants to jump, can't hardly take a walk without steppin' on a pair of toes. That wears on a soul. Ya start lookin' over to other folk to catch wind of what ya supposed to be thinkin'... That's the rot of it. Makes a man lazy. Lazy in the head. Can't be bothered to think up right and wrong for himself, so he shops out his thinkin' to others. Calls it 'The Law' and gives up on being a thinkin' soul entirely. No, can't be livin' like that, ain't nothin' a fella can build a life on. No sir."

He tapped at his temple, continuing, "There's liberty. Right here. To be free, that's a physical thin', but liberty is inside a man. In his head and his heart. When a fella takes a notion to dream – thinkin' big – that's liberty for ya. That's what the towns take away. That's what the law writes right off the books. Fella's got to be able to figure right from wrong for himself, or he'll be so tied up in his head he can't be figurin' out nothing else. Start tellin' a man what's right and what's wrong and you're tellin' him, not just that, but how to *be*."

My thoughts turned to my sister, the day before, back in Boot Hill. Up until then, I hadn't had a chance to think it over. It was all still just a blur in my head, a lingering sense of unease. Why had she done what she did? First, helping us build the engine, then betraying us – and it – to the Concession? It was inexplicable, both a personal and moral betrayal. But what the cowboy was saying fit Sophie all too well. With all the brains and all the potential, she was still tied down by her social conscience. She could see the marvel in *The Cordwainer* in one breath, understand its technical importance; and fear and loath it in another, for its selfish purpose.

"Aren't we supposed to be a Nation of Big Ideas?" I asked absentmindedly, quoting the slogan. "Doesn't that take cooperation?"

"Ha!" the cowboy laughed, mirthlessly. "Ain't nothin' but another way of sayin', 'Do what ya told'. We'll be havin' the Big Ideas, thank you very much, you folk just do what we say. Ain't no nation that has ideas, now is it? It's people. Powerful ones and weak. Ain't nobody needin' no one sitting behind no desk thinkin' up their big ideas for 'em. Seems like a fella can have his own Big Ideas all on his lonesome. God gave him at least that.

"What a fella does *need*, on the other hand, is for his Nation to get outta the way so he can make something of those Big Ideas other than just wishin'. But you don't see much of that now-a-days, no sir. Fella in the White House might *say* he wants to see Big Ideas, but he can't let go and just let folks have 'em. No, can't give up *control*. Not when ideas might make someone a little richer, or some other fella a little poorer, or might make the weather a little hotter. That right there puts a stop to just about all the good ideas – them summers just gettin' hotter and hotter – nothing you can do up against worries like that..."

We trailed off into silence, listening to Fluky and Mitty snore away. A weariness suddenly washed over me. I remembered the late hour. My brain was again starting to throb in my skull. I closed my eyes and I could feel the world spinning around me.

"You think, maybe," I stopped, picking up a thought half finished, then started again. "That maybe we've been cutting off our nose to spite our face?"

"Come again?" the cowboy said, finishing off his coffee.

"The Concession? Global overheating..." I realized I'd wandered sleepily off on my own tangent, in my head. "The summers just getting hotter and hotter..." I mused.

"Think we're heading down the wrong trail, took the wrong road?" The cowboy said, but I couldn't see him speaking in the darkness.

"Yes, I-"

"That maybe cutting back, locking things down was the wrong way to go? That in the end, we ended up consuming more, not less? That now there's so much catching up to do and we have so much less now to work with that we can't help but fall further behind, burning away hotter than ever trying to catch up, but only falling further behind, in a vicious circle – digging down deeper, down and down? Is that how it seems?"

"Yes, but-" I woke up, sitting up. The cowboy was sitting still, studying the stars. It had sounded like his voice speaking, but then again it hadn't... I shook my head, but it just made my brain spasm in pain.

177

I was about to speak, when the cowboy climbed to his feet, dusting down his pants. "Well, I can't rightly say," he shrugged. "I'm mighty grateful for the coffee and the chow," he said. He held out a hand across the fire and I shook it. For the first time I saw his face, fully lit by the fire and the feeling of recognition hit me once again.

"You're welcome," I replied. "Thanks for not shooting me back there." I pointed down, past his horse, at *The Cordwainer*.

"Fella can't be too careful in these parts," he said. "You did all right." He walked back to his horse and unhooked the bridle, patting the animal tenderly on its nose.

"Plenty of room out here for you?" I asked as he was mounting up onto this stallion.

He returned his Stetson to his head and gathered up his reins, "Always room for one more," he chuckled. He turned his horse's nose and pointed him down the hill. "Good luck with them there boots," he said back over his shoulder. "Careful there with that rollin' bathtub..."

"Good night," I called after him, waving a hand.

He cantered his horse down the hill and I noticed that a false dawn was starting, raising majestically behind the domes of Sodom and Gomorrah. He was riding into the dawn. As he passed *The Cordwainer*, I noticed the old advertisement on the side of the rear-most hopper, the one for Tom Mixx Trail Ready Cereal. The rider in the advertisement and the cowboy who'd just shared the campfire looked awfully similar...

But then I had just been shot in the head.

Chapter Twenty-Three

Right and Wrong

I went back to the fire and curled up under my dirty blanket, falling almost instantly back to sleep. When I awoke, Fluky and Mitty were up making breakfast. At my first stirring they came jumping to my side.

"How do you feel, old man?" Mitty asked, looking down at me.

"You were out all day yesterday," Fluky added. He lifted the bandage on my forehead and examined the wound. "Don't worry, ain't nothing broken. Bullet must of hit the caboose then nicked you in the head. Sure knocked ya stupid, though."

I tried to sit up, but my head was spinning.

"Easy," Mitty held me down. "Don't rush it."

"It's all right, I was up last night," I said groggily.

"Yeah, sure, just lay still."

"But I-" My head was throbbing.

I stayed horizontal for another five minutes, then Fluky helped me up to a sitting position, and force fed me a cup of coffee. It tasted as bitter and vile as it had in the middle of the night, but I choked it down and it revived me enough to let me climb to my feet.

Fluky and Mitty filled me in on the events – or lack of them – of the day I missed. They had pushed on out of Shadrach and encountered no one. They had decided to rest for the night on the hill, fearing a derailment if they continued in the dark. I asked if they had passed the cowboy or his cattle crossing the plain, but they both looked at me like I was talking nonsense. They hadn't seen a soul, man nor beast. I let it lie at that.

After eating a quick breakfast, we prepared to get underway once again. We were terribly exposed on that hillside, though a long distance from any road, but my injuries weren't so terrible that I couldn't be jostled about a bit. As we were packing up the camp, I was struck with the idea that I should have offered a pair of boots to the cowboy last night. I distinctly remember loading over a hundred pair of Boot Hill's finest, sturdiest riding boots. I could have kicked myself for not thinking of it while the cowboy had been here. Still, perhaps if I left a pair behind at the campsite, he might make his way back up here again that night and find the boots waiting.

For some reason I felt like I owed him something for his words of encouragement last night. While Fluky and Mitty were busying themselves loading up the caboose, I climbed up the side of the last hopper car in line and opened its hatch. I started fishing around for the oversized cardboard boxes that contained the style of cowboy boots that I was thinking of, when I uncovered a large hemp sack buried amongst the shoes. I gave it a tug and it seemed heavy. I didn't remember loading anything into the freight cars in sacks. I undid the tie and took a look inside.

I tossed the heavy sack down beside the smoldering fire. Fluky was packing up the billy cans. He jumped as the large sack thudded down next to him.

"What the hell?" he said looking down at the bag. Then he realized what it was. "Oh, I-"

"I can't believe it!" I began, throwing up my hands. "After all our work, after all the effort? And you do this?" I pointed accusingly at the sack.

"Now, just a second..." Fluky raised to his feet, making calming motions.

"When did you come up with this plan? Right from the beginning?" I yelled. "Did you ever give any thought to Mitty's Plan? Or was it always – right from the get-go – about this?"

"No, no, it ain't like that," Fluky stammered. "This was just sort of a last minute thing. When I went to get them guns, I sorta suggested to the fellas what we had planned. They had a real good idea."

"A *good* idea?" My brain felt like it was about to burst.

"We can double our profits here, Beanie. Think about it..." He kicked the sack with the toe of his boot. "This here one little sack, we can turn 'round and make more off than that there whole train load of boots."

"Profit?" Mitty was returning to the campfire. His ear pricked up at the mention of profit. "What can double our profits?" he asked.

"Fluky," I said without ceremony. "And his sack full of weed." I pointed at the bag in question at Fluky's feet.

"Weed? What?" Mitty looked confused.

"Now, folks are aching for this stuff in the Big City just as much as they're aching for boots," Fluky rationalized. But I'd stopped listening. I was walking off over the brow of the hill in disgust. I found a spot just out of sight from *The Cordwainer* and dropped down onto the ground.

I couldn't believe it. My head was throbbing. I felt like I was going to be sick. I'd just got shot in the head. That I could take, when I'd thought I'd got shot defending my cargo – my shipment of boots. But now... I'd got shot smuggling drugs. I lay back in the grass and let the nausea subside. The sky above me was spinning very slowly clockwise.

Was I making too much of my discovery? It wasn't like I objected to the use of the stuff. I liked to partake myself, and it was the height of insanity that pot was illegal. But something about hauling drugs... It wasn't like we were hauling legal cargo anyway. The boots, we'd stolen, and *The Cordwainer* itself existed in direct opposition to the state-assured freight monopoly that was the Concession's. But drugs...

Was I no better than Sophie? Did Mitty's Plan have to contain an altruistic component to make it acceptable to me? Had I been rationalizing the whole thing, excusing the profits I was potentially going to make because – looking at the big picture – we would be helping people in the end? Putting shoes on feet that would have otherwise remained unshod?

Was I just an insane hypocrite?

You could understand the point of view of Fluky and his weed-dealing friends. What was wrong – any more than anything else – with selling a product to people who wanted to buy it? If people wanted to smoke weed, who were we not to provide it for them? And the profit-to-weight ratio of the product... If a train was already crossing the mountains, why not throw in a bag? I took Fluky at his word that it could be worth as much as the whole train load of boots combined. Double our profits. It just made business sense.

But the cowboy, last night beside the fire, he'd been right too. Legal or illegal, it didn't matter, it was up to each and every one of us to determine our own right and wrong. Maybe I saw the boots as honest and weed as not. Maybe that didn't make a lick of sense to anyone, even me. Maybe it was hard for me to draw the line where legitimate commerce turned into exploitation. But I knew, sure as shit, that I was drawing the line here.

I wasn't out there, in the middle of nowhere, running a rocket fuel powered train across mountains for anyone's good but my own. I knew it – I had known that fact from the very beginning. I'd undertaken the execution of Mitty's Plan and the construction of *The Cordwainer* with no more noble goal in mind that my own enrichment. But I hadn't undertaken the whole enterprise to smuggle drugs.

It'd be so easy to use the cowboy's speech to justify anything that I wanted. If only I could decide right and wrong for myself, then what was there to stop me from deciding that anything and everything I decided to do was right? It'd be so easy to take that road. Or, inversely, that everything anyone else wanted to do that I didn't was wrong. Did I secretly fear other people's condemnation? Was I masking a social conscience behind all the talk of freedom and liberty?

Was I just screwing myself into the ground, turning around and around on the issue?

I pulled myself up to my feet and returned to the campfire.

Fluky and Mitty were sitting beside the fire, the last of the supplies packed up.

"The sack goes in the fire or you go on without me," I said and let it hang there in the cool morning air.

Mitty look up across his cigarette and Fluky opened his mouth to protest, "But-"

"Drugs were never part of it," I said. "That you felt you didn't need to tell the rest of us..."

"But, come on," Fluky made a sound, like a whining child. "That's cash money right there. It ain't like you're so hellfire moral about it? You smoke-"

"I said it was never a part of it," I interrupted. "If you'd thought it was a good idea, we could have discussed it from the very beginning. Then any of us who'd had a problem with it could have bowed out. But this way? No," I shook my head. It throbbed. "In the fire, or I'm walking back to Boot Hill."

Fluky looked at Mitty. Mitty's eyes were wide, he could tell I was deadly serious. Fluky was looking between the two of us. I could almost see him calculating his chances, with just Mitty for help. The mental math wasn't playing out for him, and slowly his shoulders began to sink.

"Shit," he said, grabbing the sack with both hands and lifting with all his might. He held it out, his arms fully extended and dropped it onto the smoldering fire. "Can we at least wait here till it all burns up?" he asked. "You know, breathin' deeply..."

I didn't answer. I was walking towards *The Cordwainer*, lifting a bag of supplies up onto my shoulder. Mitty fell in behind, holding a mass of the bundled blankets.

We let Fluky to mourn his loss as *The Cordwainer* built up a head of steam.

Chapter Twenty-Four

The Beginning of the Shooting War

After less than three hours of climbing through the foothills, *The Cordwainer* started down a small grade into the old logging community of Johnson City. It was a ghost town, very much like Pottersville, but it was obvious that Johnson City had never experienced the prosperity that Pottersville had once enjoyed. It was self-evidently a working class community, now long forgotten and abandoned, another victim of global overheating. With the tree canopy so precious – the only natural check on man-made carbon output – logging was one of the first industries to be regulated, marginalized, and finally made downright illegal.

No mega-gauge rail line serviced Johnson City, and with every means of self sufficiency removed, the town must have quickly died. There was no sign of human habitation as we rolled through the outlying structures. Nature was quickly reclaiming Johnson City, with brambles and trees tearing down the small, compact cottages and the rusting, forgotten logging equipment.

We were alone in Johnson City, or so we thought. We had no qualms about rolling through the center of town as the sun hung high in the sky. There'd be no crowd waiting to watch our passing here, like back in Shadrach. We steamed casually on. We thought we'd be alone in Johnson City, right before the first shot rang out through the warm air.

I was resting in the caboose, with the table down, attempting to rest my head, when the first shot echoed through the trees. Fluky was with me. Mitty was at the controls. It seems that he'd shown himself, the day I was in and out of consciousness, as quite adept at piloting *The Cordwainer*. We'd never credited

Mitty with ownership of a pair of particularly keen eyes, but he had almost a sixth sense for the lay of the track ahead. Fluky said they'd avoided a pair of derailments the day before simply because Mitty had been at the controls, and he was more than happy to let Mitty sit at the controls.

When the shooting started, Mitty instantly cut off all the power. *The Cordwainer* came rolling to a halt, on a slight downward grade, as another shot rang out. Fluky and I plainly heard the ricochet from the prow of the train and leapt to our feet. We met Mitty scrambling back along the running boards, half ducked down for cover.

"What the hell?" Fluky yelled forward.

"Black car!" Mitty yelled back. "Parked on the tracks!"

I risked poking my head up over the top of the hopper cars and strained to look towards the horizon. Sure enough, not two hundred yards down the grade, at what possibly amounted to the center of Johnson City, was the second black car, parked across the tracks, with two dark figures hiding behind it for cover. A third shot rang out and I saw the muzzle flash over the hood of the car. They were shooting at us with handguns. It was extreme range, but I heard the terrifying whiz of the bullet pass through the air above me.

They were shooting at us!

"When'd this become a shootin' war?" Fluky asked, ducking as the bullet whizzed by.

It was my fault, I realized; I'd fired the first shot. All right, it'd been a dud, but the evidence was there. Of course, they wouldn't be asking any more questions, taking any prisoners, not after we'd started shooting at our perusers back in Shadrach. No one had been hurt, but they wouldn't be taking any chances.

Another shot and another ricochet off the HTP tank at the nose of *The Cordwainer*. The HTP! If a bullet punctured that tank... I had first-hand experience with a BLEVE already, and wasn't eager to be in the vicinity of another.

"We got to back it up!" I yelled.

"Back it up? Dang thing ain't got no *reverse*!" Fluky yelled at me. For the first time the overconfidence we had shown during the whole affair hit home. No reverse. Of course not, why would we want to ever go backwards – back to Boot Hill?

"If a bullet punctures that fuel tank!" I yelled. "If they get a lucky shot and hit a fuel line!"

"I know, I know!" Fluky yelled back.

"Perhaps we should execute 'Protocol Ohm's Law'!" Mitty yelled to Fluky, ignoring me.

"Hell!"

"What's 'Protocol Ohm's Law'?" I asked, looking between Fluky and Mitty.

"Nothin'," Fluky shook his head.

"It seems befitting!" Mitty added.

"Oh, hell!"

"If you two have an idea..." A shot rang out, we all ducked.

"Ah, the tartarhead is gonna get us all killed!" Fluky bellowed, but he was fiddling with the cover of the hopper car he was holding onto the side of.

"What are we doing?" I asked as I tried to help.

"Get the covers off," he said. "Get in. On top of the boots. Don't touch anythin' metal."

We slid the cover off each hopper car and Mitty and I climbed in amongst the boots. The shooting continued intermittently, occasional shots plinking off something metal. Fluky moved up to the cockpit of the train, keeping low and out of the line of fire. He opened up a cowling on the engine, fiddled around inside for a few seconds as shots skipped off the engine around him, then he was up in the cockpit at the controls. The second he had the train moving, he leapt from the cockpit and landed in the center of the closest hopper car, in amongst the shoes.

The Cordwainer was rolling forward, towards where the black car sat parked on the tracks. We kept our heads down as the shooting intensified and Fluky rolled closer. We weren't moving fast, perhaps two or three miles an hour. Fluky must have barely turned the potentiometer. There was a crescendo of gunshots as the train rolled up to the road block, only halting for the Concession men to reload. *The Cordwainer* ran directly into the side of the black car – at limited speed, but with great mass – and pushed the car along the tracks for a few feet. But it was all too heavy for the train to push too far and the whole mass of steel came grinding to a halt.

Whatever "Protocol Ohm's Law" was it must have failed. Perhaps if Fluky had gotten more of a run up. But using the HTP tanker as battering ram would have been insanity. As it was, only the cow catcher at the prow of the train had hit the parked car. Now we were sitting ducks, hidden down in the hoppers full of boots. All the Concession goons had to do was climb aboard and shoot us like fish in a barrel.

I peeked over the rim of my hopper as the first of the Concession men came out from behind cover. There seemed to be three of them in their black suits, holding automatic handguns, training them along the length of *The Cordwainer.* The first man cautiously came up beside the cockpit of the engine, covering it with his gun. When he found it empty, he shifted his handgun to his other hand and reached out for the small ladder that brought you from ground level up to the running boards of the train.

He grabbed hold of the ladder and stopped.

I couldn't quite make out why he had paused and a second Concession man came up beside him. The second man gave the first a few words of encouragement, then gave his friend a helpful push up onto the ladder. Instantly, the second man froze to the spot. I raised my head up for a better look, unsure what was happening. From my new vantage point I could see the two men locked together, shaking slightly in place. I placed a hand on the edge of the hopper car, to lean out, and got a solid electric shock from the metal of the hopper car. The whole train was electrified!

I was so surprised by the shock that I almost missed what happened next. A third Concession man come around the other side of *The Cordwainer.* He was distracted by the behavior of his comrades and caught off guard when Mitty let out a banshee yell from within his hopper. It was a blood curdling scream, like the onrush of a berserker. Mitty jumped to his feet and leapt into the air above the third Concession man. The poor Concession man had only a second to react in shock – nowhere near enough time to raise his gun – before Mitty came crashing down, more projectile than combatant, onto his target.

Fluky jumped forward, animal-like, and landed on his thick-soled boots on the roof of the cockpit. With a swift kick he dislodged the two Concession men from their frozen positions. They crumpled in a heap to the ground. Fluky jumped down, ready to strike, but his two targets were already incapacitated.

It was the fourth Concession man that surprised us.

Luckily, after seeing the fate of his friends, the fourth Concession man decided that it was time to beat a retreat. He was hidden away behind the wheel of the black car as the action had unfolded around him. He fired the engine of the black car to life and slammed the car into gear. It squealed out, laying a track of rubber on the cement, as I jumped down from my hopper car. I scooped up the handgun dropped by the man Mitty had literally flattened and I raised it, pointing after the escaping car. If I'd understood the safety, perhaps I'd have gotten a shot off, but by the time I had the lever on the side pushed down, the black car was already swerving wildly onto the dirt of the rural highway, heading east.

So that was "Protocol Ohm's Law". One more thing no one had bothered to tell me about. Fluky had had the idea and discussed it with Mitty. The risk of igniting the HTP was a real possibility, he'd realized, so he'd shelved the whole idea. Mitty, it seems, had not. With *The Cordwainer* running on rubber tires and the crossbars being tipped in rubber to prevent wear, it was almost totally insulated from ground. It wasn't a half bad idea, apart from the fact that it could have blown us all to kingdom come.

The two electrocuted Concession men were unconscious but still very much alive. The one Mitty had flattened was in worse shape; it looked like Mitty had quite seriously broken his leg. He was conscious and very unhappy, but I kept his gun pointed at him and let him cuss at us while we got *The Cordwainer* ready for the rails again. One of the front wheels had derailed when we'd hit the car, so we cranked it up and pulled it back on the track. We took their guns and extra magazines and left the Concession men beside the track as we continued to steam off through Johnson City. We figured their fourth companion would be back soon enough with the cavalry, whoever that would be, and they'd be picked up.

It was a better deal, we were sure, than they would have given us.

Chapter Twenty-Five

Marmont

We were giddy, on a battle high, as *The Cordwainer* rolled out of Johnson City. Perhaps from this elation, we let our guard fall a little. Outside of Johnson City, we soon found ourselves amongst the high pines. The grade was climbing steeply now as the land raised up into the mountains, and *The Cordwainer* began to strain heavily to pull its load. Even with the fuel value and the potentiometer fully open, the train was managing little more than a walking pace. A fact Fluky took full advantage of anytime he needed to pee, by leaping from the cockpit, doing his business in the bushes, and making it back in time to catch the passing caboose. Mitty and I, being less athletic, simply opened the rear doors of the caboose and peed out onto the tracks. But each to his own.

It was late afternoon when the trees around us finally broke and we found ourselves amongst cultivated, terraced slopes either side of the Stephenson gauge tracks. It was obvious that the hillsides had been planted long after the end of the service on the Northern Pacific, as many of the bushes – vines perhaps – crisscrossed over the tracks. *The Cordwainer* unthinkingly pushed its way though, cutting a swath of destruction up the hillside.

Grapes, I realized, pulling a bunch off the running board near the cockpit. The vines were grape vines. I tasted one and spat it out. Bitter. Mitty's map told us that we were no more than a mile or two from the town of Lode, the last settlement we'd encounter before the pass through the mountains. But the map gave the impression that Lode was a mining community. We had little reason to suspect that it would be anything other than a ghost town, like Johnson City.

But acres upon acres of grape vines planted as far as the eye could see either side of *The Cordwainer* told us that Lode was potentially neither abandoned nor focused on mining.

We caught glimpses of figures amongst the vines as evening began to set in. People out tending to their crops. Dark, Negro faces, most women, watched in horror as we tore our way through their vines. In all honesty, we were as shocked to see such faces as they were to see a peroxide fueled train suddenly steam its way through their pastoral calm.

Black faces? It was perhaps the last thing I had expected to see in the mountains. Boot Hill may have been almost completely Caucasian, except for a few Oriental faces like Fluky, but the Big City was a far more cosmopolitan place. America, however, remained a tightly segregated place. To see colored people outside of an urban setting. In the mountains above Boot Hill. Tending to grapes. It was a shock.

Of course there was the stereotype of the poor, rural Southern black field hand, but we were a thousand miles away from the cotton fields of Virginia. And none of the vine tenders I saw as we cut through the vineyard fit the stereotype I had in my head. They were all dressed in blue coveralls and boots, like my Worker B's back on Number Six. They watched us with open-mouthed befuddlement as *The Cordwainer* rolled by. Where exactly were we?

If the sight of the vines and their colored vine tenders had come as a shock, it was nothing compared to the surprise that was coming next.

The Cordwainer finally broke through the tangle of vines and crested a small rise. Down in a valley, directly in line with the Stephenson gauge tracks, where on the map it told us the town of Lode lay, was the loveliest little French village you could imagine. A cluster of old, stone buildings with shingle roofs were nestled into the trees beside a medieval church complete with steeple. A majestic white stone château sat on the hillside overlooking it all. In the cockpit, Mitty, at the controls, cut out the engines, bringing us to a halt. All three of us climbed up onto the top of the hoppers and stared at the sight in slack-jawed amazement.

It was beautiful. Like a place out of a dream. The postcard setting for a postcard town. It couldn't be real, it just couldn't.

But there it was, directly in the path of the Stephenson rails. If we'd been less taken aback, if it had been any normal sort of town, we'd have approached it with so much more care. But the whole place was like a dream. When the sound of a car motor rose up from the valley below, none of us reacted. It was only when it was too late that we realized that a car was driving out of that most perfect of sights and heading towards us.

In our good fortune, it was not a black sedan. It was green, army style jeep, speeding towards us, loaded with men in brown uniforms. When we realized what it was, who was approaching, we attempted to get *The Cordwainer* once again underway, but it was too late. The jeep pulled up beside the train and unloaded off the back three men with rifles. They cocked their guns and pointed them up at us, yelling incoherently. I stood motionless on top of a hopper car, wisely not reaching for the automatic in my belt. To add to the confusion, all the soldiers seemed to be black too, like the vine tenders out in the fields.

They yelled and manhandled Fluky, Mitty and myself off the train. We were pushed up against the hood of the jeep and searched. The three automatics we had taken from the Concession goons were found. It was then that I realized that the men in the jeep were not soldiers. They wore army pea coats, yes, and carried Garands, but their military clothes were mixed in with civilian attire. One of the men was wearing running shoes that I recognized as a style we made in Boot Hill.

With the three of us safely secured, and constantly covered by at least one gun barrel, the men from the jeep turned their attention to *The Cordwainer.*

"What the hell is this thing?" one of the men said from the running board beside the cockpit. He was looking in at the controls.

"Is it a truck or a train?" another commented, bending over, looking under the chassis. "It got wheels like a truck but it's running on the tracks..."

"What inside of there?" yet another yelled up to the first. The man at the cockpit moved back and lifted the cover on the first hopper slightly.

"Looks like boxes..."

"Boxes of what?"

The first man reached in and came out with a shoe box. He removed the lid, throwing it away, and pulled out a pair of work boots. "Boots?" he said in disbelief.

"Boots?" the man covering us with his rifle turned around in disbelief, momentarily forgetting about his prisoners.

"Boots," The first one confirmed, throwing the pair of boots down for inspection.

"Boots!" Mitty said happily, smiling. Our guard suddenly remembered us and brandished the gun at us.

"That whole train is full of boots?" the guard asked Mitty down the length of the gun.

"Yes, ten thousand pairs!" Mitty volunteered.

"What the hell? What sort of crazy people are you?"

"Oh, we're not crazy," Mitty smiled, looking all the more crazy.

"Then what the hell is that thing?" our guard gestured at *The Cordwainer.*

"It's our train, it runs on hydrogen peroxide. Beanie here built it. Well, not exactly. His blew up, but his sister built us-"

"I asked you 'what the hell is that thing'?" the guard interrupted, poking Mitty in the chest with his barrel.

"It's very temperamental!" I replied, yelling up to the man on the running board, who had returned to the cockpit and was leaning in, fiddling with controls. At my warning, he ducked back out and dropped down off the running board. "As my friend said, it's just a train. We're on our way with a shipment of footwear, bound for the Big City. We're sorry for any damage we did to your vines back there, but they've grown up over the tracks. If we'd realized we'd be steaming through your fields..."

"You're them..." The man sitting behind the wheel of the jeep spoke up. He'd been silent up until then, watching, holding an automatic in his right hand.

"Yes, perhaps..." I replied. I was confused, but I thought it best not to contradict the men with the guns.

"You're them, from on the radio..." he continued. "You have to be, from Boot Hill..."

"Yes, that's us!" Mitty spoke up.

"Oh my God..." he was happy, amused. "I can't believe it. Right here in Marmont."

"Sorry, where?" I asked.

"Marmont," he said, pointing off towards the sleepy Gallic town with his handgun.

"Oh, our map said this was Lode."

"Yes, maybe, once upon a time..." he replied, still obviously amused by our presence. Then he realize that our guard was still pointing a gun at us. "Hey, José, point that thing somewhere else. Do you realize who these guys are?"

"Some crazy sons-of-bitches?" our guard replied, lowering his rifle.

"These are the guys the radio was squawking on about, José! The big, bad desperados that shot their way out of Boot Hill, killing hundreds! Don't they just look like a gang of big, bad desperados to you, José?"

Our guard smirked.

"We- we haven't killed anyone..." I protested.

"Oh, yes?" the driver of the jeep didn't seem surprised. "Well, that wasn't what the radio had to say. Said we should be on the lookout for the outlaws that shot up Boot Hill. Armed and dangerous, you're supposed to be. Can't say the three of you look all that dangerous, though, even if you are armed. The radio didn't say anything about a train full of boots, either. Said something about running guns for the Polypigs..."

"We ain't got any guns!" Fluky exclaimed, almost perfectly timing his protests to the uncovering of the .38 revolvers in the caboose. "Well, none that we ain't carryin' for self defense only..."

The driver behind the wheel of the jeep gave us all a wide, toothy grin.

"You're injured," he said, pointing at the bandage around my head. He put his gun away and reached down to turn on the ignition. "Get in," he ordered as the engine turned over. He turned to the men with rifles, "You guys stay here and guard that... thing."

The man driving the jeep was named Mitchell. Young and sharp-eyed, dressed in an army jacket and pants, he drove Fluky, Mitty and myself at a high rate of speed back down the narrow country lane – back towards town. He chatted pleasantly as he piloted the jeep, giving the impression we were honored guests, not prisoners.

In answer, when I queried if the town was actually Lode or Marmont, he replied, "There was a town here once, but I can't recall the name. Lode sounds as good a name as any. Mining town, when there was still mining to be done. This," he pointed proudly towards the rapidly approaching town, "is Marmont."

"But," I didn't know exactly how the phrase it. "It's a French..."

"Bordeaux, to be exact." he agreed with a chuckle, yelling over the noise of the engine. "You see, back in the War, after D-day, when Patton was pushing into France from Spain, the Nazis took a page from the Russian play book, started a scorched earth policy. As they retreated and the Americans advanced, they burned all the crops, poisoned the water. Did this all the way across the Bordeaux region. Seeded the vineyards with radium. Nothing can grow there again for two thousand years. Destroyed the French wine industry. Whole region of France was completely depopulated after the War. Nothing but ghost towns."

The jeep pulled off the dirt of the twisting country lane and onto Marmont's cobbled streets. The town was bustling with people, turning to glance at the Jeep as it sped down the street. Two things were instantly obvious as we rode through town: Everyone in Marmont was black, and everyone is Marmont carried a gun. The whole place had an air of a military camp, crossed with a sleepy, industrious rural community. Even the women, in peasant skirts and blouses, carried guns in holsters on their hips.

"So there's this General, Molloy. He's with Patton during the big push into Paris, and afterward sees the destruction the Nazis left behind. Later on he's Interior Secretary during Kennedy's first term. Reads in a report that the eastern slopes of these mountains are prime wine-growing country. Perfect combination of rain and sun. Totally unexploited. Rare opportunity. Remembers all those forgotten Bordeaux villages back in France, just sitting idle, and gets the hair to break one down, brick by brick, and ship it over here to America."

"You're joking," I said as the jeep skidded to a halt in front of a Tabac near the center of the town. Mitchell threw on the parking brake and cut out the engine.

He kept talking as he climbed out of the vehicle, "No, no joke! Completely serious. Government is going to jump-start a wine industry in the Northwest. Tap into an under-serviced market. Bring Bordeaux to the U.S. So they reassemble the whole town here in the mountains. Buildings, churches, châteaus and all."

We climbed out of the jeep after Mitchell and followed him through the front door of the Tabac. Inside, there were two men leaning at the counter, wearing berets, talking to a very attractive dark-skinned woman behind the counter.

"Amélie," Mitchell said as he stepped through the door, a tiny bell chiming our presence. The girl behind the counter turned to look and then did a double-take at the sight of Fluky, Mitty and myself walking into the store. She audibly gasped. "I have a patient for you."

The two men in berets, with submachine guns propped up against the counter, eyed us suspiciously from head to toe. There was a tense moment of silence, as no one reacted. Mitchell sensed the tension and gestured towards a small metal bistro table off in a back corner of the shop.

We all crossed the store and sat down at the table. The two men at the counter tracked us closely. Mitchell waved the girl over and she came around the counter cautiously. There was a swift, hushed exchange of words and the girl turned on her heels, and then she scurried back behind her counter.

"You'll have to forgive the reception," Mitchell began, loud enough to be heard by the two men at the counter. "You see, Marmont has something of a siege mentality, surrounded as we are. Anyone with your complexion is automatically treated as a threat."

"We didn't mean to..." I began, drying my sweaty palm on my pants. "We're not..."

"No, no," Mitchell smiled. "I understand. But as for the rest..." he nodded his head towards the counter. The two men standing there took the hint and turned away from us, lighting up cigarettes and leaning back up against the counter.

"Why is-" I began, but was interrupted as the girl returned to our table. She was carrying a tray with a first-aid kit, a bottle of wine – a real glass bottle, not a carton – and four short, squat glasses. She put the tray down on the table and picked up the first-aid kit as Mitchell reached for the bottle of wine. As the girl began to remove the bandages from my forehead, Mitchell took out a pocket knife, folded out a corkscrew and pulled the cork from the bottle. He poured wine into the four glasses and passed them around.

Mitchell drank deeply, quickly finishing off his glass, and reached for the bottle to pour another. "Our local offering," he said, filling his glass. He looked at the label. "Last year's. Quite excellent. Please, give it a try." He gestured towards the glasses in front of us.

I reached for mine as the young girl opened the first-aid kit and began to doctor my head. The wine was excellent. Dry, but full bodied. I couldn't remember the last time I'd tasted anything like it – had a glass of wine at all, for that matter. Mitty and Fluky tentatively tasted theirs. Their reaction was more subdued. Neither of them had ever really been wine people.

I was starting to let my guard down as the wine warmed my belly. Mitchell was watching our expressions for hints of approval. I smiled, trying to indicate my pleasure, when Mitty interrupted, blurting out, "Why is everyone in this town colored?"

The girl's hand slipped and painfully jabbed at my bruise. I yelped in pain. The two men at the bar again turned around to regard us with suspicion. Fluky visibly flinched.

But Mitchell let out a deep belly laugh. The tension was broken. The two men at the counter saw Mitchell's reaction and let out strained chuckles themselves. The girl apologized and returned to dressing my head wound.

"So, this Molloy character," Mitchell continued, "hauls this whole Bordeaux town across the Atlantic, through the Panama Canal, and drops it right here, in the middle of some of the finest New World wine country you could possibly imagine. He spares no expense. He searches the world for exactly the right type of grapes to grow given the climate. Mix of Cabernet and Merlot and Syrah. The perfect mix for the perfect claret. Only one thing missing from his grand plan: The people to occupy his village. He couldn't box up the Frenchies and ship them along with the stone. No, not with the government footing the bill. He'd have to populate this new town with *American* vintners. 'Cause, ain't a whole hell of a lot of them sitting around, unemployed. Not even with a brand new, state-of-the-art, wine-making operation in the offering. But that doesn't deter old Molloy.

"Now, this is about the time the Supreme Court hands down Brown vs. Board of Education, about twenty years ago, telling the government they got to end segregation – separate but equal. There's a big push in the Administration behind this, to mainstream the Negro community – the old white, Southern power bloc being their number one political enemy. Molloy figures, if he's got to train up a whole new generation of American vintners, why not train up a whole new generation of *black* American vintners?"

I looked at Mitchell with a mix of shock and surprise. I looked over at the two men at the counter and up at the beautiful young girl tending to my forehead. If I hadn't seen it for myself I wouldn't have believed it.

"Only the best and brightest, you understand, with agricultural experience. Talent held down by white oppression. Packed us up and moved us all out to this part of the country, it having no great history of acrimony between the races – the West."

"Then what's with all the guns?" Fluky asked, finishing off the last of his wine. Mitchell picked up the bottle and again refilled all our glasses.

"In the beginning," he said, tasting his wine, "Things were peaceful. But then we had the army here, keeping order. A whole platoon. Buffalo soldiers, sure, but regular army. A few years pass, however, and the Administration starts to balk at the expense. The budget is getting tighter. They pull out the Negro platoon. Of course, everyone and his uncle Ed thinks this means it's open season on Marmont. All this time, the government has been funding and supplying us. We got stuff that the rest of the nation has been having to do without. Gas, diesel. We look like a big, round, juicy peach to all the locals. One they just have to come in and pluck. But that Negro platoon, before leaving, sort of forgot to pack up a lot of their equipment. You know how wasteful the army can be. But it's nice of them to leave behind a few extra guns and trucks so we're able to still defend ourselves. Well, the locals quickly learned that Marmont was no easy mark – we were ready to protect what they had."

The girl was finished dressing my head. She closed up the first-aid kit and took it with her back behind the counter.

"And the government didn't intervene?" I asked.

"Intervene?" Mitchell laughed. "Once we showed that we could defend ourselves – were willing to fight – they sent *more* guns. And food and clothes and what have you."

The girl returned with another tray. This one with a loaf of bread and a small plate of butter. Real butter! Not margarine! She put the tray down in the center of the table and took the empty wine bottle and tray away. Mitchell reached forward and pulled off a chunk of the bread and buttered it. Seeing our lascivious stares, he pushed the bread and butter towards us. Fluky, Mitty and I quickly scrambled to help ourselves.

Mitchell went on, "See, no one in the Administration wanted to see Marmont fail. It was the shining jewel in their domestic policy – showing their material commitment to their policies. The success of their progressive agenda. That they couldn't afford to protect us, as the years when on, greatly upset them, but when we proved we could protect ourselves, they were more than happy to give us what they could."

"That's amazing," I said, halfway between rapture and disbelief. "This - this is all amazing." I whirled a hand around my head, gesturing to everything.

"It is," Mitchell agreed. "We've had to fight hard to protect it. As the shortages have worsened, as things have became more dire in the outside world, the attacks have become more concerted. Early on, they came in ones or twos, thinking we'd make easy pickings, but lately... with the Polypigs..."

"And the government just kept supplyin' you?" Fluky asked. "All these years? When other folks are going short on the bare essentials?"

"They found us useful," Mitchell stately plainly.

"Now this is mighty nice," Fluky said, holding up his glass. "But it ain't *that* nice."

Mitchell looked at us across the bistro table, sizing us up. For a moment, I though Fluky had managed to finally insult him; but instead, he jumped to his feet and said, "Come on," waving for us to follow. We stood up, tentatively, looking at each other in confusion. We followed Mitchell back out into the street under the watchful eyes of the two men at the counter, and back into the jeep. Mitchell fired up the engine and we were again rocketing through the narrow cobble streets of Marmont, climbing up the hill toward the château.

"Of course, up here, there's no Concession train service. We have to truck everything in and out," Mitchell said as he drove. "With the price of diesel, that's prohibitively expensive. We try and be as self-sufficient as possible – keeping livestock, fabricating most of our own equipment – but we can't provide completely for our own needs. There's no land here to farm, to grow grain... If the Administration was to ever pull its support for Marmont, the wolves would set upon this town without mercy. We'd be a ghost town in a week."

We had arrived in the courtyard of the château. Mitchell parked the jeep abruptly and leapt free of it on the gravel of the courtyard. He crunched off across the gravel, still speaking, assuming our attention. We followed him across the courtyard and down through a basement entrance. The warmth of the day gave way to a cool, dry stone cellar, dominated by massive casks, ten feet each in diameter.

"Luckily, there is a lot of demand for the product we produce," Mitchell said, his voice echoing around the basement. "Without it, the nation would be in a much tougher position than it currently finds itself – and times are pretty bad. Everyone looks to the government to assure the supply and availability of our product. If it ever vanished from store shelves... well, it'd be all out war. That's why the Administration is so keen on keeping Marmont armed and supplied. Without us, the whole country could collapse into anarchy. It's a matter of national security to keep Marmont fully operational – a matter of maintaining domestic tranquility."

"Really?" I replied, as we moved quickly through the cellar of casks. "But I've never even heard of your wine before..."

"Of course not," Mitchell said as we reached a door at the far end of the cellar. He reached down to turn the handle, but paused before turning it. He finished his thought, "Nobody wants to drink colored wine."

He swung the door open and we stepped through, into a section of the cellar at least as large as the one we were departing. I was instantly hit by the pungent aroma, a smell both instantly overpowering and yet somehow familiar. Beyond the door, the cellar was dominated by giant vats of bubbling liquid and large contraptions of copper tubing. It instantly reminded me of The Shop – the dying vats where hemp was bleached of its natural hue. I was no expert in wine production, but nothing in this room looked like it was used in making wine.

"The wine is mostly for our consumption," Mitchell said, as Fluky, Mitty and myself looked up at the vast maze of copper and glass. "And occasionally some power brokers – those in the know. This here is the reason for Marmont's existence, the grease that keeps the wheels of America turning."

I breathed in again, the heady aroma, and the realization came washing over me, "McTavish," I said.

"I take it you're familiar with the product."

"This is where they make McTavish?!" Fluky said with glee, like a child finding Santa Claus's Workshop.

"For the western seaboard," Mitchell confirmed. "There's a dozen other distilleries dotted around the country, all making a product sold behind the label 'McTavish' from various sugar sources – corn, barley, fruit. Perhaps I'm biased, but I think we, by far, make the best-tasting version. Grapes add a subtle undertone to the whiskey."

"I've died and gone to heaven..." Fluky said solemnly.

Mitchell ushered us out, back into the wine cask section of the cellar, closing the door behind us.

He started off again, back across the cellar floor, back along the path we had followed to the door. "Of course, making large quantities of cheap liquor was never the intent. Marmont, from the beginning, was supposed to be a model community. A template for further experiments of its type. But the expense of our upkeep always required that we produce something... tangible. More than a few hundred cases of wine a season.

"The irony of it all, of course, isn't lost on anyone," Mitchell said as we came out of the cellar back into the courtyard. We walked across the gravel towards the jeep, where he paused before he climbed back into it. "To have all of this – for the government to have gone to such outrageous expense – for the mere production of cheap booze to keep the population docile... To be taught the fine craft of wine making, only to waste our talents on mass production of slop..."

Mitchell climbed back into the jeep and we loaded up beside him. He fishtailed the jeep around in the loose stone of the courtyard and exploded out back onto the streets of Marmont, driving wildly. He drove with complete abandon but significant skill, never missing a turn or coming near a pedestrian. I gripped the dash of the jeep tightly as we sped over the cobbles of the beautiful town. I was reminded of the many journeys I'd taken in Fluky's wrecking truck between Boot Hill and Pottersville, but Fluky was an amateur behind the wheel compared to Mitchell.

He followed the tight streets until we came to the square that faced onto the large, gothic church whose spire I'd seen from *The Cordwainer*. The square was fronted on its three other sides by numerous small, welcoming cafés. To one of these, Mitchell drove his jeep, parking at a curb beside its empty outdoor tables. It was, perhaps, too early for dinner, but Mitchell took a table out in the sun.

Chapter Twenty-Six

The Fallacy of Merit

"As I said," Mitchell said, as Fluky, Mitty and myself sat down at his table. "The irony isn't lost on anyone. But there is a certain inevitability to it, to our ignominious fate." A waiter, discreet in the background, appeared to welcome us all. Mitchell ordered wine, the waiter bowed and quickly vanished.

"This hardly seems ignominious..." Mitty questioned, looking around. It was the beginning of a lovely, warm summer evening. The mountains rose majestically all around us. If there was a more perfect spot on the planet I didn't know of it. The fresh air and the smell of cooking food in the restaurants all around; people enjoying the evening sitting in the square beside the small fountain at its center; bicycles riding by, ridden by young, beautiful, dark-skinned women. It felt like paradise.

"Perhaps," Mitchell shrugged. "But unsustainable. The cost, to run this town, for the value of the product that it produces. There will be a dark day soon when the cost and the value of Marmont must be reconciled," Mitchell said hauntingly, then shifted, "But it is an honor that you gentlemen were able to see Marmont at its best. To have such celebrities as yourselves, here at my table..."

The wine arrived. The waiter presented the bottle to Mitchell for his inspection. Approved, the waiter proceeded to open the bottle and pour out a small amount for Mitchell to sample. He sniffed it, tasted it, and nodded his acceptance.

"We're not celebrities," I said, expectantly watching my glass fill with red wine. "We're businessmen."

"Yes," Mitchell smiled. "And in this day-and-age, that means instant celebrity status. To be such a thorn in the side of the Concession, that pleases people no end – it please me no end.

To be desperados, outlaws, for what you're attempting to do. That fires the imagination – invigorates people."

I remembered the street in Shadrach. The line of dour faces on either side of the tracks. "We're just out trying to make a buck," I said honestly.

Mitchell shrugged, tasting his wine. "Now-a-days, that's damn near sedition."

I returned his shrug.

"Pursuit of the almighty buck has become a much maligned pastime by those of more refined sensibilities; but what is a dollar but a store of value – a metric to gauge the relative worth of one item compared another? Does a dollar, in itself, have any value greater than the value you assign to a product you wish to purchase with it? If the pursuit of a buck is reworded to indicate the buck's true roll as a unit of exchange, does it take on a more altruistic air? If you rephrased your comment to be: 'We're just out trying to create value', would you say it with such a sinister tone? No? Perhaps not.

"High-minded ideals might lead us to believe that money is the root of all evil, but if we pause to consider that the creation of wealth is merely the creation of value, we can see that money is at the root of very little at all except the value it represents, and the relative moral implications of that value, good or bad. That 'value' and 'values' are the same word, give or take a letter, is an illuminating coincidence: That our sense of value influences our values is a self-evident truth: We assign a higher value to things we value – we are willing to sacrifice more for that which we think is important. If money has little meaning beyond its store of value, then it's a simple translative operation to come to the conclusion that we assign a higher dollar value to things that conform to our values. To say that money is the root of all evil is a judgment call on the moral character of the pursuer of the money in question, not the money. The idiom never applies to one's own pursuit of cash – that's morally acceptable, of course, since it's obtained by a person of good moral character. Namely oneself.

"If, again, you rephrased your comment to 'we're just out trying to pursue our values', I think you might – again – say it with modicum of pride."

The waiter returned to refill our glasses. Mitchell ordered without help of the menu: Hors d'oeuvres, a beef main course, a salad course for four and more wine. The waiter nodded and turned on his heels to vanish back into the shadows of the café.

"I've never heard money spoken of in that way," I said.

"Misunderstanding value and money is at the center of all this," Mitchell said, with a gesture to the town of Marmont. "That is why I have such an interest in it. That this town was a gift from the centralized government, paid for by the taxes of the people of the United States, greatly burdens the people who live and work here."

"Wish I had your burden," Fluky smirked.

"Perhaps. But with all this handed up to us as a reconciliation for past wrongs, presents itself as a terrible moral hazard to the good people who chose to take the gift. That it was done for the best and most honest of reasons limits none of the ethical impact – absolves us of none of the risks."

"I don't follow." I shook my head.

"A fiscal transaction," Mitchell began, "has comparative advantage. Both parties profit from the interaction. One party gets the goods they purchased and the other gets money in proportion to the other party's value of the goods. It's a mutually beneficial situation because both parties profit: One in the goods they might not have otherwise been unable to obtain, the other in the difference between the value they assign to the good they sold and the value the purchaser assigns to them. Both parties profit, or the transaction would never have taken place.

"A charitable transaction, on the other hand, is not a mutually beneficial interaction. Ostensibly, one party is giving up something for the benefit of another – the giver is losing to the benefit of the receiver – but that's misguided. Charity is a double-edged sword. Look deeper, and you'll see that such a transaction proves itself to be a mutually *detrimental* situation. The giver loses the gift, correct, but the receiver also loses the *value* of the gift. Having not earned the gift, the receiver is unable to correctly value its worth – understand the gift in the context of its real cost. And, as I said, with value and values differing by only one letter..."

"Someone once told me," I began, thinking back to the cowboy sitting beside the campfire, "That you can only decide right from wrong for yourself. That no one else can dictate that to you."

"True," Mitchell agreed. The hors d'oeuvres were here. Pâté. There was silence as everyone hungrily dug into the appetizer. After chewing and swallowing, Mitchell continued, "It is true that the human soul is the only moral actor. But that in no way implies there is no such thing as right or wrong, right thinking from bad, no correct solution to difficult problems.

"Right and wrong can only be weighed by the individual, it is true, but that does not make it a subjective act. Right thinking leads to right actions, which receive rewards; wrong thinking leads to wrong actions, which are punished – not by any higher authority, but by the circumstances of life itself. But no individual is born with an innate sense of right and wrong. That we learn growing up, and through cxpcricnccs in our life. A misunderstanding of value distorts a person's sense of right and wrong, leading to suffering. One might conclude that it is a fickle, unjust universe, but that's simply the wrong thinking feeding on itself. Right thinking comprehends that right thinking leads to rewards, and that right thinking is based on solid values, and those values based on an honest, complex understanding of value.

"Take away the opportunity for people to make reasonable assessments of value for themselves and you take away the ability of people to change wrong thinking into right. Enter the government, with its unique power to redistribute wealth, and the misguided desire to build a better world, and you have a serious distortion to everyone's sense of value, as it shifts resources around, trying to help for the greater good.

"You can sympathize with their motivations – admittedly, even admire them. After all, it is incumbent on the runner who falls behind in the race to run twice as fast to have any hope of catching the leader. For the betterment of society – for the betterment of all – is it not the responsibility of the government to give the slower runner a helping hand?

"But the analogy is misleading, it implies that life is a merit based competition – the race being won by the fastest runner – but success in life is not so easily granted to the best and the brightest. Wealth and brains might be a great asset, but life is full with examples of the victory going to someone other than the most worthy. Why? Perhaps, because life is not a meritocracy.

"And a good thing too, for a meritocracy is simply another form of autocracy. Should we wish to live under the thumb of a self-appointed class simply because they are genuinely our betters? No, life rewards the maximization of value, not merit, and value is a truly democratic proposition.

"If right thinking leads to better decisions, which in turn lead to success; life is therefore predisposed to reward those with the best values – the keenest understanding of value – not those with the most money, or the best education, or the brightest ideas, or most powerful connections. And values are universal, both good and bad. A poor man can be true of heart just as easily as a rich man can be corrupted by his power. In fact, there's a predisposition for those conditions: Poverty teaching the harsh lessons and a sharp understanding of value, with wealth granting little but idleness and complacency.

"But government, with its munificence, is hell bent on helping for the wrong reasons. It is a poor student of the distinction between value and merit. Even at its best, progressive government is an attempt to reward merit – at its worse, it's an attempt to redefine it."

The main course arrived: Beef medallions in red wine sauce. The aroma was intoxicating. The plates were placed on the table and I quickly picked up my knife and fork. The dish was as exquisite as everything else about Marmont. I ate hungrily, as did Mitchell, Fluky and Mitty. We all remained silent until everyone's plate was clean. More wine was poured and the waiter reappeared to clear the dishes.

"Then you're saying," I said, picking up the conversation again after wiping my mouth clean with my napkin, "that you'd have been better off if the government had never given you this town?"

"No, of course not," Mitchell replied, leaning back in his chair, satisfied with his meal. "But Marmont is symptomatic of the society at large: An unsustainable high ideal. To run Marmont at a loss has required the redistribution of many resources. That redirection has required austerity in other areas of society. To fund us – to pay for this meal," Mitchell pointed at the table in front of us. Our salads came just in time to punctuate Mitchell's point. "Many other people have had to go without. Why? Because the government has decided that the merit of Marmont outweighs the cost to the society as a whole. But does its value? And has the government created the merit in Marmont that it was hoping to create? Has giving us this, without demanding its value in payment, taught the people of Marmont anything? Except how to be dependent on government?

"And that's the irony of Marmont: A grand experiment to foster merit in a world that does not reward it; a massive redistribution of wealth, only to manufacture the sedative to mollify the unfortunates whose wealth had to be redistributed to pay for it; a lesson in merit that's taught only dependence. That is Marmont, what you see around you. Why, I say that a dark day will soon come, when Marmont's value must be reconciled with its cost. It is this dark day that is coming, not just for Marmont, but for the whole nation. The bills that we've incurred must one day be paid in full. Mark my words."

Chapter Twenty-Seven

Red Line

Evening had fully fallen on Marmont's town square as the cheese plate and coffee emerged from within the café. The crowd in the square was growing thicker as people shuffled to and fro from the various cafés. The dinner hour was starting in earnest. All around us, the outdoor tables were filling with people, laughing and yelling out salutations to friends passing by. The air was beginning to chill and the sunset behind the mountains was coloring the sky a deep saffron. Mitchell's mood had grown grim as he finished his monologue, staring down into his coffee, contemplating the fate he had outlined so succinctly.

I felt the need to comfort him, assure him that things were really not as bad as all that. But I couldn't bring myself to make an utterance. I drank my coffee and sliced off cheese, topping it with quarters of apple and pear. I watched the faces of the other patrons sitting at the tables around us at the café; happy, warm, energetic faces enjoying a beautiful evening at the tail end of a beautiful summer. Here in Marmont.

Mitchell finished the last of his coffee and pulled himself up out of his seat. He clapped his hands together, rubbing is palms, announcing, "But I've wasted enough of you gentlemen's time. You have a train to catch!"

"What?" The three of us said in unison, equally insulted by the proposition that we should move even an inch after such an outstanding meal.

"We're free to go?" I asked. Perhaps I had already assumed it, but the fact had not been explicitly stated. It was not three hours ago that we'd been under an armed guard.

"Of course!" Mitchell said, with a dismissive wave. "I could never live with myself if I delayed you gentlemen any longer. Not with such an important mission to perform."

"What?" Fluky said despondently. "Leave?" But Mitchell was already on his way, returning back to his jeep. Fluky looked between Mitty and myself, all of us silently communicating our deep and resounding disappointment. "Why would anyone ever wanta leave this place?"

The summer evening. The food. Despite Mitchell's dire prognostications, I had to agree with Fluky. But I wearily pulled myself to my feet, and put a hand under Fluky's arm, pulling him to his. I moved him physically back to the jeep, lifting his dead weight back into the rear set.

Mitchell again fired the engine to life and accelerated in a wide arc around the square. Back, speeding through town, he drove rapidly up towards the winding country path and *The Cordwainer* – back to our train and his men faithfully standing guard.

He kept up the conversation as he drove, "I have to admit that I'm envious – envious of you gentlemen, with your very own enterprise sitting there, that you have struggled for and fought for and feared you'd lose at every turn." A heavy truck turned out onto the country road, forcing Mitchell to swerve. We missed it only by inches, but Mitchell hardly paused. "I can only envy you. With all of that within your grasp, almost in the free and clear, without owing it to anyone or anything..."

The jeep skidded to a halt twenty yards from the engine of *The Cordwainer*, right back at the spot where our detour had begun. Mitchell pulled on the handbrake and killed the engine, but he didn't step out of the car, "That you are up against great odds, I concede to you. That you may end up paying an awful price to find out the value of your enterprise, I sympathize. But I suggest that perhaps no one has yet fully grasped the value of the endeavor you have chosen to undertake, its true value beyond the simple worth of your cargo."

The men Mitchell had posted to guard our train came over to the jeep, grumbling about the lateness of the hour. Mitchell ignored them, hands still on the wheel, speaking into the evening air.

"That the Concession has reacted so violently to your enterprise, that it has conscripted the government into helping it, that it is acting to stop you any way it can, is only understandable. To allow you to slip through, even this one train with the world watching on, would so undermine its legitimacy... It would set an example for everyone living under the Concession's thumb that there can be commerce outside of its direct control."

He nodded at *The Cordwainer*, sitting quietly on the tracks, "That lesson is cargo on that train, in addition to those hoppers full of boots. And the Concession is hell bent on making sure that the three of you pay the full bill, for the whole value of everything you're hauling. Yes, what you are attempting to do is dangerous; and yes, those opposing you will kill you if they must. But to cross these mountains and to deliver your cargo into the Big City... it would be to earn the right to say you did this thing, and that the profits from the enterprise were honestly yours and fairly earned. The value of that, I can only envy. That's value only you three – when you reach the terminus of these tracks – will truly be able to understand."

Fluky, Mitty and I climbed slowly out of the jeep, letting Mitchell's words slowly sink in. His men quickly and noisily took our places in the jeep, complaining about the cold. I came around to the driver's side and held out a hand for Mitchell to shake. He took it and shook it warmly.

"These tracks," he said, pointing his free hand over his shoulder, back towards town, "are old but still serviceable. We've maintained them for some distance into town – we use them at harvest. They will lead you below the village, through the saddle of the valley. As the valley climbs again, on the far side of town, the land will open up onto our Commons. The old tracks bisect this. You can rest the night there in perfect safety. I'll inform the town that, at sunrise, if they make their way to the commons with goods for trade, you'll be waiting."

"All right..." I replied.

"Beyond that, it's a steep climb, along the north side of a valley. There's a tunnel, still passable, which will bring you out at the mouth of the pass." Mitchell turned over the engine of the jeep, took off the brake and put the jeep in reverse. He looked back over his shoulder as if to pull out, but paused, "All summer, army trucks have been moving up that valley. Word is, the army has the Polypigs penned up in that pass – penned up from the west and the east. Every other day we see planes, circling. You might need these." He leaned back and took our pistols off one of his men, handing them back one at a time. "Remember: The word on the radio is you're running guns up to the Polypigs; the army won't want you hauling that load of yours through their lines. And as for the Polypigs... well, you can never predict their reaction. They raided into Marmont once or twice a few years ago, but we bloodied their nose well enough they haven't tried since."

"Thanks," I said, handing pistols back to Fluky and Mitty, holding mine by its barrel. "Thank you for everything... for dinner."

"You're welcome," Mitchell replied. Again, looking back over his shoulder. He accelerated quickly back, turning the jeep, then slammed it into first. "Remember, sunrise on the commons!" he yelled as the jeep sped away. "I'll bring wine!" his voice vanished into the distance.

What a singular evening. It felt like a dream. My belly was still full, but already my memory was beginning to fade as to the details of the dinner and conversation with Mitchell. The reality of *The Cordwainer* – its physical fact – came flooding back, pushing out everything else from my mind. I loaded my pistol and returned it to my waistband and climbed up onto the running board beside the cockpit. Fluky was already inside, looking over the gauges.

"That was one crazy-ass dinner party," he said, turning on the valve for the fuel tanks. Mitty was forward, by the flywheel, turning it by hand. As soon it was spinning under its own power, steam began to pour from the exhaust pipe.

"Food for thought," I said.

"You wanta hang around over there in that there meadow? For tradin'? We could push on in the dark, maybe make up some lost time."

"Mitchell said he'd bring wine," I smiled. "Seems like that's worth the wait."

"Hell yeah," Fluky agreed.

In the encroaching dark, we moved *The Cordwainer* slowly down through the valley, past the low, squat barn-like building that covered the valley floor, and up into the wide open, treeless field that constituted Marmont's Commons. The town glittered silently across the valley from us as we locked down the train for the night, and huddled up in the caboose attempting to catch what sleep we could before sunrise.

I was blissfully lost to the world when the first of the villagers came across the valley bearing goods in trade. One became two and two quickly became a crowd as the whole town of Marmont evidently had woken with the sun and made its way to the Commons. We did a brisk business. Bread, cheese, cured meats – the caboose was quickly full of all the food and provisions we could possibly require for the rest of our journey. Mitchell showed up with two cases of Marmont's best claret, in real glass bottles, like had been served to us the evening before. This we traded him for a dozen pairs of boots and three pairs of loafers.

Many, however, came with cold hard cash in hand, and we started selling boots to these people at thirty dollars a pair. It quickly became obvious that we were well below market value – the demand could have easily bore a higher price – but in part I was considering the hospitality Marmont had shown us when I'd decided on the thirty dollar figure. I felt no need to maximize our profits here, as much as I knew Mitchell would object. Thirty dollars, to me, seemed fair, and by nine o'clock, we had sold over three hundred pairs. Mostly, to people buying six or seven pairs at a time, stocking up. As the crowd began to disperse, Fluky and I looked down into our hands and realized we had over ten thousand dollars between us. It was more money than I had ever seen in my life – more money that I could have earned in two years working at The Shop. We tried hard to stay calm, not to be overwhelmed by the extent of our success. In the caboose, we found a hemp sack and filled it with the cash, stowing it away under one of the bench seats.

I should have been watching Mitty. While Fluky and I were trading for goods and cash, he was near the rear of the train making deals for himself – quite astutely, I should add. He was not taking advantage of anyone or being taken advantage of. He came away with over a thousand dollars of his own from our morning of trading. But the problem was, he also came away with a shiny Thompson submachine gun and a pair of rotary magazines he traded for sixty pairs of boots. I was flabbergasted: Mitty with a machine gun! I almost made him give it back, but he was vague about exactly who he had traded with and what exactly for. The sun was rising in the sky and we were eager to continue our journey... and... well, the damn thing made him so *happy*... sitting on the roof of the caboose holding the gun across his lap.

By ten, our profits nestled snugly away out of sight, we had the turbine of *The Cordwainer* belching steam and the nose pointed up towards the steep climb, and the tall pines above us. The valley that divided us from Marmont began to open up towards the south as we climbed, the tracks splitting away from the mountain road that climbed the opposite face of the valley. A morning mist hid the valley floor beneath us as the rock walls climbed steeply up the mountainside to our right.

The Cordwainer scuttled along the thin ledge between cliff face and precipice, gaining altitude with every hour of our journey. Perhaps it was my imagination, but the ledge that the rails clung to began to grow thinner as we climbed. If we were to derail here... I tried not to think about it. I was in the rear, in the caboose with Mitty, while Fluky was at the controls. I had to resist the urge to look out and over the edge as we steamed on. I knew it'd do me no good to know how far the fall really was.

"Quite the ride, wouldn't you say?" Mitty said. He was sitting at the bench across the table from me, gripping the table's edge with white knuckles. With each big lurch this way or that he flinched visibly.

"Stimulating," I agreed. I reminded myself that a century of rail freight had ridden these rails daily, without a mishap. Of course, the track back then had had the benefit of routine maintenance. Nothing and no one had traveled these tracks in over thirty years. We hit a solid bump and I could feel the caboose list dangerously to the left. I grabbed at the table's edge, like Mitty, hanging on for dear life.

"I've been thinking," Mitty began. The cigarette in its holder had burned down to its nub. Mitty hadn't attempted to replenish it; to do so would have required letting go of the table. "What Mitchell said back there, in Marmont..."

"Yeah..."

"Well, that is us, isn't it?"

"What?" I hadn't been listening, looking tentatively out the caboose's left window. "What's us?"

"The slowest runners. Well, at least me. Back of the pack, so to speak." He paused as the train gave another lurch. "But if everything he said – if the race isn't won by the fastest. Well, I'm better off being me, aren't I? In the end. That I could do this." A hand came up momentarily to gesture around the caboose, but quickly clamped back down tight as *The Cordwainer* wavered. "It proves it, doesn't it?"

"Yes, Mitty," I replied with a smile. "I think it does."

Mitty smiled back, making himself ever so slight taller in his seat.

Then *The Cordwainer* lurched again.

But this time it was different. Until that moment, as *The Cordwainer* circled clockwise around a rock face, the old rusty tracks had been tipping us left and right, but this lurch was backwards. *The Cordwainer* was suddenly picking up speed. Mitty and and I looked at each other with concerned interest. That was wrong – if anything we needed to slow down our accent, not speed it up.

I pulled myself to my feet, up onto the table, and slipped through the sunroof of the caboose. I yelled a query up the length of the train to Fluky in the cockpit. He was hunkered down over the controls. At the sound of my voice, he glanced back and then started pointing frantically to the port side of the train. I looked off into the mist, attempting to make out what he was gesturing at.

At first, it was all a haze – a wet, misty blob of gray – then something through the clouds resolved into view, a silhouette of something up against the south wall of the valley. I strained my eyes to see through the mist. The haze began to clear and I could, momentarily, make out the outline of a canvas-covered truck, parked on the mountain road, idle in the distance. My brain took a moment to center itself on its significance.

The Army.

If only the fog has remained as thick as we pushed on up along the edge of valley, but luck was not on our side. The heavy truck, still in the distance, began to resolve into ever clearer focus. The mist was lifting. I pulled myself up out of the caboose and scrambled across the hopper cars toward the cockpit. By the time I had reached Fluky in the cockpit, the scene had cleared enough for me to plainly make out the sandbagged machine gun nest, pointed west up the valley.

"Fluky!" I yelled, and he turned to face me. I could see his fist had the big red button on the console mashed down. *The Cordwainer* was picking up steam as diesel was injected into the hydrogen peroxide mix. The steam from the exhaust had turned black, thick with the soot of the burning petroleum.

Across the valley, I could see that we'd been spotted. Figures were moving behind the sandbags, but the machine gun was pointing in the wrong direction – up into the mountains – they weren't prepared for any threats approaching from the east. They were scrambling to move their weapon, bring it around to bear across the valley.

"Fluky!" I yelled again, though I'm not entirely sure why I wanted his attention. He didn't raise his hand up off the big red button, but he pointed frantically towards the nose of the train. I looked up, my attention had been so absorbed with the threat across the chasm of the valley I hadn't bothered to look where we were going. Small in the distance, but distinctly there, was the mouth of a tunnel cut into the cliff face. It was perhaps a quarter mile ahead, but the distance between us and it was entirely open to the far side of the valley. If they got that machine gun brought around... *The Cordwainer* was picking up steam, but...

The machine gun belched a few test rounds of fire. I heard the whiz of the bullets over my head and the bone-shaking crack as they hit the cliff wall. I dropped flat to my belly, hugging the roof of the foremost hopper. Then a long burst of fire came and I pressed my face firmly down against the steel. I could hear the sound of ricochets all around me. I dared not move. I stole a quick glance up and could see Fluky curled up in a ball as low down in the cockpit as possible, his hand shooting up bolt straight, keeping his palm on the red button.

The mouth of the tunnel was approaching.

There was a pause in the shooting and I took the opportunity to slide off the right side of the hopper onto the running board, with only inches between me and the moving rock face. I was more satisfied with the cover this position afforded me, and risked raising up my head high enough to look across the valley. The machine gun was jammed or out of ammunition; the two men manning it were pulling off a belt and putting on another one. The gun was resting unattached to any mount on top of the stacked sandbags, slightly off kilter. They'd had to dismount it from its base to bring it around to bear. They finished up whatever they were working on and the gun barked to life again. I ducked down, dropping to my knees on the running board, but not before I saw how much the machine gun was kicking around as they fired it. They weren't going to hit anything that way.

The tunnel was well within view now. I could see into its darkness as a chain of massive thumps slammed into the side of the hoppers. I ducked down deeper, almost laying flat on the running board, fearing the bullets would cut right through the hoppers full of boots. Another burst of fire came and flecks of rocks rained down from above me.

Then, from the rear of the train, I heard another string of shots – this time much closer and louder. I looked up, heaving myself up to my knees to see. Mitty had his upper torso through the sunroof of the old woody station wagon, the Thompson in his hands. He had let rip with a long stream of fire from one of the rotary magazines. Cigarette in its holder, pinched between his lips, he had a look of dogged determination on his face. The hose of bullets seemed to fly wildly across the valley, harmlessly peppering the far cliff wall; but Mitty's torrent of fire seemed to do its trick. The men manning the far machine gun ducked down behind the cover of their sandbags. When Mitty's weapon ran dry, they tentatively poked their heads up over the edge, then frantically attempted to return the machine gun to action. But we were another two hundred feet closer to the tunnel by the time they managed to bring their gun back to bear.

They had the rear of *The Cordwainer* in their sights by then, and Mitty and the caboose took an awful hail of fire. Mitty dropped down back through the sunroof and the wood of the old station wagon threw up a cloud of splitters. I feared that Mitty had been hit and pulled myself to my feet to move back toward the rear of the train; but before I could move, I was distracted by a call from Fluky. I turned to look and noticed the walls of the fast approaching tunnel. There wouldn't be room for me and it along the side of the train. I quickly shimmied back and slipped into the gap between two hopper cars as the tunnel engulfed us.

Still the machine gun rattled away, sending bullets down the tunnel after us. We plunged into darkness, deeper and deeper, until the sound of gunfire faded behind us. Then I could feel the speed of *The Cordwainer* yield. The choking steam of the exhaust abated, and the train slowly began to roll to a halt.

In the darkness I fumbled for a hand hold and pulled myself blindly up and onto the roof of a hopper. There was a number of feet of clearance here, and I reached up on my knees until I touched the dank, soot-encrusted ceiling of the tunnel. My eyes were adjusting to the darkness, but still there was little I could make out: The faint glow of the tunnel's mouth in the distance behind us and the soft luminescence of *The Cordwainer's* turbine cowling in front of me. Fluky must have really red lined her to make it glow like that, I contemplated. I could hear the hiss of steam as water condensed on the engine and evaporated again – the creaking of the steel as the turbine cooled.

I was contemplating moving – if I should fumble around in the dark – when then beam of Mitty's pen light came flicking from the rear of the train. It danced around like a miniature spotlight across the ceiling of the tunnel, then scanned down until it was shining right in my face.

"Are you okay, Mitty?" I asked, raising a hand to shield my eyes.

"I'm hunky dory," Mitty replied. "But a case of that Marmont wine was forced to give its life so others might live..."

"Fluky?" I called back up toward the nose of the train.

"Yeah, yeah," Fluky replied. "Can't kill ol' Fluky that easy."

"And *The Cordwainer*?" I asked. "The engine?"

"Buried that temperature needle right past the red line. Think that maybe we should let her cool down a little."

"They had a machine gun," I stated. "They were trying to shoot us with a machine gun." I breathed heavily, the adrenaline only then starting to hit me, making me dizzy.

"Yeah, good thing they can't shoot worth shit." Fluky laughed.

"They seemed to be getting the hang of things near the end there," Mitty added. His pen light was flashing between the faces of Fluky and me.

"Shit, shine that damn thing someplace else!" Fluky objected, holding up a hand. Then he asked Mitty, "Were that you? At the end there, rat-a-tattin' away?"

"Yes!" Mitty said with pride, holding something up in the darkness. I could just make out the shape of the submachine gun in his hand. "However, I don't believe I hit anything."

"Didn't much matter," I said. "It was good shooting nevertheless. You got another drum for that saw?"

"Somewhere in the caboose."

"You might want to load it up and keep an eye peeled that way," I pointed in the dark, mostly for my own benefit. "Can't imagine they'll be in any serious rush to follow us down into the tunnel, but might as well be on the safe side."

"Understood," Mitty snapped to attention, then the pen light flashed around and snaked back into the caboose. Fluky and I were left again standing in the blackness.

"Mitchell said the pass is just beyond the other end of this tunnel." I could just make out Fluky's silhouette against the glow of the turbine cowling. "We must have run the army's eastern position. It'll be Polypig country from here on out; at least until we reach whatever machine gun emplacement the army had waiting on the west side of the pass."

"Just full of good news, ain't ya?"

"We still have our weapons... *The Cordwainer* is still moving under her own steam..."

"Heck," Fluky sneered in the dark. "What I want to live forever for, anyway?"

Chapter Twenty-Eight
Uncle Sam Slams the Door

It was well towards evening before we again risked turning over the engine. It had quickly cooled down and faded out of sight in the blackness of the old railway tunnel, but what damage had been caused to the turbine's internals by overheating it, we could only guess. Nothing, however, seemed to be amiss as we returned fuel to the expansion chamber. Our escape from the army's machine gun had completely drained the small diesel tank; there'd be no more boosts of power from the large, red button on the console.

With the flywheel again spinning, we started to steam along the dark length of the old Northern Pacific tunnel. It felt impossibly long, crawling along with the potentiometer only slightly turned. It was a silent testament to a past age of engineering greatness, that such a thing as the tunnel had once been possible. It made me feel small, despite the engineering tasks I had recently undertaken.

That once people dug so deep and so far into the earth... It put the construction and operation of *The Cordwainer* into perspective. We were, in any serious evaluation, just parasites living off the labors of a past civilization. I thought of the trains that had rumbled through this darkness. Perhaps someday men would again build things like tunnels and railroads, once the problems of global overheating had been solved and the death-grip of the Concession had been loosened on the nation. But until then, we could only walk in the footsteps of those who had come before us – ride the rails they had laid down.

The light at the end of the tunnel slowly resolved itself at the very limit of my vision. Soon we'd be out of the tunnel and into the light again, into the pass that marked the halfway point of our journey.

The sun was setting majestically before us as we alighted the tunnel and steamed out between the steep, green slopes that climbed quickly up on both sides of tracks. Back in the daylight, we could finally assess the damage that had been done to *The Cordwainer.* A long snake of bullet holes ran the whole length of the port side of the train. The rear of the old station wagon caboose looked like a large animal had been chewing on the wood. One of the rear doors was completely demolished, and much of the paneling hung loose off the frame. The floor of the caboose was slick with contents of a dozen bottles of wine, shot to pieces by the machine gun. It was a devastating loss, but most of our other provisions had survived the firefight.

We made ourselves a dinner of bread and cheese and sat on the bullet-riddled benches in the caboose to eat it. We were again safely nestled amongst the tall pines and steep hillsides of the mountains, and we let ourselves relax our guard. If it was true, that we were now fully within the domain of the Polypigs, there seemed little reason to twist ourselves into knots worrying ourselves about it. On the Northern Pacific rails, we were more than twenty miles off any normal means of cresting the mountains, and there was no reason to believe that we wouldn't sneak through the hills unnoticed by a small band of poorly equipped, desperate rebels with bigger things to worry about than the presence of one simple train.

The U.S. Army, first and foremost, must have been high on their list of concerns. If that machine gun nest behind us had constituted the front line of the army's offensive, then they had the Polypigs bottled up in the mountains tightly indeed. I was more concerned about what army defenses there would be west of the pass that we still needed to navigate past. We had made it past the first gun emplacement with the help of our diesel injectors. But they were now empty. The next machine gun nest we encountered we'd have to pass without that extra boost of speed.

Nothing about that excited me.

But the army were not going to be content to just wait for us to emerge from the pass.

Perhaps the fiction that we were carrying weapons for the Polypigs had been accepted at face value within the higher ranks of the military. Perhaps our continual existence had proven too galling for the Concession and they'd pulled in political favors to make sure we never emerged from the mountains alive. Whatever the truth, the distant drone of a plane's engine was our first ominous indication that all was not well.

We frantically scanned the sky, climbing out onto the roof of the train. Mitty was the first to spot the black dot of an airplane approaching from the south. As it neared, we strained our eyes against the failing light to make out the shape of the airplane. Fluky was the first to call it: P-51 Mustang, its unmistakable squared wings forming a crucifix in the sky. It appeared to have something large and heavy slung from its belly, throwing off its profile. A large bomb or extended flight fuel tank, we hypothesized aloud.

As the plane came closer, Fluky scrambled up to the front of the train to man the cockpit, as I found my spot again on a running board, almost out of sight. Mitty retrieved his Thompson from the caboose and made sure the bolt was back. What he thought we was going to do with it, I didn't know, but he took a knee on the roof of the caboose and held the weapon at his side.

The plane crossed *The Cordwainer's* tracks on a perpendicular course, not fluttering its wings.

For a moment I thought we'd been passed by. After all, the whole universe didn't revolve around us. If the army was hunting Polypigs in these hills, there was no reason to believe that the plane would have any interest in a homemade train steaming through the mountains.

But my small glimpse of relief faded as the Mustang banked to the west once it'd passed over us. It circled in a great arc until it was parallel with the tracks we were running on, and then it proceeded to dive directly towards us.

Fluky was in the cockpit, but there was little he could do. The potentiometer was already fully on. *The Cordwainer* was making a good twenty, thirty miles an hour up the grade. The P-51

Mustang had its nose pointed down towards us. Its wings began to scream from its velocity as it dived. I ducked down lower onto the running board of the train and I saw Mitty flop down face first onto the roof of the caboose, covering his head in his arms. The fighter plane pulled up out of its dive perhaps two hundred feet above us, leveling out, filling the pass with the ear-splitting roar of its engine. Once past us, it pulled up and banked to the south, then wiggled its wings and banked again to the east, circling. They were coming around again, for another pass.

"Fluky!" I yelled as the plane was lining up on us, this time to dive at our rear. "Faster, Fluky! Faster!"

Fluky looked back at me and threw up his hands. He turned back to the console and ineffectually pounded on the red button. There were a few puffs of black smoke mixed in with the stream of the exhaust, but *The Cordwainer* was gaining no speed.

"I think he means business this time!" I yelled, climbing up off of my perch along the side of the train. I took the pistol out of my belt and made sure it was loaded. I flicked off the safety and turned to face the approaching plane, feet straddled wide on the roof of the hopper. "Fluky, do something!" I screamed back over my shoulder.

"What the fuck you want me to do?" he screamed back. He was frantically flipping at controls, reading dials. But he was right, what could he do? This was all the speed *The Cordwainer* had. It wasn't like we could ever outrun a diving P-51 anyway, not even at ten times the speed we were going.

I raised my gun and fired it importantly into the air. I didn't know what I might accomplish, but at least I was doing *something*. Mitty was still laying with his face hidden in the roof of the caboose. My shots startled him, and he rolled over onto his back, raising his Thompson and braced its stock against the roof he was laying on. He opened fire, throwing lead up into the sky and brass off the left side of the train.

The Mustang was barreling down towards us. Both Mitty and I were emptying our weapons into the sky. At two hundred feet, the plane again leveled off and rushed past us with a deafening roar. This time, however, the Mustang didn't bank away once it had cleared the length of our train. It stayed level, flying over the tracks in front of us, as the mountain pass rose up quickly on either side of it. At the moment when I thought the plane was about to crash – snap its wings off against the canyon walls – it pulled up. But the black cargo that had been slung under its belly continued straight on. It flew, like a thrown stone, in a parabolic arc until it vanished from sight deep into the mountain pass before us.

The plane was climbing up almost vertically, frantically attempting to grab altitude. I watched in open mouthed wonder as it arced away, my handgun lolling uselessly at my side.

Then the earth picked itself up and threw me from the train.

The earth shattering shock of the P-51's bomb shook the mountain pass, knocking *The Cordwainer* off its tracks and me off of its roof. I came crashing down into the underbrush beside the rails, landing hard on my back. The world was caving in around me. Rubble was rolling down off the pass walls, raining down around me. *The Cordwainer* steamed off the tracks, collided with the pass wall and buckled in the middle – the hopper cars turning over onto their sides, spilling boots. In front of us, deeper into the pass, the two opposing sides of the mountains were collapsing down, sliding together, slamming closed the pass with a million tons of trees and rocks. I attempted to jump to my feet but my legs gave out from underneath me. I fell back down amongst the brambles and *The Cordwainer* came to rest, a mass of twisted metal, thrown on its side and back. The engine let out a pained hiss as steam escaped from a thousand tight seams that were suddenly let loose.

I lay on my back for a moment, watching the Mustang arc in the sky. It turned its nose south again and leveled itself out, perhaps at two or three thousand feet. Its job here was done, and it was turning for home.

I groaned and lay motionless in the brambles, afraid to move. If I looked up and saw the destruction, it would be real, but while I lay still... I could hear Fluky yelling in the distance, screaming for a fire extinguisher. There were some unintelligible screams, then the unmistakable whoosh of a chemical extinguisher. Then there was silence, punctuated randomly by a few more blasts of compressed chemicals.

I eventually took hold of myself, faced reality, and pulled myself up to a sitting position. The situation was far worse than I could have possibly feared. Fluky and Mitty were upright, standing on the tracks with their backs to me, looking down at the wreckage that had once been *The Cordwainer*. She had completely come apart, spilling her cargo and flipping onto her side. Only the caboose still sat upright, vaguely on the tracks, completely decoupled from the rest of the train. I pulled myself to my feet and looked down toward the pass. I could see nothing over two hundred yards away but dust and rubble. The pass had completely collapsed in on itself. Even if *The Cordwainer* had still been rail worthy – if the bomb hadn't shaken us all free of the tracks – there'd be no place to go. The path ahead was closed. We had failed. The all-consuming, gut-wrenching horror of the realization hit me. I fell back down to my knees.

Fluky and Mitty spun around at the sound of my groans. They skipped across the empty tracks and helped me to my feet, asking after my welfare. I waved them off, again able to stand under my own power. Now I wanted to smash something. I picked up a twisted piece of metal and threw it angrily towards the impassable pass. I screamed and bellowed and kicked at the rails, cussing at the sky and at everyone and everything I could think of.

When I calmed down, I turned to the others. Mitty was silent, still holding the extinguisher in his right hand. Fluky was bleeding from his forehead, wiping the blood out of his eyes with his filth-covered sleeve. No one had to say anything.

Nobody bothered.

We found two unbroken bottles of Marmont claret in the caboose and a crushed carton of McTavish that had magically not broken open. Fluky hopped up onto the side of one of the overturned hoppers and Mitty and I sat on the bullet hole ridden tailgate of the old caboose. We proceeded to get drunk as fast as we could, cutting the corks out of the bottles with a knife and chugging the wine quickly down. The McTavish tasted especially rancid as a chaser to the wine, but we gulped it down in big mouthfuls and passed the cartons around.

The night fell quickly, without any real indication of twilight. By the time the stars came out, the three of us were having a merry old time, despite or dire situation. Miraculously, we were able to laugh at our predicament, with the help of the booze. Everything we had worked so hard for, for so long, was laying in pieces all around us. Fluky was joking, though fits of laughter, that the HTP tank would rupture next and blow us all to hell. And despite the very real possibility of that actually happening, I was laughing along with him.

Mitty had recovered his machine gun from the wreckage. It was empty now, all its rotary magazines spent, but he let it rest across his lap as he drank his share of the whiskey. I noted, probably for the first time in ten years, that Mitty didn't have a cigarette or its holder protruding from his mouth. He chuckled that he had finally smoked the last one in his last pack. This the three of us found uncontrollably hysterical. Oh, how far up shit creek were we, if even Mitty was even out of smokes? It wasn't funny, not a bit of it, but we couldn't stop laughing.

When the whiskey was finally gone, our mood turned more somber. Facing the facts could not be avoided: We were stranded in the mountains with very little food or water and without transportation, surrounded by hostile forces and cut off from the west by a rock slide and east by a waiting machine gun emplacement. If by some miracle the elderly tunnel behind us had survived the explosion and was still passable... We fell into silence and I looked up at the stars above me. It was another clear night, with the constellations bright in the sky.

"What we gonna do?" Fluky said, pulling his shirt tighter in around him. The chill of the mountain night was beginning to set in.

"Marmont must be under twenty miles back along these tracks..." Mitty pointed back toward the mouth of the tunnel, indistinguishable from the cliff face in the light.

"The town of Taggart is perhaps twice that, that way," I said, pointing at the rubble-clogged pass.

"That's quite a hike." Fluky picked up the empty carton of McTavish and shook it, holding it up over his tilted-back mouth. He got a drop or two, but that was it.

"We can carry fifty, sixty pairs of boots on our backs," I pointed to where the cargo of *The Cordwainer* had spilled out over the tracks. "We could easily turn that into two or three thousand dollars in Taggart. Along with what we made in Marmont, that's going on fifteen grand. Split three ways, that not so bad. I couldn't make that in a year working at The Shop."

"But then what?" Mitty asked forlornly.

"Then what? We hop the mega-gauge to the Big City. Disappear."

"With five grand? That won't last long," Fluky snorted.

"It's what we got. There ain't any good options here."

"If we returned to Marmont," Mitty continued. "Perhaps Mitchell would let us stay."

"And what?" I asked. "Wait around for the Concession to figure out what happened to us? Wait for the goons in the black Cadillacs to come searching for us? Head back to Shadrach? Boot Hill? No, there isn't anything for us back that way but a jail cell. That way," I pointed at the rubble. "In the Big City, we got a fighting chance – maybe no one will be able to find us. I still have friends, I know people in town. We'd have a shot."

"Then what? Change our names?" Fluky asked. "And lose our chits? Ain't gonna be another Class A for you, you understand, not unless your name is Andy Rice. And if you use that name, they're gonna find you, just as easy as if you were back in Boot Hill. Least back there we got family. Friends. We might make a go of it."

"That's insane! You want to go to jail?" I almost yelled.

"No, but in Boot Hill-"

There was a sound in the darkness that made Fluky come up short. We all stopped to listen. We had been making a whole hell of a lot of noise. First laughing and carrying on, then arguing at full volume. Our voices must have echoed for miles in the hills. Mitty raised his empty sub machine gun and Fluky reached into his belt for his automatic. I slowly reached down and picked up the first heavy item that I touched with my hand: A section of one of the crossbars. There was another rustle amongst the trees and we all simultaneously rose to our feet.

"Who's there?" Fluky yelled out, his pistol drawn. I took a few steps toward the tree line and raised up my iron bar. Suddenly, an anger rolled over me. If there were soldiers in these hills, come to check on their handiwork, then I wanted a piece of them – for everything they'd cost me. I was wildly unconcerned with the danger, oblivious to the fact they were probably well armed. I wanted blood. I stepped closer to the tree line, desperately looking for a head to cave in.

"Come on, you sons-of-bitches!" I yelled. "You think you can fuck with us, huh?"

I glared into the blackness, threatening the trees.

"We're not here to fuck with anyone," a voice said, very close, in the darkness.

I think I leapt three feet back, tripping on a rail and landing on my ass. Fluky brought his gun up, but before he could react, behind him, a young girl materialized out of the darkness. She had a revolver in her hand and she pushed it against Fluky left ear. Mitty came around with his Thompson, but something cracked him square in the face, sending him reeling. He hit the ground next to me on the tracks, his nose bleeding.

Out of the tree line a small figure stepped – taller than a child but not big enough to be an adult. The gleam of a gun barrel proceeded it and drew my attention. The figure walked with a strange gait, dropping down onto the tracks with pained stiltedness.

"Looks like you boys have had a hard day." The figure walked along the tracks, moving awkwardly, and showed itself to be a small, middle-aged woman whose limbs seemed just barely under her control. The small carbine she held, however, wavered very little as she moved towards us, keeping us covered. "Seems like someone went to a lot of trouble to put your little train there out of commission."

"I-I-" I stammered.

"I was up there," she said, pointing up into the darkness with an arm that seemed incapable of raising above her shoulder. "Saw the whole goddamn thing. You folks are just lucky that pilot didn't decided to drop that three hundred pounder right on top of you. Wouldn't have been a shoelace left of the whole kit and caboodle."

"What? Shoelace?" I pulled myself up to a sitting position. The woman with the carbine was looking past me at the wreckage of *The Cordwainer*. The man who had hit Mitty in the face came out of the darkness with a short club in his hand, watching us intently. The young girl with the revolver to Fluky's ear hadn't moved. Wisely, Fluky hadn't moved either.

"You're those Boot Hill Boys, aren't you?" The woman asked, looking down at me. "From the radio. What'd you call it? *The Cordwainer*?"

"Yes, yes..."

"Radio said you were running us guns. That would have been nice. I don't see any guns in there though, just a bunch of boots. That a shame, a mighty big shame. We could have used a train load of guns." The large man with the short club picked up Mitty's Thompson and tossed it to the woman. She caught it with her free hand and looked it over. "Well, here's one at least."

"And another," The young girl said, taking Fluky's automatic out of his hand.

"Running guns?" I looked up at the woman and squinted, the wheels in my brains starting to turn.

"That's right," The woman said, reading my expression, looking down at me with a smile. "We're the Polypigs."

Chapter Twenty-Nine

The Polypigs

"But you're a-" I started and stopped. The woman had helped me to my feet with her strangely twisted, crooked left hand. She had introduced herself as Majorette, though if that was her name or some sort of rank, she didn't clarify.

"A woman? A cripple?" she asked, indignantly.

"No, no!" I scrambled. She laughed. "I just thought..."

"What?"

"That you were supposed to be bigamists..." It sounded silly the moment it came out of my mouth. Majorette, the large man and the young girl laughed.

"What if we are? Only men can be bigamists?" Majorette offered her misshapen hand to Mitty and pulled him up to a standing position. She looked up into Mitty's bloodied nose, reached up and twisted on it to check the bone. Mitty screamed, but she seemed satisfied. "You'll live," she said, giving Mitty a pat on his large stomach, directly at her eye level.

"I-I-" I stammered again. I was slowly becoming aware of more people dropping down onto the tracks in the dark. Lots of people, shadowy figures with weapons coming closer.

"This is my daughter, Rachael," she indicated the young girl with the revolver in Fluky's ear. "And that's husband number three, Al," she pointed at the large man standing menacingly with the club.

"Number three?!" I exclaimed.

"Six," Majorette snapped off, unprompted.

"Six?"

"Husbands," she reaching down and picked up one of the empty bottles of wine. She sniffed it and looked at the label.

"Total. Before you feel obliged to ask. Though two are dead now." She held up the wine bottle for me to see. "You boys stop in Marmont?"

"Yes." There were a dozen more standing amongst the wreckage of *The Cordwainer* now. Rough, scruffy-looking people, in many layers of clothes, rummaging through the wreckage like heavily armed hobos.

"You meet Mitchell?"

"Yes," I replied in surprise.

"He feed you?" she asked, with an edge in her voice.

"Yes..."

"Yes, he fed me too when I was there," Majorette nodded, dropping the bottle.

"*Six*?" I repeated. "You?"

"Me," Majorette replied, offended. "The cripple."

"No, no!" I tried to backpedal.

"We make do," she continued. "Not a lot of women, here about, you see?" She gestured at the other Polypigs, digging in the rubble. They were predominantly male.

"No."

"You have to learn to adapt, living the way we do," Majorette was looking around at the destruction littered across the tracks. "Now," she began, slinging her carbine over her shoulder. Rachael took this as a cue and lowered the gun from Fluky's head. "What are we going to do about this?"

"Do?" I parroted.

"Yes, to get you boys back on the tracks."

"What?"

"Get you boys rolling again. These boots are destined for the Big City, are they not?"

"Well, yes, but..." I looked off into the darkness, at the million tons of dirt and rock I knew were blocking the tracks.

"Well, don't let this little bump in the road stop you. You know what they say about spilled milk."

"You want to *help* us?" Fluky said, hand to his ear, a phantom gun still tickling it.

"Of course."

"Well, folks in these hills are sure friendly," Fluky quipped.

"We were expecting you," Rachael said, holstering her pistol. "We've been waiting. Thought they'd got you further down in the valley, but then we heard the machine gun, knew you were on your way. Didn't expect you to stop in Marmont for tea."

"But-" I started and stopped, then started again. "We're not running guns."

"No. Boots. I can see," Majorette kicked a loose boot and sent it skipping down the tracks.

"You want our boots?" I asked.

"No!" she said, then paused, adding, "Well, perhaps some."

"Then I don't understand. Why were you waiting for us?"

"We heard about you on the radio," Rachael replied.

"But *we're not running guns*," I almost pleaded.

"No," Majorette smiled. "Something much better."

The Polypigs were already at work all around me. What I had at first taken to be opportunistic salvaging amongst the wreckage quickly turned out to be a concerted effort to clean up the debris of *The Cordwainer*. I looked around to see that boots were already being collected in a single location and a team of Polypigs seemed to be assessing the damage to the upturned train cars themselves. I watched on in confusion, still unclear to their motivations. Majorette excused herself for a moment to give orders to a few scrubby-looking young men, while Rachael herded Mitty, Fluky and myself to a spot by the tracks safely out from under foot.

Pack animals emerged from the blackness, led by children of various ages. From the mules, ropes and pulleys started to be unloaded. Despite appearances, the Polypigs worked with an organized efficiency. They were prepared, ready for our arrival. Ready to tackle exactly the sort of mess we had suddenly found ourselves thrust into.

As Majorette returned to speak with us, one of the hopper cars was already righted onto its wheels.

"You knew we were coming?" I asked, after Majorette had barked an order to a teenage Polypig, leading a pack of mules.

"Yes, we already said-"

"And you knew they'd bomb the pass?" I asked in disbelief.

"Oh, hell no!" Majorette laughed. "Not in my wildest imagination... but we knew, if they couldn't stop you further down the mountain, they'd stop you here. And for good. I was expecting troops, tanks, a gun fight... but that plane... You three have made someone, somewhere, very angry – very angry indeed."

"But your men, the mules..."

"We came prepared to detour you. There's a trail. Wide, but not excessive. The state thugs won't be watching it. We hatched this little plan when we heard the warning go up over the radio. We were west, raiding the border towns when we heard it. It took us two days to rustle up the livestock and the equipment. But we didn't have to steal it. When word got around on the west side of the mountains – when word got around about what you were really up to. As Rachael said, your reputation precedes you. There's very little that could make Polypigs and Monogamists stop shooting at each other long enough to cooperate, but word of your impending arrival was enough to get that done. Folks in the towns west of the mountains actually *gave* these mules and these ropes to us. Can you believe that? So we could wait for you here, and detour you around the pass. That's the kind of fire you lit under folk on the other side of these mountains."

"All this? To help us?" Mitty asked, as another hopper car was righted.

"All this to buy a pair of boots!" Majorette chuckled and slapped Mitty again in the gut. "But, of course, we were expecting real locomotives. We were expecting to have to haul your whole cargo all the way down off the mountain, but these tinker toys... what is that thing? A windup toy?" Majorette pointed at *The Cordwainer's* engine.

"It runs on hydrogen peroxide," I replied in shocked awe. "No carbon emissions..."

"Well aren't you three just the sweetest little things?" Majorette said with sarcasm. "Saving the planet, too..." She stepped away to bark some orders at the group that was hooking the mules up to the engine, trying to right it. A team of eight mules had already been hooked up to a hopper car – its load of boots having been unloaded and loaded into sacks slung across the backs of a fleet of mules – and it was moving back along the tracks, away from the pass. The other two cars and the caboose were also being unloaded and hitched. The sheer number of hands working away at *The Cordwainer*... It was like a small swarm of dirty, ragged young children had descended out of the hills to pull the train back up onto its wheels and haul it off.

Fluky, Mitty and I could do nothing but watch.

The engine of *The Cordwainer* turned out to be too heavy to lift off its side by the mules and horses the Polypigs had available. As the night rolled on, and more of *The Cordwainer* was moved back down the tracks, talk turned to removing the fuel tank from the engine so the chassis could be righted. When Fluky and I overhead this, we had to intervene. Despite the ruthless efficacy with which the Polypigs had gone to work, they obviously had no real concept of what they were attempting to take apart and put back together. We were quick to dissuade Majorette from disassembling the HTP fuel tank, considering the chance of an explosion. Fluky quickly showed how the turbine and generator might be unbolted safely from the chassis. This, the Polypigs did, after Fluky had correctly corked the input fuel line. Then the turbine and generator were soon hauled off, slung between the backs of four of the strongest of the pack animals.

The Cordwainer's engine, with fuel tank still attached, was then righted – the tank by that point in the journey already almost two-thirds empty.

With the last of *The Cordwainer* resurrected from where it had crashed, Majorette and Rachael led the three of us up off the tracks and up into the tree line, climbing steeply away from the blocked pass. Two hundred yards into the trees we met up with the sections of the train being hauled up a narrow dirt path by straining, unhappy mules.

"There is no way we can ever thank you for this," I said as we joined the wagon train climbing the mountainside along the thin trail.

"Get your train to the Big City, with all your cargo, and it will be thanks enough," Majorette replied.

"I don't see-" I huffed. It was a steep climb. "I don't see how that helps you."

"You might say we're in the same line of business. Me and you."

"Boots?" Mitty asked.

"Chaos."

"We're not-" I began and stopped myself. After everything the last few days, I thought better of trying to contradict anyone.

"If you succeed in this quest of yours," Rachael spoke up. She was walking behind us all. "If you actually deliver your product to market, it will be quite the finger in the eye to the Concession. That three yokels with no resources can do what the Concession can't..."

"You're fightin' the Concession?" Fluky asked. "I thought you were fightin' the government?"

"They're one in the same," Rachael replied. "The line where one stops and the other begins is nonexistent. Kick one and the other rubs its ass in pain."

"We're not like you," I said.

"No," Rachael agreed.

"We're not rebels."

"No."

"I *voted* last November," I said, as if that explained it all.

"Well, good for you..." Rachael chuckled in the dark behind me. I turned to look at her, incredulous, but Majorette threaded one of her twisted hands under my arm and led me on.

"Don't mind her," Majorette began, leaning in to whisper comfortingly. She patted my arm. "You make her nervous."

"She makes me nervous," Fluky said, look back over his shoulder.

"We don't get many chances to interact with what you'd call 'normal' folk. We're very insular up here, you understand."

"We weren't trying to start any trouble," I said. The climb was starting to flatten out. A hopper car up ahead was jammed on some rocks. Voices were yelling in the dark and mules were whinnying as they strained against their harnesses. "We're very grateful for your help, but we can't claim to be sympathetic to your cause."

"But your actions say otherwise," Rachael answered. We paused as the Polypigs scrambled around the hopper car, putting beams under the stuck tire and prying it over the rock. Then suddenly – explosively – everything was moving again.

"All we wanted to do was sell some boots in the Big City. If anything, if we have any gripes at all, it's against the Concession."

"You really still see a distinction between the Concession and the State, don't you?"

"Shouldn't I?"

Majorette still had a hold of my arm and pulled me closer to speak up into my ear, "Who do you think we're rebelling against, dear?"

"Well... the government," I replied.

"No," she shook her head like a disappointed teacher. "Government we like – governments we elect. Rebels rebel against the State."

"What, like Utah?" Fluky asked, breathing heavy from the climb.

"No. *The* State, dear. Big 'S'. That which rules, but is not answerable to the people. The top down system of control that extends from, but does not include, the Executive Branch at the point, to your local mail carrier at the base. The State, dears. The monstrosity that we fool ourselves we control, but in reality controls us. That is who we're fighting against."

"And that's not the government?"

"No," Majorette said firmly. "That the distinction between the two has been lost is the great tragedy of progressivism. To legitimize the vast expansion of the state, to authorize the million tiny tweaks and controls placed on civil society, the State has consumed the legitimacy of democratic government. You voted for it, and therefore you have given your approval to be governed by the State, they argue. But no one votes to elect the State. It is eternal, outliving governments and administrations. We vote, in a democracy, for a government, which we assume oversees the State. But the days when elected officials had the power to control the agents of the State has long since passed by. The tail now wags the dog. The State controls the government and persists it. It's the enemy."

We had reached the summit of the narrow trail. The Polypigs were stopping here, in the dark, to rest the animals. There wasn't a man nor beast within ear shot that wasn't huffing with exhaustion. It was a clear night and the stars were twinkling in the sky above us. Our breath was misting in the air in front of our faces. Majorette found a grassy spot by the edge of the trail and dropped her bent body down onto it. I didn't need to wait for an invitation to rest. I sat down next to her as Fluky and Mitty collapsed next to us on the grass. Only Rachael remained standing, seemingly untaxed. She was watching the trail in both directions furtively, as if expecting company.

"And the Concession is part of this State?" I blew out a cloud of steam. "I though it was a private company. Amalgamated Holdings..."

"Oh, it's a for-profit company all right. With a board of directors and shareholders and a balance sheet – no State agency. But the Concession and its ilk are, nevertheless, fully vested appendages of the Beast. The State, you see, is a parasitic entity, dependent on the rest of civil society for succor. It can produce nothing, you understand, but consumes a great deal. It is wholly dependent on other entities for its survival, but it hamstrings the entities at every turn with the costs and trouble of carrying the State on their backs. For these companies to ever hope to thrive under this almost unbearable weight, they're forced to demand protections. They argue that they can't carry the State and the burden of a competitive marketplace. And rightly so.

"The State, more than happy to preserve that status quo, provides these protections. And this is the birth of the Concession and its ilk. Not entirely part of the ever-expanding State – enough to still remain productive – but wholly dependent on the protections of the State for its survival. The two live in symbiosis – the State and its Corporatist extremities."

"And that's how the Concession can call out the Army Air Corp, to swat a fly with a three-hundred-pound bomb," Rachael added.

"Yes," Majorette went on. "The State might be completely incapable of the production of any useful goods or service, but it has one dimension that no other social entity can deliver: A monopoly on violence. In fact, it is often argued that the State is defined as nothing more than that. The only institution in civilized society with the power to righteously act with violence, through its military and its police. Much of civil society's purpose is to maintain this monopoly. Laws are created, police patrol, courts are brought to order, all with the purpose of severely punishing those who'd challenge the State in this arena."

"Like you Polypigs."

"Like the Polypigs," Majorette agreed.

The moon was high in the sky and the last sections of *The Cordwainer* were making their way over the summit. The turbine and generator, slung between their mules, came by our small, grassy spot and started on down again without resting. *The Cordwainer's* engine with its tank of HTP came up behind, a dozen mules hee-hawing as their drivers whipped them on. For a moment, I feared that it wouldn't make the last push over the summit; but one last great exertion of will, and the whole engine car was over the hump and moving down the west side of the mountain. Polypigs leapt and stumbled forward to slow its descent – the great weight they had lifted up the hill, now becoming a great weight they had to lower down.

"I still don't see how a train full of boots is at all helpful to you," I asked, watching *The Cordwainer's* engine descend into the darkness.

"It's all a question of sovereignty." Majorette climbed to her feet, helping me to mine. The hopper cars were starting again down the hill, along the narrow trail. They'd been waiting for the engine to pass, I realized. Its weight they understandably didn't want coming down the trail behind them.

"Sovereignty?" Of everything I was expecting her to say, that perhaps was the last thing.

"Yes, who has it. Genuinely. Naturally. Self evidently, perhaps. Tell me, by what power does a king rule?"

"By the grace of God," Mitty answered.

"And our Government?"

"By the consent of the people," Mitty said again.

"And is one source of authority more valid that the other?"

"Of course, the consent of the people-"

"-Is merely a woolly abstraction, like power being a gift from God. Can you rightly say that 'the people' consent to anything? Is it not correct to say that each individual, within 'the people', consents individually to the legitimacy of a democratic government? That each man and woman, in their own heart, decided – perhaps not consciously – to accept the authority of an elected government? To not resist, to not rebel, to go along as ordered by the powers-that-be?"

"I guess..." I shrugged, watching my feet in the dark. The trail was now falling away as fast as it had risen east of the mountains. It was tricky going in the moonlight, finding a footing. If the cars of *The Cordwainer* had not proceeded us and dug deep ruts, it might have been a hard descent.

"And is this not really the source of a government's authority? The individual? Isn't this the reason for our Bill of Rights? The realization that power stems not from the people, but the individual, and this individual has powers and rights above and beyond those of the collective whole?

"This is sovereignty. Authority, we can concede, but sovereignty is the source from which all authority originates, which cannot be relinquished or transfered. If sovereignty sits within the individual, not within God or 'the people' or any other abstract entity, then is not the individual the arbiter of society?"

"The source of right and wrong," I said, mostly to myself.

"Exactly!" Majorette happily agreed. "But when God, or 'the people' or the State is risen up in importance above this sovereignty, then the individual must be suppressed, less it finds its feet and exercises its natural rights. To keep the individual down, the State monopolizes away whole swaths of society, which otherwise would be dominated by the will of the individual. Violence, predominantly. But here – in America in 1973 – commerce very much as well.

"You might not think you're a revolutionary, dear, but your actions, as pure or as selfish as they might be, have butted up against and challenged one of the State's strongest monopolies. To challenge one monopoly is to challenge them all, and that is why the State has reacted to your enterprise with such surprising violence. You have performed an act of violence against it, and it is retaliating.

"So, perhaps now you can understand why we say our causes are alike – why the State sees us as common enemies. Perhaps we attack the State with violence and you attack the State with boots, but neither assault can they tolerate and still hope to maintain their iron grip on society. By helping you across these mountains we help ourselves, open up a second front in our rebellion against the State. You might disapprove of being treated so, but you must come to understand that we are compatriots fighting in a common cause, albeit by different means."

Chapter Thirty

The Parable of the Witch Doctor

The sun rose soberly behind us, filling the sky with warming color long before the first rays of light could been seen over the mountains. By early morning, we were back down on the tracks, on the other side of the rock slide. We had passed over the mountains that were no longer passable. The engine made if first, along with its turbine and generator, and by the time Fluky, Mitty, Majorette, Rachael and myself had descended onto the tracks, much of *The Cordwainer* was starting to take shape.

In the half light of dawn, Fluky quickly got to work re-bolting the parts of the engine back onto its chassis. This required the construction of a crude a-frame. But the Polypigs were more than capable at that simple task of engineering. After Fluky had described what he needed, a band of scruffy young men had gotten to work falling small trees and stripping them of their foliage. Within an hour, Fluky was carefully guiding the turbine cowling back into place, with a dozen Polypigs ready with tools to bolt it down.

While all of this was happening up front, I oversaw the delivery of the almost endless caravan of mules carrying our cargo of boots. A human chain was established to unload the mules and redeposit the boots back in their hoppers. The Polypigs worked with military precision, jumping to attention anytime Majorette barked an order. I supposed the discipline was what had kept them alive so long, living in the mountains fighting the State. That it had been mustered and directed to our benefit, I could scarcely believe.

There was very little for me to actually, physically do – the Polypigs had little need for help outside of their own ranks. It had to satisfy myself to just sit with Majorette and watch the events unfold, offering advice or a preference when solicited.

"It seems," I commented idly to Majorette as the work bustled on around me, the morning passing by, "incumbent on us all to at least attempt to work for change through a peaceful process..." What she had said in the night, crossing the mountains, was sitting uncomfortably in my belly. That Mitty's Plan – *The Cordwainer* – was analogous to the Polypig rebellion. "I mean, you say the Government can no long control the State, but I..." I trailed off, not sure exactly what I wanted to say.

"Let me tell you a story," Majorette began. "There once was a man who suffered from headaches – crippling migraines. He is suffering so acutely, he decides to go see a witch doctor, hoping for some relief. The witch doctor tells him that the source of his headaches is an evil spirit that is trapped in his brain, pushing on the inside of his skull, attempting to break out. The only way to cure the headaches, the witch doctor insists, is to hammer a nail into the man's head, thereby letting the evil spirit escape.

"Now, the man is understandably skeptical. Letting the witch doctor hammer a nail into his head sounds extremely dangerous, potentially deadly. But the headaches are so bad, the man is willing to give it a try. To be safe, the man tells the witch doctor to hammer the nail in slowly, a little at a time, and keep a check on his vital signs. If anything starts to look amiss, the man will call the operation off, evil spirit or no.

"So the witch doctor starts hammering, as the man suggested, a little bit at a time. Tap, tap, tap, then he checks on the man's heartbeat. Still okay. Tap, tap, tap, checks his heart again. So far so good. Tap, tap, tap. Ahh! The man screams. The doctor checks the man's heart rate and his pulse is running. Stop, stop, stop! the man pleads, and the witch doctor agrees. Take it out! he screams in pain, and the witch doctor turns the hammer around to pull the nail out. There's a gush of blood as the nail is removed and the man's heart begins beating even faster. Not knowing what else to do, the witch doctor pushes the nail back in, stopping the flow of blood. The man's heart beat slows a little, but the pain in his head is still there... not to mention the nail.

"The man wisely decides to seek a second opinion. He calls together all of the best witch doctors from all of the villages around to come look at his problem. They come and examine the nail in his head and they confer with the original witch doctor. There's much muttering and nodding and poking at the patient's head. The size and weight of the nail is discussed, as is the nature of the spirit still trapped within the man's aching skull.

"The conference of witch doctors eventually comes to a consensus: The spirit in the man's head evidently is not the type that wishes to be freed. It is causing the pain, the rapid heart beat, rebelling against the attempts to remove it from the man's head. The spirit must be extracted from the skull as quickly as possible, lest it kill the man as it attempts to fight off the attack. The gaggle of witch doctors, therefore, starts gleefully hammering the nail further into the man's head, causing his heartbeat to race to dangerous extremes.

"The man is screaming in pain, his heart seems ready to explode in his chest. The man pleads for the witch doctors to stop with the hammering. The witch doctors reluctantly capitulate to the man's bloodied request, and stop forcing the nail any further into the man's brain. The man, at the very limits of his tolerance, collapses into unconsciousness. The witch doctors are mystified at this consequence.

"Along comes a bright, young witch doctor, who looks over the unconscious patient. He proposes a radical diagnosis: That the man's state of unconsciousness has been caused by a nail hammered into his head, and removing that nail must now be the top priority, lest the man succumb to his wounds. The other witch doctors throw their arms up in disgust. 'Nonsense!' they say, whatever damage the nail has done is insignificant to the damage the spirit inside the man's head is causing. If the nail is removed now, it will anger the spirit that, for the moment, seems to be resting.

"But the young witch doctor is unconcerned with predictions of woe and proceeds to pull the nail free with one mighty tug. A stream of blood follows the nail out of the man's skull, sending the man into cardiac arrest, killing him completely.

"Murder! The other witch doctors scream, pointing accusing fingers at the young witch doctor. Now the evil spirit is free and angry to be so unceremoniously removed from its home. Now it will hunt us all down and haunt us all! they bellow, and fall upon the young witchdoctor and beat him to death with their bone clubs, killing him for his blasphemy."

"I don't understand," I said, Majorette had seemingly finished with her story.

"The moral of this story is," she said with a smile, watching the human chain of Polypigs load the last of the boots into the third hopper car, "more often than not, the doctors are worse than the disease."

Majorette stood up and barked an order to one of her people, raising one of her short, twisted arms almost above her shoulder.

Chapter Thirty-One

Fluky Bows Out

The Cordwainer was coming together, west of the rock slide, once again straddling the tracks of the old Northern Pacific Railroad.

It was beginning to look very much like its old road-worn, bullet-ridden, well-used self as the hopper cars were slowly refilled with their cargo. Fluky had the engine reassembled, bolted down, but managed to "Protocol Ohm's Law" himself and six Polypigs attempting to power up the traction motors. No one was seriously injured, but there was much grumbling and complaining from everyone involved. It took Fluky most of the rest of the day, with limited tools, to track down the short to the motor of the rear-most car. He simply cut the HT leads leading to the bad motor. With it being a downward descent from there on out, he figured we could reach the Big City with just the two remaining motors.

Darkness descended upon us before *The Cordwainer* was ready on the tracks. We tinkered away, late into the evening, realigning this and that. Before midnight, we joined the Polypigs at their campfire and attempted to get some rest before daybreak.

The Polypigs were slumbering in clusters on the hard ground, each wife with her various husbands sleeping around her. With their work complete, they had all helped themselves to a shiny new pair of boots from our hoppers – the best hemp walking shoes Boot Hill had to offer – and they all slept with them on their feet, their guns tucked up inside their bedrolls. We didn't begrudge them their prize. For the price of fifty or sixty pairs of boots, *The Cordwainer* had been picked up from where it had derailed, carried around the blocked pass and reassembled on the other side.

In all honesty, I was still a little fuzzy as to the Polypigs true motivations. I doubted I'd ever completely understand their actions. Everything Majorette had said about a common cause, the State/Concession duality, hardly explained the level of dedication the Polypigs had shown in getting *The Cordwainer* running on tracks once again. Perhaps what Mitchell had said about our journey inspiring others was turning out to be prophetic. Perhaps the odyssey of *The Cordwainer* had taken on a meaning greater than just the profits that Fluky, Mitty and I hoped to make.

Whatever their reasons, I was keenly aware of how much in the debt of the Polypigs we really were. Part of me hoped we really would strike a disruptive blow to those the Polypigs considered enemies by bringing our cargo of boots to the Big City. Even if I didn't share their cause, it would be close to the only way to pay in full the debt we owed to them. But I seriously doubted our little enterprise amounted to that much – could create such serious waves – regardless of the value assigned to it by others.

With the first light of dawn, *The Cordwainer* had a full head of steam and we were on our way once again. We only made it a few yards before derailing a hopper car. The crossbars were understandably misaligned. With the help of a few mules and Fluky's innovative jacks, we had the train quickly on the tracks again.

Our next attempt to continue our journey got us a quarter mile down the tracks before derailing again. This time we were on our own. We lifted *The Cordwainer* back onto the track and got her underway again, but a number of the crossbars were horribly twisted from the accident. Fluky adjusted everything, spending some time under the chassis of each car until he was satisfied with his calibrations, but there was little else we could do but cross our fingers and hope the train didn't derail at a critical moment – like during the approach to the next machine gun nest the army inevitability had positioned in front of us on the tracks. The last thing we needed to do was make ourselves a sitting duck for a thirty-caliber machine gun.

Along with helping themselves to some boots, the Polypigs had also confiscated all our guns – the Thompson, the automatics we'd taken from the Concession goons, and the old Smith & Wesson thirty-eights. We expressed concern to Majorette about the next machine gun emplacement, that we'd potentially need to defend ourselves, but she assured us we had no need for concern. Three miles down the slope of the mountain we caught sight of what she had been alluding to: The sandbagged emplacement, smoldering quietly in the morning air. Three scruffy Polypigs, holding rifles, were picking through the debris. They looked up as we rounded the bend, raising their hands in a friendly salute. We waved back as the train steamed past, the body of a soldier laying dead just off to the side of the tracks.

That was the last I was ever to see of the Polypigs – perhaps the last anyone ever saw. By Christmas of that year, the government had declared victory in their campaign against the Polypigs, pulling the army back out of the mountains. It pains me to think that Majorette and the others, after everything they had done for us, might have met with such an ignominious end. But whether there was any truth to the government's claims, I could never verify. And by that Christmas, the troops the government had fighting in those mountains were beginning to sorely be needed elsewhere.

The Cordwainer steamed into the town of Taggart late that afternoon, to a hero's welcome. A large crowd – perhaps the whole town – was waiting beside the tracks. It was a scene that would be repeated time and again in each of the small communities that we passed through, descending down the west side of the mountains: A line of poor, hardworking men and women waiting, ready with cold hard cash in hand, looking to do business, grateful for our presence.

In Taggart, we started selling boots at $100 a pair, quickly selling six hundred in twenty minutes. It almost turned into a mob scene, the crowd rushing on *The Cordwainer* as we started to unload stock. It was a quick, cheap lesson in pricing our product correctly, for the safety of our customers as well as ourselves. $100 was well below market, though the same pair of boots could be bought in the town's Concession Store for $2.25, if they could be bought at all.

As *The Cordwainer* steamed on for the next town of Rearden, we bumped the price up to $150. This had the desired affect of making the eager mob of customers waiting for us in the center of town a little more leery of our product. There was some grumbling about highway robbery. That was a good indication we were hitting the sweet spot: High enough to sting, but low enough that we still were doing a brisk business.

We sold over a thousand pairs in Rearden. We had our first attempt at a wholesale purchase. The Manager of the local Concession Store somehow appeared with $10,000 in hand, looking for two thousand pairs. We turned this offer down, despite the tempting sight of the bag full of cash. We hadn't come all that way, suffered through so many hardships, to sell off our going concern. We sold directly to customers with money in the pocket – two or three pairs of boots at a time.

While in Rearden, while Mitty and I were sitting on the tailgate of the caboose, collecting money and checking boots for style and size, Fluky was back in the hoppers pulling stock down for the customers. While we were frantically doing business, I noticed out of the corner of my eye that Fluky had stepped away from the hoppers and was talking with a man beside the train. The man was tall and young and of some Oriental heritage. He was conferring with Fluky, quietly but seriously. At the time, I gave the sight no mind, but the same conversation was repeated again in the next town we stopped in, and then the next. The third time, the young man was joined by two older, well-dressed men.

After Rearden, we stopped in the orchard town of San Anconia, where we did just as brisk a business as we had come to expect. The day was winding on, and we sold a little over eight hundred pairs of shoes before dusk was completely upon us. We pulled out of town in the twilight, stopping *The Cordwainer* amongst the apple trees for the night, and counted our money. Inconceivably, we had over $300,000 all loose and flapping around in the caboose. $300,000! In tens and twenties and fives. More money than I'd ever seen in my life – more money that my tiny, pea brain had ever considered to even exist. And we had just emptied a single hopper; two more were almost untouched. We filled three large hemp sacks to the top and still had notes fluttering around loose in the caboose.

We sat in the moonlit night, each with our share of the loot in a sack in front of us, and ate some cheese and bread we still had left over from our trading in Marmont.

We were rich.

We could stop right there, leave *The Cordwainer* in that orchard, and have enough money to last each of us twenty years.

We were still fifty miles from the Big City, steaming through the hinterlands – small, poor farming communities. The mega-gauge Concession behemoths didn't service Taggart, Rearden or San Anconia; they took their goods to market by horse and cart. And we'd still made over a third of a million dollars.

The nearer to the City we came, the wealthier the communities would become. Perhaps tomorrow, $150 for a pair of boots would get us mobbed again. We'd have to raise the price to $200, $300... whatever the market could bear.

And there was still the Big City ahead of us.

The next morning, we rose before dawn and steamed into the town of Galt, just after breakfast. Sure enough, we set our price at $200 and still did a raging businesses. There was a rumor in the crowd, however, that the National Guard had been called out in the next town down the tracks, Wyatt, where a crowd of customers had formed late yesterday, expecting the late arrival of *The Cordwainer.* As the night rolled on and there was no sign of our appearance, they'd started to riot, smashing the windows of the town's Concession Store, and looting its contents. We'd be steaming right into the middle of this tense situation if we departed Galt, people told us. Best to stay where we were and sell our shoes there.

It was here in Galt that Fluky had his clandestine conversation with that same young man and the two older, Japanese-looking men. While Mitty and I were collecting money, he stepped aside and talked to the three men beside an old, rusty Buick. The conversation was brief and they had quickly come to some form of agreement. They shook hands and Fluky returned to *The Cordwainer,* while the other three men climbed into the rusty Buick and drove off.

We took the advice of the crowd and spent the rest of the day in Galt. There was no shortage of customers. When we began to run dry of townsfolk to sell to, a slow trickle of out-of-town customers began to appear. They came on horseback and by the wagon load. People from the surrounding territory were converging on Galt, cash in hand.

By evening, foot traffic from Wyatt started to show up with more news about the events in that town. Sure enough, the Mayor had declared a state of emergency after the looting of the Concession Store, and the National Guard was patrolling the streets. When word arrived that *The Cordwainer* was in Galt, much of the town of Wyatt up and walked the twelve miles between the two communities.

We'd be doing no business in Wyatt, we realized, but we'd need to pass through there, and Hammond and Mulligan, before we'd even have the remotest chance of steaming on to the Big City. We could stay in Galt, it seemed, and let the whole state west of the mountains make its way to us, and sell off our stock just as well, but it seemed as something of an anti-climax. We'd set out to deliver a cargo of boots to the Big City for sale, and that was what we still intended to do. National Guard or not.

But just to be safe, we spent the night in the Galt's town square, talking turns on watch.

We had sold nearly fifteen hundred pairs of boots that day – some people buying a dozen pairs at a time – almost doubling our take to $600,000. The bank manager of the local Federal Savings and Loan, seeing the sheer value of cash on hand, had come to us around dinner time and strongly suggested we deposit our profits in his bank. He'd cook the books, he said, to hide the identity of the depositors. We'd turned down his offer, but he had, for the price of ten pairs of boots, exchanged our fives, tens and twenties for hundred dollar bills – an almost unheard-of, magic artifact to us. This allowed our profits to fit comfortably in a single sack, which was unnerving in itself. We were totally without weapons and surrounded on all sides by eager customers. Perhaps far too eager, if Wyatt was any gauge.

I took first watch and spent most of the evening dealing with a steady stream of customers. One or two at a time they came up to buy boots until two in the morning. At two, I woke Mitty and went to sleep myself. I slept the sleep of the dead, in the caboose, wrapped in Mitty's dirty blankets. Sometime in the night Mitty woke Fluky to relieve him, laying down next to me and falling fast asleep.

I was awoken in the morning by the first of the new day's customers, rapping on the side of *The Cordwainer*. There was already over a dozen people waiting patiently for our store to open, standing in the town square of Galt. Someone had brought coffee and handed Mitty and me a cup. I looked around bleary-eyed, wondering why Fluky wasn't handling the morning rush.

That was when I realized he was gone.

He'd left in the night, taking an even third of the money we'd made. At first, I thought we'd been robbed and Fluky kidnapped, but the reality of the situation sank in when I saw the other $400,000 dollars sitting untouched in the hemp sack under the seat of the caboose.

Fluky was gone. It made no sense. I looked around the town square, hoping something about it would give me a clue to why Fluky would vanish in the middle of the night. Of course, there was nothing. No large sign, explaining the significance of the rusty, old Buick. No rusty, old Buick itself keeping an eye on us. It was simply gone, with Fluky along with it. I was mystified. Mortified. I felt betrayed.

Fluky... Fluky, of all people. If Mitty had wandered off in the night, I wouldn't have thought twice about it. I'd have been concerned for his safety, but I wouldn't have felt betrayed. No, Mitty's allegiances had always been ephemeral – his attention easily taken. But Fluky... *The Cordwainer* was his more than anyone's. He'd worked so hard to build it.

The whole plan to sell boots in the Big City might have been Mitty's idea, but if the whole enterprise had failed, he wouldn't have lost any sleep. It was just another harebrained scheme in a hare brain that was chock full of them.

The engine, to actually be functional, had needed to be something other than my design. In the end, I had contributed very little to the construction of *The Cordwainer*. Apart from the realization that I wasn't smart enough to attempt to do the thing I was attempting, I had made a very small contribution. It really wasn't my train any more than it was Mitty's. The engine was Sophie's design, but she'd rejected it out of hand as something evil and contemptuous.

That left only Fluky. It was his sweat and blood and tears that hand gone into the construction of the whole thing. More than anyone else, he deserved to reap the full harvest of its reward. But here he was, gone. Vanished with his share of the profits. His fair share, admittedly, but a drop in the bucket to what we might realize once we'd reached the Big City. Why would he abandon it all so close to our victory? Bow out when we were so close to to understanding the full value of the cargo we were hauling, like Mitchell had predicted?

For the first time in my life, I began to think that Fluky might be a coward. Despite a lifetime of knowing different – despite a week of being shot at and kidnapped and rammed and bombed – I wondered if the prospect of steaming *The Cordwainer* through a gauntlet of National Guard troops had rattled Fluky. It was nonsense, of course, that Fluky could be scared off. Nothing in life had even put a fright in the Fluky, but I was angry and injured and looking for answers.

Fine, if Fluky wanted to chicken out and hide away instead of seeing the things he started through to the end... Fine. I wouldn't begrudge him that. It simply meant more profits for me and Mitty.

If I'd known the truth, if Fluky had stopped to explain it, perhaps I would have sympathized with his actions. But he'd always been so secretive about his religion – its connection to the plight of the repatriated Japanese. If I'd only known – no, I would never have understood. Perhaps that's why Fluky left as he did, in the night, in an old, rusty Buick driven by two older, Japanese men, with $200,000 in hundred dollar bills in a hemp sack under his arm.

Mitty took it harder than me. I think Fluky and I were as close to family as Mitty had ever had– as near to parents as anyone had been to him. For Fluky to let out like that... well, Mitty had never known his father, but I think the pain of his absence was alleviated some by Fluky's foulmouthed, belittling abuse. When the full weight of Fluky's absence started to dawn on Mitty, he excused himself and climbed up in the cockpit of *the Cordwainer's* engine for most the rest of the day.

I was too busy to think about it. Most of the rest of the town of Wyatt showed up that morning, eager to buy what we were selling. I bumped the price up to $250, and still sold four hundred pairs of shoes on my own. Word with the Wyatt townsfolk, however, was that the National Guard had been ordered to let *The Cordwainer* through. We were not to stop and trade at any more towns on the way – not Hammond or Mulligan or in the suburbs of the Big City – but no one was to waylay us on our journey into the heart of the Big City.

Chapter Thirty-Two

Mitty Speaks Up

Maybe Fluky was smart, getting out while the getting was good. By noon, the stream of customers from Wyatt had died to a trickle and I took the chance to buy some food and bring it to Mitty, sulking up in the cockpit of *The Cordwainer.*

"Eat," I ordered from the running board, handing a sandwich in Mitty. He took it and removed the brown paper, taking a bite, sullenly. "I think it's time to steam on," I said, taking a bite of my own sandwich. "See what awaits us in Wyatt."

Mitty chewed contemplatively, "What do you think happened to Fluky?"

"I don't know," I answered honestly.

"He wouldn't have left... abandoned us..."

"No."

"Something must have happen."

"No."

"Then-" Mitty started then stopped, taking another bite of his sandwich. "He wouldn't have just run away..."

"Nevertheless, here we are."

"He might be back," Mitty said hopefully, "thinking we were waylaid here in Galt for the interim..."

"No," I replied gravely. "He took his share."

"He wouldn't have just run away..." Mitty repeated, dejected.

"We're moving out in twenty minutes," I said, dropping down off the running board. "I'll secure the load."

"But... Wyatt. The National Guard?" Mitty remembered, leaning out the cockpit.

"Ordered to let us through, so I hear. We're going to take this train all the way to the Big City, Mitty. Fluky or not. There, we can see what's waiting for us – what little surprise the Concession has for us at the end of the line."

We were moving again and rolling out of Galt after half a dozen more transactions out of the back of the caboose. If we'd waited for a complete end to the stream of customers, we'd never have left town. One determined young man sprinted after our departing train with a wad of bills in his hand, which I grabbed as I tossed a pair of shoes back at him.

We were out of the mountains now, into the lush open green of the foothills above the Big City. Wyatt was a sleepy farming community that looked idyllic as we wound our way down off the hills towards it. On closer inspection, however, it seemed significantly more hard done by. The looting of the Concession Store seemed to have turned into an all-out riot through town. We saw windows of houses smashed and doors pulled off their hinges as we came through the outskirts of town. The streets were abandoned. For the first time since crossing the mountains, there was no welcoming crowd of people waiting for our train.

We saw a single National Guard trooper as we neared the center of town. He was standing guard with a rifle, and looked taken aback to see us steam by. As we crossed Wyatt's Main Street, a number of baby-faced young soldiers appeared from the surrounding buildings to watch us pass by. We didn't slow, despite some of the troopers waving for us to do so – waving money in their hands. We were out of Wyatt as quickly as we had entered, with no confrontations.

Hammond was a different case entirely. The National Guard had been turned out here also, but a throng a people waited along the tracks, hoping to catch a glimpse of our passing. A great yell went up when we came into view, and people waved and cheered as we pulled into town. Only a line of troopers on either side of the tracks stopped the people from mobbing the train.

These troops were focused on their duty of crowd control. Very few of the troopers even looked over their shoulders to see our train passing. They were facing a crowd that could have easily turned ugly at any moment, but the celebratory mood of the crowd remained gay as we steamed straight on through the center of town, neither stopping nor slowing down. That day, turning out and seeing *The Cordwainer* pass was a special event, enough for the people of Hammond. No commerce was really necessary. Mitty and I waved from the cockpit of the train, the cheers raising our spirits a little after the inexplicable loss of Fluky.

The reception we received in Hammond, however, started me thinking about exactly what would be waiting for us in the Big City. If we were becoming so popular, if we could turn out a crowd just to see our passing, the powers-that-be in the Big City had a real problem on their hands. What would we find at the terminus of the Northern Pacific? Cheering crowds? Or a riot in progress?

The bomb in the pass now made so much more sense to me. If *The Cordwainer* had simply vanished in the mountains, lost in the crossing, attacked by Polypigs, it would have been so much easier to explain. But now we were in the lowlands, only hours from the Big City, the eyes of the whole region watching. It would have been best to stop us before we triumphantly rolled our stock into the abandoned freight yards of the old railroad. But to attack our train now would reverberate up and down the tracks like a shock wave. Everyone we had dealt with, sold a pair of boots to, knew we were not criminals. Flouting the law, yes, but not criminals. We were a genie the government could never put back into the bottle. Better we had vanished in the mountains never to be found. But we had survived, and we had made it through the pass, and now we were at their very doorstep. What could they do when we rolled into the Big City with our train load of boots?

Mulligan gave me a glimpse of exactly what would be waiting for us at the end of the line.

They had time to prepare. They had made banners.

Passing through Mulligan was, perhaps, as close to riding on a float in Mardi Gras as I will ever come. As the late afternoon light was fading, the town of Mulligan was in full parade spirit. There was yelling and whistles and a brass band playing in the town square. Confetti came tumbling down out of the upper windows of the building facing onto the tracks. The same thin khaki line of National Guard troopers stood between the merriment and the tracks, but they did little to dampen the spirits of the partygoers.

If, in Hammond, we had been a spectacle, in Mulligan we were out-and-out heroes. Word of *The Cordwainer* was traveling down the tracks faster than our real engine could carry us. The story was picking up more stream than our turbine could produce. The whole enterprise had left the land of actual events and entered into the realm of mythic folk law. Mitty and I waved to the screaming crowds as we steamed through Mulligan, but didn't slow *The Cordwainer* down in the slightest.

We had a date in the Big City.

Outside of Mulligan, the terrain bottomed out, flattening for the approach to the big lake that edged the Big City. I caught my first glimpse of the skyscrapers of the Big City there, as the sun was setting behind them. We'd be running the last twenty miles of our journey, around the south end of the big lake, in darkness. I moved up from the caboose to the running board beside the cockpit, where Mitty was crouched behind the controls. I took in the beautiful view, with our goal finally in sight, and smiled up at Mitty.

"There she is!" I yelled over the whir of the engine.

Mitty pulled himself halfway out of the cockpit to get a better view, sitting on the edge. He laughed a belly laugh as he saw the city for the first time – for the first time in his life. "Bully!" he yelled.

"An hour and this will all be over!"

"For good or ill."

"Yes."

"What's the final take?" Mitty asked, not taking his eyes off the view.

"A quarter of a million each, you and I," I replied.

"Bully," he said, with a deep and abiding appreciation. "What do you think they're going to do?" Mitty asked after a pause. "When we get to the city?"

"I don't know, if the reception is anything like Mulligan..."

"We'll be heroes!"

"Heroes for a day..."

"But still... heroes..."

"I didn't think we would strike such a nerve. Shadrach, Marmont, the Polypigs, Galt..."

"A ray of light, in a gray world..." Mitty said thoughtfully. He took his cigarette holder out of his pocket and put it into his mouth. He'd long ago smoked the last of his cigarettes, but he sucked on the empty holder, contentedly.

"I still don't see exactly what we did..." I said, more to myself than to Mitty.

"I think," Mitty began, not looking away from the sunset. "For a decade, the President has been telling us all that we're still a Nation of Big Ideas. Well, I think we've shown them all, somehow with this train, that we're a nation still capable of small ones, too."

I looked up at Mitty in disbelief. Shock. For once, I didn't interrupt.

"Incremental changes. Each fellow working to make things better. All the global overheating has got us thinking of things backwards. Big solutions to big problems. But that isn't how you solve big problems. No sir. Even a dummy like me knows that. Break it down into its component parts, like this train, and deal with each part independently. Fix the things you can fix and mitigate the impact of the rest. Start worrying about the whole big problem and you lose perspective, try and bite off too much. But if you can make the problems small enough, and numerous enough, you can solve them each in turn. And before you know it, you've solved the bigger problem, too.

"No, the whole global overheating thing has everyone thinking there aren't any solutions to people's problems 'cause there aren't solutions to the problems that are big enough. Summers just keep getting hotter and hotter, no matter what folks do. They suffer, they sacrifice, they do without, but nothing helps the temperature at all. But instead of a million different people attacking the problem in a million different ways we got one fellow, right at the top, trying to solve it all at once. Can't be done, no sir, no matter how smart you are, no matter how many strings you can pull.

"So, when people see a problem being solved, even a small one, like putting boots on people's feet, they applaud it. They applaud us, you and I, Beanie, for solving that problem. That it is, perhaps, inconsequential in the grand scheme of things, doesn't really matter. After so many years, after so many setbacks, it's a gain – it's a win. It's something people can get behind and cheer. And cheer they are, Beanie, for what we've done. For this train."

I hung to the running board in silence as *The Cordwainer* steamed toward the Big City. Mitty removed his empty cigarette holder and returned it to his pocket, slipping back into the cockpit and looking over the gauges.

I made my way back along the length of the train, past the bullet-ridden hopper cars, now mostly empty, and dropped back into the caboose. I dug the hemp bang containing our profits from underneath the seat and opened it up. I took a look at the stacks of crisp $100 bills inside. $500,000. More money than I could have ever dreamed of seeing in my life. Right there in my hands. I pulled the tie closed on the sack and climbed out of the caboose again, working along the running board back towards the engine.

"Here," I said, handing the bag through the window of the cockpit.

"What?" Mitty took the sack, looking at me cross-eyed.

"Take it," I said.

"Put it back in the caboose," Mitty tried to hand the bag back.

"No," I corrected. "Take it all. All the money, the whole half million."

"What?"

"You're getting off."

"What?!"

"Off the train, before we get to the Big City. There's Hoovervilles all along the track to the south of the city, I'll drop you off there. You're half way to looking like a hobo already, you'll blend right in."

"No!" Mitty protested.

"No," I insisted and poked the sack. "They're not going to take this away from us. Not what we've rightfully earned. Someone has to take this train right to the end of the line, but two of us don't have to. You're getting off, before we reach the terminus. You can hold on to my share, I'll find you later, then we can split it up.

"But take it and run, Mitty. Get off this train before we reach the station. We might be heroes today, Mitty, but today's heroes are tomorrow's villains. Mitchell was right, the Concession aims to make us pay the full price for the cargo we've hauled.

Not just the boots, but all the troubles we've caused along the way. They'll need their patsy, their villain to parade before the public, but they won't need two. I'm volunteering for this Mitty. The whole thing – this whole train – it was your idea. It was Fluky who built it. What did I do? Realize I was too stupid to build the engine I said I thought I could build? That was my whole contribution to this enterprise, Mitty, until right now. This I can do, I can bring this train home and I can stand by it. I can stand by what we built and let them vilify me for it."

"We can both-" Mitty began.

"You're no dummy, Mitty," I interrupted. "But you and I both know this is no job for you. They'd twist your words, Mitty, use them against you. You can take the money and you can hide. That you can do. I'll take this train to the end of the line and we'll meet up later, after it's all blown over. I know I can trust you with my share of the profits, Mitty, just as you would trust me. You're getting off the train, Mitty, with all of the cash."

"I-" Mitty started and stopped. He looked at me and I stared back as *The Cordwainer* rattled along down the tracks. The big lake was now fully in view, shimmering off to our right in the moonlight. Here and there amongst the trees, small housing developments showed themselves – clutches of well wishers beside the tracks waving flags, cheering. Here, the rails must have been in use by the local trolley cars, as small neighborhood stations facing onto the tracks. It wouldn't be long now, and we'd been on the outskirts of the Big City. Almost to the end of the line.

Mitty pulled his bulk out of the cockpit of *The Cordwainer*, slinging the hemp bag of hundred dollar bills over his shoulder.

Chapter Thirty-Three

End of the Line

I slowed *The Cordwainer* down to a walking pace as the Big City began to grow up around us. As the terrain became more urban, the lights of the freight yards and storehouses of the southern section of the city began to glitter all around us. Here, the semi-permanent shantytown of Hooverville lined the tracks on either side, almost overlapping them. The shantytown had stood on the banks of the railroad since the Northern Pacific trains had still run down the line, a transient community of the city's great swath of unemployables that never managed to really transition to anywhere else.

In amongst the makeshift, tin-roofed shacks, Mitty leapt down off the running board of the train. He landed awkwardly, stumbled, but managed to maintain his feet. I caught one last glimpse of him as I leaned out of the cockpit, vanishing into the darkness as the train steamed on. He pulled himself up straight and snapped off his best military salute. I held up a single hand in a silent goodbye, and then he was lost amongst the detritus. Gone.

I settled myself into the cockpit's small, uncomfortable seat, and turned up the potentiometer, steaming faster towards the lights of the Big City.

After everything, I would have to see off the last mile of *The Cordwainer's* journey on my own. Two hundred miles lay behind me. Boot Hill was little more than a distant memory. Fluky was gone, Mitty was free. I looked down at the dash of the cockpit to where Fluky had suction-cupped the googly-eyed Jesus, and for the first time I realized he was gone, too. If he'd fallen off in the crash, if a Polypig had taken a shine to him, if Fluky had retieved his small totem before he'd abandoned the train, I didn't know. It left me at the controls of our train, alone. No weapons, no money, no googly-eyed Jesus. Nothing to show for my pains.

The lights of the city were growing brighter in front of me.

The Northern Pacific rails terminated in the city at a Union Station of its own. Converted to a central trolley hub, I remembered it from my time at University as a dingy, depressing place, filled with bums and workaday commuters, waiting for various trolley routes. It was a hazy structure in my memory, something I could remember, but not quite totally picture in my mind. Its exact shape – if it sported a clock tower – I couldn't quite recall.

As *The Cordwainer* rounded its last bend and turned its nose north toward a well illuminated, epic Romanesque structure, sitting on the horizon where the tracks beneath me eventually converged, no feeling of familiarity welled up inside me – no instant hit of recognition. That was the Big City's Union Station? I didn't remember the old platforms being so... well lit. As *The Cordwainer* rolled closer, the rumbling of a distant crowd began to join the nearby hum of the train's turbine. I began to make out spotlights pointing up at the clock tower of the station, illuminating it against the night. Closer still, and I could make out the shape of a platform, raised up at the terminus of the tracks. A large banner hung above it. I couldn't yet make out what it said, but a tightness in my stomach made me shift in my seat. I kept the potentiometer open, keeping the train at perhaps an even thirty miles an hour. Off to the left and right I could see figures in the dark, attempting to run alongside the train. They sprinted for a few yards, as far as their legs could take them, until the trail left them behind, exhausted in the dust.

There was an explosion of sound and more spotlights lit up the night when I was perhaps two hundred yards out. I slacked back on the potentiometer as the spotlights swept down, shining directly into my face. I held out a hand to shield my eyes, but the red blotches were already dancing on my retinas. A band was playing, I could hear it, over the din of the cheering crowd.

Closer and closer I rolled the train, driving blind, until I was passing between the spotlights, into the station itself. For the first time I could see the welcome that had been waiting for me: A massive crowd, perhaps thousands, thronging to the left and the right of the rails, up on the platforms. At the end of the tracks, above the large metal bumpers built to stop trains from rendezvousing with the Pacific, a grand stage had been erected; like a political rally, with bunting and all the trimmings. The banner above the stage read: "Welcome Boot Hill Banditos". A collection of well dressed, powerful-looking men stood on the stage applauding.

I cut out the potentiometer and let *The Cordwainer* coast. She slowed herself and bumped to a halt up against the bumper, her HTP tank clanking up against it like a bell.

The crowd came streaming down off the platforms, dropping down onto the tracks, cheering me. I pulled my head out of the cockpit and people were already climbing up onto the running boards, yelling congratulations. It was a mob scene, but a mob scene of good will. When I'd freed myself from the cockpit and down onto the running board, I was spontaneously scooped up by the crowd and carried on people's shoulders. Hands were being thrust up to me to shake, a continual series of pats on the back almost knocked me off my perch.

The crowd passed me from one pair of shoulders to another until I was up on the platform with the important-looking, powerful men. There was another series of handshaking with each and every dignitary. It was a blur of "well done" and "good show" all around. I turned and waved to the crowd, getting caught up in the festivities of it all. It was my first chance to really look around the old station – at the carnival the place had become.

The source of the music was a large fiddle and banjo band, perhaps twenty or thirty members, playing away with all their hearts from the top of an old wagon pulled out to the end of one of the platforms. On another, a preacher had set up a pulpit, and was vigorously delivering a fire and brimstone sermon to a crowd that was gleefully ignoring him. A mob of people were jammed shoulder to shoulder between them, and between the walls of the station and our stage. Through the large archways into the concourse, more people could be seen attempting to catch a glimpse of the goings-on on the platform. It was quite a crowd, quite a turn-out.

From below me a familiar voice called out, catching my attention. I looked down and scanned the crowd to see my father in amongst the throng. He seemed terribly small, crushed between two policemen. He was waving at me, smiling. The policemen were attempting to make their way towards the stage, but not managing to gain much ground. When I held out a hand and attempted to reach out to my father, the crowd around him parted a little and he was able to push forward. Soon he was up on the stage next to me and I was shaking his hand warmly. He attempted to yell something salutatory over the noise, but I couldn't make out a word.

A microphone was handed up out of the crowd. One of the dignitaries took it and spoke into it. Nothing could be heard. Somewhere, someone turned something up and the white-bearded man spoke again. This time his voice boomed out over the crowd.

"Thank you! Thank you!" He said, waving a calming hand. "I know you will all join me in welcoming the Boot Hill Bandito here to Seattle!" he said, and then even with the amplification his voice was lost behind the roar of the crowd. When the applause finally abated, he was already speaking, "...fresh from his arduous journey, filled with many dangers, across treacherous and outlaw infested mountains, to bring here, to us, a shipment of much needed, much demanded supplies, straight from the Concession factory, there in Boot Hill, here to the Big City!"

The crowd roared again. I let it wash over me like a wave. Of everything I had expected to happen at the end of my journey, a party was low on the list. After Mulligan I'd had an inkling, but nothing like this. Police, the Army, I might have expected. I had hoped I might sneak into town undetected; but this... and my father standing beside me with his arm around me, with a bright smile on his face, enjoying the moment. It was hard to believe.

"...And it is my great honor to inform you all," the white-bearded man was still speaking. "That the endeavors of this young man have not gone unnoticed. Scientists from the University are already meeting with the designer of this fabulous new engine, and are looking at the possibilities of using the technology you see here before you, to power

Concession trains, on standard routes! To help get this country moving again! To put an end to these interminable shortages that have so devastatingly gripped our nation!"

The crowd went wild again. Loud applause. The band struck up, gaily playing a tune.

Only I stood there in shocked silence.

What? I looked at my father. He was beaming at me, clapping along with the band. Suddenly, I realized what was happening – what the welcoming committee meant. This was no celebration of me – no congratulatory slap on the back for the success of *The Cordwainer*. The Concession – the Government – unable to bury us in the mountains, were co-opting what we had achieved, attempting to absorb our success. If you couldn't beat us, they were going to join us. Or have us join them. Now I realized why my father was there, why Sophie would be in the Big City, also.

The full weight of what was happening hit me. The whole thing was slipping out of my control. This party was a far worse welcome than police or National Guard would have been. A direct assault I could have handled. But to be co-opted.

Then I realized that I was the man of the hour. All those faces looking up to me in admiration. To see me and the train was the reason all these people had come out in the middle of the night, not to hear speeches from the Concession. The fight was far from over. I realized I still had an ace up my sleeve to play. I stepped forward, slipping out from under my father's arm and stepped up beside the white-bearded man, who later I'd learn was the Mayor of the Big City. I shook his hand, warmly, and he shook it back. And without giving him the chance to protest, I took the microphone from his hand.

"Thank you! Thank you!" I spoke into it. The crowd roared. I let them applaud as long as they liked, egging the crowd on. The Mayor next to me look slightly concerned, but smiled and slapped me on the shoulder. "Thank you to everyone who came out at this late hour to witness the final moments of my journey." More applause. "Myself and my friends, we've brought boots to your town." I paused as the crowd whooped and yelled. "But I implore you all, not to forget the circumstance that put us in this position – what institutions and what entities have caused the shortages that have so besieged us all..."

The Mayor next to me chuckled, slapped me one last time on the back, and attempted to reach for the microphone. I caught his hand in mine and continued speaking, "The Concession, ladies and gentlemen," I went on, "are the enemy here. They attempted to stop *The Cordwainer* – our train – at every turn. Look at the train, ladies and gentlemen, look at the bullet holes-" I was interrupted as the Mayor tired to break away from my grip. We scuffled for a moment as he attempted to grab the microphone from me. I managed a few more monosyllables into the microphone before it was cut off at the source. The Mayor and I, however, continued to wrestle for it, until a number of the other dignitaries grabbed me by my arms and pulled me away.

The Mayor took up the microphone, straightened his jacket, and attempted to speak, hearing nothing over the speakers. He leaned over the edge of the stage and yelled to have the microphone turned back on. It subsequently was, and he started to speak to the crowd again, but the mood of the gathered mob had already changed. My job was done. There was no more applauding or spontaneous eruptions of song, just low murmuring in the crowd.

The two policemen who'd escorted my father up onto the stage now appeared and escorted me and my father back down off it. We were bustled out of the station and into a police car before the Mayor had finished speaking to the crowd. But it was already obvious that the crowd had turned against him. *The Cordwainer* sitting in the station in front of him, fully in view for everyone to see, was more than enough of a counterpoint to the promises the Mayor was attempting to make to the people.

A train full of boots versus a Mayor full of hot air... The boots were going to win every time.

From the train station, we were whisked to a nearby hotel, to a fifth-floor room overlooking the station. Little was said to my father or me, in the car or when we reached the hotel, and food and drink were brought up from the kitchens. But the pair of policemen that remained outside in the corridor, behind the hotel room's firmly locked door, indicated that we were not exactly honored guests. My father and I ate sandwiches and drank coffee in silence.

Outside the window, down at the old Union Station, the festival was still raging. I could still faintly hear the music, but the speeches had ceased.

It was morning before the locked door to our room opened up again. I caught a few hours sleep, tired down to my bones. When I awoke, the party across the street, down at the station, was still rolling on. It had spilled out into the square that faced onto the station; thousands were milling in the streets. Nothing exactly was happening, but the people were still there. As if waiting for something.

The morning consisted of a steady stream of men in suits asking questions. The whereabouts of Fluky and Mitty were a high priority for all of them. I was glad that I could say, with all honesty, that I had no idea where either of them were. The various men who came to interrogate me – obviously middle-management types, low-hanging bureaucrats, with titles like Deputy Comptroller for the Northwest Region – seemed particularly keen to wheedle out of me exactly what had become of the money I had earned selling boots along the rails down the west face of the mountains. They seemed to have a pretty good idea exactly how much I should have had on hand, arriving in the Big City. Perhaps they'd gotten to that banker in Galt. It wouldn't have surprised me. The absence of the money was a great source of consternation for them; and as the morning rolled by, the long stream of servile flatterers became more and more pointed in their questioning.

I had nothing to tell them. I truthfully stated that Fluky and Mitty had divided up the money and departed the train before we'd reached the city. But that answer satisfied no one. I wasn't aware of it at the time, and it was many years later when I finally came to comprehend the exact reasoning behind their obsession with the money: It was all that the powers-that-be – all the Concession or the government – had to pin on me.

Below in the station, that night before, after my father and I had been removed from the stage and the Mayor had been booed off, various members of the crowd had taken up the microphone and had something of a town meeting. The arrival of *The Cordwainer* had stirred up a groundswell of dissatisfaction amongst those who'd turned out to see my arrival. The Mayor's speech, and our subsequent fisticuffs, hadn't sat well with the crowd. They had resolved themselves to remain at the station until I was returned and was able to finished my remarks, apropos the arrival of the train and the related shortages.

The Concession, and their government handlers, had shifted into serious damage control. They'd managed to put an emergency block on the morning papers, which would have reported *The Cordwainer's* arrival and the resulting demonstration – it had been easy enough, the Concession being the newspaper publisher and only distributor. But the evening papers would not be so easy to skip. A whole day without papers, and rumors would begin to circulate. The Concession realized that they needed to control the spin on the story, get their version out officially in the paper; and this instigated the steady stream of sycophantic middle-management types parading through my hotel room. They needed dirt on me, something to smear me with. And half a million in ill begotten profits, they figured, could just about do it.

Without the cash, without the mercenary, profiteering angle, they had nothing. The thefts – the boots, the peroxide, the parts – it was all nothing that would play well in print. Before, they'd tried to portray *The Cordwainer* as outlaws and it had backfired on them, playing out with a whole Robin Hood angle. All they had now was that we were dirty, rotten capitalists. And without the capital, that was going to be hard to prove.

By the evening, our handlers had left my father and me alone. We ate dinner in the room, behind the door still guarded by policemen, and watched evening fall outside the windows. The crowds in the square and the station had grown. Word of mouth had called people out and it seemed, from five stories up, that the protests had started in earnest. At dusk, the microphone of the stage cracked to life again, booming around the station and out into the streets beyond. I couldn't make out exactly what anyone was saying, but the speeches sounded sufficiently inflammatory.

Slowly and quietly, police were gathering to encircle the station.

The kindly waitress who had brought my father and me all our meals sneaked in a carton of McTavish with our evening coffee. She had given me a knowing wink when she'd brought the tray in, covered by the cloth. For a second I'd panicked, fearing it was going to be a handgun, but I was infinitely relieved to raise the cloth and find only the whiskey. My father and I poured coffee cups full of the bitter, sour brown liquid and toasted each other's health. The McTavish still tasted vile, but I couldn't drink it without a slight smile on my face, thinking back to Mitchell and the Château Marmont.

"Andy, Andy..." my father shook his head after his third cup. He'd been handling the whole affair, our arrest, quite well up until then. "Why did you have to do this?"

I was silent, drinking my whiskey.

"Now we're..." He pointed at the locked door. "They'll never..."

"It seemed like a good idea back home. Once we were in the hills, though, it got complicated," I replied moodily.

"But, you could have gotten yourself *killed*," he emphasized. "And for what?"

"Money," I said flatly.

"What money? They've been asking you all day about the money. Was there any money?"

I didn't reply. I looked at my father over the rim of my cup. He shook his head, as if to retract the question, "Just a stupid risk for nothing."

"You've always told stories about the War," I said. "Of you and Mr. Salmon, in France, liberating Paris. That was a risk. You couldn't have been any older than me back then."

"Yes, son," my father said, condescendingly. "But that was the *War*."

"And that makes a difference?" I reacted angrily. "That somehow makes it okay? That the government said you could? Are those the only adventures we're allowed? The only risks we can take? Those that are duly authorized and approved by the State?" I finished off the last of my scotch, standing up and crossing to the window, pointing. "I did a good thing here, Dad. Look how those people have reacted. We've shaken things up, made people realize their discontent with the status quo. Wasn't that worth the risk?"

"Son, there could be a riot!" my father protested.

"Yes, and isn't it about time? Things are broken, Dad, and people are sick and tired of waiting around for a fix. What's wrong with all of us fixing things for ourselves? Huh? Why do we have to wait for the sanctioned solution? If the solution is within the grasp of each and every one of us? Why can't we take it?"

"Son-" he began, but was interrupted as the loudspeakers outside cut out. It had been droning on all evening with speaker after speaker, but now it fell suddenly silent. I looked down from my fifth-story perch to see that the spotlights that had been illuminating the Union Station clock tower were also dark. The power had been cut. Momentarily, the lights in the hotel room died out, too. I watched as the crowd in the square in front of the station churned restlessly. They could feel it as well as I could: The sudden change in the air. "What's happening?" my father asked, joining me at the window.

"I think the protest has outstayed its welcome."

I could see in the gloom, mounted policemen moving down the side streets. Long, thin spear-length batons, like whips, in their hands.

Behind us, I heard the lock in the door turn. But the door didn't open. A beam of a flashlight momentarily appeared at the foot of the door, but then vanished.

I crossed the room and tried the handle. The door opened. I looked cautiously out into the dark corridor though a crack in the door. The corridor was empty of policemen, guarding either side of the door. There was no one. I though of our kindly, sympathetic waitress, looking down at the key in the lock. I opened the door fully to let myself out.

"Where are you going?" my father asked, grabbing at my arm.

"Anywhere but here," I replied truthfully.

"Son, no!"

I pulled my arm free. My father didn't make another attempt to stop me.

"What are you going to do?" he asked as I moved quickly across the corridor and tried a nearby door to a stairwell. It was dark in there too, but it appeared to be empty.

"With no job opportunities, and a history of criminal behavior?" I said, trying to answer the question for myself, too. "Perhaps I'll go into politics?"

"Andrew, wait," my father appealed, still standing in the doorway to our hotel room, afraid to step out in the dark corridor.

"Goodbye, Dad," I said, stepping towards the stairwell door. But I paused, suddenly thinking of Barry's watch around my wrist. I slipped it off, looked at the time through the broken crystal and handed it to my father. He said nothing. There was nothing to say.

I turned and pushed through the stairwell door, letting it swing closed behind me. The stairs were engulfed in blackness. My hand found the railing and I was moving down; circling and circling.

I'd find a fire exit at ground level, out into some back alley, and then I'd be free on the streets. There'd be no cops, I knew; they'd all be busy advancing on the station – advancing on the station and the protesters and *The Cordwainer* and that last hopper car full of boots. I'd be five miles away, in an after-hours bar I knew near the campus of the University, before anyone returned to the hotel to check on me. They'd find only my father. I would be free.

But I had no plans of hiding. No, not from the Concession, or the government, if they wanted to find me. I'd make my whereabouts well known. What was happening across the street, what was happening in that station, was the direct result of my actions. I would have to take responsibility.

For good or ill, I would have to let the world judge me for what I had done. What I had started. Started in a makeshift train, powered by rocket fuel, piloted across the mountains and through many dangers by three losers from Boot Hill.

I was proud to say that was what I had done, and I was responsible.

Epilogue

I was never to see either Mitty or Fluky again.

Fluky was lost to his Japanese American revolution, draped in the mysticism of his inexplicable religion. Many years later, I would receive word that he died of non-combat related injuries during the Okinawa Insurrection. The exact details of his death remain murky, as most everything about the military's crackdown on the island remains to this day, but it seems that Fluky had taken to heart the words Majorette had spoken that night up in the pass – her call to revolution. How much the funds raised by the adventures of *The Cordwainer* went to fund this revolution, I cannot say. $200,000 may seem like a handsome sum, but I doubt it goes very far towards overthrowing a government.

I could do nothing but mourn his passing when word of his death reached me. I knew he'd died in a cause he believed in. That the Okinawa Insurrection would pull hard on the loose threads that held the patchwork of allegiances together that made up the American Government, Fluky would not live to see.

By then, I had been elected to a seat in the Senate, running on the popularity that the affair of *The Cordwainer* had earned me. I ran for office without help of either of the dominant political parties. I was a sitting Senator when the unthinkable finally happened. That I'd worked so diligently to undermine the very institution of which I was a member, gave me no comfort.

When the polite tolerance maintained between the various political factions that made up the Kennedy government finally broke down, and the militias and the gangs took to the streets of the Capitol, jostling for power, I could take little pleasure in the havoc. By then, of course, the shortages and the Concession's inability to address them had resulted in widespread famine and suffering. There was very little of the nation left that wasn't directly under military control. The implementation of martial law on the capital hardly shocked anyone. But the army had little better luck addressing the needs of a hungry population than the civilian administrations that had come before it. It was not long before the people's wrath turned on the military junta that had stepped into the power vacuum.

When the army began to fight amongst itself for food and fuel, the end was almost finally upon us.

As for Mitty, I had no word for many, many years; and then, in the end, only the slightest hint to his eventual fate. Perhaps fifteen years after the journey of *The Cordwainer*, I was serving on a transition committee within the Provisional Government, attempting to ascertain exactly how much, and to whom, America was in debt. It was a maddening affair, attempting to untangle the accounting shenanigans of a hundred years of blissfully ignorant administrations. In an attempt to get a hand on the ocean of figures, we reached out to some of the newly burgeoning private industries for technical assistance.

In the Big City, at the terminus of *The Cordwainer's* adventure, a new high technology sector had begun to grow. They were building new, revolutionary "counting machines", and many in the Provisional Government saw these machines as the panacea to all our ills. We put out a request for bids, and one such company that submitted paperwork listed amongst its principle investors someone named John Mitty.

I contacted that company, attempting to track down this John Mitty, but was quickly frustrated in my search. The computer company could only tell me their John Mitty was a silent partner, of reclusive tendencies, who had nothing to do with the day-to-day operation of the firm. I made repeated calls, even making the trip out west to visit their offices, but with little success.

The company would eventually win the contract to supply the Provisional Government with counting machines. But apart from that single line on that single disclosure form, there was never again any mention of anyone by the name of John Mitty.

Perhaps it was all a coincidence, but the thought that *The Cordwainer* profits had been used in such a way captivated me.

Mitty a reclusive millionaire?

Perhaps one day I will see him again – get to shake his hand, and talk over old times – but until that day, the image of Mitty locked away in some palatial mansion somewhere, meticulously overseeing his investments; taking time, now and again, to look over a map or two of the European Theater; to trace out the path of Patton's Army, from Izpegi Pass to Paris. That thought makes me smile.

Or perhaps, back in Hooverville, Mitty has remained to this day. Sleeping in the shanties, with the other hard-luck candidates, eating beans from a can, warmed against the encroaching cold of the night by a half million dollars lining the inside of his clothes.

That thought makes me smile, too.

About the Author

Christopher Blankley was born in the United Kingdom, and now resides in Seattle, Washington with his wife and two children. He is also the author of a series of steampunk adventure novels for young adults, *The Bobbies of Bailiwick*.

His shoe size is 9½.